BY JOHN GRISHAM

JOHN GRISHAM

———

A
TIME
FOR
MERCY

A NOVEL

DELL BOOKS
New York

2021 Dell Books Mass Market Edition

Copyright © 2020 by Belfry Holdings, Inc.

All rights reserved.

Published in the United States by Dell, an imprint of
Random House, a division of
Penguin Random House LLC, New York.

DELL and the HOUSE colophon are registered trademarks of
Penguin Random House LLC.

Originally published in hardcover in the United States by
Doubleday, an imprint of Knopf Doubleday Publishing Group,
a division of Penguin Random House LLC, in 2020.

ISBN 978-0-593-15781-7
Export edition ISBN: 978-0-593-35688-3
Ebook ISBN 978-0-385-54597-6

Cover design: John Fontana
Cover photograph: David Keochkerian/Trevillion Images

Printed in the United States of America

randomhousebooks.com

2 4 6 8 9 7 5 3

Dell mass market edition: July 2021

To the memory of

SONNY MEHTA

Knopf Chairman, Editor in Chief, Publisher

A TIME FOR MERCY

1

The unhappy little home was out in the country, some six miles south of Clanton on an old county road that went nowhere in particular. The house could not be seen from the road and was accessed by a winding gravel drive that dipped and curved and at night caused approaching headlights to sweep through the front windows and doors as if to warn those waiting inside. The seclusion of the house added to the imminent horror.

It was long after midnight on an early Sunday when the headlights finally appeared. They washed through the house and cast ominous, silent shadows on the walls, then went away as the car dipped before its final approach. Those inside should have been asleep for hours, but sleep was not possible during these awful nights. On the sofa in the den, Josie took a deep breath, said a quick prayer, and eased to the window to watch the car. Was it weaving and lurching as usual, or was it under control? Was he drunk as always on these nights or could he have throttled back on the drinking? She wore a racy negligee to catch his attention and perhaps alter his mood from violence to romance. She had worn it before and he had once liked it.

The car stopped beside the house and she watched him get out. He staggered and stumbled, and she braced herself for what was to come. She went to the kitchen where the light was on and waited. Beside the door and partially hidden in a corner was an aluminum baseball bat that belonged to her son. She had placed it there an hour earlier for protection, just in case he went after her kids. She had prayed for the courage to use it but still had doubts. He fell against the kitchen door and then rattled the knob as if it were locked; it was not. He finally kicked it open and it slammed into the refrigerator.

Stuart was a sloppy, violent drunk. His pale Irish skin turned red, his cheeks were crimson, and his eyes glowed with a whiskey-lit fire that she had seen too many times. At thirty-four, he was graying and balding and tried to cover it up with a bad comb-over, which after a night of bar-hopping left long strands of hair hanging below his ears. His face had no cuts or bruises, perhaps a good sign, perhaps not. He liked to fight in the honky-tonks, and after a rough night he usually licked his wounds and went straight to bed. But if there had been no fights he often came home looking for a brawl.

"The hell you doin' up?" he snarled as he tried to close the door behind him.

As calmly as possible, Josie said, "Just waitin' on you, dear. You okay?"

"I don't need you to wait on me. What time is it, two in the mornin'?"

She smiled sweetly as if all was well. A week earlier, she had decided to go to bed and wait him out there. He came home late and went upstairs and threatened her children.

"About two," she said softly. "Let's go to bed."

"What're you wearin' that thing for? You look like a real slut. Somebody been over here tonight?"

A common accusation these days. "Of course not," she said. "I'm just ready for bed."

"You're a whore."

"Come on, Stu. I'm sleepy. Let's go to bed."

"Who is he?" he growled as he fell back against the door.

"Who is who? There's no one. I've been here all night with the kids."

"You're a lyin' bitch, you know that?"

"I'm not lyin', Stu. Let's go to bed. It's late."

"I heard tonight that somebody saw John Albert's truck out here coupla days ago."

"And who is John Albert?"

"And who is John Albert, asks the little slut? You know damned well who John Albert is." He moved away from the door and took steps toward her, unsteady steps, and he tried to brace himself with the counter. He pointed at her and said, "You're a little whore and you got old boyfriends hangin' around. I've warned you."

"You're my only boyfriend, Stuart, I've told you that a thousand times. Why can't you believe me?"

"Because you're a liar and I've caught you lyin' before. Remember that credit card. You bitch."

"Come on, Stu, that was last year and we got through it."

He lunged and grabbed her wrist with his left hand and swung hard at her face. With an open hand he slapped her across the jaw, a loud popping sound that was sickening, flesh on flesh. She screamed in pain and shock. She had told herself to do anything but scream because her kids were upstairs behind a locked door, listening, hearing it all.

"Stop it, Stu!" she shrieked as she grabbed her face and tried to catch her breath. "No more hittin'! I promised you I'm leavin' and I swear I will!"

He roared with laughter and said, "Oh really? And where you goin' now, you little slut? Back to the camper in the woods? You gonna live in your car again?" He yanked her wrist, spun her around, threw a thick forearm around her neck, and growled into her ear. "You ain't got no place to go, bitch, not even the trailer park where you was born." He sprayed hot saliva and the rank odor of stale whiskey and beer into her ear.

She jerked and tried to free herself but he thrust her arm up almost to her shoulders as if trying mightily to snap a bone. She couldn't help but scream again and she pitied her children as she did so. "You're breakin' my arm, Stu! Please stop!"

He lowered her arm an inch or two but pressed her tighter. He hissed into her ear, "Where you goin'? You got a roof over your head, food on the table, a room for those two rotten kids of yours, and you wanna talk about leavin'? I don't think so."

She stiffened and wiggled and tried to break free, but he was a powerful man with a crazy temper. "You're breakin' my arm, Stu. Please let go!"

Instead, he yanked hard again and she yelled. She kicked back with her bare heel and hit his shin, then spun around and with her left elbow caught him in the ribs. It stunned him for a second, did no damage, but allowed her to pry herself free, knocking over a kitchen chair. More noise to frighten her children.

He charged like a mad bull, grabbed her by the throat, pinned her to the wall, and dug his fingernails into the flesh of her neck. Josie couldn't yell, couldn't swallow or breathe, and the mad glow in his eyes told her this was their last fight. This was the moment he would finally kill her. She tried to kick, missed, and in a flash he threw a hard right hook that landed square on her chin, knocking her out cold. She crumpled to the floor and landed on her back with her legs spread. Her negligee was open, her breasts exposed. He stood for a second or two and admired his handiwork.

"Bitch hit me first," he mumbled, then stepped to the fridge where he found a can of beer. He popped the top, had a sip, wiped his mouth with the back of a hand, and waited to see if she might wake up or whether she was down for the night. She wasn't moving so he stepped closer to make sure she was breathing.

He had been a street brawler all his life and knew the first rule: Nail 'em on the chin and they're out for good.

The house was quiet and still, but he knew the kids were upstairs, hiding and waiting.

DREW WAS TWO years older than his sister, Kiera, but puberty, like most normal changes in his life, was coming late. He was sixteen, small for his age and bothered by his lack of size, especially when standing next to his sister, who was struggling through another awkward growth surge. What the two didn't know, yet, was that they had different fathers, and their physical development would never be in sync. Heredity aside, at that moment they were bound together as tightly as any two siblings while they listened in horror as their mother suffered another beating.

The violence was spiraling and the abuse was more frequent. They were begging Josie to leave and she was making promises, but the three of them knew there was no place to go. She assured them things would get better, that Stu was a good man when he wasn't drinking, and she was determined to love him to better health.

No place to go. Their last "home" had been an old camper in the backyard of a distant relative who was embarrassed to have them on his property. All three knew they were surviving life with Stu only because he owned a real house, one with bricks and a tin roof. They were not hungry, though they still had painful memories of those days, and they were in school. Indeed, school was their sanctuary because he never came near the place. There were issues there—slow academic progress for Drew, too few friends for both of them, old clothes, the free-lunch lines—but at least at school they were away from Stu, and safe.

Even when sober, which, mercifully, was most of the time, he was an unpleasant ass who resented having to support the children. He had none himself because he had never wanted them, and also because his two prior marriages ended not long after they began. He was a bully who thought his home was his castle. The kids were unwelcome guests, perhaps even trespassers, and therefore they should do all the dirty work. With plenty of free labor, he had an endless list of chores, most designed to disguise the fact that he himself was nothing more than a lazy slob. At the slightest infraction, he cursed the kids and threatened them. He bought food and beer for himself and insisted that Josie's meager paychecks cover "their" side of the table.

But the chores and food and intimidation were nothing compared to the violence.

JOSIE WAS BARELY breathing and not moving. He stood above her, looked at her breasts, and as always wished they were larger. Hell, even Kiera had a bigger rack. He smiled at this thought and decided to have a look. He walked through the small dark den and began to climb the stairs, making as much noise as possible to frighten them. Halfway up he called out in a high-pitched, drunken, almost playful voice, "Kiera, oh Kiera . . ."

In the darkness, she shuddered in fear and squeezed Drew's arm even tighter. Stu lumbered on, his steps landing heavy on the wooden stairs.

"Kiera, oh Kiera . . ."

He opened Drew's unlocked door first, then slammed it. He turned the knob to Kiera's and it was locked. "Ha, ha, Kiera, I know you're in there. Open the door." He fell against it with his shoulder.

They were sitting together at the end of her narrow bed, staring at the door. Jammed against it was a rusted metal shaft Drew had found in the barn, and with it he had rigged a doorstop that they prayed would hold. One end was wedged against the door, the other against the metal bed frame. When Stu began rattling the lock, Drew and Kiera, as rehearsed, leaned on the metal shaft to increase the pressure. They had practiced this scenario and were almost certain the door would hold. They had also planned an attack if the door came flying open. Kiera would grab an old tennis racket and Drew would yank a small tube of pepper spray out of his pocket and blast away. Josie had bought it for the kids, just in case. Stu might beat them again, but at least they would go down fighting.

He could easily kick in the door. He had done so a month earlier, then raised hell when a new one cost him a hundred dollars. At first he insisted that Josie pay for it, then wanted money from the kids, then finally stopped bitching about it.

Kiera was rigid with fear and crying quietly, but she was also thinking that this was unusual. On the prior occasions when he had come to her room, no one else was at home. There had been no witnesses and he had threatened to kill her if she ever told. Stu had already silenced her mom. Did he plan to harm Drew too, and threaten him?

"Oh Kiera, oh Kiera," he sang stupidly as he fell against the door again. His voice was a little softer, as if he might be giving up.

They pressed on the metal shaft and waited for an explosion, but he went silent. Then he retreated, his steps fading on the stairs. All was quiet.

And not a sound from their mother, which meant the end of the world. She was down there, either dead or unconscious because otherwise he would not have climbed the stairs, not without a nasty fight. Josie would claw his eyes out in his sleep if he harmed her children again.

SECONDS AND MINUTES dragged by. Kiera stopped crying, and both of them sat on the edge of the bed, waiting for something, a noise, a voice, a door being slammed. But, nothing.

Finally, Drew whispered, "We have to make a move."

Kiera was petrified and couldn't respond.

He said, "I'll go check on Mom. You stay here with the door locked. Got it?"

"Don't go."

"I have to go. Something happened to Mom, otherwise she'd be up here. I'm sure she's hurt. Stay put and keep the door locked."

He moved the metal shaft and silently opened her door. He peeked down the stairs and saw nothing but darkness and the faint glow of a porch light. Kiera watched and closed the door behind him. He took the first step down as he clutched the can of pepper spray and thought how great it would be to blast that son of a bitch in the face with a cloud of poison, burn his eyes

and maybe blind him. Slowly, one step at a time without making a sound. In the den he stopped dead still
and listened. There was a distant sound from Stu's bedroom down the short hallway. Drew waited a moment
longer and hoped that maybe Stu had put Josie to bed
after slapping her around. The light was on in the
kitchen. He peeked around the door face and saw her
bare feet lying still, then her legs. He dropped to his
knees and scurried under the table to her side where he
shook her arm roughly, but didn't speak. Any sound
might attract him. He noticed her breasts but was too
frightened to be embarrassed. He shook again, hissed,
"Mom, Mom, wake up!" But there was no response.
The left side of her face was red and swollen, and he
was certain she wasn't breathing. He wiped his eyes and
backed away, and crawled into the hallway. At the end
of it Stu's bedroom door was open, a dim table light was
on, and after he focused Drew could see a pair of boots
hanging off the bed. Stu's snakeskin pointed-toes, his
favorites. Drew stood and walked quickly to the bedroom, and there, sprawled across the bed with his arms
thrown open wide above his head and still fully dressed,
was Stuart Kofer, passed out again. As Drew glared at
him with unbridled hatred, the man actually snored.

Drew ran up the stairs, and as Kiera opened the
door, he cried, "She's dead, Kiera, Mom's dead. Stu's
killed her. She's on the kitchen floor and she's dead."

Kiera recoiled and shrieked and grabbed her brother.
Both were in tears as they went down the stairs and to
the kitchen where they cradled their mother's head.
Kiera was weeping and whispering, "Wake up, Mom!
Please wake up!"

Drew delicately grabbed his mother's left wrist and
tried to check her pulse, though he wasn't sure he was
doing it properly. He felt nothing.

He said, "We gotta call 911."

"Where is he?" she asked, glancing around.

"In the bed, asleep. I think he passed out."

"I'm holding Mom. You go call."

Drew went to the den, turned on a light, picked up the phone, and dialed 911. After many rings the dispatcher finally said, "911. What's your emergency?"

"My mother has been killed by Stuart Kofer. She's dead."

"Son, who is this?"

"I'm Drew Gamble. My mother is Josie. She's dead."

"And where do you live?"

"Stuart Kofer's house, out on Bart Road. Fourteen-fourteen Bart Road. Please send someone to help us."

"I will, I will. They're on the way. And you say she's dead. How do you know she's dead?"

"'Cause she ain't breathing. 'Cause Stuart beat her again, same as always."

"Is Stuart Kofer in the house?"

"Yep, it's his house and we just live here. He came in drunk again and beat my mother. He killed her. We heard him do it."

"Where is he?"

"On his bed. Passed out. Please hurry."

"You stay on the line, okay?"

"No. I'm checkin' on my mom."

He hung up and grabbed a quilt from the sofa. Kiera had Josie's face cradled in her lap, gently rubbing her hair as she wept and kept saying, "Come on, Mom, please wake up. Please wake up. Don't leave us, Mom." Drew covered his mother with the quilt, then sat by her feet. He closed his eyes and pinched his nose and tried to pray. The house was still, silent; the only sounds were Kiera's whimpering as she begged her mother. Minutes passed and Drew willed himself to stop crying and do something to protect them. Stuart might be asleep back there but he might wake up, too, and if he caught them downstairs he would fly into a rage and beat them.

He had done that before: get drunk, rage, threaten, slap, pass out, then wake up ready for another round of fun.

Then he snorted and made a drunken noise, and Drew was afraid he might wake himself from his drunkenness. Drew said, "Kiera, be quiet," but she did not hear him. She was in a trance, pawing at her mother as tears dripped from her cheeks.

Slowly, Drew crawled away and left the kitchen. In the hall he crouched and tiptoed back to the bedroom where Stuart hadn't moved. His boots still hung off the bed. His stocky body was spread across the covers. His mouth was open wide enough to catch flies. Drew stared at him with a hatred that almost blinded him. The brute had finally killed their mother, after months of trying, and he would certainly kill them next. And no one would bother Stuart for it because he had connections and knew important people, something he often bragged about. They were nothing but white trash, castaways from the trailer parks, but Stuart had clout because he owned land and carried a badge.

Drew took a step back and looked down the hall where he saw his mother lying on the floor and his sister holding her head and moaning in a low pained hum, completely detached, and he walked to a corner of the bedroom, to a small table on Stuart's side of the bed where he kept his pistol and his thick black belt and holster and his badge in the shape of a star. He took the gun out of the holster and remembered how heavy it was. The pistol, a Glock nine-millimeter, was used by all deputies on the force. It was against the rules for a civilian to handle it. Stu cared little for silly rules, and one day not long ago when he was sober and in a rare good mood he walked Drew to the back pasture and showed him how to handle and fire the weapon. Stu had been raised with guns; Drew had not, and Stu poked fun at the kid for his ignorance. He boasted of killing his first deer when he was eight years old.

Drew had fired the gun three times, badly missing an archery target, and was frightened by the kick and noise of the gun. Stu had laughed at him for his timidity, then fired six quick rounds into the bull's-eye.

Drew held the gun with his right hand and examined it. He knew it was loaded because Stu's guns were always at the ready. There was a cabinet in the closet packed with rifles and shotguns, all loaded.

In the distance Kiera was moaning and crying, and before him Stu was snoring, and soon the police would come barging in and they would eventually do as little as they had done before. Nothing. Nothing to protect Drew and Kiera, not even now with their mother lying dead on the kitchen floor. Stuart Kofer had killed her, and he would tell lies and the police would believe him. Then Drew and his sister would face an even darker future without their mother.

He left the room holding the Glock and slowly walked to the kitchen, where nothing had changed. He asked Kiera if their mother was breathing and she did not respond, did not interrupt her noises. He walked to the den and looked out the window into the darkness. If he had a father he didn't know him, and once again he asked himself where was the man of the family? Where was the leader, the wise one who gave advice and protection? He and Kiera had never known the security of two stable parents. They had met other fathers in foster care, and they had met youth court advocates who had tried to help, but they had never known the warm embrace of a man they could trust.

The responsibilities were left to him, the oldest. With their mother gone, he had no choice but to step up and become a man. He and he alone had to save them from a prolonged nightmare.

A noise startled him. There was a groan or a snort or some such noise from the bedroom and the box spring and mattress rattled and heaved, as if Stu was moving and coming back to life.

Drew and Kiera could not take any more. The moment had come, their only chance to survive was at hand, and Drew had to act. He returned to the bedroom and stared at Stu, still on his back and dead to the world, but oddly one boot was off and on the floor. Dead was what he deserved. Drew slowly closed the door, as if to protect Kiera from any involvement. How easy would it be? Drew clasped the pistol with both hands. He held his breath and lowered the gun until the tip of the barrel was an inch from Stu's left temple.

He closed his eyes and pulled the trigger.

A TIME FOR MERCY   15

2

Kiera never looked up. She stroked her mother's hair and asked, "What did you do?"

"I shot him," Drew said matter-of-factly. His voice had no expression, no fear or regret. "I shot him."

She nodded and said nothing else. He went to the den and looked out the front window again. Where were the red and blue lights? Where were the responders? You call and report your mother has been killed by a brute and no one shows up. He turned on a lamp and glanced at the clock. 2:47. He would always remember the exact moment he shot Stuart Kofer. His hands were shaking and numb, his ears were ringing, but at 2:47 A.M. he had no regrets for killing the man who'd killed his mother. He walked back to the bedroom and turned on the ceiling light. The gun was beside Stu's head, which had a small, ugly hole in the left side. Stu was still looking at the ceiling, now with his eyes open. A circle of bright red blood was spreading in an arc through the sheets.

Drew walked back to the kitchen, where nothing had changed. He went to the den, turned on another light, opened the front door, and took a seat in Stu's recliner. Stu would have a fit if he caught anyone else sitting on his throne. It smelled like him—stale cigarettes, dried sweat, old leather, whiskey and beer. After a few minutes, Drew decided he hated the recliner, so he pulled a small chair to the window to wait for the lights.

The first were blue, blinking and swirling furiously,

and when they topped the driveway's last incline Drew was stricken with fear and had trouble breathing. They were coming to get him. He would leave in handcuffs in the rear seat of a deputy's patrol car, and there was nothing he could do to stop it.

The second responder was an ambulance with red lights, the third was another police car. Once it was known that there were two bodies and not just one, another ambulance arrived in a rush, followed by more law enforcement.

Josie had a pulse and was quickly loaded onto a stretcher and raced away to the hospital. Drew and Kiera were sequestered in the den and told not to move. And where would they go? Every light in the house was on and there were cops in every room.

Sheriff Ozzie Walls arrived by himself and was met in front of the house by Moss Junior Tatum, his chief deputy, who said, "Looks like Kofer came home late, they had a fight, he slapped her around, then passed out on his bed. The kid got his gun and shot him once in the head. Instant."

"You talked to the kid?"

"Yep. Drew Gamble, age sixteen, son of Kofer's girl-friend. Wouldn't say much. I think he's in shock. His sister is Kiera, age fourteen, she said they've lived here about a year and that Kofer was abusive, beat their mom all the time."

"Kofer's dead?" Ozzie asked in disbelief.

"Stuart Kofer is dead, sir."

Ozzie shook his head in disgust and disbelief and walked to the front door, which was wide open. Inside, he stopped and glanced at Drew and Kiera who were sitting beside each other on the sofa, both staring down and trying to ignore the chaos. Ozzie wanted to say something but let it pass. He followed Tatum into the bedroom, where nothing had been touched. The gun was on the sheets, ten inches from Kofer's head, and there was a wide circle of blood in the center of the bed. On the other side, the bullet's exit had blown out a section of the skull, and blood and matter had been sprayed against the sheets, pillows, headboard, and wall.

At the moment, Ozzie had fourteen full-time deputies. Now thirteen. And seven part-timers, along with more volunteers than he cared to fool with. He'd been the sheriff of Ford County since 1983, elected seven years earlier in an historic landslide. Historic because he was, at the time, the only black sheriff in Mississippi and the first ever from a predominantly white county. In seven years he'd never lost a man. DeWayne Looney had his leg blown off in the courthouse shooting that put Carl Lee Hailey on trial in 1985, but Looney was still on the force.

But there, in all its ghastliness, was his first. There was Stuart Kofer, one of his best and certainly his most fearless, dead as a doornail as his body continued to leak fluids.

Ozzie removed his hat, said a quick prayer, and took a step back. Without taking his eyes off Kofer, he said, "Murder of a law enforcement officer. Call in the state boys and let them investigate. Don't touch anything." He looked at Tatum and asked, "You talked to the kids?"

"I did."

"Same story?"

"Yes sir. The boy won't talk. His sister says he shot him. Thought their mother was dead."

Ozzie nodded and thought about the situation. He said, "All right, no more questions for the kids, no more interrogation. From this point on, everything we do will be picked through by the lawyers. Let's take the kids in, but not a word. In fact, put 'em in my car."

"Handcuffs?"

"Sure. For the boy. Do they have any family around here?"

Deputy Mick Swayze cleared his throat and said, "I don't think so, Ozzie. I knew Kofer pretty well and he had this gal livin' with him, said she had a rough background. One divorce, maybe two. I'm not sure where she's from but he did say she ain't from around here. I came out here a few weeks ago on a disturbance call, but she didn't press charges."

"All right. We'll figure it out. I'll take the kids in. Moss, you ride with me. Mick, you stay here."

Drew stood when asked and offered his hands. Tatum gently cuffed them in the front and led the suspect out of the house and to the sheriff's car. Kiera followed, wiping tears. The hillside was manic with a thousand flashing lights. Word was out that an officer was down, and every off-duty cop in the county wanted a look.

OZZIE DODGED THE other patrol cars and ambulances and weaved down the drive to the county road. He turned his blue lights on and hit the gas.

Drew asked, "Sir, can we see our mother?"

Ozzie looked at Tatum and said, "Turn on your tape recorder."

Tatum removed a small recorder from a pocket and flipped a switch.

Ozzie said, "Okay, we are now recording anything that's said. This is Sheriff Ozzie Walls and today is March twenty-fifth, nineteen ninety, at three fifty-one in the morning, and I'm driving to the Ford County jail with Deputy Moss Junior Tatum in the front seat, and in the backseat we have, what's your full name, son?"

"Drew Allen Gamble."

"Age?"

"Sixteen."

"And your name, Miss?"

"Kiera Gale Gamble, age fourteen."

"And your mother's name?"

"Josie Gamble. She's thirty-two."

"Okay. I advise you not to talk about what happened tonight. Wait until you have a lawyer. Understand?"

"Yes sir."

"Now, you asked about your mother, right?"

"Yes sir. Is she alive?"

Ozzie glanced at Tatum, who shrugged and said into the recorder, "As far as we know, Josie Gamble is alive. She was taken from the scene in an ambulance and is probably already at the hospital."

"Can we go see her?" Drew asked.

"No, not right now," Ozzie said.

They rode in silence for a moment, then Ozzie said, in the direction of the recorder, "You were the first on the scene, right?"

Tatum said, "Yes."

"And did you ask these two kids what happened?"

"I did. The boy, Drew, said nothing. I asked his sister, Kiera, if she knew anything, and she said her brother shot Kofer. At that point I stopped askin' questions. It was pretty clear what happened."

The radio was squawking and all of Ford County, even in the darkness, seemed to be alive. Ozzie turned down the volume and went silent himself. He kept his foot on the gas and his big brown Ford roared down the county road, straddling the center line, daring any varmint to venture onto the pavement.

He had hired Stuart Kofer four years earlier, after

Kofer returned to Ford County from an abbreviated career in the army. Stuart had managed a passable job in explaining his dishonorable discharge, said it was all about technicalities and misunderstandings and so on. Ozzie gave him a uniform, put him on probation for six months, and sent him to the academy in Jackson where he excelled. On duty, there were no complaints. Kofer had become an instant legend when he single-handedly took out three drug dealers from Memphis who had gotten lost in rural Ford County.

Off-duty was another matter. Ozzie had dressed him down at least twice after reports of drinking and hell-raising, and Stuart, typically, apologized in tears, promised to clean up his act, and swore allegiance to Ozzie and the department. And he was fiercely loyal.

Ozzie had no patience with unpleasant officers and the jerks didn't last long. Kofer was one of the more popular deputies and liked to volunteer in schools and with civic clubs. Because of the army he had seen the world, an oddity among his rather rustic colleagues, most of whom had hardly stepped outside the state. In public he was an asset, a gregarious officer who always had a smile and a joke, who remembered everyone's name, who liked to walk through Lowtown, the colored section, on foot and without a gun and with candy for the kids.

In private there were problems, but as brothers in uniform his colleagues tried to keep them from Ozzie. Tatum and Swayze and most of the deputies knew something of Stuart's dark side, but it was easier to ignore it and hope for the best, hope no one got hurt.

Ozzie glanced in the mirror again and looked at Drew in the shadows. Head down, eyes closed, not a sound. And although Ozzie was stunned and angry, it was difficult to picture the kid as a murderer. Slight, shorter than his sister, pale, timid, obviously over-whelmed, the kid could pass for a shy twelve-year-old.

They roared into the dark streets of Clanton and soon slid to a stop in front of the jail, two blocks off the square. Outside the main door to the jail a deputy was standing with a man holding a camera.

"Dammit," Ozzie said. "That's Dumas Lee, isn't it?"

"Afraid so," Tatum said. "I guess word's out. They all have police scanners these days."

"Y'all stay in the car." Ozzie got out, slammed his door, and walked straight for the reporter, already shaking his head. "You ain't gettin' nothin', Dumas," he said roughly. "There's a minor involved and you ain't gettin' his name or his picture. Get outta here."

Dumas Lee was one of two beat reporters for *The Ford County Times,* and he knew Ozzie well. "Can you confirm an officer has been killed?"

"I ain't confirmin' nothin'. You got ten seconds to get outta here before I slap cuffs on you and haul your ass inside. Beat it!"

The reporter slinked away and soon disappeared into the darkness. Ozzie watched him, then he and Tatum unloaded the kids and hustled them inside.

"You want to process them?" asked the jailer.

"No, we'll do it later. Let's just get 'em in the juvenile cell."

With Tatum bringing up the rear, Drew and Kiera were led through a wall of bars and down a narrow hallway to a thick metal door with a narrow window. The jailer opened it and they stepped into the empty room. There were two sets of bunk beds and a dirty commode in one corner.

Ozzie said, "Take off the handcuffs." Tatum snapped them off and Drew immediately rubbed his wrists. "You're gonna stay here for a few hours," Ozzie said.

"I want to see my mother," Drew said, more force-fully than Ozzie expected.

"Son, you're in no position to want anything right now. You're under arrest for the murder of a law enforcement official."

"He killed my mother."

"Your mother is not dead, thankfully. I'm about to drive to the hospital and check on her. When I come back I'll tell you what I know. That's the best I can do."

Kiera asked, "Why am I in jail? I didn't do anything."

"I know. You're in jail for your own safety, and you won't be here long. If we released you in a few hours, where would you go?"

Kiera looked at Drew and it was obvious they had no idea.

Ozzie asked, "Do y'all have any kinfolks around here? Aunts, uncles, grandparents? Anybody?"

Both hesitated then slowly shook their heads, no.

"Okay. It's Kiera, right?"

"Yes sir."

"If you had to call someone right now to come get you, who would you call?"

She looked at her feet and shook her head. "Our preacher, Brother Charles."

"Charles who?"

"Charles McGarry, out in Pine Grove."

Ozzie thought he knew all the preachers but per-haps he had missed one. In all fairness, there were three hundred churches in the county. Most were small con-gregations scattered throughout the countryside and notorious for fighting and splitting and running off their preachers. It was impossible for anyone to keep score. He looked at Tatum and said, "Don't know him."

"I do. Good guy."

"Give him a call, wake him up, ask him to get down

here." He looked at the kids and said, "We'll leave you here where you're safe. They'll bring in some snacks and drinks. Make yourself at home. I'm goin' to the hospital." He took a breath and looked at them with as little sympathy as possible. His overwhelming concern was a dead deputy and he was looking at the killer. Still, they were so lost and pathetic it was difficult to want revenge.

Kiera lifted her wet eyes and asked, "Sir, is he really dead?"

"He is indeed."

"I'm sorry, but he beat our mother a lot, and he came after us too."

Ozzie held up both hands and said, "Let's not go any further. We'll get a lawyer in here to talk to you kids and you can tell him anything you want. For now, just keep it quiet."

"Yes sir."

Ozzie and Tatum left the cell and slammed the door behind them. At the front, the jailer hung up his phone and said, "Sheriff, that was Earl Kofer, said he just heard that his son Stuart had been killed. Really upset. I said I didn't know but you need to call him."

Ozzie cursed under his breath and mumbled, "Just fixin' to do that. But I need to get to the hospital. You can handle it, can't you?"

"No," Tatum said.

"Sure you can. Give him a few facts and tell him I'll call later."

"Thanks for nothin'."

"You got it." Ozzie hustled out the front door and drove away.

———

IT WAS ALMOST 5:00 A.M. when Ozzie wheeled into the hospital's empty lot. He parked near the ER, hurried inside, and almost bumped into Dumas Lee, who was one step ahead of him.

"No comment, Dumas, and you're pissin' me off."

"That's my job, Sheriff. Just searching for the truth."

"I don't know the truth."

"Is the woman dead?"

"I'm not a doctor. Now leave me alone."

Ozzie punched the elevator button and left the reporter in the lobby. On the third floor, two deputies were waiting, and they escorted their boss to a desk where a young doctor saw them coming and was waiting. Ozzie made introductions and everybody nodded without shaking hands. "What can you tell us?" he asked.

Without looking at a chart, the doctor said, "She's unconscious but stable. Her left jaw is shattered and will need surgery soon to reset it, but it's not that urgent. Looks like she just took a shot to the jaw and/or chin and got knocked out."

"Any other injuries?"

"Not really, maybe some bruises on her wrists and neck, nothing that requires care."

Ozzie took a deep breath and thanked God for only one murder at a time. "So she'll pull through?"

"Her vitals are strong. Right now there's no reason to expect anything but a recovery."

"So when might she wake up?"

"Hard to predict, but I'd guess within forty-eight hours."

"Okay. Look, I'm sure you'll keep good records and all, but just remember that everything you do with this patient will probably be picked over in a courtroom one day. Keep that in mind. Be sure to take plenty of X-rays and color photos."

"Yes sir."

"I'll leave an officer here to monitor things."

Ozzie marched away and returned to the elevator and left the hospital. As he drove back to the jail, he grabbed his radio and called Tatum. The conversation with Earl Kofer had been about as awful as one could expect.

"You'd better call him, Ozzie. He said he's goin' over there to see for himself."

"Okay." Ozzie ended the call as he stopped in front of the jail. He held his phone and stared at it and, as always at these terrible moments, remembered the other late night and early morning calls to families; terrible calls that would dramatically change and even ruin the lives of many; calls he hated to make but his job required it. A young father found with his face blown off and a suicide note nearby; two drunk teenagers hurled from a speeding car; a demented grandfather finally found in a ditch. It was by far the worst part of his life.

Earl Kofer was hysterical and wanted to know who killed his "boy." Ozzie was patient and said he couldn't talk about the details at the moment but was willing to meet with the family, another dreadful prospect that was unavoidable. No, Earl should not go to Stuart's house because he would not be allowed in. The deputies there were waiting for investigators from the state crime lab, and their work would take hours. Ozzie suggested that the family meet at Earl's house and he, Ozzie, would stop by later in the morning. The father was wailing into the phone when Ozzie finally managed to hang up.

Inside the jail, he asked Tatum if Deputy Marshall

Prather had been notified. Tatum said yes, he was on his way. Prather was a veteran who had been a close friend of Stuart Kofer's since they were kids at Clanton Elementary School. He arrived in jeans and a sweatshirt and a state of disbelief. He followed Ozzie to his office where they fell into chairs as Tatum closed the door. Ozzie recited the facts as they knew them, and Prather couldn't hide his emotions. He gritted his teeth like a tough guy and covered his eyes, but he was obviously suffering.

After a long, painful pause, Prather managed to say, "We started school together in the third grade." His voice faded and he lowered his chin. Ozzie looked at Tatum, who looked away.

After another long pause, Ozzie pressed on. "What do you know about this woman, Josie Gamble?"

Prather swallowed hard and shook his head as if he could shake off the emotion. "I met her once or twice but didn't really know her. Stu took up with her I'd guess about a year ago. She and her kids moved in. She seemed nice enough, but she'd been around the block a few times. Pretty rough background."

"What do you mean?"

"She served some time. Drugs, I think. Has a colorful past. Stu met her in a bar, no surprise, and they hit it off. He didn't like the idea of her two kids hangin' around, but she talked him into it. Lookin' back, she needed a place to stay and he had extra bedrooms."

"What was the attraction?"

"Come on, Ozzie. Not a bad-lookin' woman, pretty damned cute really, looks good in tight jeans. You know Stu, always on the prowl but completely unable to get along with a woman."

"And the drinkin'?"

Prather removed an old cap and scratched his hair.

Ozzie leaned forward with a scowl and said, "I'm askin' questions, Marshall, and I want answers. This is no time for a cop cover-up where you look the other way and play dumb. I want answers."

"I don't know much, Ozzie, I swear. I stopped drinkin' three years ago so I don't hang out in the bars anymore. Yes, Stu was drinkin' too much and I think it was gettin' worse. I talked to him about it, twice. He said everything was fine, same as all drunks. I gotta cousin who still hits the joints and he told me that Stu was gettin' quite the reputation as a brawler, which was not what I wanted to hear. Said he was gamblin' a lot over at Huey's, down by the lake."

"And you didn't think I should know this?"

"Come on, Ozzie, I was concerned. That's why I had a chat with Stu. I was gonna talk to him again, I swear."

"Don't swear to me. So we had a deputy drinkin', fightin', and gamblin' with the riffraff, and oh by the way beatin' his girlfriend at home, and you thought I shouldn't know about it, right?"

"I thought you knew."

"We did," Tatum interrupted.

"Say what?" Ozzie snapped. "I never heard a word about domestic abuse."

"There was a report filed a month ago. She called 911 late one night and said Stu was on a rampage. We sent a car out with Pirtle and McCarver and they settled things down. The woman had obviously been slapped around but she refused to press charges."

Ozzie was livid. "I never heard about this and never saw the paperwork. What happened to it?"

Tatum shot a look at Prather, but it was not returned. Tatum shrugged as if he knew nothing and said, "There was no arrest, just an incident report. Must've been misplaced, I guess. I don't know, Ozzie, I wasn't involved."

"I'm sure no one was involved. If I looked high and low and grilled every man in my department I'm sure I wouldn't find anyone who was involved."

Prather glared at him and asked, "So you're blamin' Stu for gettin' himself shot, is that right, Ozzie? Blame the victim?"

Ozzie sank in his chair and closed his eyes.

ON THE BOTTOM bunk, Drew had curled up with his knees to his chest and was resting under a thin blanket with his head on an old pillow. He stared blankly at the dark wall. It had been hours since he said anything. Kiera sat at the foot of the bed, one hand touching his feet under the blanket and the other hand twirling her long hair as they waited for whatever might happen next. From time to time there were voices in the hallway but they faded, then disappeared for good.

For the first hour she and Drew had talked about the obvious—their mother's condition, and the stunning news that she was not dead, and then the shooting of Stu. The fact that he was dead was a relief to both of them and they felt fear but no remorse. Stu had used their mother as a punching bag, but had slapped them around too, and threatened them repeatedly. That nightmare was over. They would never again hear the sickening sounds of their mother getting smacked around by a drunken thug.

The jail cell itself was insignificant. Such crude and unsanitary conditions might bother a new offender, but they had seen worse. Drew had once spent four months in a juvenile facility in another state. Just last year they had locked Kiera up for two days in what was supposed to be protective custody. Jail was survivable.

For a little family that was always on the move, one

question before them was where to go next. Once they were with their mother they could plan their next move. They had met some of Stu's relatives and had always felt unwelcome. Stu liked to boast that he owned the house "free and clear" of debt because his grandfather had left it to him in a will. The house really wasn't that nice. It was dirty and needed repairs, and Josie's efforts to clean up were always met with disapproval. They had decided that they would not miss Stu's house.

During the second hour, they had speculated about how much trouble Drew might be facing. For them, it was a simple matter of self-defense, of survival, and of retribution. Slowly, Drew began to relive the shooting, step by step, or as much as he could remember. It had happened so fast and was a blur. Stu lying there, redfaced with his mouth open, snoring away as if he'd earned a good night's sleep. Stu reeking of alcohol. Violent Stu who could awaken at any moment and slap the kids around for the fun of it.

The pungent smell of spent gunpowder. The flash of blood and matter hitting the pillows and the wall. The shock of seeing Stu's eyes roll open after he was shot.

As the hours passed, though, Drew had grown quieter. He pulled the blanket to his chin and said he was tired of talking. She watched him slowly curl into himself and stare blankly at the wall.

3

The jail was filled with off-duty deputies and Clanton policemen and other miscellaneous personnel, some with affiliations to the department, others without. They smoked cigarettes, drank coffee, ate stale pastries, and spoke in subdued conversations about their fallen comrade and the dangers of the work. Ozzie was busy in his office, on the phone, making calls to the state police and the crime lab, ducking calls from reporters and friends and strangers.

When Reverend Charles McGarry arrived he was escorted to the big office where he shook hands with Ozzie and took a seat. Ozzie gave the details and explained that Kiera had asked to see their preacher. She said there was no family in the area and they had nowhere else to go. She was in the cell with her brother but Ozzie did not anticipate charges against her. There were two other juvenile cells but they were occupied, and she really didn't need to stay in jail anyway.

The preacher was only twenty-six years old and trying his best to lead a country church, one that Ozzie had visited when campaigning but with a different pastor back then. He was a pleasant young man who was obviously overwhelmed by the situation. He had been hired by the Good Shepherd Bible Church only fourteen months earlier, his first assignment since finishing seminary. He took a cup of coffee from Tatum and gave what little history he knew of the Gamble family. Josie and the kids had first shown up about six months back when a church member mentioned to McGarry that they might need some help. He went to their home on a weeknight and was treated rudely by Stuart Kofer. As he left, he invited Josie to their Sunday service. She and the kids had attended a few times, but she let him know that Kofer did not approve of their churchgoing. Without Stu's knowledge, McGarry had counseled her twice and been stunned by her background. She'd had both kids out of wedlock as a teenager, served time for drug possession, and admitted to a lot of bad behavior, which she promised was all in the past. While she was locked up, her kids had been placed in foster care and an orphanage.

"Can you take the girl somewhere safe?" Ozzie asked.

"Sure. She can live with us for the time being."

"Your family?"

"Yes. I have a wife and toddler and we're expecting. We live in the parsonage next to the church. It's small but we can find room."

"Okay. You take her home, but she can't leave the area. Our investigator will want to talk to her."

"No problem. How much trouble is Drew in?"

"A ton. He won't be getting out of jail anytime soon, I can promise you that. He'll remain in the juvenile cell and I'm sure the court will appoint him a lawyer in a day or so. We're not talkin' to him until then. The case looks open and shut. He admitted to his sister that he shot Kofer. No other suspects. He's in a lot of trouble, Reverend, a lot of trouble."

"Okay, Sheriff. Thanks for your consideration."

"Don't mention it."

"And I'm sorry for your loss. This is hard to believe."

"It is. Let's walk over to their cell and get the girl."

McGarry followed Ozzie and Tatum through the

crowded reception room and it grew quiet. The preacher got some stares as if he had already joined the opposing team. He was there to offer support for the killer's family. In a strange place and even stranger situation, the preacher did not realize the significance of the harsh looks.

The jailer opened the cell door and they stepped inside. Kiera hesitated as if uncertain, then she stood and ran to McGarry. His was the first trusted face she had seen in hours. He squeezed her tight, rubbed her head, whispered that he was there to get her, and that her mother was going to be all right. She clutched him tightly as she sobbed. The embrace dragged on, and Ozzie shot a look at Moss Junior.

Let's move along now.

In the darkness of the bottom bunk, Drew had all but disappeared under the blanket and had not moved a muscle since they entered. McGarry finally managed to gently push Kiera back a few inches. With his fingers he tried to wipe her tears, but they were rolling down her cheeks.

"I'm taking you to my house," McGarry repeated, and she tried to smile. He looked at the bottom bunk for a glimpse of Drew but there wasn't much to see. He looked at Ozzie and asked, "Can I say something to him?"

Ozzie said no with a firm shake of the head. "Let's get outta here."

McGarry took Kiera by the arm and led her out of the cell into the hallway. She did not try to speak to Drew, who was left alone in his dark world as the door closed. Ozzie led them through a side door and into the parking lot. As they were getting into McGarry's car, Deputy Swayze appeared and whispered to Ozzie.

Ozzie listened, nodded, said "Okay." He walked to

McGarry's window and said, "The hospital just called. Josie Gamble is awake and askin' about her kids. I'm goin' over and you're welcome to come wait."

AS OZZIE ROARED AWAY, again, he told himself that he just might spend the entire day running from one hotspot to another as the awful story unfolded. When he ignored a stop sign, Tatum asked, "You want me to drive?"

"I'm the high sheriff and this is important. Who'll complain?"

"Not me. Look, when you were back there with the preacher, I got a call from Looney at the scene. Earl Kofer showed up, out of his mind, said he wanted to see his boy. Looney and Pirtle have the place secured but Earl was hell-bent on gettin' inside. He had a coupla nephews with him, young bucks tryin' to be tough, and they made a big scene in the front yard. About that time the state investigators showed up with a van from the crime lab, and they were able to convince Earl that the entire house was an active crime scene and it was against the law for him to go inside. So Earl parked his truck in the front yard and just sat there with his two nephews. Looney asked him to leave but he said it was his property. Family property, he called it. I think he's still there."

"Okay, in about an hour I'm goin' to see Earl to meet with the whole family. You want to go?"

"Hell no."

"Well, you're goin' and that's an order. I need a couple of white boys backin' me up and I want you and Looney."

"Those people vote for you?"

"Everybody voted for me, Moss, don't you know

that? When you win a local race, everybody and his grandmother voted for you. I got seventy percent of the vote, so no complaints, but I have yet to meet a single person in Ford County who didn't vote for me. And they're proud of it, can't wait to go vote for me again."

"I thought it was sixty-eight percent."

"It would've been seventy if your lazy-ass people out in Blackjack had turned out."

"Lazy? My people vote like hell, Ozzie. They're tireless, relentless voters. They vote early, often, all day long, late, absentee, with real ballots, stuffed ballots, fake ballots. They vote dead people, crazy people, underage people, convicted felons who have no right to vote. You don't remember—it was about twenty years ago—but my uncle Felix went to jail for votin' dead people. Wiped out two cemeteries in one election. Still wasn't enough, and when his enemy won by six votes he got him indicted."

"Your uncle went to prison?"

"I didn't say prison. I said jail. He served about three months, said it wasn't that bad, came out a hero but never could vote again. So he learned how to stuff ballot boxes. You need my people, Ozzie, we know how to swing elections."

Ozzie again parked near the ER entrance and they hustled inside. On the third floor, the same two deputies walked him down the hall where the same young doctor was chatting with a nurse. The report was quick. Josie Gamble was conscious, though sedated because of sharp pains in her splintered jaw. Her vitals were normal. She had not been told that Stuart Kofer was dead or that her son Drew was in jail. She was asking about her children and the doctor assured her they were safe.

Ozzie took a deep breath, looked at Tatum who was

reading his mind and already shaking his head. Tatum said softly, "All yours, boss."

Ozzie asked the doctor, "Can she handle the bad news?"

The doctor smiled and shrugged and said, "Now or later. It doesn't really matter."

"Let's go," Ozzie said.

"I'll wait here," Tatum said.

"No you won't. Follow me."

FIFTEEN MINUTES LATER, Ozzie and Tatum were leaving the hospital when they noticed Pastor McGarry and Kiera sitting in the ER waiting room. Ozzie walked over and quietly explained that he had just spoken with Josie and that she was alert and eager to see Kiera. She was distraught and confused by Kofer's death and Drew's arrest and really wanted to see her daughter.

He again thanked the pastor for his help and promised to call later.

At the car, Ozzie said, "You drive," and walked to the passenger door.

"Gladly. Where to?"

"Well, I haven't seen a bloody corpse in several hours, so let's have a look at Stuart, may he rest in peace."

"I doubt he's moved much."

"And I need to speak to the state boys."

"Surely they can't screw up a case like this."

"They're good boys."

"If you say so." Tatum slammed the door and cranked the engine. Past the city limits, Ozzie said, "It's eight-thirty and I've been up since three."

"Same here, especially that bit about eight-thirty."

"And I've had no breakfast."

"I'm starvin'."

"What's open at this wonderful hour on the Sabbath?"

"Well, Huey's is probably just now closin' and they don't do breakfast. What about Sawdust?"

"Sawdust?"

"Yep, as far as I know it's the only place open this early on Sundays, at least in this part of the county."

"Well, I know I'll be welcome because they have a special door for me. Says, NEGROES ENTER HERE."

"I heard they took that down. You ever been inside?"

"No, Deputy Tatum, I have never been inside the Sawdust country store. When I was a kid here it was still used by the Klan for meetings that were not so secret. We may be living in 1990, but the people who shop and dine at Sawdust, along with those who sit by the old iron stove in the wintertime and tell nigger jokes, and those who chew tobacco on the front porch and spit on the gravel as they whittle and play checkers, are not the kind of people I want to hang with."

"They have great blueberry pancakes."

"They'll probably poison mine."

"No, they won't. Let's order the same thing, then swap after we're served. If I croak over and die, then Kofer and I can have a joint service. Damn, just think of the parade around the square."

"I really don't want to."

"Ozzie, you've been elected sheriff of Ford County by two landslides. You are the Man around here, and I can't believe you're shy about walkin' into a public café and havin' a meal. If you're afraid, I promise I'll protect you."

"That's not the case."

"A question. How many white-owned businesses

have you ducked and dodged since you ran for sheriff seven years ago?"

"Well, I haven't been to all the white churches."

"That's because it's humanly impossible to visit them all. Must be a thousand and they're still building. And I said businesses, not churches."

Ozzie pondered the question as they flew by small farms and pine forests. Finally, he said, "Only one that I can think of."

"Then let's go."

"Is that Confederate flag still flyin' out front?"

"Probably."

"Who owns the place now?"

"I don't know. I haven't stopped by in a few years."

They crossed a creek and turned onto another county road. Tatum gunned the engine as he straddled the center line. The road saw little traffic on workdays and was especially quiet on a Sunday morning. Ozzie said, "Pine Grove precinct. Ninety-five percent white and only thirty percent voted for me."

"Thirty percent?"

"Yep."

"I ever tell you about my mother's father, Grumps they called him? Died before I was born, which was probably a good thing. Ran for sheriff in Tyler County forty years ago and got eight percent of the vote. So thirty is pretty impressive."

"It didn't feel too impressive on election night."

"Give it up, boss. You won big. And this is your chance to impress the enlightened people who dine at Sawdust."

"Why is it called Sawdust?"

"Bunch of sawmills around here, lots of loggers. Tough guys. I don't know, but we're about to find out."

The parking lot was filled with pickups, some new,

most old and dented, all parked haphazardly as if their
drivers had sprinted to breakfast. An off-center flagpole
hailed the great state of Mississippi and the glorious
cause of the Confederacy. Two black bears nuzzled each
other in a cage next to the side porch. The planks
creaked as Ozzie and Moss Junior crossed them. The
front door entered into a cramped country store with
smoked meats hanging from the ceiling. The strong,
heavy aroma of frying bacon and burning wood filled
the air. Behind the counter, an old woman looked at
Tatum, then at Ozzie, and managed to nod and say,
"Mornin'."

They spoke, kept walking, and entered the café in
the rear where half the tables were crowded with men,
all white men, no women. They were eating and drinking coffee, some were smoking, and all seemed to be
chattering away, until they saw Ozzie. There was a noticeable decline in the noise, but only for the second or
two it took them to realize who he was and that both
were officers. Then, as if to prove their tolerance, they
picked up their conversations with even more vigor
and tried to ignore them.

Tatum waved to an empty table and they sat down.
Ozzie immediately busied himself with a thorough pe-
rusal of the menu, though it was unnecessary. A waitress
arrived with a pot of coffee and filled their cups.

A man at the nearest table looked for the second
time and Tatum pounced. "This place used to have famous blueberry pancakes. That still the case?"

"You betcha," the man said with a grin, then patted
his ample stomach. "That and venison sausage. Helps
me keep my figure." This got a laugh or two.

Another man said, "Say, we just heard about Stuart
Kofer." The room was instantly silent. "Is it true?"

Tatum gave a quick nod to his boss, as if to say, "This is your moment. Act like the high sheriff."

Ozzie's back was turned to at least half of the diners, so he stood and looked at them all. He said, "Yes, I'm afraid it's true. Stuart was shot and killed around three this morning, at home. We've lost one of our best."

"Who shot him?"

"I can't go into the details right now. We may have more to say tomorrow."

"We heard it was a kid livin' with him."

"Well, we've taken a sixteen-year-old boy into custody. The boy's mother was Kofer's girlfriend. That's all I can say. The state police are on the scene right now. Again, I can't say much. Maybe later."

Ozzie was smooth and friendly, and he could not have scripted what happened next. A rustic old man with dirty boots and faded overalls and a cap from a feed company said, respectfully, "Thank you, Sheriff." There was a pause. The ice was broken, and several others offered their thanks too.

Ozzie sat down and ordered pancakes and sausage. As they drank coffee and waited, Tatum said, "Not a bad campaign stop, huh, boss?"

"I never think about politics."

Tatum suppressed a laugh and looked away. "You know, boss, if you came here once a month and had breakfast, you'd get every vote."

"Don't want every vote. Just seventy percent of them."

The waitress laid a copy of the Sunday edition of the Jackson paper on the table and smiled at Ozzie. Tatum grabbed the sports section, and to pass the time Ozzie read the state news. His eyes drifted above the print and he noticed the wall to his right. In the center were two large 1990 football schedules, one for Ole Miss, one for

Mississippi State, and around them were banners for both teams and framed black-and-white photos of yesterday's heroes in various action poses. All white, all from another era.

Ozzie had starred at Clanton High and dreamed of being the first black player at Ole Miss, but he wasn't recruited. There were already two blacks in the program and Ozzie had always quietly assumed that, at that time, two were enough. He signed instead with Alcorn State, started for four years, got drafted in the tenth round, and made the L.A. Rams roster his rookie year. He played in eleven games before a knee injury sent him back to Mississippi.

He studied the faces of the old stars and wondered how many of them had actually played in a professional football game. Two other players from Ford County, both black, had made it professionally, but their photos were not on the wall either.

He lifted the newspaper an inch or two and tried to read a story, but he was distracted. The conversations around him were about the weather, a coming storm, the bass biting in Lake Chatulla, the death of an old farmer they all knew, and the latest stunts by their senators in Jackson. He listened carefully as he pretended to read and wondered what they would be discussing in his absence. Would they dwell on the same subjects? Probably so.

Ozzie knew that in the late 1960s the Sawdust had been the gathering spot for white hotheads determined to build a private school in the wake of the Supreme Court's betrayals on desegregation. The school had been built on some donated land outside of Clanton, a simple metal building with low-paid teachers and cheap tuitions that were never cheap enough. It folded after a few years of rising debts and intense pressure for countywide support of the public schools.

The pancakes and sausage arrived and the waitress refilled their cups.

"You ever had venison sausage?" Tatum asked. In his forty or so years he had barely set foot outside of Ford County, but he often assumed he knew far more than his boss, who had once traveled coast to coast in the NFL.

"My grandmother used to make it," Ozzie said. "I watched her." He took a bite, considered it, said, "Okay, a bit too spicy."

"I saw you lookin' at those photos on the wall. They need one of you, boss."

"Not really my hangout, Tatum. I can live without it."

"We'll see. It ain't right, you know."

"Drop it."

They dug into their tall stacks of pancakes, each enough for a family of four, and enjoyed a few bites. Then Tatum leaned in and asked, "So what're you thinkin' about a funeral and such?"

"I'm not family, Moss, in case you haven't noticed. I suppose that'll be up to his parents."

"Yeah, but you can't just have a service and lower him into the ground, right? Hell, he's a law enforcement officer, Ozzie. Don't we get parades and marchin' bands and drill teams and rifle salutes? I want a crowd and I want some folks really tore up and carryin' on when they bury me."

"Probably not goin' to happen." Ozzie lowered his knife and fork and slowly took a drink of coffee. He looked at his deputy as if he was in kindergarten and said, "A slight distinction, Moss. Our buddy Kofer was not exactly killed in the line of duty. Indeed, he was

off-duty and in all likelihood had been drinkin' and
carousin' and who knows what else. It might be rather
difficult to drum up support for a parade to send him
off."

"What if the family wants a show?"

"Look, they're still takin' pictures of his dead body,
so let's worry about it later, okay? Now eat. We need to
hustle over there."

BY THE TIME they arrived at Stuart's house, Earl
Kofer and his nephews were gone. At some point, they
got tired of waiting and were probably needed back
with the family. The driveway and front yard were
crowded with police cars and official vehicles: two vans
from the state crime lab, an ambulance waiting to haul
Stuart away, another one with a crew just in case they
were needed; even a couple of volunteer fire department vehicles were in place to assist, as usual, with the
congestion.

Ozzie knew one of the state investigators and got a
quick briefing, not that it was needed. They looked at
Stuart again, in exactly the same spot as before, the only
difference being the darkened shades of the blood on
the sheets around him. The stained and spattered pillows were gone. Two technicians in head-to-toe hazmat
garb were slowly lifting samples from the wall above the
headboard.

"Fairly cut-and-dried, I'd say," the investigator said.
"But we'll take him in anyway for a quick autopsy. I
take it the kid is still in jail."

"Yep," Ozzie replied. Where else would the kid be?
As always at these crime scenes, Ozzie found it difficult
to stomach the arrogance of the state boys who rolled
in with their airs of superiority. He wasn't required to

call them to the scene, but in murder cases that led to murder trials he had learned that jurors tend to be more impressed with experts from the state police. In the end, nothing mattered but convictions.

"Has he been printed?" the investigator asked.

"No. We thought we'd let you guys do that."

"Good. We'll go by the jail and fingerprint him and scan for gunshot residue."

"He's waiting."

They stepped outside where Tatum fired up a cigarette and Ozzie took a paper cup of coffee from a fireman who'd brought his thermos. They loitered a bit, with Ozzie trying to delay his next stop. The front door opened again and a technician began backing out slowly, pulling the gurney with Stuart wrapped tightly in sheets. They rolled him down the brick walkway, lifted him into an ambulance, and closed the door.

EARL AND JANET Kofer lived a few miles away in a low-slung 1960s-style ranch house where they had raised three sons and a daughter. Stuart was their oldest child and because of this had inherited from his grandfather ten wooded acres and the house where he lived and died. The Kofers as a clan were not wealthy and did not own a lot of land, but they had always worked hard, lived frugally, and tried to avoid trouble. And there were plenty of them, scattered around the southern part of the county.

In his first run for public office, in 1983, Ozzie was never certain how the family voted. However, four years later and with Stuart wearing a uniform and driving a shiny patrol car, Ozzie got every vote in the family. They proudly displayed his yard signs and even wrote small checks for his campaign.

Now, on this awful Sunday morning, they were all waiting for their sheriff to pay his respects and answer their questions. For a show of support, Ozzie had Tatum at the wheel, followed by a car with Looney and Mc-Carver, two other white deputies. It was, after all, Mississippi, and Ozzie had learned where to use his white deputies and where to use his black ones.

As expected, the long front drive was lined with cars and trucks. On the porch, one group of men smoked and waited. Not far away under a sourwood tree another group did the same. Tatum parked and they got out and began walking across the front lawn as relatives stepped forward with their somber greetings. Ozzie and Tatum, and Looney and McCarver, worked their way toward the house, shaking hands, offering condolences, grieving with the family. Near the front, Earl stood and stepped down and thanked Ozzie for coming. His eyes were red and wounded and he began sobbing again as Ozzie shook his hands with both of his and just listened. A crowd of men gathered around the sheriff and expected to hear something.

Ozzie met their sad and troubled eyes, nodded, tried to appear just as hurt. He said, "Really not much to add to what you already know. The call came across at two-forty this morning, call from the son of Josie Gamble, said his mother had been beaten and he thought she was dead. When we got there we found the mother unconscious in the kitchen being tended to by her daughter, age fourteen. The daughter said her brother had shot Stuart. Then we found Stuart in the bedroom, on his bed, a single gunshot to the head, by his service pistol, which was on the bed. The boy, Drew, wouldn't talk so we took him in. He's in jail now."

"No doubt it's the boy?" someone asked.

Ozzie shook his head. No. "Look, I can't say much

right now. Truth is we don't know much more than what I just told you. I'm not sure there's that much more to it, really. Maybe we'll know something tomorrow."

"He ain't gettin' outta jail, right?" asked another.

"No, no way. I expect the court will appoint him a lawyer real soon, and at that point the system takes over."

"Will there be a trial?"

"I have no idea."

"How old is this boy?"

"Sixteen."

"Can they treat him like an adult, put his ass on death row?"

"That's up to the court."

There was a pause as some of the men studied their feet while others wiped their eyes. Softly, Earl asked, "Where is Stuart now?"

"They're takin' him to Jackson, state crime lab, for an autopsy. Then they'll release him to you and Mrs. Kofer. I'd like to see Janet, if that's okay."

Earl said, "I don't know, Sheriff, she's in bed and surrounded by her sisters. I'm not sure she wants to see anybody. Give her some time."

"Of course. Please pass along my condolences."

Two other cars were arriving, and out on the highway another had slowed. Ozzie killed a few awkward minutes and then excused himself. Earl and the others thanked him for coming. He promised to call tomorrow and keep them informed.

4

Six days a week, every day but Sunday, Jake Brigance allowed himself to be dragged out of bed at the unholy hour of 5:30 A.M. by a noisy alarm clock. Six days a week he went straight to the coffeepot, punched a button, then hurried to his own private little bathroom in the basement, far away from his sleeping wife and daughter, where he showered in five minutes and spent another five with the rest of his ritual before dressing in the clothes he'd laid out the night before. He then hurried upstairs, poured a cup of black coffee, eased back into his bedroom, kissed his wife goodbye, grabbed his coffee, and, at precisely 5:45 closed the kitchen door and stepped onto the rear patio. Six days a week he drove the dark streets of Clanton to the picturesque square with the stately courthouse anchoring life as he knew it, parked in front of his office on Washington Street, and, at 6:00 A.M., six days a week, walked into the Coffee Shop to either hear or create the gossip, and to dine on wheat toast and grits.

But on the seventh day, he rested. There was never an alarm clock on the Sabbath, and Jake and Carla reveled in a long morning's rest. He would eventually stumble forth around 7:30 and order her back to sleep. In the kitchen he poached eggs and toasted bread and served her breakfast in bed with coffee and juice. On a normal Sunday.

But nothing about this day would be normal. At 7:05 the phone rang, and since Carla insisted that the phone be located on his night table, he had no choice but to answer it.

"If I were you I'd leave town for a couple of days." It was the low raspy voice of Harry Rex Vonner, perhaps his best friend and sometimes his only one.

"Well good morning, Harry Rex. This better be good."

Harry Rex, a gifted and devious divorce lawyer, ran in the dark shadows of Ford County and took enormous pride in knowing the news, the dirt, and the gossip before almost anyone not wearing a badge.

"Stuart Kofer got shot in the head last night. Dead. Ozzie picked up his girlfriend's boy, sixteen-year-old kid without a trace of peach fuzz, and he's at the jail just waitin' on a lawyer. I'm sure Judge Noose knows about it and is already thinkin' about the appointment."

Jake sat up and propped up his pillows. "Stuart Kofer is dead?"

"Deader'n hell. Kid blew his brains out while he was sleepin'. Capital, dude, death penalty and all. Killing a cop will get you the gas nine times outta ten in this state."

"Didn't you handle a divorce for him?"

"His first one, not his second. He got pissed off about my fee and became a disgruntled client. When he called about the second, I told him to get lost. Married a couple of crazies, but then he had a fondness for bad women, especially in tight jeans."

"Any kids?"

"None that I know of. None that he knew of either."

Carla scurried out of bed and stood beside it. She frowned at Jake as if someone was lying. Three weeks earlier, Officer Stuart Kofer had visited her class of sixth graders and given a wonderful presentation on the dangers of illegal drugs.

"But he's only sixteen," Jake said, scratching his eyes.

"Spoken like a true liberal defense lawyer. Noose will be callin' you before you know it, Jake. Think about it. Who tried the last capital murder case in Ford County? You. Carl Lee Hailey."

"But that was five years ago."

"Doesn't matter. Name another lawyer around here who'll even think about taking a serious criminal case. Nobody. And more important, Jake, there's no one else in the county who's competent enough to take a capital case."

"No way. What about Jack Walter?"

"He's back in the sauce. Noose got two complaints last month from disgruntled clients and he's about to notify the state bar." How Harry Rex knew such things was always a marvel to Jake.

"I thought they sent him away."

"They did, but he came back, thirstier than ever."

"What about Gill Maynard?"

"He got burned in that rape case last year. Told Noose he'd surrender his license before he got stuck with another bad criminal appointment. And he's pretty awful on his feet. Noose was beyond frustrated with the guy in the courtroom. Give me another name."

"Okay, okay. Let me think a minute."

"A waste of time. I'm tellin' you, Jake, Noose will call you sometime today. Can you leave the country for a week or so?"

"Don't be ridiculous, Harry Rex. We have motions before Noose at ten Tuesday morning, the rather insignificant matter of the *Smallwood* case? Remember that one?"

"Dammit. I thought it was next week."

"Good thing I'm in charge of the case. Not to mention such trivial matters as Carla and her job and Hanna and her classes. It's silly to think we can just disappear. I'm not running, Harry Rex."

"You'll wish you had, believe me. This case is nothin' but trouble."

"If Noose calls, I'll talk to him and explain why I can't get involved. I'll suggest that he appoint someone from another county. He likes those two guys in Oxford who'll take anything, and he's brought them in before."

"Last I heard they're swamped with death row appeals. They always lose at trial, you know. Makes the appellate stuff go on forever. Listen to me, Jake, you do not want a dead-cop case. The facts are against you. The politics are against you. There's not a chance in hell the jury will show any sympathy."

"Got it, got it, got it, Harry Rex. Let me drink some coffee and talk to Carla."

"Is she in the shower?"

"Well, no."

"That's my favorite fantasy, you know."

"Later, Harry Rex." Jake hung up and followed Carla to the kitchen where they brewed coffee. The spring morning was almost warm enough to sit on the patio, but not quite. They settled around a small table in the breakfast nook, with a pleasant view of the pink and white azaleas blooming in the backyard. The dog, a recent rescue effort they called Mully but who, so far, answered to nothing except food, emerged from his turf in the washroom and stared at the patio door. Jake let him outside and poured two cups.

Over coffee, he repeated everything Harry Rex said, except the parting shot about Carla in the shower, and they discussed the unpleasant possibility of getting dragged into the case. Jake agreed that the Honorable Omar Noose, his friend and mentor, was unlikely to appoint another lawyer from the rather shallow pool of talent that was the Ford County bar. Almost to a man, or to a person since there was now one female lawyer, they avoided jury trials, preferring instead to do the paperwork required of their quiet little office practices. Harry Rex was always up to a good courtroom brawl, but only in domestic relations cases tried before judges; no juries. Ninety-five percent of the criminal cases were settled with plea bargains, thus avoiding trials. Small tort cases—car wrecks, slip-and-falls, dog bites— were negotiated with the insurance companies. Usually, if a Ford County lawyer stumbled onto a big civil case he rushed to Tupelo or Oxford and associated a real trial lawyer, one experienced in litigation and not terrified of juries.

Jake still dreamed of changing this, and at the age of thirty-seven he was trying to establish a reputation as a lawyer who gambled and got verdicts. Without a doubt his most glorious moment had been the not-guilty verdict for Carl Lee Hailey five years earlier, and he had been certain in its aftermath that the big cases would find their way to his door. They had not. He still threatened to try every dispute, and this worked well, but the rewards were still paltry.

The *Smallwood* case, though, was different. It had the potential of being the biggest civil case in the county's history, and Jake was the lead counsel. He had filed the lawsuit thirteen months earlier and had since spent half his time working on it. He was now ready for the trial and yelling at the defense lawyers for a date.

Harry Rex had not mentioned the role of the county's part-time public defender, and with good reason. The current P.D. was a bashful rookie whose early job approval ratings were about as low as they could get. He took the job because no one else wanted it, and because the position had been vacant for a year, and because the county reluctantly agreed to increase the salary to $2,500 a month. No one expected him to survive another year. He had yet to try a case all the way to a jury's verdict and showed no interest in doing so. And, most important, he had never even watched a capital murder trial.

Not surprisingly, Carla immediately felt sympathy for the woman. Even though she had liked Stu Kofer, she also knew that some off-duty cops could behave as badly as anyone. And if domestic violence was a factor, the facts would only become more complicated.

But she was wary of another high-profile, controversial case. For three years after the trial of Carl Lee Hailey, the Brigance family had lived with a deputy parked in front of their house at night, and threatening phone calls, and hateful glares from strangers in stores. Now, in another nice home and with that case even further behind them, they were slowly adjusting to a normal life. Jake still carried a registered gun in his car, which she frowned on, but the surveillance was gone. They were determined to enjoy the present, plan for the future, and forget the past. The last case Carla wanted was one that might attract headlines.

As they were chatting quietly, Miss Hanna appeared in her pajamas, sleepy-eyed and clutching, still, her favorite stuffed cub, one that she had never slept without. The cub was threadbare and far past its useful shelf life, and Hanna was nine years old and needed to move on, but a serious discussion about such a transition was being postponed. She crawled into her father's lap and closed her eyes again. Like her mother, she preferred a quiet entry into the morning with as little noise as possible.

Her parents stopped talking about the legal stuff and switched to Hanna's Sunday school lesson, one she had not yet read. Carla disappeared and returned with the study guide, and Jake began reading about Jonah and the Whale, one of his least favorite Bible stories. Hanna wasn't impressed with it either and seemed to doze. Carla busied herself in the kitchen with breakfast—oatmeal for Hanna, poached eggs and wheat toast for the adults.

They ate quietly and enjoyed the peaceful moments together. Cartoons on television were usually prohibited on Sundays, and Hanna didn't think to ask. She ate little, as usual, and reluctantly left the table for a bath.

At 9:45, they were dressed in their Sunday finest and headed for worship at the First Presbyterian Church. Once loaded in the car, Jake couldn't find his sunglasses, and hustled back inside, turning off the ever-present alarm system as he entered.

The phone on the kitchen wall started ringing and the caller ID flashed a number—same area code but a different prefix that looked familiar. Could be Van Buren County, next door. No name, caller unknown, but Jake had a hunch. He stared at the phone, either unable or unwilling to answer, because something told him not to. Besides Harry Rex, who dared call on a peaceful Sunday morning? Lucien Wilbanks maybe, but it wasn't him. It must be important and it must be trouble, and for seconds he just stood there gawking at the phone, transfixed. After the max of eight rings, he waited for the recording light to blink and punched a button. A familiar voice said: "Good morning, Jake, it's Judge Noose. I'm at home in Chester and headed to church. You probably are too and I'm sorry to disturb, but there's an urgent matter in Clanton and I'm sure you've heard about it by now. Please call me as soon as possible." And the line went dead.

He would remember that moment for a long time— standing in his kitchen, dressed in a dark suit as if filled with confidence, and staring at the telephone because he was too afraid to answer it. He could not remember ever feeling like such a coward and vowed that it would never happen again.

He set the alarm, locked the door, and walked to the car with a big fake smile for his girls and got in. As he backed out of the drive, Hanna asked, "Where are your sunglasses, Daddy?"

"Oh, I couldn't find them."

"They were on the counter by the mail," Carla said.

He shook his head as if it didn't matter and said, "Didn't see them and we're running late."

THE LESSON IN the men's Bible class was a continuation of the study of Paul's letter to the Galatians, but they never got around to it. A policeman had been murdered, a local boy whose parents and grandparents were from the county, along with other family members scattered about. Much of the discussion was about crime and punishment, with the mood running strongly in favor of swift retribution, regardless of how young the killer might be. Did it really matter if he was sixteen or sixty? It certainly didn't matter to Stu Kofer, whose stock seemed to rise by the hour. A bad kid pulling a trigger can do just as much damage as a serial killer. There were three lawyers in the class, and the other two held forth with no shortage of opinions. Jake was passive but deep in thought, and tried not to appear troubled.

His Presbyterian brethren were considered a bit more tolerant than the fundamentalists down the street—the Baptists and Pentecostals who loved the death penalty—but judging by the thirst for vengeance in the small classroom Jake figured the boy who killed Stu Kofer was headed to the gas chamber at Parchman.

He kept trying to dismiss it all, because it would be someone else's problem. Right?

At 10:45, with the pipe organ roaring away and calling all to worship, Jake and Carla made their way down the aisle to the fourth pew from the front, right side, and waited for Hanna to come bouncing in from her Sunday school class. Jake chatted with old friends and acquaintances, most of whom he rarely saw outside of church. Carla said hello to two of her students. First Presbyterian averaged 250 congregants for the morning service, and it seemed as if most were milling around and exchanging greetings. There was a lot of gray hair, and Jake knew their minister was concerned about the flagging popularity of worship among younger families.

Old Mr. Cavanaugh, a perpetual grouch who most people tried to avoid but who wrote bigger checks than any other member, grabbed Jake by the arm and said, much too loudly, "You ain't gettin' involved with that boy who killed our deputy, are you?"

Oh, the retorts he would love to use. First: Why can't you ever mind your own business, you cranky old bastard? Second: You and your family have never thrown me a dime in legal work, so why are you now concerned with my law practice? Third: How can the case possibly affect you?

Instead, Jake looked him square in the eye and without a trace of a smile replied, "Which deputy are you talking about?"

Mr. Cavanaugh was taken aback, paused just long enough for Jake to free his arm, and managed to ask, "Oh, you haven't heard?"

"Heard what?"

The choir erupted in a call to worship and it was time to be seated. Hanna appeared and wedged herself between her parents, and not for the first time Jake smiled at her and wondered how long these days would last. She would soon start bugging them to let her sit with her friends during "Big Church," and then not long after that boys would enter the picture. Don't look for trouble, Jake reminded himself. Just enjoy the moment.

The moments, though, were difficult to enjoy. Not long after the preliminary announcements and the first hymn, Dr. Eli Proctor assumed the pulpit and delivered the somber news that everyone already knew. With a bit too much drama, at least in Jake's opinion, the pastor told of the tragic loss of Officer Stuart Kofer as if in some way it directly affected him. It was an irritating habit, one that Jake occasionally mentioned to Carla, though she had no patience for his complaints. Proctor could almost cry when describing typhoons in the South Pacific or famines in Africa, disasters that no doubt deserved the prayers of all Christians, but were on the other side of the world. The pastor's only connection was the cable news shared by the rest of the country. He managed, though, to be more profoundly touched.

He prayed long and hard for justice and healing, but was a bit light on mercy.

The youth choir sang two hymns and the service switched gears. When the sermon started, at precisely 11:32 by Jake's watch, he tried gamely to absorb the opening paragraph but was soon lost in the near dizzying scenarios that might be played out in the days to come.

He would call Noose after lunch, that much was certain. He had great respect and admiration for his judge, and this was strengthened by the fact that Noose felt the same way about him. As a young lawyer, Noose had gotten himself involved in politics and gone astray. As a state senator, he had narrowly missed an indictment and was humiliated at reelection time. He once told Jake that he had wasted his formative years as a young lawyer and had never honed his courtroom skills. With great pride he had watched Jake grow up in the courtroom, and still relished his not-guilty verdict in the Hailey trial.

Jake knew it would be next to impossible to say no to the Honorable Omar Noose.

And if he said yes and agreed to represent the kid? That kid sitting over there in the jail, in the juvie cell that Jake had visited many times? What would these fine folks, these devout Presbyterians, think of him? How many of them had ever seen the inside of a jail? How many had an inkling of how the system worked?

And, crucially, how many of these fine law-abiding citizens believed every defendant had the right to a fair trial? And the word "fair" was supposed to include the assistance of a good lawyer.

The common question was: How can you represent a man who's guilty of a serious crime?

His common response was: If your father or son was charged with a serious crime, would you want an aggressive lawyer or a pushover?

Typically, and with no small measure of frustration, he was again busying himself with thoughts about what others might think. A serious flaw for any lawyer, at least according to the great Lucien Wilbanks, a man who had never worried about the concerns of others.

When Jake finished law school and found himself working in the Wilbanks law firm under Lucien's tutelage, his boss had proclaimed such gems as: "Those pricks down at the Rotary Club and the church and the coffee shop will not make you a lawyer and will not make you a dime." And, "To be a real lawyer, first you grow a thick skin, and second you tell everybody but your clients to go to hell." And, "A real lawyer is not afraid of unpopular cases."

Such was the atmosphere of Jake's apprenticeship. Before he was disbarred for all manner of bad behavior, Lucien was a successful lawyer who made a name for himself representing the underdogs—minorities, unions, poor school districts, abandoned kids, the homeless. Because of his brazenness, though, and his self-awareness issues, he often failed to connect with juries.

Jack pinched himself and wondered why he was thinking of Lucien during the sermon.

Because if he still had a license to practice law, Lucien would be calling Noose and demanding that he, Lucien, be appointed to represent the kid. And since all other locals were running from the case, Noose would appoint Lucien and everyone would be pleased.

"Take the damned case, Jake!" he could hear him yelling.

"Every person is entitled to a lawyer!"

"You can't always pick your clients!"

Carla realized he was drifting and shot him a look. He smiled and patted Hanna's knee, but she quickly shoved his hand away. After all, she was nine years old.

IN THE PARLANCE of the Bible Belt, those within the faith used many words and terms to describe those outside of it. On the harsher end of the spectrum, the "lost" were referred to as heathen, unsaved, unclean, hellbound, and just old-fashioned sinners. More polite Christians called them nonbelievers, future saints, backsliders, or—the favorite—unchurched.

Whatever the term, it was safe to say that the Kofers had been unchurched for decades. Some distant cousins were members of congregations, but as a rule they as a clan had avoided involvement with the Word. They were not bad people, they had just never felt the need to pursue the holier way. They had had their chances. Dozens of well-meaning country preachers had tried to reach them, to no avail. And it was not unusual for traveling evangelists to target them and even call them by name in fiery sermons. They had often been at the top of prayer lists and subjected to door-to-door solicitations. Through it all, they had resisted all efforts to follow the Lord and were quite content to be left alone.

On that somber morning, though, they needed the embrace and sympathy of their neighbors. They needed the usual outpouring of love and compassion of those closer to God, and it wasn't there. Instead, they huddled en masse at Earl's home and tried to cope with the unimaginable. The women sat and cried with Janet, Stu's mother, while the men stayed outside on the porch and under the trees, smoking, cursing quietly, and talking of revenge.

THE GOOD SHEPHERD Bible Church met in a picturesque white-frame building with a tall steeple and a manicured cemetery behind it. The building was historic, 160 years old, and had been built by Methodists, who handed it down to some Baptists, who disbanded and left it vacant for thirty years. The church's founders had been an independent group, not fond of denominational labels and the rampant fundamentalism and political leanings that had swept through the South in the 1970s. The church, with about a hundred members, had bought the building out of foreclosure, renovated it with great care, and welcomed more enlightened souls who were weary of the prevailing dogma. Women were elected as elders, a radical notion that gave rise to the whispered claim that Good Shepherd was a "cult." Blacks and all minorities were welcome, though they worshipped elsewhere, for other reasons.

On that Sunday morning, attendance was up slightly as the members met to learn the latest details of the killing. Once Pastor Charles McGarry let it be known that the accused, young Drew Gamble, was practically one of them, and that his mother, Josie, was in the hospital, badly injured after a brutal beating, the church circled its wagons and embraced the family. Kiera, still in the jeans and sneakers she wore during the terrible ordeal of the night before, sat through Sunday school in a small classroom with other teenage girls and tried to comprehend where she was. Her mother was in the hospital and her brother was in the jail, and she had already been told that she could not go back to the house to gather her things. She tried not to cry but couldn't help herself. During the worship hour she sat on the front pew with the pastor's wife on one side, holding her arm, and a girl she knew from school close on the other. She managed to stop the tears but she couldn't think clearly. She stood for the hymns, old songs she had never heard before, and she closed her eyes tight and tried to pray along with Pastor Charles. She listened to his sermon but heard nothing. She had not eaten in hours but had declined food. She could not imagine going to school tomorrow and decided she would not be forced to do so.

All Kiera wanted was to sit on the edge of her mother's hospital bed, with her brother on the opposite side, and touch her arms.

5

Sunday lunch was a light salad and soup, the usual unless Jake's mother was in the mood to put on a spread, a treat that happened about once a month. But not today. After a quick lunch, he helped Carla clear the table and stack the dishes and toyed with the idea of a Sunday nap, but Hanna had other plans. She wanted to take Mully for a walk to the city park and Carla volunteered Jake for the adventure. He was fine with it. Anything to kill time and avoid the return call to Judge Noose. By two he was back and Hanna disappeared into her room. Carla boiled water and served them green tea at the breakfast table.

She asked, "He can't make you take the case, can he?"

"I really don't know. I've thought about it all morning and I can't remember a case where the court tried to appoint a lawyer and he refused. Circuit judges have enormous power and I suppose Noose could make my life miserable if I said no. Frankly, that's why you don't say no. A small-town lawyer is dead if he alienates his judges."

"And you're worried about *Smallwood*?"

"Of course I'm worried about it. Discovery is almost complete and I'm pestering Noose for a trial date. The defense is stalling as always but I think we have them on the run. Harry Rex thinks they might be ready to talk settlement, but not until they're staring at a firm trial date. We need to keep Noose happy."

"Are you saying he might carry a grudge from one case to the next?"

"Omar Noose is a wonderful old judge who almost always gets it right, but he can also be prickly. He's human and makes mistakes, and he's also accustomed to getting whatever he wants, at least in his own court-room."

"So he would allow one case to affect another?"

"Yes. It has happened."

"But he likes you, Jake."

"He sees himself as my mentor and he wants me to do great things, and that's a perfect reason to keep the old guy happy."

"Do I get a vote in this?"

"Always."

"Okay. This is not the Hailey case. There is no racial tension here. As far as I know, everybody is white, right?"

"So far."

"So the Klan and those crazies won't show up this time. To be sure, you'll rankle some people who want to string the kid up right now and they'll resent any law-yer who takes his case, but doesn't that go with the territory? You're a lawyer, the best in my opinion, and right now there's a sixteen-year-old boy in serious trouble and he needs help."

"There are other lawyers in town."

"And which one would you hire if you were facing the death penalty?"

Jake hesitated too long and she said, "See."

"Tom Motley is a promising trial lawyer."

"And one who doesn't get his hands dirty on the criminal side. How many times have I heard you give that rant?"

"Bo Landis is good."

"Who? I'm sure he's great but his name doesn't ring a bell."

"He's young."

"And you would trust him with your life?"

"I didn't say that. Look, Carla, I'm not the only lawyer in town and I'm sure Noose can twist somebody else's arm. It's not uncommon in nasty cases like this to appoint a lawyer from outside the county. Remember that terrible rape out in Box Hill three or four years ago?"

"Sure."

"Well, we begged off and Noose protected us by hooking in a lawyer from Tupelo. No one here knew him and he handled it as well as could be expected. Bad facts."

"And that was a plea bargain, right?"

"Yes. Thirty years in prison."

"Not enough. What are the chances of a plea bargain in this case?"

"Who knows? We're talking about a minor, so Noose might cut him some slack. But there'll be a big push for blood. The death penalty. The victim's family will make noise. Ozzie will want a big trial because one of his boys is dead. Everybody's up for reelection next year so it's a perfect moment to get tough on crime."

"It doesn't seem right to send a sixteen-year-old kid to death row."

"Try telling that to the Kofer family. Don't know them, but I'll bet they're thinking about the gas chamber. If some guy harmed Hanna, you wouldn't be too concerned about his age, would you?"

"Probably not."

They took a deep breath and allowed this sobering thought to pass.

"I thought you were ready to vote," Jake said.

"I don't know, Jake. It's a tough call, but if Judge Noose pushes hard I don't see how you can say no."

The phone rang and they stared at it. Jake walked over and looked at the caller ID. He smiled at Carla and said, "It's him." Jake grabbed the receiver, said hello, then pulled the cord halfway across the kitchen and took a seat with his wife at the breakfast table.

They waded through the pleasantries. Families were all fine. The weather was changing. Terrible news about Stuart Kofer. They both professed admiration. Noose had spoken to Ozzie, and Ozzie had the kid locked away, safe and secure. Good ole Ozzie. Most sheriffs Noose dealt with would've had the kid on the rack and signing a ten-page confession.

Hitting his stride, Noose said, "Jake, I want you to represent this kid through the preliminaries. Don't know if it'll turn into a capital case but that's always a real possibility. Nobody else in Clanton has any recent experience with the death penalty and you're the lawyer I trust the most. If it goes capital, then we'll revisit your representation and I'll try to find someone else."

Jake closed his eyes and nodded and, at the first pause, jumped in. "Judge, you and I both know that if I step in now there's an excellent chance I'll be stuck with it all the way."

"Not necessarily, Jake. I just spoke with Roy Browning over in Oxford, damned fine lawyer, you know him, Jake?"

"Everybody knows Roy, Judge."

"He has two capital trials this year and is swamped, but he has a young partner who he thinks highly of. He promised me they would take a look at the case down the road if it goes capital. Right now, though, Jake, I want someone in that jail talking to the kid and keep-

ing the police away from him. I don't want to be faced
with some bogus confession or a jailhouse snitch."

"I trust Ozzie."

"And so do I, Jake, but this is a dead policeman, and
you know how worked up those boys can get. I would
just feel better if that kid had some protection right
now. I'll make the appointment good for thirty days.
You get over there and see the kid, then we'll meet at
nine Tuesday morning before the Civil Docket. I believe you have motions pending in the *Smallwood* case."

"But I knew the victim, Judge."

"So what? It's a small town and everybody knows
everybody, right?"

"You're pushing pretty hard, Judge."

"I'm sorry, Jake, and sorry to be bothering you on a
Sunday. But this situation can get dicey and needs a
steady hand. I trust you, Jake, and that's why I'm asking
you to step in. You know, Jake, when I was a young
lawyer I learned that we don't always get to choose our
clients, right?"

And why not, Jake asked himself. "I'd like to discuss
this with my wife, Judge. As you know, we went through
a lot five years ago with Hailey and she may have an
opinion or two."

"This is nothing like Hailey, Jake."

"No, but it is a dead policeman, and any lawyer who
represents the alleged killer will face a backlash from
the community. As you say, it's a small town, Judge."

"I really want you to step up to the plate here, Jake."

"I'll discuss it with Carla and I'll see you first thing
Tuesday morning, if that's all right."

"The kid needs a lawyer now, Jake. As I understand
things, he has no father and his mother is in the hospital
with injuries. There's no other family in the area. He's
already admitted to the killing, so he needs to shut up.

Yes, we both trust Ozzie but I'm sure there are some hotheads around the jail who cannot be trusted. Discuss it with your wife and call me back in a couple of hours."

There was a loud click and the line was dead. His Honor had just given an order and hung up.

THE MARCH WINDS picked up late in the afternoon and the temperature dropped. With his girls lost in an old movie in the den, Jake left his house and went for a long walk through the quiet streets of Clanton. He often spent an hour or two alone in his office late on Sundays, reviewing the files he had not managed to close the previous week and deciding which ones to postpone next. At the moment he had eighty open files, but only a handful were decent cases. Such was the practice of law in a small, poor town.

These days his world was consumed with *Smallwood*, and most other matters were being ignored.

The facts were as simple as they were complicated. Taylor Smallwood, his wife Sarah, and two of their three children were killed instantly when their small import collided with a train at a dangerous crossing near the Polk County line. The accident happened around ten-thirty on a Friday night. A witness in a pickup truck a hundred yards behind the family said the red flashing crossing lights were not working at the time of the collision. The train's engineer and brakeman swore that they were. The crossing was at the foot of a hill that dropped fifty degrees from a crest half a mile up.

Two months earlier, Sarah had given birth to their third child, Grace. At the time of the accident, Grace was being kept by Taylor's sister who lived in Clanton.

Typically, such a sensational accident sent the local bar into a frenzy as every lawyer in town searched for an angle to land the case. Jake had never heard of the family and struck out immediately. Harry Rex, though, had handled a divorce for Sarah's sister and she was pleased with the results. As the vultures were circling, he struck quick and got a contract signed by various family members. He then dashed to the courthouse, set up a guardianship for Grace, the sole heir and plaintiff, and filed a $10 million lawsuit against the railroad, Central & Southern.

Harry Rex knew his limitations and realized that he might not connect with jurors. He had a much better plan. He offered Jake half the fee if he would step in as lead counsel, do the heavy lifting, and push hard for a trial. Harry Rex had seen the magic with the Hailey jury. He had sat mesmerized like everyone else as Jake pleaded for his client's life, and he knew that his younger friend had a way with jurors. If Jake could just land the right cases, he would someday make a lot of money in the courtroom.

They shook hands on the deal. Jake would take an aggressive role and lean on Judge Noose to speed things along. Harry Rex would work in the shadows, plowing through discovery, hiring experts, intimidating insurance lawyers, and, most important, picking the jury. They worked well together, primarily because they gave each other plenty of room.

The railroad tried to remove the case to federal court, a less friendly jurisdiction, but Jake blocked the move with a series of motions that Noose granted. So far, their judge had shown little patience with the defense lawyers and their usual stalling tactics.

The strategy was straightforward: just prove the crossing was dangerous, badly designed, not properly maintained, well known as a place of near misses, and that the warning lights had failed that night. The defense was just as simple: Taylor Smallwood hit the four-teenth boxcar without ever touching his brakes. How do you not see, whether at night or in clear daylight, a railroad boxcar that is fifteen feet tall, forty feet long, and covered with bright yellow reflective warning stickers?

The plaintiff had a strong case because the damages were enormous. The defense had a strong case because of the obvious facts.

For almost a year, the railroad's insurance lawyers had refused to discuss settlement. However, now that the judge was setting a trial date, Harry Rex believed some money might be on the table. One of the defense lawyers was an acquaintance from law school and they had been drinking together.

JAKE PREFERRED HIS office when it was empty, which was rare these days. His current secretary was Portia Lang, a twenty-six-year-old army veteran who would be leaving in six months to start law school at Ole Miss. Portia's mother, Lettie, had inherited a small fortune in a will dispute two years earlier, and Jake had battled an entire squad of lawyers to uphold the will. Portia had been so inspired by the case that she decided to go to law school. Her dream was to become the first black female lawyer in Ford County, and she was well on her way. Far more than a secretary, Portia not only answered the phone and ran interference with the clients and foot traffic, she was also learning legal research and wrote clearly. They were negotiating a deal in which she would continue to work part-time while in school, but both knew it would be nearly impossible the first year.

To complicate their lives, Lucien Wilbanks, the

owner of the building and former owner of the law firm, was now in the habit of arriving for work at least three mornings each week and generally making a nuisance of himself. Disbarred years earlier, Lucien could not take cases or represent clients, so he spent too much of his time sticking his nose into Jake's business and unloading unsolicited advice. He often claimed to be studying for the bar exam, a monumental challenge for an old man with much of his mental strength sapped by years of heavy drinking. Lucien claimed that by keeping hours at the office he stayed away from the whiskey cabinet at home, but before long he was sipping at his desk. He had assumed ownership of a small downstairs conference room, far away from Jake but too close to Portia, and usually spent the afternoons snoring off his liquid lunches with his feet on his desk.

Lucien had made one crude comment of a sexual nature to Portia, after which she threatened to break his neck. They had been civil ever since, though she was happier when he was absent.

To round out the firm's lineup, most of the typing was being done by a twenty-hour-a-week former client named Beverly, a perfectly nice lady of middle age whose entire existence revolved around smoking cigarettes. She chain-smoked, knew the habit was killing her, and had tried every gimmick on the market to quit. The addiction prevented her from keeping a full-time job, and a husband. Jake fixed her an office behind the kitchen where all windows and doors could be left open and she could peck away in a blue haze. Even then, everything she touched reeked of stale smoke and Jake was worried about how long she would last. He quietly speculated to Portia that lung cancer might get her before he was forced to terminate her employment. But Portia did not complain, nor did Lucien, who still smoked cigars on his porch and often smelled of old fumes himself.

Jake eased upstairs to his grand office and did not turn on the lights because he did not want to attract attention. Even on Sunday afternoons, he had heard people knocking on his door. Not often, though. Not often enough. Some days he wondered where the next clients were coming from. Others, he wanted to get rid of all of them.

In the semidarkness, he stretched out on the old leather sofa purchased by the Wilbanks brothers decades earlier, and he stared at the dusty fan hanging from the ceiling and wondered how long it had been there. How much of the practice of law had changed over the years? What were the ethical dilemmas faced by those lawyers back then? Did they worry about taking unpopular cases? Were they afraid of a backlash if they represented murderers?

Jake chuckled at the stories he'd heard about Lucien. He had been the first, and for years the only, white member of the county's chapter of the NAACP. And later, the same for the ACLU. He had represented unions, a rarity in rural north Mississippi. He sued the state over the lousy schools for blacks. He sued the state over capital punishment. He sued the city because it refused to pave the streets in Lowtown. Until he was disbarred, Lucien Wilbanks had been a fearless lawyer who never hesitated to fire off a lawsuit when he thought one was needed, and never failed to help a client who was being mistreated.

On the sidelines now for the past eleven years, Lucien was still a loyal friend who reveled in Jake's success. If asked, there was no doubt in Jake's mind that Lucien would advise him to not only take on the defense of young Drew Gamble but to do so with as much noise as possible. Proclaim innocence! Demand a speedy trial! Lucien had always believed that every person charged with a serious crime deserved a good lawyer. And, Lucien had never, throughout his colorful career, dodged the attention that a bad client could bring.

Jake's other close friend, Harry Rex, had already weighed in and there was no reason to revisit the question with him. Carla was on the fence. Noose was waiting by the phone.

He wasn't worried about the Kofers. He didn't know them and believed they lived in the southern part of the county. Jake was thirty-seven years old and had practiced law successfully for twelve years without that family. He could certainly prosper in the future without knowing them.

He was thinking about the cops—the city policemen, and Ozzie, and his deputies. Six days a week, Jake had breakfast four doors down at the Coffee Shop, and Marshall Prather was often there, waiting with the morning's first insult. Jake had done legal work for many on the force and knew that he was their favorite lawyer. DeWayne Looney had testified against Carl Lee Hailey, and had stunned the jury by admitting he admired the man who blew off his leg. Mick Swayze had a crazy cousin that Jake had successfully shipped off to the state mental hospital, at no charge.

Granted, the legal work wasn't much—wills and deeds and small stuff that Jake charged little for. Pro bono work was not unusual.

As he studied the ceiling fan, he had to admit that not a single law enforcement officer had ever brought him a decent case. And wouldn't they understand if he represented Drew? Sure they were in shock at the murder of a colleague, but they realized that someone, some lawyer, had to represent the accused. Might they feel better if the lawyer was Jake, a friend they trusted?

Was he about to make a courageous decision, or the biggest mistake of his career?

He finally walked to his desk, picked up the phone, and called Carla.

Then he called Judge Noose.

6

I t was dark when he left the office and even darker as
he walked around the deserted square. It was almost
eight on a Sunday night and not a single store or café
was open. The jail, however, was bristling with activity.
As he turned down the street and saw the fleet of patrol
cars parked haphazardly around the buildings, and the
news trucks—one from Tupelo, one from Jackson—and
the crowd of men loitering outside smoking and talking quietly, a sharp pain hit low in his stomach. He felt
as though he was walking directly into enemy territory.

He knew the layout well and decided to duck down
a side street and enter the sprawling office complex
through a rear door. The buildings had been enlarged
and renovated over time and with no clear plan as to
what might be constructed next. Along with the twenty
or so cells and holding rooms and reception areas and
cramped hallways, the complex housed the sheriff's department on one end and the Clanton City Police on
the other. For the sake of simplicity, all of it was simply
referred to as the "jail."

And on that dark night the jail was packed with
every person even remotely connected to law enforcement. It was indeed a brotherhood; the comfort in
being with others who wore the badge.

A jailer told Jake that Ozzie was in his office with
the door locked. Jake asked him to inform the sheriff
that he needed to speak with him and would wait outside near the yard, a fenced area where the inmates

often played basketball and checkers. In good weather, Jake and the other lawyers in town would sit on an old picnic table under a tree and chat with their clients through the chain-link fence. At night, though, the yard was dark as all prisoners were locked away. Their small cell windows were secured by rows of thick bars.

At that moment, Jake had no clients serving time in the jail, other than his latest one. He had two boys at the state penitentiary at Parchman, both for selling drugs. One had a mother with a big mouth and was blaming Jake for their family's demise.

A door opened and Ozzie appeared, alone. He strolled over, in no hurry, as if his shoulders were weighted, as if he hadn't slept in days. Instead of extending a hand, he cracked his knuckles and gazed across the yard.

"Rough day," Jake said.

Ozzie grunted and said, "The worst one yet. Got the call at three this mornin' and haven't slowed down since. It's tough losin' a deputy, Jake."

"I'm sorry, Ozzie. I knew Stu and liked him. I can't imagine what you guys are going through."

"He was a great guy, kept us all in stitches. Maybe a darker side, but we can't talk about that."

"And you've met with his family?"

Ozzie took a deep breath and shook his head. "I drove out, paid my respects. They're not the most stable people I've met. They've called here this afternoon askin' about the boy. Two of them showed up at the hospital, said they wanted to talk to the boy's mother. Crazy stuff like that. So now I've got a deputy parked outside her room. You better watch these guys, Jake."

Just what the little Brigance family needed. More crazies to worry about.

Ozzie cleared his throat and spat on the ground. "I just talked to Noose."

"So did I," Jake said. "He wouldn't take no."

"He told me he leaned on you, said you didn't want to get involved."

"Who would, Ozzie? Certainly nobody from around here. Noose promised me he would try to find a lawyer from outside the county, so I'm just sort of standing in for the preliminaries. At least that's the plan."

"You don't sound too sure."

"I'm not. These cases are not easy to get rid of, especially when the rest of the bar goes into hiding and won't take calls from the judge. There's a good chance I'll get stuck with it."

"Why couldn't you just say no?"

"Because Noose is standing on my neck and because there's no one else, not now anyway. It's hard to say no to a circuit judge, Ozzie."

"Sounds like it."

"He pushed pretty hard."

"Yeah, that's what he said. I guess we're on opposite sides here, Jake."

"Aren't we usually on opposite sides? You bring 'em in, I try to get 'em off. Both doing our jobs."

"I don't know. This seems different. I've never buried a deputy before. Then we'll have a trial, a big one, and you'll do what good lawyers are supposed to do. Get the kid off, right?"

"That day is far away, Ozzie. I'm not thinking about a trial right now."

"Try thinkin' about a funeral."

"I'm sorry, Ozzie."

"Thanks. Should be a fun week."

"I need to see the kid."

Ozzie nodded to a row of windows on the back side of the jail's most recent addition. "Right there."

"Thanks. Do me a favor, Ozzie. Marshall, Moss, De-Wayne, those guys are my friends, and they won't like this at all."

"You got that right."

"So at least be honest and tell them that Noose appointed me, and that I didn't ask for the case."

"I'll do that."

THE JAILER OPENED the door and switched on a dim light. Jake followed him inside as his eyes tried to refocus in the semidarkness. He had been in the juvie cell before, many times.

The normal procedure would have been to handcuff the inmate and walk him down the hall to an interrogation room where he would meet face-to-face with his lawyer while a jailer stood guard just outside the door. No one could remember a lawyer being attacked in the jail by his client, but they were cautious nonetheless. There was a first time for everything and the clientele was not the most predictable.

However, it was obvious to Ozzie and the jailer that this inmate posed no threat. Drew had completely withdrawn and refused all food. He had said nothing since his sister left twelve hours earlier.

The jailer whispered, "Shall I leave the door open, just in case?"

Jake shook his head no and the jailer left, closing the door behind him. Drew was still on the bottom bunk, using as little space as possible. Under a thin blanket, he was curled with his knees to his chest and his back to the door, wrapped tight and warm in his own little dark cocoon. Jake pulled over a plastic stool and sat down, making as much noise as possible. The kid did not flinch, did nothing to acknowledge the presence of his visitor.

Jake adjusted to the utter stillness, then coughed and said, "Say, Drew, my name is Jake. Are you there? Anybody home?"

Nothing.

"I'm a lawyer and the judge has assigned me to your case. I'll bet you've met a lawyer before, right, Drew?"

Nothing.

"Okay. Well, you and I need to be friends because you're about to spend a lot of time with me, and with the judge, and with the court system. You ever been to court before, Drew?"

Nothing.

"Something tells me that you've been to court."

Nothing.

"I'm a good guy, Drew. I'm on your side."

Nothing. A minute passed, then two. The blanket rose and fell slightly as Drew breathed. Jake could not see if his eyes were open.

Another minute. Jake said, "Okay, can we talk about your mother, Drew? Josie Gamble. You know she's okay, right?"

Nothing. Then a slight movement under the blanket as he slowly uncurled his legs and stretched them.

"And your sister, Kiera. Let's talk about Josie and Kiera. They're both safe right now, Drew. I want you to know this."

Nothing.

"Drew, we're not getting anywhere here. I want you to turn around and look at me. It's the least you can do. Roll over and say hello and let's have a chat."

The boy grunted the word "No."

"Great, now we're getting somewhere. You can talk

after all. Ask me a question about your mother, okay? Anything."

Softly, he asked, "Where is she?"

"Turn around and sit up and look at me when you talk."

He rolled over and sat up, careful not to hit his head on the frame of the top bunk. He pulled the blanket tight around his neck as if it protected him and leaned forward with his feet hanging free. Dirty socks, shoes over by the commode. He stared at the floor and huddled under the blanket.

Jake studied his face and was certain there had to be a mistake. Drew's eyes were red and puffy from a day spent under the covers and probably no small amount of crying. His blond hair was wild and in need of a trim. And he was tiny.

When Jake was sixteen years old he was the starting quarterback for Karaway High School, ten miles from Clanton. He also played basketball and baseball and was shaving, driving, and dating every cute girl who would say yes. This kid belonged on a bike with training wheels.

Chatter was important and Jake said, "Paperwork says you're sixteen years old, right?"

No response.

"When's your birthday?"

He stared at the floor, motionless.

"Come on, Drew, surely you know your own birthday."

"Where's my mother?"

"She's at the hospital and she'll be there for a few days. She has a broken jaw and I think the doctors want to operate. I'm going by there tomorrow to say hello and I'd like to tell her that you're okay. Under the circumstances."

"She's not dead?"

"No, Drew, your mother is not dead. What do you want me to say to her?"

"I thought she was dead. So did Kiera. We both thought Stu had finally killed her. That's why I shot him. What's your name?"

"Jake. I'm your lawyer."

"The last lawyer lied to me."

"Sorry about that, but I'm not lying. I swear I don't lie. Ask me something now, anything, and I promise I'll give you a straight answer without lying. Try me."

"How long will I be here in jail?"

Jake hesitated and said, "I don't know and that's not a lie. It's the truth, because right now nobody knows how long you'll stay in jail. A safe answer would be 'a long time.' They're going to charge you with killing Stuart Kofer, and murder is the most serious crime of all."

He looked at Jake and with red moist eyes said, "But I thought he killed my mother."

"I get that, but the truth is, Drew, that he didn't."

"I'm still glad I shot him."

"I wish you had not."

"I don't care if they keep me in prison forever because he can never hurt my mother again. And he can't hurt Kiera and he can't hurt me. He got what he deserved, Mr. Jake."

"It's just 'Jake,' okay? Drew and Jake. Lawyer and client."

Drew wiped his cheeks with the back of his hand. He closed his eyes tightly and began shaking, shivering as if the chills were sweeping through him. Jake pulled down another thin blanket from the top bunk and draped it over his shoulders. He was sobbing now, shaking and sobbing with tears dripping off his cheeks. He cried for a long time, a small, pitiful, terrified little boy so utterly alone in the world. More of a little boy than a teenager, Jake thought more than once.

When the shaking stopped, Drew went back into his own world and refused to speak, refused to acknowledge Jake's presence. He wrapped himself in the blankets, lay down, and stared blankly at the mattress frame above him.

Jake brought up his mother again, but it didn't work. He mentioned food and soft drinks but there was no response. Ten minutes passed, then twenty. When it became apparent that Drew was not going to respond, Jake said, "Okay, I'm outta here, Drew. I'll see your mother in the morning and tell her you're doing just great. While I'm away, you are not to speak to anyone else. No jailer, no policeman, no investigator, nobody, you hear? Which, for you, should not be a problem. Just say nothing until I get back."

Jake left him much as he'd found him, lying still, trance-like, staring wide-eyed but seeing nothing.

He closed the door behind him. At the desk he signed out, avoided some familiar faces, and left the jail on foot for the long walk home.

OUT OF CURIOSITY, he took a detour near the square and saw an office light on, as he'd expected. Harry Rex often locked himself away late at night, especially on Sunday, to catch up with the madness that was his practice. During most days his dingy waiting room was filled with warring spouses and other unhappy clients, and he spent more time refereeing than settling disputes. In addition to that stress, his fourth marriage was not going well and he preferred the late-night tranquility of his office over the tension around the house.

Jake tapped on a window and entered through a rear door. Harry Rex met him in the kitchen and removed two cans of beer from the fridge. They settled into a cluttered workroom beside his office. "Why are you out so late?" he asked.

"Stopped by the jail," Jake said, and Harry Rex nodded as if this was no surprise.

"Noose hazed you into it, right?"

"He did. Said the appointment was only for thirty days, just to get the kid through the preliminaries."

"Bullshit. You'll never get rid of this case, Jake, because no one else'll take it. I tried to warn you."

"You did, but it's pretty hard saying no to the circuit judge, Harry Rex. When was the last time you looked at Noose and said no to a favor?"

"I stay away from Noose, not my domain. I prefer chancery court where we don't have juries and the judges are afraid of me."

"Chancellor Reuben Atlee is not afraid of anybody."

Harry Rex swallowed some beer and looked at Jake in disbelief. He took another swallow and kicked back in an old wooden swivel. He'd lost fifty pounds the year before but had now regained at least that much, and because of his bulk he struggled to lift both feet to the table. But they made it, in ragged old jogging shoes that Jake could swear he'd been wearing for at least the past decade. Feet in place, cold beer in hand, he continued pleasantly. "A really stupid move on your part."

"I may have stopped by for a beer but not for any abuse."

As if he didn't hear him, Harry Rex said, "My phone has been ringin' all day as the gossip spread and I heard from people I thought were dead, hoped most of them were anyway, but, seriously, a murdered deputy? This county has never seen one of those, and so folks are prattlin' away right now. And tomorrow and the next day and the rest of the week, that's all this town will talk about. How much they all loved Stuart Kofer. Even the wags who hardly knew him will discover a deep admiration for the guy. And can you imagine the funeral or memorial or whatever Ozzie will put on with the family? Hell, you know how much cops love parades and funeral processions and burials with guns and cannons. It'll be quite the show with the whole town tryin' to get into the act. And when they're not weepin' over Kofer they'll be vilifying his killer. Sixteen-year-old punk shot him with his own gun in his own bed. Cold-blooded murder. Let's string him up now. As always, Jake, the guilt will rub off on the lawyer, on you. You'll do your best to represent your client and they'll hate you for it. It's a mistake, Jake, a big one. You'll regret this case for a long time."

"You're assuming too much, Harry Rex. Noose assured me it's only temporary. I'll meet with him Tuesday to discuss the possibility of approaching some of the national child advocacy groups to get some help down here. Noose knows the case is not good for me."

"Y'all talk about *Smallwood*?"

"Of course not. That would be highly inappropriate."

Harry Rex snorted and swallowed more beer.

It was unethical to discuss a hotly contested case with the presiding judge when the opposing lawyers knew nothing of the conversation. Especially a phone chat on a Sunday afternoon that was initiated for other reasons. But such ethical formalities had never impressed Harry Rex.

He said, "Here's what might happen, Jake, and this is my biggest fear. Right now those sumbitches on the other side of *Smallwood* are gettin' nervous. I've convinced Doby that they don't want to mess with you in your courtroom, in front of a Ford County jury. You're good and all that but not nearly as good as I've made you out to be. I've blown a lot of smoke up his ass and he's not much of a trial lawyer anyway. His partner is better, but they're from Jackson and that can be a long ways off. Sullivan will be sitting at the table with them but he's not a factor. So we're talkin' trial dates for *Smallwood* and I have a hunch the railroad will start droppin' hints about a settlement. However." A gulp of beer and the can was empty. "Yesterday you were the golden boy with a fine reputation, but that started changin' today. By the end of the week your good name will be mud because you're tryin' to spring the kid who murdered our deputy."

"I'm not sure it was murder."

"You're crazy, Jake. Have you been hangin' around Lucien again?"

"No, not today. It could be insanity. Could be justifiable homicide."

"Could be. Could be. Let me tell you what it will be. It'll be suicide for you and your law practice in this small and unforgiving town. Even if you keep Noose happy, it'll still kill *Smallwood.* Can't you see that, Jake?"

"You're overreacting again, Harry Rex. There are thirty-two thousand people in this county and I'm sure we can find twelve who've never heard of me or Stuart Kofer. The railroad's lawyers can't point at me in the courtroom and say, 'Hey, that guy represents cop killers.' They can't do that and Noose won't let them try."

Harry Rex jerked his feet down as if he'd had enough, and he lumbered out of the room, went to the kitchen, fetched two more beers, and brought them to the table. He popped a top and began pacing along the far end of the table. "Here's your problem, Jake. Your problem is that you want to be the center of attention. That's why you fought to hang on to the Hailey case when all the black preachers and organizers and radicals were tellin' Carl Lee to ditch the white boy before they sent his black ass to Parchman. You fought to keep the case and then you defended him brilliantly. You love it, Jake. I don't expect you to admit it, but you love the big case, the big trial, the big verdict. You love being in the very center of the arena with all eyes on you."

Jake ignored the second can and took a sip from his first.

"What's Carla's opinion?" Harry Rex asked.

"Mixed. She's tired of me carrying a gun."

Harry Rex drank some beer and stopped to stare at a bookcase filled with thick, leather-bound law treatises no one in his office had touched in decades. Not even to dust. Without looking at Jake, he asked, "Did you say the words 'justifiable homicide'?"

"I did."

"So you're already at trial, right, Jake?"

"No, I'm just thinking out loud. Just a habit."

"Bullshit. You're already at trial and plannin' the defense. Did Kofer beat the woman?"

"She's in the hospital with a concussion and a broken jaw that will require surgery."

"Did he beat the kids?"

"I don't know."

"So there was a pattern of Kofer comin' home drunk late on Saturday night and slappin' everybody around. And the way you see the defense is that you'll in effect put him on trial. You'll slander his good name by exposin' all of his sins and bad habits."

"It's not slander if it's true."

"That could be a very nasty trial, Jake."

"I'm sorry I mentioned it, Harry Rex. I don't plan on being anywhere near that courtroom."

"Now you're lyin'."

"No, I think about trials because I'm a lawyer, but this one is for someone else. I'll get through the preliminary stuff, then unload the kid."

"I doubt that. I truly doubt that, Jake. I just hope you're not screwin' up *Smallwood*. Truthfully, I really don't give a damn what happens to Stuart Kofer or his girlfriend and kids and people I've never met, but I do care about *Smallwood*. That case could be the biggest payday in our lousy little careers."

"I don't know. I got a thousand bucks for the Hailey case."

"And that's about all you'll get for this turkey too."

"Well, at least we have Noose on our side."

"For now. I don't trust him as much as you do."

"Have you ever met a judge you trusted?"

"No. Nor a lawyer."

"Look, I gotta go. I need a favor."

"A favor? Right now I'd like to choke you."

"Yeah, but you won't. Tomorrow morning at six, I'll walk into the Coffee Shop and say hello to Marshall Prather. Same routine. Might be another deputy or two at the table. I need a wingman."

"You've lost your mind, Jake."

"Come on, pal. Think of all the crazy stuff I've done for you."

"Nope. You're on your own. Tomorrow mornin' you get another dose of life as a small-town criminal lawyer."

"And you're afraid to be seen with me?"

"No. I'm afraid of wakin' up that early. Beat it, pal. You're makin' your own decisions these days, without regard to others. I'm pissed and I plan to stay that way for a long time."

"I've heard that before."

"This time I mean it. You wanna play radical lawyer, get your buddy Lucien to join you for breakfast. See how the locals enjoy him."

"He can't get up that early."

"And we know why."

WITH HANNA TUCKED IN for the night and Jake out roaming the streets, Carla watched television and waited on the ten o'clock news. She started with the Tupelo station where, as expected, the murder of Stuart Kofer was the lead story with a large color image of the deputy in his nicely starched uniform posted as background. Details were still under wraps. A suspect, a minor, name not given, was in custody. There was footage of an ambulance leaving Kofer's property with, presumably, a dead body inside but none visible. No comment from the sheriff or anyone else with authority. No comments anywhere, yet the intrepid reporter on the scene managed to ramble on about the killing for a solid five minutes while saying almost nothing. Filler was added with live shots of the Ford County Courthouse and even the jail, where some patrol cars were filmed coming and going. Carla switched to a Memphis station and learned even less, though for good measure the story included something vague about a "domestic disturbance," with the mild implication that Kofer had been called to the scene to break up a fight and somehow got hit in the crossfire. There was no reporter on the scene to get to the bottom of things. Evidently, a weekend intern at a news desk was ad-libbing. Another Memphis station spent half its time recapping the city's own daily carnage of home invasions, gang wars, and random murders. It then went south to the Kofer story and the real news that, allegedly, he was the first county officer to be killed "in the line of duty" since a moonshiner shot two deputies in 1922. Not surprisingly, the reporter spun things to give the impression that the county was still rife with illegal whiskey, drugs, and other lawlessness, a far cry from the safe streets of Memphis.

Jake walked in during the last report, and Carla turned off the television and briefed him on the others. He wanted some decaf coffee. She brewed a pot and they had a cup at the breakfast table where the long day had begun.

He replayed his conversations with Ozzie, Drew, and Harry Rex, and he confessed that he was not looking forward to the coming week. She was sympathetic but obviously worried. She wanted the case to simply go away.

7

After the Sunday night service at Good Shepherd, Reverend McGarry convened a special meeting of the board of deacons. Seven of the twelve were present, four women and three men, and they gathered in the fellowship hall with cookies and coffee. Kiera was next door in the small church parsonage, with Meg McGarry, the pastor's wife, eating a sandwich for dinner.

The young preacher explained that since Kiera had no other place to go at the moment, she would be staying with them until—until what? Until a relative showed up to claim her, which didn't appear likely? Until some court somewhere issued an order? Until her mother was discharged and could leave town with her? Regardless, Kiera was now an unofficial ward of the church. And she was traumatized and needed professional help. Throughout the afternoon she had talked of nothing but her mother and brother and her desire to be with them.

Meg had called the hospital and talked to an administrator who said that, yes, they could provide a foldaway bed for the girl to stay with her mother. Two of the lady deacons volunteered to spend the night down the hall in the waiting room. There was a discussion about food, clothing, and school.

Charles was of the firm opinion that Kiera should not return to classes for at least a few days. She was far too fragile and there was the near certainty that another student would say something hurtful. It was finally agreed that the school attendance issue would be dealt with on a day-by-day basis. One member of the church taught algebra at the middle school and would talk to the principal. Another member had a cousin who was a child psychologist and she would inquire about counseling.

Plans were formulated, and at ten o'clock they drove Kiera to the hospital where the staff had arranged a bed next to her mother's. Josie's vitals were normal and she said she felt okay. Her swollen and bandaged face, though, told another story. A hospital gown was provided for Kiera, and when the nurses turned down the lights, she was sitting at her mother's feet.

AT 5:30 A.M. Jake's alarm clock started making noises. He silenced it with a slap and rolled back under the covers. So far, he had slept little and was not ready to begin his day. He burrowed deep, found Carla's warm body, moved closer but was met with resistance. He withdrew, opened his eyes and thought about his newest client sitting in jail, and was about to surrender to the morning when thunder rolled in the distance. A cold front was expected, with potential storms, and perhaps it wasn't safe to venture out. Another reason to sleep more was the desire to avoid the Coffee Shop on this dark day, when all the chatter and gossip would be about poor Stu Kofer and the teenage thug who murdered him.

Yet another reason was the fact that he was not due in court or anywhere else the entire day. As the reasons accumulated he felt them closing in, smothering him, and eventually he drifted off.

Carla wakened him with a pleasant kiss on the cheek and a cup of coffee, then she was off to rouse Hanna and get her ready for school. After two sips, Jake thought about the newspapers and hopped out of bed. He pulled on some jeans, found the dog, leashed him, and went outside. The morning editions from Tupelo, Jackson, and Memphis were strewn along his drive, and he quickly scanned each. All had the Kofer story on the front page. He tucked them under his arm, made the block, and returned to the kitchen where he poured more coffee and spread out the papers.

The gags were holding; no one was talking. Ozzie wouldn't even confirm that he was the sheriff. Reporters had been shooed away from the crime scene, the jail, the home of Earl and Janet Kofer, and the hospital. Officer Kofer was thirty-three, an army veteran, single with no children, four years as a deputy. The sparse details of his bio were spread thin. The Memphis paper covered the story of Kofer's deadly run-in with some drug dealers three years earlier on a rural road near Karaway, a shoot-out that left the bad guys dead and Lieutenant Kofer only slightly wounded. A bullet grazed his arm and he refused hospitalization and never missed a day of work.

Jake was suddenly in a hurry. He showered, skipped breakfast, kissed his girls goodbye, and headed to the office. He needed to visit the hospital and it was imperative that he see Drew again. He was convinced the kid was traumatized and needed help, medical as well as legal, but he wanted to pick the right moment for another attorney-client consultation.

Evidently, others felt differently. Portia was at her desk, standing, holding the receiver of her phone, looking puzzled. Her customary smile was missing as Jake walked into the office.

"This man just yelled at me," she said.

"Who was it?"

She put the receiver away, picked up the Tupelo paper, pointed to the black-and-white photo of Stuart Kofer, and said, "Said he was his father. Said his boy got shot yesterday, shot dead, and that you're the lawyer for the kid who shot him. Talk to me, Jake."

Jake tossed his briefcase onto a chair. "Earl Kofer?"

"That's him. Sounded crazy. Said the kid, Drew somebody, didn't deserve no lawyer, crazy stuff like that. What's the deal?"

"Have a seat. Is there any coffee?"

"It's brewing."

"Noose appointed me to the case yesterday. I met with the kid last night at the jail, so, yes, our little law firm now represents a sixteen-year-old boy who will probably be indicted for capital murder."

"What about the public defender?"

"He couldn't defend a bully in kindergarten and everybody, especially Noose, knows it. He called around and couldn't find anyone else and he thinks I know what I'm doing."

Portia sat down, tossed the newspaper aside, and said, "I like it. This will really liven up the place. Almost nine o'clock on a Monday morning and we've already had our first nasty phone call."

"There will probably be others."

"Does Lucien know?"

"I haven't told him. And Noose is promising that he'll replace me in thirty days, just wants me to handle the preliminary stuff."

"Did the boy shoot him?"

"He didn't talk much. In fact he clammed up and went into a daze. I think he needs some help. Based on what Ozzie said, he shot him once in the head with his own gun."

"Do you—did you know Kofer?"

"I know all the cops, some better than others. Kofer seemed to be a good guy, a friendly sort. Last month he spoke to Carla's sixth graders about drugs and she said he was wonderful."

"Not a bad-lookin' boy, for a white guy."

"I'm going to the hospital in about an hour to see the kid's mother. Looks like Kofer may have knocked her around some before his big moment. You want to go?"

Portia finally smiled and said, "Of course. I'll get you some coffee."

"What a good little secretary you are."

"I'm a paralegal slash research assistant, soon to be law student, and before you know it I'll be a full-blown partner around here and you'll be fetching *me* coffee. One milk, two sugars."

"I'll write that down." Jake climbed the stairs to his office and took off his jacket. He had just settled into his leather swivel when Lucien arrived, before the coffee.

"Heard you got a new case," he said with a smile as he fell into a chair, one that he still owned because he owned all the other furniture as well as the building itself. Jake's office, the grandest one, had belonged to Lucien before he was disbarred in 1979, and to his father before he was killed in a plane crash in 1965, and to his grandfather who built the Wilbanks firm into a powerhouse until Lucien took over and ran off all the paying clients.

Jake should have been surprised that Lucien knew, but he wasn't. Like Harry Rex, Lucien seemed to hear the hottest news first, though both had entirely different sources.

"Noose appointed me," Jake said. "I didn't want the case, still don't."

"And why not? I need some coffee."

Usually, on a Monday morning, Lucien did not bother with pushing himself out of bed, showering and shaving, and putting on semi-respectable clothes. Since he couldn't practice law, his Mondays were normally spent on the porch trying to drink off the weekend's hangover. The fact that he was awake and fairly presentable meant he wanted details.

"It's coming," Jake said. "Who told you?" A worthless question that was never answered.

"Sources, Jake, sources. And why don't you want the case?"

"Harry Rex is afraid it might somehow damage the *Smallwood* settlement."

"What settlement?"

"He thinks they're getting ready to put money on the table. He also thinks that this killing could damage my stellar reputation as a noted trial lawyer. He thinks the public will turn on me and we won't be able to pick fair and open-minded jurors."

"When did Harry Rex become an expert on juries?"

"He thinks he's an expert on people."

"I wouldn't let him in front of my jury."

"That's my job. I have the charisma."

"And the ego, and right now your ego is telling you that you're far more popular than you really are. Defending this kid will not affect your railroad case."

"I'm not sure. Harry Rex thinks otherwise."

"Harry Rex can be stupid."

"He's a brilliant lawyer who happens to be my co-counsel in what just might be the biggest case of our struggling careers. You don't agree with him?"

"I seldom do. Sure, you'll take some heat for defending an unpopular client, but what the hell? Most of my clients were unpopular, but that didn't mean they were bad people. I didn't care what these yokels thought about me or them. I had a job to do and it was completely unrelated to the gossip in the coffee shops and churches. They may talk about you behind your back but when they get in trouble they'll want a lawyer who knows how to fight, and fight dirty if necessary. When's the kid going to court?"

"I have no idea, Lucien. I plan to talk to the D.A. and to Judge Noose this morning. There's also the matter of youth court."

"Not a youth court matter, not in this backward state."

"I know the law, Lucien."

"A charge of murder is automatically excluded from youth court jurisdiction."

"I know the law, Lucien."

Portia opened the door and eased in with coffee and cups on a tray.

Lucien continued his lecture. "It really doesn't matter how young the kid is either. Twenty years ago they put a thirteen-year-old on trial for murder down in Polk County. I knew his defense lawyer."

"Good morning, Lucien," Portia said politely as she poured coffee.

"Mornin'," he said without looking at her. In the early days of her employment he enjoyed long, leering stares. He had touched her a few times, on the arms and shoulders, just little affectionate pats that meant nothing, but after some stern warnings from Jake and a direct threat of bodily harm from Portia, he'd backed off and grown to admire her.

"We had another call, Jake, about five minutes ago," she said. "Anonymous. Some hick said if you tried to get this boy off like you got that Hailey nigger off, there would be hell to pay."

"I'm sorry he said that, Portia," Jake said, stunned.

"It's okay. I've heard it before and I'm sure I'll hear it again."

"I'm sorry too, Portia," Lucien said softly. "Real sorry."

Jake waved at a wooden chair next to Lucien and she sat down. In unison, they sipped their coffee and thought about the N-word. Twelve years earlier, when Jake finished law school and arrived in Clanton as the rookie, the word was commonly used by white lawyers and judges as they gossiped and told jokes and even did their business without an audience. Now, though, in 1990, its usage was fading and it was deemed improper, even low-class, to use it. Jake's mother hated the word and had never allowed it, but, growing up in Karaway, Jake knew that his home was different in that respect.

He looked at Portia, who at the moment seemed less bothered than the two men, and said, "I'm really sorry you heard that in this office."

"Hey, I'm okay. I've heard it my entire life. I heard it in the army. I'll hear it again. I can deal with it, Jake. But, just to clear the air here, all the players involved are white. Right?"

"Yes."

"So, we shouldn't expect the Kluckers and those guys to show up, like Hailey, right?"

"Who knows?" Lucien said. "There are plenty of nuts out there."

"You got that right. Not yet nine on a Monday morning and two calls already. Two threats."

"What was the first one?" Lucien asked.

"The father of the deceased, a man named Earl

Kofer," Jake said. "I've never met him but it looks like that might change."

"The father of the deceased called the lawyer of the person arrested for the killing?"

Jake and Portia nodded. Lucien shook his head, then he smiled and said, "I love it. Makes me wish I was back in the trenches."

The desk phone rang and Jake stared at it. Line three was blinking and that usually meant Carla was calling. He slowly lifted the receiver, said hello, and listened. She was at school, in her classroom, first period. The secretary in the principal's office down the hall had just answered the phone, and a man who refused to give his name asked if Jake Brigance's wife worked there. He said he was a good friend of Stuart Kofer, said Kofer had a lot of friends, and that they were upset because Carl Lee Hailey's lawyer was now trying to get that kid out of jail. Said jail was the only thing keeping the boy alive at the moment. When she asked his name for the second time, he hung up.

The secretary informed the principal, who told Carla, then called the city police.

WHEN JAKE WHEELED to a stop in front of the school, he parked behind two patrol cars. An officer named Step Lemon, a former bankruptcy client of Jake's, was at the front door and greeted Jake like an old friend. Lemon said, "The call came from a pay phone at Parker's store, down by the lake. That's as far as we can dig. I'll get Ozzie to ask around at the store but my guess is it's a waste of time."

Jake said, "Thanks," and they stepped inside where the principal was waiting with Carla, who seemed thoroughly unflustered by the phone call. She and Jake walked away for some privacy. "Hanna's fine," Carla whispered. "They checked on her right away and she knows nothing."

"The asshole called the school where you work," Jake whispered.

"Watch your language. It's just some nut, Jake."

"I know. But nuts can do stupid things. We've had two calls at the office already."

"Do you think it'll blow over?"

"No. There are too many big events just around the corner. The boy's first court appearance. Kofer's funeral. More court appearances, and one day there might be a trial."

"But you're just temporary, right?"

"Right. I'll see Noose tomorrow and tell him what's going on. He can find another lawyer from outside the county. You're okay?"

"I'm fine, Jake. You didn't have to race over here."

"Yes I did."

He walked out of the building with Officer Lemon, shook hands with him and thanked him again, and got in his car. Instinctively, he slid back the lid of his console to make sure his automatic pistol was still there. It was, and he cursed it, and shook his head in frustration as he drove away.

At least a thousand times in the past two years he had vowed to put his firearms away and retrieve them only for hunting. But the gun nuts were loose and more rabid than ever. It was safe to assume that in the rural South every vehicle had a weapon. Old laws had made it necessary to hide them, but newer ones had brought them out into the open. Get a permit these days and you could hang rifles in your rear window and strap a

six-shooter on your hip. Jake despised the idea of keeping guns in his car, his desk at work, his nightstand at
home, but once they take shots at you, burn your house,
and threaten your family, notions of self-preservation
become priority one.

8

A Mrs. Whitaker and a Mrs. Huff introduced themselves in the third-floor waiting room and asked if Jake and Portia would like something to eat. The Good Shepherd Bible Church was in the process of laying siege. The coffee tables and counters were covered with food, and more was on the way. Mrs. Huff explained that the ladies of the church were working shifts now, keeping a watchful eye on Josie Gamble down the hall in that room with a bored deputy sitting outside the door in a rocker. As Mrs. Huff talked, Mrs. Whitaker placed two thick slices of triple-fudge cake on paper plates and handed one to Portia and one to Jake. Since it was not physically possible to decline the cake, they took small bites with plastic forks as Mrs. Huff went through the results of Josie's latest tests, with no respect for privacy.

When Jake was finally allowed to speak and told them that he was the court-appointed lawyer for Drew, the ladies were visibly impressed and offered coffee. Jake introduced Portia as his paralegal, but it wasn't clear if they knew what that meant. Mrs. Whitaker said her nephew was a lawyer over in Arkansas, and, not to be outdone, Mrs. Huff said her brother had once served on a grand jury.

The cake was delicious and Jake asked for another, smaller slice, and accepted some coffee to wash it down. When he glanced at his watch Mrs. Whitaker informed him that Josie's door was closed because she was being examined by her doctors. It wouldn't take long, she assured him, as if she was now well versed on hospital procedures.

Since both ladies seemed hell-bent on talking nonstop, Jake sat down and began asking questions about the Gamble family. Mrs. Whitaker got the jump on her rival and explained that they, mother and children, had been worshipping at Good Shepherd for the past few months. One of the deacons, Mr. Herman Vest they thought it was, had met Josie where she worked at the car wash in Clanton and struck up a conversation, as he was prone to do. Mr. Vest enjoyed meeting new people and inviting them to church. Mr. Vest, if it was indeed him, had passed along her name to their pastor, Brother Charles, and he had followed up with a home visit, one that reportedly did not go well because the man of the house, Officer Stuart Kofer, may he rest in peace, had been quite rude to their pastor.

Additionally, it was obvious that Josie was living with the man without the benefit of holy matrimony, living in open sin, so that gave them all additional ammo for their prayer lists.

Nevertheless, Josie and the kids visited one Sunday morning. The church always took great pride in welcoming visitors. That was one reason its enrollment had almost doubled since Brother Charles had arrived. One big happy family.

Mrs. Huff barged in at this point because she had something special to offer. Kiera at the time was only thirteen years old, fourteen now, and Mrs. Huff taught the young teenage girls in a Sunday school class. Once Mrs. Huff, as well as the rest of the church, came to realize what awful things Josie and the kids had been through, they really took them in. Mrs. Huff had a special interest in Kiera, who at first was extremely shy and introverted. About once a month Mrs. Huff invited the class to her house for pizza, ice cream, and a scary-movie sleepover, and she coaxed Kiera into joining them. The other girls were terrific, some knew her from school, but she had a difficult time relaxing at the little party.

Portia had put down her cake and was taking notes. When Mrs. Huff paused for a breath, Portia pounced with "When you say the family had been through some awful things, what do you mean? If you don't mind telling us."

These two women would tell anything. But they did glance at each other as if thinking perhaps they should throttle back. Mrs. Huff said, "Well, when they were younger they were separated. Not sure how or why, but I think Josie, and she is a dear, had to go away, maybe got in some trouble, you know? The kids were sent away. Something like that."

Mrs. Whitaker added, "Drew's teacher said the class was doing pen-pal letters to boys and girls in orphanages and Drew said he'd been there once, to an orphanage, and he wasn't ashamed to talk about it. Seems like he's more outgoing than his sister."

"Any family around here?" Jake asked.

Both ladies shook their heads. No. Mrs. Huff said, "And I'm not sure how or why she took up with that Kofer fellow. He had a bad reputation in the area."

"For what?" Portia asked.

"Well, there were a lot of rumors about the guy, down our way. Even though he was a deputy, he had a darker side."

Jake was keen to pursue the dark side when a doctor walked in. The ladies proudly introduced him to the family's lawyer and his paralegal. As in most hospitals, the presence of a lawyer chilled the conversation with the doctor. He assured them the patient was doing fine, still in pain, but getting restless. Once the swelling was under control, they would do the surgery to reset the broken bones in her cheek and jaw.

"Can she talk?" Jake asked.

"A little. She struggles but she wants to talk."

"Could we see her?"

"Sure, just don't overdo it, okay?"

Jake and Portia hurried from the room as Mrs. Whitaker and Mrs. Huff were pointing the doctor toward the latest casseroles and talking about lunch. It was 10:20.

The deputy on hall duty was Lyman Price, probably the oldest member of Ozzie's force and the one least able to stalk drug dealers and chase down criminals. When he wasn't pushing papers around his desk at the jail, he worked the courtrooms keeping order in the court. Killing hours outside a hospital room was another perfect job for old Lyman.

He greeted Jake with his usual gruffness, with no hint of an edge because of the Kofer business.

Jake knocked on the door as he opened it and smiled at Kiera, who was sitting in a chair, reading a teen magazine. Josie was on her back but propped up and alert. Jake introduced himself and Portia, and said hello to Kiera, who put down the magazine and stood near her mother's feet.

Jake said they would just be there for a moment, but he had met with Drew the night before and promised him that he would see his mother and make sure she was okay. She grabbed his hand and squeezed it and through the gauze mumbled something like "How is he?"

"He's okay. We're on our way back to the jail to see him now."

Kiera had moved closer and was sitting on the edge of the bed. Her eyes were moist and she wiped her cheeks, and Jake was struck by the fact that she was much taller than her brother, though two years younger. Drew could pass for a little boy far away from puberty. Kiera was physically mature for her age.

"How long in jail?" Josie asked.

"A long time, Josie. There's no way to get him out for weeks or months. He'll be charged with murder and face a trial and that'll take a lot of time."

Kiera leaned forward with a tissue and wiped her mother's cheeks, then wiped her own. There was a long silent pause as a monitor beeped and nurses laughed in the hallway. Jake flinched first and was suddenly eager to leave. He clutched Josie's hand, leaned down and said, "I'll be back. Right now we're going to check on Drew."

She tried to nod but the pain hit and she grimaced. Backing away, Jake handed Kiera a business card and whispered, "There's my number." At the door he turned around for a last glance and saw the two clutching each other in a tight embrace, both crying, both terrified of the unknowns.

It was a heartbreaking image that he would never forget. Two little people facing nothing but fear and the wrath of the system, a mother and daughter who'd done nothing wrong but were suffering mightily. They had no voice, no one to protect them. No one but Jake. A voice told him that they, along with Drew, would be a part of his life for years to come.

THE CHIEF PROSECUTOR for the Twenty-second Judicial District—Polk, Ford, Tyler, Milburn, and Van Buren counties—was the district attorney, Lowell Dyer, from the even smaller town of Gretna, forty miles north of Clanton. Three years earlier, Dyer had challenged the great Rufus Buckley, the three-term D.A. who many believed would one day become governor, or at least try. With as much ceremony, publicity, grandstanding, and outright hotdogging as the state had ever seen, Buckley had prosecuted Carl Lee Hailey five years earlier and begged the jury for death. Jake convinced them otherwise and handed Buckley his greatest defeat. The voters then gave him another one, and he limped back to his hometown of Smithfield and opened a small office. Jake and virtually every other lawyer in the district had quietly supported Lowell Dyer, who had proven to be a steady hand at a rather dull job.

Monday morning was anything but dull. Dyer had taken a call late Sunday night from Judge Noose, and the two had discussed the Kofer case. Ozzie called early Monday morning, and by 9:00 A.M. Dyer was meeting with his assistant, D. R. Musgrove, to consider their options. From the outset, there was little doubt that the State wanted to push for a capital murder indictment and seek the death penalty. A man of the law had been murdered in his own bed, by his own gun, in cold blood. The killer had confessed and was in custody and, though only sixteen, he was certainly old enough to know right from wrong and appreciate the nature of his actions. In Dyer's world, the Good Book taught an eye for an eye, a tooth for a tooth, vengeance is mine saith the Lord. Or something like that. The exact wording from the Bible was really not that important, because capital punishment was still favored by an overwhelming majority of the population, especially those concerned enough to vote. Polls and public opinion surveys were of no consequence in the rural South, because the issue had long since been settled and public

sentiment had not changed. Indeed, when Dyer ran for
office he said several times on the stump that the problem with the gas chamber was that it was not being
used enough. This had really pleased the crowds, or at
least the white ones. In black churches, he had avoided
the issue altogether.

The law currently considered murder to be exempt
from youth court jurisdiction if the accused was at least
thirteen years old. A twelve-year-old could not be prosecuted in circuit court, the tribunal for all criminal
prosecutions. No other state had such a low threshold.
In most, the defendant had to be at least sixteen to be
tried as an adult. Up north, a few states had bumped the
age up to eighteen, but not in the South.

Though the gravity of the moment throttled his enthusiasm, Lowell was secretly delighted to have such an
important case. In his three years, he had not indicted
anyone for capital murder, and as a prosecutor who saw
himself getting tougher and tougher, he had grown
frustrated with such a bland docket. If not for the production and peddling of drugs, and the gambling sting
run by the Feds with local help, he'd have little to do.
He had tried a drunk in Polk County for vehicular
homicide and put him away for twenty years. He had
won two bank robberies in Milburn County, same defendant, but the guy had escaped and was still on the
lam. Probably still robbing banks.

Before the Kofer killing, Lowell was spending his
time on a joint task force of prosecutors trying to fight
the cocaine plague.

But with the Kofer killing, Lowell Dyer was suddenly the man in the middle. Unlike his predecessor,
Rufus Buckley, who would have already called at least
two press conferences, Lowell avoided the reporters
Monday morning and went about his business. He

spoke to Ozzie again, and Noose, and he placed a call to Jake Brigance but got voicemail. Out of respect, he called Earl Kofer and passed along his sympathies while promising a full measure of justice. He sent his investigator to Clanton to start digging.

And he took a call from a pathologist at the state crime lab. The autopsy revealed that Kofer died of a single bullet wound to the head, in through the left temple, out through the right ear. Nothing really remarkable, but for the fact that his blood alcohol level was .36. Point-three-six! Three and a half times the state's limit of .10 to be legally drunk behind the wheel. Kofer was six feet one inch tall and weighed 197 pounds. A man that size, and that drunk, would have a difficult time doing anything—walking, driving, even breathing.

As a small-town lawyer with fifteen years' experience, Lowell had never seen or heard of a case involving such a high level of alcohol. He expressed disbelief and asked the pathologist to test the blood again. Lowell would review the autopsy report as soon as he received it, and in due course he would hand it over to the defense. There would be no way to conceal the fact that Stuart Kofer was blind drunk when he died.

No set of facts was ever perfect. Every prosecution, as well as every defense, had its flaws in the proof. But for a deputy to be so raging drunk at two in the morning presented a lot of questions, and just hours after landing the case of a lifetime Lowell Dyer had his first doubt.

JAKE DROPPED PORTIA off at the square and drove to the jail. It was still busier than usual and he did not want to go inside and face the stares. But as he parked on the street he said to himself, "What the hell? You can't defend a cop killer and still be loved by the cops."

If they resented Jake for doing his job, a job that no one else wanted but had to be done, then he couldn't worry about it. He entered the front room where the deputies liked to kill time gossiping and drinking gallons of coffee, and said hello to Marshall Prather and Moss Junior Tatum. They nodded because they had to, but within seconds Jake realized the battle lines had been drawn.

"Is Ozzie in?" he asked Tatum, who shrugged as if he had no clue. Jake kept walking and stopped at Doreen's desk. She was Ozzie's secretary and guarded his door like a Doberman. She also wore a full uniform and carried a gun, though it was no secret she had no law enforcement training and could not legally make an arrest. It was assumed she could use the pistol but no one had dared to test her.

"He's in a meeting," she said coolly.

"I called half an hour ago and we agreed to meet at ten-thirty," Jake said as politely as possible. "It's ten-thirty."

"I'll buzz him, Jake, but it's been a crazy morning."

"Thank you."

Jake walked to a window that overlooked a side street. Beyond it was the first cluster of office buildings that lined the south side of the square. The dome of the courthouse rose above the buildings and the stately oaks that were two hundred years old. As he stood there he was aware that the usual chatter and banter behind him had died down. The deputies were still around, but now so was the defense lawyer.

"Jake," Ozzie called as he opened his door.

Inside his office, the two old friends stood and looked at each other across the big desk.

Jake said, "We've already had two threatening phone calls at the office, and someone called the school asking about Carla. Wouldn't leave a name, of course, they never do."

"I know about the call to the school. What am I supposed to do, Jake? Tell people not to call your office?"

"Have you spoken with Earl Kofer?"

"Well, yes, twice. Yesterday at his farm and this morning on the phone. We're tryin' to work out some details about the funeral, Jake, if that's okay."

"I'm not thinking about the funeral, Ozzie. Could you politely inform Mr. Kofer to inform his people, whoever the hell they are, that they need to back off and leave us alone."

"So you're certain it's the family?"

"Who else would it be? I'm told they're a bunch of hotheads. They're obviously upset about the killing. Who wouldn't be? Just stop the threats, okay, Ozzie?"

"I think you're upset too, Jake. Maybe you should settle down first. Nobody's been hurt, other than Stuart Kofer." Ozzie took a deep breath and slowly eased into his chair. He nodded and Jake sat down too.

Ozzie said, "Record the calls and bring them to me. I'll do what I can. You want security again?"

"No. We got tired of that. I'll just shoot them myself."

"Jake, I really don't think you have anything to worry about. The family is upset but they're not crazy. We'll get through the funeral, maybe things will settle down. You'll be off the case soon, right?"

"I don't know. I hope so. Have you checked on the boy this morning?"

"I talked to the jailer. Kid's really shut down."

"Has he eaten anything?"

"Some chips maybe, drank a Coke."

"Look, Ozzie, I'm no expert, but I think the kid is traumatized and needs help. He could be in the middle of some type of a breakdown, for all we know."

"Forgive me, Jake, but I'm not feelin' the sympathy."

"I get that. I'll see Noose in the morning before the Civil Docket, and I plan to ask him to send the kid to Whitfield for tests. I need your help."

"My help?"

"Yes. Noose admires you, and if you agree that the kid needs to see a professional, then he might go along. The kid is in your custody and you know more about his condition than anyone else right now. Bring the jailer over and we'll meet with Noose in his chambers. Off the record. You won't have to testify or anything. The rules are different for minors."

Ozzie gave a sarcastic laugh and looked away. "Let me get this straight. This kid, regardless of his age, murdered my deputy, whose memorial service or funeral or whatever you white folks call these events, has not yet been planned, and here I am with the defense lawyer who's askin' me to help out with the defense. Right, Jake?"

"I'm asking you to do what's right here, Ozzie. That's all."

"The answer is no. I haven't even seen the kid since they brought him in. You're pushin' too hard, Jake. Back off."

Ozzie was glaring across the desk when he gave the warning, and Jake got the message. He got to his feet, said, "Okay. I'd like to see my client."

HE TOOK HIM a can of Mountain Dew and a package of peanuts, and after a few minutes managed to coax

Drew from under the covers. He sat on the edge of his bed and opened the drink.

"I saw your mother this morning," Jake said. "She's doing great. Kiera is with her at the hospital and there are some folks from the church taking care of them."

Drew's eyes never left his feet as he nodded. His blond hair was stringy, matted, dirty, and his entire body needed a good scrubbing. They had yet to dress him in the standard orange jail jumpsuit, which would be an improvement over the cheap and wrinkled clothes he wore.

He kept nodding and asked, "What church?"

"I believe it's called the Good Shepherd Bible Church. The pastor is a guy named Charles McGarry. You know him?"

"I think so. Stu didn't want us to go to church. Is he really dead?"

"He's dead, Drew."

"And I shot him?"

"Sure looks that way. You don't remember?"

"Sometimes I do, sometimes I don't. Sometimes I think I'm dreaming, you know? Like right now. Are you really here, talking to me? What's your name?"

"Jake. We met last night when I stopped by. Do you remember that?"

A long silence followed. He took a sip and then tried to open the peanuts. When he couldn't, Jake gently took the package, tore the top, and gave it back.

Jake said, "This is not a dream, Drew. I'm your lawyer. I've met your mother and sister and so now I represent the family. It's important for you to trust me and talk to me."

"About what?"

"About what. Let's talk about the house where you

live with Kiera and your mother and Stuart Kofer. How long have you lived there?"

More silence as he stared at the floor, as if he'd heard nothing Jake said.

"How long, Drew? How long did you live with Stuart Kofer?"

"I don't remember. Is he really dead?"

"Yes."

The can slipped from his hand and hit the floor with foam splashing near Jake's feet. It rolled a bit, then stopped but continued leaking the soda. Drew did not react to the dropped can, and Jake tried his best to ignore it too as the puddle inched closer to his shoes. Drew closed his eyes and began to make a low humming sound, a soft painful groan that came from somewhere deep within. His lips began moving slightly, as if he was mumbling to himself. After a moment, Jake almost said something to interrupt him, but decided to wait. Drew could have been a monk in a deep trance-like meditation, or a mental patient drifting away again, into the darkness.

But Drew was a wounded child in need of help that Jake was unqualified to give.

9

By noon Monday Ozzie was fed up with the crowds and noise, the off-duty guys hanging around to gather or spread the latest gossip, the retired cops just wanting to be part of the brotherhood, the useless reserves taking up space, the reporters, the nosy old ladies from town stopping by with brownies and doughnuts as if massive quantities of sugar would help in some way, the curious with no discernible reason for being there, the politicians hoping their presence would remind the voters that they believed in law and order, and friends of the Kofers who thought they were helping the situation by offering their support for the good guys and supporting the boys in blue. Ozzie ordered everyone who wasn't on duty out of the building.

For over thirty hours he had worked hard at maintaining the facade of a pro untouched by the tragedy, but fatigue was settling in. He had barked at Doreen, who barked back. The tension was palpable.

He gathered his A-team in his office and, politely, asked Doreen to guard the door and hold all calls. Moss Junior Tatum, Marshall Prather, and Willie Hastings. None were in uniform, nor was Ozzie. He passed around sheets of paper and asked them all to take a look. After enough time, he said, "Point-three-six. Can any of you remember catchin' a drunk driver who registered point-three-six?"

The three veterans had seen it all, or thought so.

Prather said, "I've had a couple of threes, but nothin' higher. Not that I can remember."

Moss Junior shook his head in disbelief and said, "Not here."

Hastings said, "Butch Vango's boy was point-three-five. I think that's the record for Ford County."

"And he died," Prather said.

"Next day at the hospital. I didn't bring him in so I didn't do the test."

"There was no test," Prather said. "He wasn't drivin'. They found him lyin' in the middle of Craft Road one mornin'. Called it alcohol poisonin'."

"Okay, okay," Ozzie said. "Point is, our fallen brother was saturated with enough booze to kill most men. Point is, Kofer had a problem. Point is, Kofer was out of control and we didn't know the extent of it, did we?"

Prather said, "We talked about this yesterday, Ozzie. You're tryin' to blame us for not rattin' out a fellow officer."

"I am not! But I smell a cover-up. There were at least two incident reports filed after Kofer's girlfriend called when he slapped her around. I never saw them and now I can't find them. We've looked all mornin'."

Ozzie was the sheriff, elected and reelected by the people, and the only person in the room who was required to face the voters every four years. The other three were his top deputies and owed him their paychecks and careers. They understood the relationships, the issues, the politics. It was imperative that they protect him as much as possible. They weren't sure if Ozzie had actually seen the memos, and they weren't sure how much he knew, but at that moment they were on board with whatever image he wanted to project.

Ozzie continued, "Pirtle and McCarver filed one about a month ago after she called the dispatcher late

one night, then she refused to press charges so nothin'
happened. They swear they filed the report, but it ain't
here. Turns out that four months ago the girlfriend
called the dispatcher, same crap, Kofer came home
drunk, slapped her around, Officer Swayze made the
call but she wouldn't press charges. He filed the report,
now it's gone. I never saw it, never saw either one.
Here's the problem, boys. Jake stopped by an hour ago.
He's been appointed by Noose and he claims he doesn't
want the case, says Noose will find somebody else as
soon as possible. We can't be sure of that and it's out of
our control. For now, Jake is the lawyer and it'll take
him about five minutes to sniff out missin' paperwork.
Not now, but down the road if this thing goes to trial. I
know Jake well, hell we all know him, and he'll be a
step ahead of us."

"Why would Jake get involved?" Prather asked.

"As I said, because Noose appointed him. The kid
has to have a lawyer and, evidently, no one else would
take it."

"I thought we had a public defender," Hastings said.
"I like Jake and I don't want him on the other side."
Willie Hastings was a cousin to Gwen Hailey, mother
of Tonya, wife of Carl Lee, and in their world Jake Brigance walked on water.

"Our public defender is a greenhorn who's yet to
handle a serious case. I've heard that Noose doesn't like
him. Look, guys, Omar Noose is the circuit judge and
has been for a long time. Love him or hate him, but he
rules the system. He can make or break a lawyer and
he's quite fond of Jake. Jake couldn't say no."

"But I thought Jake was just doin' the preliminary
stuff until they brought in somebody else?" Prather
asked.

"Who knows? A lot can happen and it's still early.

They may have trouble findin' somebody else. Also, Jake's an ambitious lawyer who likes the attention. Keep in mind he was hired and trained by Lucien Wilbanks, a radical in his day who would defend anyone."

"I can't believe it," Tatum said. "Jake did a land deal for my uncle last year."

Ozzie said, "He said they're already gettin' phone calls, threats. I'm gonna ride out again and talk to Earl Kofer, pay my respects and such, talk about the burial, and make sure those folks are under control."

"The Kofers are okay," Prather said. "I know some of them and they're just in shock right now."

"Aren't we all?" asked Ozzie. He closed the file, took a deep breath, and looked at his three deputies. He settled on Prather and finally asked, "Okay, let's hear it."

Marshall tossed his sheet of paper on the desk and lit a cigarette. He walked to a window, cracked it for ventilation, and leaned against the wall. "I talked to my cousin. He wasn't out with Kofer Saturday night. He called around and got the scoop. Seems there was a card game at Dog Hickman's cabin near the lake. Poker, low stakes, not a high-dollar crowd, but an unnamed player showed up with some shine, peach flavored, fresh from the still, and they got into it. Everybody got wasted. Three of them passed out and stayed there. They don't remember much. Kofer decided it would be smart to drive home. Somehow he made it."

Ozzie interrupted with "Sounds like Gary Garver's still."

Prather took a drag and stared at the sheriff. "I didn't ask for names, Ozzie, and none were offered, except for Kofer and Dog Hickman. Kofer's dead and the other four are kinda scared right now."

"Scared of what?"

"I don't know, maybe they feel some responsibility.

They were gamblin' and hittin' the moonshine and now their buddy is dead."

"They must be stupid."

"I didn't say they weren't."

"If we start raidin' dice and poker games we'll have to build a new jail. Get me their names, okay, and assure them that they will not be charged."

"I'll try."

"Get their names, Marshall, because you can bet that Harry Rex Vonner will have the names by tomorrow, and Jake'll get to them first."

Moss Junior said, "They've done nothin' wrong. What's the big deal? The only crime here is murder and we got the killer, right?"

"Nothin' is that simple," Ozzie said. "If this thing goes to trial you can bet your ass the defense lawyer, whoever it is, will make hay out of Kofer's bad behavior that led to the shootin'."

"They can't do that," Prather said. "He's dead."

"And why is he dead? Is he dead because he came home drunk and fell asleep and this stupid kid thought it would be fun to blow his brains out? No. Is he dead because his girlfriend wanted his money? No, Marshall. He's dead because he had the bad habit of gettin' bombed and punchin' her around and her boy tried to protect her. This will be an ugly trial, boys, so just get ready for it. That's why it's imperative now that we know everything that happened. Start with Dog Hickman. Who can talk to him?"

"Swayze knows him," Willie said.

"Okay. Get Swayze to run him down as soon as possible. And make sure these clowns know we're not after them."

"Got it, boss."

———

WITH CARLA TEACHING school and spending many of her evenings preparing lesson plans and grading papers and trying to monitor Hanna's homework, there was little time for the kitchen. The three ate dinner together most evenings at exactly seven. Jake occasionally stayed at the office until late or was out of town, but the life of a small-time practitioner did not require much time on the road. Dinner was always something quick and as healthy as possible. A lot of chicken and vegetables, baked fish, few breads or grains, and they avoided red meat and added sugar. Afterward, they hustled to clear the table and tidy up the kitchen and get on with more pleasant matters like television, reading, or playing games once Hanna had finished her homework.

On perfect nights, Jake and Carla enjoyed walks through the neighborhood, short little excursions with the doors locked and Hanna safe in her room. She refused to walk with them because being all alone in the house was such a cool move for a big girl. She would settle in with Mully the mutt and read a book as the house became quiet and still. Her parents were never more than ten minutes away.

After one of the longest Mondays in recent memory, Jake and Carla locked the doors and walked to the edge of the street where they paused by the dogwoods and enjoyed the aroma. Their home, known as the Hocutt House, was one of twenty on a shady old street eight blocks from the Clanton square. Most of the homes were owned by elderly pensioners who struggled to keep up with the ever-increasing maintenance, but a few had been reclaimed by younger families. Two doors down was a young doctor from Pakistan who at first

had not been well received because no one could pro-
nounce his name and his skin was darker, but after three
years and thousands of consultations he knew more secrets than anyone in town and was widely admired.
Across the street from him and his pleasant wife lived a
young couple with five children and no jobs. He
claimed to run the family timber business his grandfather started and handed down, but he seldom left the
country club. She played golf and bridge and spent
most of her time supervising the staff that was raising
her brood.

Besides those two homes, though, and the Hocutt
House, the rest of the street was dark, as the older folks
turned in early.

Carla suddenly stopped, pulled on Jake's hand, and
said, "Hanna's alone."

"So?"

"You think she's safe?"

"Of course she's safe."

Nonetheless, they instinctively turned around. After
a few steps, Carla said, "I can't do this again, Jake. We've
just settled into a normal routine and I really don't want
to start worrying again."

"There's nothing to worry about."

"Oh really?"

"Okay, yes, there's something to worry about, but
the threat level is low. A few strange phone calls here
and there, all made by cowards who wouldn't give their
names and hid behind pay phones."

"I think I've heard this before, right before they
burned down our house."

They walked a few steps, still holding hands. "Can
you get rid of the case?" she asked.

"I just got it yesterday."

"I know. I remember. And you see Judge Noose in the morning?"

"Bright and early. For motions in *Smallwood*."

"Will you talk about this case?"

"I'm sure we will. It's the only case that's being discussed anyway. Drew needs help right now, or at least he needs to be seen by a professional. If I get the chance I'll ask Noose about it. And if by chance he's found another lawyer, then I'm sure he'll tell me."

"But that's unlikely?"

"Yes, it's unlikely this soon. I'll do the preliminary stuff, make sure the kid's rights are protected, try to get him some help and so on, and then in a few weeks I'll push Noose hard to find a replacement."

"Promise."

"Yes, I promise. You doubt me?"

"Sort of, yes."

"Why?"

"Because you care, Jake, and I already get the sense that you're worried about this kid and his family and you want to protect them. And if Judge Noose has a difficult time finding another lawyer, it'll be easy for him to just lean on you again. You'll be in place. The family will trust you. And, be honest, Jake, you enjoy being in the center of the ring."

They turned into their narrow driveway and admired their lovely home, all safe and quiet.

Jake said, "I thought you wanted me to represent the kid."

"I thought so too, but that was before we started getting phone calls."

"They're just phone calls, Carla. Nothing counts until they start shooting."

"Well, that makes me feel better."

———

ACCORDING TO EARL'S lawyer, the property was owned solely by Stuart, having been passed down through probate, courtesy of his grandfather who died twelve years earlier. The two ex-wives were long gone and their names had never been on the deed. Stuart fathered no known children. He died without a will, and under Mississippi law the property would be inherited by his parents, Earl and Janet, and his younger siblings, in equal shares.

After dinner Monday night, Earl and his two surviving sons, Barry and Cecil, drove to the house for the first look around since it was released by the state investigators that afternoon. It was not a visit they wanted to make, but it had to be done. When Earl parked behind Stuart's pickup and turned off the headlights, they sat and stared at the dark house, a place they had known forever. Barry and Cecil asked if they could remain in the car. Earl said no, it was important for them to see where he died. In the rear seat, Barry tried to muffle his sobs. Finally, they got out and walked to the front door, which was not locked.

Earl braced himself and entered the bedroom first. The mattress had been stripped of its sheets and blankets, and a large, hideous stain of dried blood dominated the center of it. Earl backed into the only chair in the room and covered his eyes. Barry and Cecil stood in the door and gawked at the gruesome spot where their brother had breathed his last. There were specks of blood on the wall above the headboard and a hundred tiny divots where the technicians had removed matter for whatever was to be done with it later. The room smelled of death and evil, and a sharp pungent odor not unlike that of roadkill grew heavier the more they inhaled.

Ozzie said they could burn the mattress. They dragged it through the kitchen and across the small wooden deck to a spot in the backyard. They did the same with the headboard, frame, box springs, and pillows. No one would ever again sleep on Stuart's bed. In a small closet in the hall, they found Josie's clothes and shoes, and after taking stock of her belongings, Earl said, "Let's burn 'em too." In a dresser they found her undergarments, pajamas, socks, and so on, and in the bathroom they found her hair dryer and toiletries. Her purse was on a kitchen counter by the phone, and beside it was a set of car keys. Cecil left the keys and did not look inside the purse, but tossed it onto the mattress with the rest of her things.

Earl poured lighter fluid and lit a match. They watched the fire grow quickly and took a step back. "Get the kids' stuff too," he said to Cecil and Barry. "They ain't comin' back here."

They raced upstairs to the boy's room and grabbed everything that might burn—bed linens, clothing, shoes, books, a cheap CD player, banners on the wall. Barry cleaned out the girl's room. She had a few more items than her brother, including some stuffed bears and other animals. In her closet he found a box of old dolls and other toys, which he hauled downstairs and outside and happily tossed on the roaring fire. They inched away from it and, mesmerized, watched it grow until it began to die out.

Barry asked his father, "What about her car?"

Earl sneered at the old Mazda parked beside the house and for a moment thought about torching it, too. But Barry said, "I think she owes money on it."

"Better leave it alone," Earl said.

They had discussed gathering Stuart's personal effects, his guns and clothing and such, but Earl decided they could do it later. The house had been in the family for a long time and was secure. He would change the locks tomorrow and drive over to check on it each day. And he would pass along the word, through Ozzie, that there was no reason for that woman or her kids or any of her friends to ever set foot on Kofer property again. Ozzie could deal with her car.

DOG HICKMAN RAN the only motorcycle shop in town and sold new and used bikes. Though he was familiar with illegal activities, he had been smart enough to avoid getting caught and had no record, other than an old drunk-driving conviction. The police knew him well, but since he didn't bother people he was left alone. Dog's vices were primarily gambling, bootlegging, and dealing in pot.

Mick Swayze had traded several motorcycles with Dog and knew him well. He stopped by the shop after dark on Monday and, after assuring him that he was off-duty, took a beer. Mick got right to the point and promised Dog that Ozzie was not looking for people to accuse. He just wanted to know what happened on Saturday night.

"I'm not worried about Ozzie," Dog said confidently. They were outside, leaning on his Mustang, smoking cigarettes. "I've done nothin' wrong. I mean I wish I hadn't drunk so much so maybe I could've stopped Stu before he got lit, you know? I should've stopped him, but I didn't do anything wrong."

"We know that," Swayze said. "And we know there were five of you at your cabin, passin' around a jug. Who were the other three?"

"I ain't snitchin'."

"How can you snitch, Dog, if there's no crime?"

"If there's no crime, what are you doin' here askin' questions?"

"Ozzie wants to know, that's all. Kofer was one of us and Ozzie liked him a lot. We all liked Stuart. Good cop. Great guy. He was also drunk as a skunk, Dog. Point-three-six."

Dog shook his head in disbelief at this news and spat on the ground. "Well, I'll tell you the truth. When I woke up yesterday mornin' my head felt like it was point-five-five. I stayed in bed all day and barely got out this mornin'. Crazy shit, man."

"What was it?"

"Fresh batch from Gary Garver. Peach flavored."

"That's three. Who were the other two?"

"This is confidential, right? You ain't tellin' nobody."

"Got it."

"Calvin Marr and Wayne Agnor. We started off with a case of beer, just playin' poker in my cabin, no big plans really. Then Gary showed up with two quarts of his good stuff. We all got hammered. I mean, blacked out. First time in a long time and it was bad enough to make me think about quittin'."

"What time did Kofer leave?"

"Don't know. I wasn't awake when he left."

"Who was awake?"

"Don't know, Mick. I swear. I think we all passed out and things went black. I don't remember much. At some point in the night, have no idea when, Stu and Gary left the cabin. When I woke up late Sunday, Calvin and Wayne were still there, in rough shape. We got up, tried to stir around, drank a couple of beers to kill the pain, then the phone rang and my brother told me Stu was dead. Shot in the head by some kid. Hell, he was just there, right there at the card table, shufflin' cards and sippin' peach whiskey from a coffee cup."

"You been hangin' out with Stu?"

"I don't know. What kind of question is that?"

"A simple one."

"Not as much as a year ago. He was losin' control, Mick, you know? We'd play poker once a month, usually at the cabin, and you could always count on Stu to overdo things, drink too much. Who am I, right? But there was talk about Stu. Some of his friends were concerned. Hell, we all drink too much, but sometimes it's the drunks who see what's really goin' on. We figured Ozzie knew about it and turned a blind eye."

"I don't think so. Stu showed up for work every day and did his job. He was one of Ozzie's favorites."

"Mine too. Everybody liked Stu."

"Will you talk to Ozzie?"

"Well, I don't want to."

"No rush, but he'd just like to have a chat. Maybe after the funeral."

"Like I got a choice?"

"Not really."

10

As with most hot courthouse rumors, the source would never be known. Did it spring to life behind a hint of the truth, or was it someone's idea of a joke down in the Office of Land Records on the first floor? Did a bored lawyer create the fiction with one eye on the clock to see how soon the story would make the rounds and find its way back to him? Since the courthouse, indeed the entire town, was still buzzing with the details of the murder, it was not too far-fetched to believe that someone with a bit of authority, perhaps a deputy or a bailiff, might have said something like "Yep, we're bringin' the boy over today."

At any rate, early Tuesday morning half the county knew for a fact that the kid who killed Stuart Kofer would appear in court for the first time, and for good measure the rumor was soon amended to include the irresistible fact that he would probably be *released*! Something to do with his age.

On a routine day, the Civil Docket attracted only a few lawyers who had motions pending, never a crowd of spectators. But on Tuesday, the gallery was half full as dozens gathered in the main courtroom to witness this horrendous miscarriage of justice. The clerks checked and rechecked the docket to see if they had missed something. Judge Noose was not expected until almost ten, when the first motion hearing was supposed to start. When Jake ambled in at nine-thirty he at first thought he had somehow chosen the wrong date. He whispered to a clerk and was told about the rumor.

"That's odd," he whispered back as he scanned the hard faces staring at him. "Seems like I'd know it if my client was coming to court."

"That's usually the way we do things," she whispered back.

Harry Rex arrived and began insulting an insurance lawyer. Others milled about with eyes on the crowd and wondering what was the attraction. Bailiffs and deputies huddled to one side, aware of the rumor but unaware of any orders to bring the defendant over from the jail.

Lowell Dyer entered through a side door and greeted Jake. They agreed to have a word with Noose as soon as possible. At ten, His Honor called them back to his chambers and offered them coffee as he lined up his second round of daily medications. His robe was hanging on the door and his jacket was draped over a chair. "How's the defendant?" he asked. Noose had always been gaunt with a long, lanky frame and a sloping nose that was often redder than the rest of his pale skin. He had never looked that healthy, and to watch him knock back an impressive collection of pills made the lawyers wonder just how sick he might be. But they didn't dare ask what was ailing him.

Jake poured two cups of coffee into paper cups, and he and Lowell sat across from the judge. Jake replied, "Well, Judge, the kid is not doing too well. I saw him this morning for the third straight day and he's shutting down. I think he's traumatized and having some sort of breakdown. Can we get him evaluated and perhaps treated? This might be a sick little boy."

"Boy?" Lowell asked. "Try telling that to the Kofers."

"He's sixteen, Jake," Judge Noose said. "Hardly a boy."

"Wait till you meet him."

"Evaluated where?" Lowell asked.

"Well, I'd prefer that the pros do it, down at the state hospital."

"Lowell?"

"The State objects, as for right now anyway."

"I'm not sure you have the right to object, Lowell," Jake said. "There's no case yet. Shouldn't you wait until you get the indictment?"

"I suppose."

"Here's the problem," Jake said. "The kid needs help right now. Today. This very moment. He's suffering from some type of trauma and he's not improving sitting over there in the jail. He needs to be seen by a doctor, a psychiatrist, someone a lot smarter than we are. If that doesn't happen, then he may continue to deteriorate. At times he refuses to talk to me. He can't remember from one day to the next. He's not eating. He's having crazy dreams and hallucinating. At times he just sits and stares and makes this weird humming noise like he's lost his mind. Don't you want a healthy defendant, Lowell? If the boy's crazy as a loon, you can't put him on trial. There's no harm in at least getting someone, some doctor, to take a look."

Lowell looked at Noose, who was chewing a pill that must have been bitter.

Noose said, "Crime, suspect, arrest, jail. Looks to me like the defendant needs a first appearance."

"We'll waive it," Jake said. "There's nothing to be gained by hauling the kid over in a police car and dragging him into a courtroom. He simply can't handle that right now. I'm being honest here, Judge, I don't think the kid knows what's happening around him."

Lowell smiled and shook his head as if he had doubts. "Sounds to me like you're already laying the ground-work for an insanity plea, Jake."

"I am not, because Judge Noose here has promised me that he'll find another lawyer to handle the trial, if there is a trial."

"Oh, there will be a trial, Jake, I can promise that," Lowell said. "You can't kill a man in cold blood and walk away."

"Nobody's walking away here, Lowell. I'm just wor-ried about this kid. He's detached from reality. What's the harm in having him evaluated?"

Noose had finished with his meds and was choking them down with a glass of water. He looked at Jake and asked, "Who would do it?"

"State Health has a regional office in Oxford. Maybe we can send him over there to be examined."

"Can they send someone over here?" Noose asked. "I really don't like the idea of the defendant leaving jail so soon."

"Agreed," Lowell said. "They haven't had the funeral yet. I'm not sure the kid would be safe outside the jail."

"Fine," Jake said. "I don't care how we do it."

Noose raised his hands and called for order. "Let's agree on a plan here, fellas. I assume, Mr. Dyer, that you plan to seek an indictment for capital murder, is this correct?"

"Well, Judge, it's still a bit early, but, yes, that's how I'm leaning as of today. It appears as if the facts call for such an indictment."

"And when would you present this case to your grand jury?"

"We meet here in two weeks, but I can always call it early. Do you have a preference?"

"No. The grand jury is really none of my business.

Mr. Brigance, how do you see the next few weeks un-folding?"

"Thank you, Your Honor. Since my client is so young I will have no choice but to ask you to transfer his case over to youth court."

Lowell Dyer bit his tongue and gave Noose plenty of room to respond. Noose looked at him with raised eyebrows and Dyer said, "Of course, the State will oppose such a motion. We believe the case belongs in this court and that the defendant should be tried as an adult."

Jake did not react. He took a sip of coffee and glanced at a legal pad as if he knew this was coming, which in fact he did because there was no chance at all that the Honorable Omar Noose was going to allow the Ford County Youth Court to handle such a serious crime. Lesser offenses committed by teenagers were often sent down—car theft, drugs, small-time larcenies and burglaries—and the juvenile judge was known to be judicious in dealing with them. But not serious crimes involving bodily harm, and certainly not murders.

Most white Southerners firmly believed that a sixteen-year-old like Drew Gamble who shot a man sleeping in his own bed must be tried as an adult and given a harsh sentence, even death. A small minority felt otherwise. Jake wasn't sure, yet, how he felt, though he already doubted whether Drew had the wherewithal to understand criminal intent.

Jake also knew the political realities. Next year, 1991, both Omar Noose and Lowell Dyer faced reelection—Dyer for the first time, Noose for the fifth. Though His Honor was pushing seventy and took a lot of meds he was showing no signs of slowing down. He enjoyed the job, the prestige, the salary. He had always faced light opposition—few lawyers were willing to challenge a sitting and entrenched judge—but there was always the chance of that screwball election where an underdog caught fire and the voters decided they wanted a new face. Three years earlier, Noose had been hounded by a quack of a lawyer from Milburn County who made a bunch of wild claims about lenient sentences in criminal cases. He got a third of the vote, which was not unimpressive for a complete unknown with little credibility.

Now, a more ominous threat was looming. Jake had heard the rumors and he was sure Noose had heard them too. Rufus Buckley, the ex–district attorney, the showboat Dyer had defeated in a close election, was reportedly making waves and dropping hints about wanting Noose's seat on the bench. Buckley had been banished to the sidelines, where he spent his days in a small office down in Smithfield drafting deeds and fuming and plotting his comeback. His greatest loss was the not-guilty verdict of Carl Lee Hailey, and he would forever blame Noose. And Jake. And everyone else remotely connected to the case. Everyone but himself.

"File your motion in due course," Noose said, as if he'd already made up his mind.

"Yes sir. Now, about the psychiatric examination."

Noose stood and grunted and walked to his desk where he took a pipe from an ashtray and stuck the stem between his stained teeth. "And you think this is urgent?"

"Yes I do, Judge. I'm afraid this kid is slipping as the hours pass."

"Has Ozzie seen him?"

"Ozzie's not a shrink. I'm sure he's seen him because he's at the jail."

Noose looked at Dyer and asked, "And your position on this?"

"The State is not opposed to an exam but I don't want that kid out of jail for any reason."

"Got that. Okay, I'll sign the order. Do you have other business today?"

Dyer replied, "No sir."

"You're excused, Mr. Dyer."

THE CURIOUS CONTINUED to stream into the courtroom. The minutes passed and Judge Noose did not appear. Near the jury box, Walter Sullivan sat with his co-counsel, Sean Gilder, an insurance lawyer from Jackson who was defending the railroad in the *Smallwood* case. They spoke in low voices about this and that, lawyer talk for the most part, but as the crowd grew Walter began to realize something.

Harry Rex's instincts were correct. The lawyers for the railroad and its insurance company had finally agreed to approach Jake with the idea of a preliminary chat about a settlement. But they planned to be extremely cautious. On the one hand, the case was dangerous because the damages were high—four dead family members—and Jake would be trying the case on his turf, indeed in the very courtroom where they were now sitting and from which he walked out with Carl Lee Hailey as an innocent man. But on the other hand, the railroad and insurance lawyers were still confident they could win because of liability issues. Taylor Smallwood, the driver, had hit the fourteenth boxcar of a moving freight train without, evidently, touching his brakes. Their expert estimated his speed at seventy miles per hour. Jake's expert thought it was closer to sixty.

The speed limit on that forlorn stretch of road was only fifty-five.

There were other issues to worry about. The railroad crossing had historically been badly maintained, and Jake had the records and photos to prove it. There had been other accidents, and Jake had those reports enlarged and ready to show to his jury. The only known eyewitness was an unstable carpenter who had been following the Smallwood car perhaps a hundred yards behind, and he was adamant in his deposition that the red flashing lights were not working at the time. However, there were rumors, still unsubstantiated, that the gentleman had been drinking in a honky-tonk.

That was the terrifying aspect of going to trial in Ford County. Jake Brigance was an upstanding young lawyer with an impeccable reputation and could be trusted to play by the rules. However, his clique included Harry Rex, also his co-counsel, and the loathsome Lucien Wilbanks, neither of whom spent much time worrying about the ethics of the profession.

Thus, there was the potential for a huge verdict, but the jury could just as easily blame Taylor Smallwood and find in favor of the railroad. With so many unknowns, the insurance company wanted to explore settlement. If Jake wanted millions, then the negotiations wouldn't last long. If he chose to be more reasonable, they could find common ground and make everyone happy.

Walter tried few cases himself, preferring instead to be the local guy when the big firms from Jackson and Memphis rolled in and needed a presence. He collected modest fees for doing little more than using his connections and helping to weed out potential problems during the selection of the jury.

As the courtroom buzzed with quiet gossip and

speculation, Walter realized that Jake was about to become the most unpopular lawyer in town. Those folks packing into the pews were not there to support Drew Gamble and whatever family he might have. No sir. They were there to get a hateful look at the killer and silently rage against the injustice of treating him with sympathy. And if Mr. Brigance somehow worked his magic again and got the kid released, there might be trouble in the streets.

Sullivan leaned toward his co-counsel and said, "Let's get through the motions and not broach the idea of settlement, not today anyway."

"And why not?"

"I'll explain later. There's plenty of time."

ACROSS THE COURTROOM, Harry Rex chewed on the ragged end of an unlit cigar and pretended to listen to a bad joke from a bailiff while glancing at the crowd. He recognized a girl from high school, couldn't remember her last name back then but he knew she had married a Kofer. How many of these people were related to the victim? How many would resent Jake Brigance?

As the minutes dragged on and the crowd grew, Harry Rex confirmed his original fear. His buddy Jake was taking a case that would pay peanuts and, in doing so, risking a case that could be a bonanza.

11

Late Tuesday morning, Pastor Charles McGarry, his wife, Meg, and Kiera arrived at the hospital and went to the waiting room on the third floor where they checked in with the crew from his church. They had things well under control and were feeding half the hospital's staff and some of its patients as well.

Few things excite country folk more than a trip to the hospital, either as visitors or patients, and the members of the tiny church were rallying around the Gamble family with great love and enthusiasm. Or at least around Josie and Kiera. Drew, the accused killer, was locked away and none of their concern, which was fine with them. But the mother and sister had done nothing wrong and were in dire need of sympathy.

Josie's room was busy with nurses preparing her for the trip. Kiera hugged her and then backed into a corner where Charles waited and watched. Her doctors were convinced that there was a better reconstructive specialist in the larger hospital in Tupelo, where her surgery was scheduled for early Wednesday morning.

She managed to swing her feet off the bed, stand alone, and walk three steps to the gurney where she settled in as nurses restrung tubes and wires. She tried to smile at Kiera, but her face was swollen and covered with gauze.

They followed her down the hall, where she passed the admiring crowd from Good Shepherd, and to the service elevator and down to the basement where an

ambulance was waiting. Kiera left with Charles and
Meg and hustled to his car. They followed the ambulance away from the hospital, out of town, and into the
countryside. Tupelo was an hour away.

AS JAKE WAS trying his best to sneak out of the
courthouse through a rear door, someone called his
name. Oddly enough, it was Ozzie, who knew the secret passages and rooms as well as anyone. "Got a minute?" he said as they stopped beside two ancient vending
machines. Ozzie preferred to be noticed around the
courthouse, shaking hands, slapping backs, lots of laughs,
a big personality, ever the politician shoring up his base.
To find him lurking in the shadows could only mean
that he didn't want to be seen chatting with Jake.

"Sure," Jake said, as if he or anyone else in the county
could say no to Ozzie.

He handed Jake a square envelope with the words
SHERIFF'S DEPARTMENT stamped on the front. "Earl
Kofer called this mornin' and had his nephew bring
these by the jail. It's the keys to Ms. Gamble's car. We
went out and got the car, brought it in, it's parked behind the jail. Just so you'll know."

"I didn't realize I represented Josie Gamble."

"You do now, or at least everybody thinks so. Earl
was quite clear. She is never to set foot on that property
again. They've changed the locks and if they see her
they'll probably start shootin'. She and the kids didn't
have much in the way of clothes and such, but it's all
been destroyed. Earl bragged about burnin' it last night
along with the bloody mattress. Said he almost burned
the car too but figured she owed money on it."

"Just tell Earl to keep his matches dry, okay?"

"I'd like to avoid Earl myself for a few days."

"Was he in court this morning?"

"I think so, yes. He doesn't like the fact that you're representin' the guy who killed his son."

"I've never met Earl Kofer and there's no reason he should be concerned with my law practice."

"There's also a paycheck in there."

"Ah, good news."

"I wouldn't get excited. Seems she worked at the car wash north of town and they owed her for last week. Probably not much. Somebody brought that to the jail too."

"So she's fired?"

"Looks that way. Somebody said she was also workin' at a convenience store over by the high school. You checked this gal out?"

"No, but I'm sure you have."

"She was born in Oregon, thirty-two years ago. Her father was in the air force, not a pilot, and they moved around. She grew up on the base in Biloxi but her father got killed in some kind of explosion. She dropped out of school at sixteen when she gave birth to Drew. The proud papa was some tomcat named Barber, but he disappeared a long time ago. Two years later she had the girl, different daddy, some dude named Mabry. He probably never knew it. She lived here and there, the record is spotty. When she was twenty-six she married a gentleman named Kolston, but the romance broke up when he went to prison for thirty years. Drugs. Divorce. She served two years in Texas for dealing and possession. Not sure what happened to the kids because, as you know, that family court stuff is sealed. Needless to say, they've had a rough time. Things'll get worse."

"I would say so. They're homeless. She's unemployed, facing surgery tomorrow, no place to go when she's released from the hospital. Her daughter is living with their preacher. Her son is in jail."

"You want sympathy, Jake?"

Jake took a deep breath and studied his friend. "No."

Ozzie turned to leave and said, "When you get the chance, ask that kid why he pulled the trigger."

"He thought his mother was dead."

"Well, he was wrong, wasn't he?"

"Yes he was. So let's kill him, too."

Jake held the envelope and watched the sheriff disappear around a corner.

FROM YEARS OF observation and experience, Jake had become an expert on the rhythm and flow of commerce around the square, and he knew that at four-thirty in the afternoon the Coffee Shop would be deserted and Dell would be behind the counter wrapping cheap flatware with paper napkins and waiting for the clock to hit five so she could call it a day. During breakfast and lunch she oversaw the gossip, stirring it up when things were slow, throttling it back when it became too vicious. She listened hard, missed nothing, and was quick to reprimand a raconteur who veered off script. Foul language was not tolerated. A dirty joke could get you banned. If a customer needed to be insulted, she was quick with a quip and didn't care if he never came back. Her recall was legendary and she had often been accused of quickly scribbling down notes to herself to record important rumors. When Jake needed the truth, he ventured over at four-thirty and sat at the counter.

She poured coffee and said, "We missed you these past two mornings."

"That's why I'm here now. What are they saying?"

"It's big news, obviously. First murder in five years, since Hailey. And Stu was a popular guy, good deputy, came in here for lunch every now and then. I liked him. Nobody knows the kid."

"They're not from here. The mother met Kofer and a romance ensued. Pretty sad little family, really."

"That's what I hear."

"Am I still the favorite lawyer?"

"Well, they're not going to talk about you with me close by, now are they? Prather said he wished they could find another lawyer, said Noose dumped the kid on you. Looney said you had no choice, said Noose would replace you later. Stuff like that. No criticism yet. You're worried about it?"

"Sure. I know these guys well. Ozzie and I have always been close. It's not comforting to know that the cops are pissed off."

"Watch your language. They're okay, I think, but you need to show up tomorrow and see how they act."

"I plan to."

She paused and glanced around at the empty café, then leaned in a bit closer. "So, why did the kid shoot him? I mean, he did do it, right?"

"There's no doubt about that, Dell. I won't let them interrogate the kid but they don't have to. His sister told Moss Junior that he shot Stuart. Doesn't give me much to work with, you know?"

"So, what was the motive?"

"I don't know, and I'm not that involved. Noose told me to just hold the kid's hand for the first month until he finds someone else. If it goes to trial maybe they'll find a motive, maybe not."

"Are you going to the funeral?"

"The funeral? I haven't heard."

"Saturday afternoon, at the National Guard Armory. Just heard about it."

"I doubt if I'll be invited. You going?"

She laughed and said, "Of course. Name the last funeral I missed, Jake."

He could not. Dell was known for attending two and sometimes three funerals a week and fully recapping each as she served breakfast. For years Jake had heard tales of open caskets, closed caskets, long sermons, bawling widows, jilted children, family dustups, beautiful sacred music, and bad organ recitals.

"I'm sure it will be a show," he said. "It's been decades since we buried an officer."

"You want some dirt?" she asked as she once again glanced around the café.

"Of course."

"Well, word is that his people are having trouble getting a preacher. They don't do church, never have, and all the preachers they've stiff-armed over the years are saying no. Can't blame them, can you? Who'd want to stand up at the pulpit and say all the usual happy stuff about a man who never darkened their door?"

"So, who's officiating?"

"Don't know. I think they're still scrambling. Come back in the morning and maybe we'll know something."

"I'll be here."

THE TABLE IN the center of Lucien's downstairs workroom was covered with thick lawbooks, legal pads, and discarded papers, as if the two non-lawyers had been plowing through research for days. Both wanted to be lawyers and Portia was well on her way. Lucien's glory days were far in the past but he still, at times, found the law fascinating.

Jake walked in, admired the mess, and pulled up another mismatched chair. "So, please tell me your brilliant new legal strategies."

"Can't find one," Lucien said. "We're screwed."

Portia said, "We've tracked down every youth court case over the past forty years and the law doesn't budge. When a kid, a person under the age of eighteen, commits a murder, rape, or armed robbery, original jurisdiction is in circuit court, not juvenile."

"What about an eight-year-old?" Jake asked.

"They don't rape much," Lucien mumbled, almost to himself.

Portia said, "In 1952, an eleven-year-old boy in Tishomingo County shot and killed an older kid who lived down the road. They kept him in circuit court and put him on trial. He was convicted and sent to Parchman. Can you believe that? A year later the Mississippi Supremes said he was too young and kicked it back to youth court. Then the legislature got involved and said the magic age is thirteen and older."

Jake said, "It doesn't matter. Drew is not even close, at least in age. I'd put his emotional maturity at about thirteen, but I'm not qualified."

"Have you found a psychiatrist?" Portia asked.

"Still looking."

"And what's the goal here, Jake?" Lucien asked. "If he says the boy is certified batshit crazy, Noose ain't movin' the case. You know that. And can you really blame him? It's a dead cop and they have the killer. If the case went to youth court the kid would be found guilty and put away in a kiddie jail. For two years! And the day he turns eighteen, youth court loses all jurisdiction and guess what happens."

"He walks," Portia said.

"He walks," Jake said.

"So you can't blame Noose for keeping the case."

"I'm not trying to plead insanity here, Lucien, not yet anyway. But this kid is suffering from something and needs professional help. He's not eating, bathing, is barely talking, and he can sit for hours staring at the floor and humming as if he's dying inside. Frankly, I think he needs to be moved to the state hospital and put on medication."

The phone rang and they stared at it. "Where's Bev?" Jake asked.

"Gone. It's almost five," Portia said.

"Out for more cigarettes," Lucien said.

Portia slowly lifted the receiver and said, quite officially, "Law office of Jake Brigance." She smiled and listened for a second and asked, "And who's calling, please?" A brief pause as she closed her eyes and racked her brain. "And this is in regard to which case?" A smile, then: "I'm sorry but Mr. Brigance is in court this afternoon."

He was always in court, according to the office's rules of engagement. If the caller was a non-client or other stranger, he or she was left with the impression that Mr. Brigance practically lived in the courtroom and getting an appointment for an office consultation would be difficult and probably expensive. And this was not unusual among the bored and timid office practitioners in Clanton. On the other side of the square, a worthless lawyer named F. Frank Mulveney trained his part-time secretary to go one step further and gravely inform all callers that "Mr. Mulveney is in *federal* court." No lowly state work for F. Frank. He was off to the big leagues.

Portia hung up and said, "A divorce."

"Thank you. Any more cranks today?"

"Not that I know of."

Lucien stared at his wristwatch as if waiting for an alarm. He stood and announced, "It's five o'clock. Who wants a drink?"

Jake and Portia waved him off. As soon as he was gone, she asked quietly, "When did he start drinking here?"

"When did he stop?"

12

The only child psychologist working for the state in north Mississippi was too busy to return phone calls. Jake assumed this meant that a request, if somehow made, that she drop everything and hustle over to the jail in Clanton would not be well received. There were no such specialists in private practice in Ford County, or anywhere else in the Twenty-second Judicial District for that matter, and it took Portia two hours on the phone to finally locate one in Oxford, an hour to the west.

On Wednesday morning, Jake talked to him briefly before the guy said he could evaluate Drew in a couple of weeks, and in his office, not at the jail. He did not make house calls. Nor did the two in Tupelo, though the second one, a Dr. Christina Rooker, warmed up quickly when she recognized the identity of the potential patient. She had read about the murder of the officer and was intrigued by what Jake told her on the phone. He described Drew's condition, appearance, behavior, and near catatonic state. Dr. Rooker agreed that the situation was urgent and agreed to see him the following day, Thursday, in her office in Tupelo, not at the jail in Clanton.

Lowell Dyer objected to Drew's leaving for any reason, as did Ozzie. Judge Noose was hearing motions at the Polk County Courthouse in Smithfield. Jake drove forty-five minutes south, walked into the courtroom, and waited until some rather long-winded lawyers finished their bickering and His Honor had a few moments to spare. In chambers, Jake again described his client's condition, explained that Dr. Rooker felt the matter was urgent, and insisted that the kid be allowed out of the jail for an examination. He posed no safety or flight risk. Hell, he was barely capable of feeding himself. Jake finally convinced the judge that the ends of justice would be served by getting the defendant some immediate medical help.

"And her fee is five hundred dollars," he added on his way out of the door.

"For a two-hour consultation?"

"That's what she said. I promised her we, the State, because you and I are now on its payroll, right, would cover it. And that brings up the matter of my fees."

"We'll discuss them later, Jake. I have lawyers waiting."

"Thanks, Judge. I'll call Lowell and Ozzie and they'll bitch and cuss and probably come crying to you."

"That's part of my job. I'm not worried about them."

"I'll tell Ozzie that you want him to drive the kid to Tupelo. He'll like that."

"Whatever."

"And I'm filing a motion to transfer the case to youth court."

"Please wait until there's an indictment."

"Okay."

"And don't waste a lot of time on the motion."

"Is that because you don't plan to waste a lot of time with it?"

"That's correct, Jake."

"Well, thanks for the candor."

"As always."

———

AT EIGHT O'CLOCK Thursday morning, Drew Gamble was led to a small dark room and told by the jailer that it was time for a shower. He had declined earlier requests and needed a good scrubbing. He was given a bar of soap and a towel and told to hurry, there was a five-minute limit on showers throughout the jail, and also warned that the hot water, if any, would last for only the first two minutes. He closed the door, stripped, and tossed out his soiled clothing, which the jailer collected and took to the laundry. When Drew was finished, he was given the smallest orange jumpsuit available and a pair of well-used rubber shower shoes, also orange in color, and taken back to his cell where he declined a plate of eggs and bacon. Instead, he munched on peanuts and drank a soda. As usual, he did not speak to the jailers even when spoken to. They had at first assumed their prisoner had some serious attitude but soon realized that his mind was functioning at a very low level. One whispered to another, "His light's barely on but nobody's home."

Jake arrived just before nine with two dozen fresh doughnuts that he passed around the jail in an effort to score points with old friends who now viewed him as an enemy. A few were taken but most were ignored. He left one box at the front desk and walked back to the jail. Alone with Drew in his cell, he offered his client a doughnut, and, to his surprise, he ate two of them. The sugar seemed to jack up his energy and he asked, "Is something going on today, Jake?"

"Yes. You're taking a trip to Tupelo to see a doctor."

"I'm not sick, am I?"

"We'll let the doctor decide that. She'll ask you a lot of questions about yourself and your family, and where you've lived and all that, and you need to tell the truth and answer to the best of your ability."

"Is she a shrink or something?"

The use of the word "shrink" caught Jake off guard. "She's a psychiatrist."

"Oh, a shrink. I've met one or two before."

"Really? Where?"

"They put me in jail one time, in the juvenile pen, and I had to see a shrink once a week. It was a waste of time."

"But I've asked you twice if you've ever been to juvenile court and you said no."

"I don't remember you asking me that. Sorry."

"Why were you in the juvenile pen?"

Drew took another bite of a doughnut and thought about the question. "And you're my lawyer, right?"

"This is the fifth straight day I've come here to the jail to talk to you. Only your lawyer would do that, right?"

"I really want to see my mom."

Jake breathed deeply and told himself to be patient, something he did with every visit. "Your mother had surgery yesterday, they reset her jaw, and she's doing fine. You can't see her now but I'm sure they'll allow her to come here for a visit."

"I thought she was dead."

"I know you did, Drew." Jake heard voices in the hall and looked at his watch. "Here's the drill. The sheriff will drive you to Tupelo. You'll sit in the backseat, probably alone, and you are not to say a word to anyone else in the car. Understand?"

"You're not going?"

"I'll be in my car behind you, and I'll be there when you meet the doctor. Just don't say anything to the sheriff or his deputies, okay?"

"Will they talk to me?"

"I doubt it."

The door opened and Ozzie barged in with Moss Junior behind him. Jake stood and offered a terse "Mornin' gentlemen," but they only nodded. Moss Junior unsnapped the cuffs from his belt and said to Drew, "Stand up please."

Jake asked, "Does he have to wear handcuffs? I mean, he's not going anywhere."

"We know our job, Jake, same as you," Ozzie said like a real smart-ass.

"Why can't he wear street clothes? Look, Ozzie, he's going for a psychiatric evaluation, and sitting there in an orange jumpsuit will not help matters."

"Back off, Jake."

"I'm not backing off. I'll call Judge Noose."

"You do that."

The jailer said, "He doesn't have any extra clothes. Just one change, and it's in the laundry."

Jake looked at the jailer and asked, "You don't allow the kids to have any clothes?"

Ozzie said, "He's not a kid, Jake. He was in circuit court last time I checked."

To benefit nothing, Moss Junior said, "They burned all his clothes. Same for his mother and sister."

Drew shuddered and took a deep breath.

Jake looked at Drew, then looked at Moss Junior and asked, "Was that really necessary?"

"You're askin' 'bout more clothes. Ain't got 'em."

Ozzie said, "Let's go."

Every office had leaks, and Ozzie had been burned on occasion. The last thing he wanted was a front-page photo of him trying to sneak the accused killer out for a visit to a psychiatrist. His car was waiting behind the jail, with Looney and Swayze standing guard and prepared to shoot any reporter they saw. The getaway went smoothly, and as Jake raced to keep up with them in his

Saab, he could barely see the top of Drew's blond hair in the rear seat.

DR. ROOKER'S OFFICE was one of a dozen in a professional office building not far from downtown Tupelo. As directed, Ozzie turned into a service drive behind the building and was met by two marked patrol cars from the Lee County sheriff's department. He parked, got out, left Moss Junior in the front seat to guard the defendant, and went inside with the local deputies to check out the premises. Jake remained in his car, not far from Ozzie's, and waited. What else could he do? Driving over, he had called Portia who had called the hospital for information about Josie Gamble. Portia had learned nothing and was waiting for a return call from a nurse.

Half an hour dragged by. Moss Junior finally got out and lit a cigarette, and Jake walked over for a chat. He glanced into the rear seat and saw Drew lying down with his knees pulled to his chest.

Jake nodded at him and asked, "Did he say much?"

"Not a word, nothin', course we didn't pry. That's a sick puppy, Jake."

"What do you mean?"

"Have you heard that hummin' sound he does? Just sits there with his eyes closed and sorta hums and groans at the same time, like he's in another world."

"I've heard it."

Moss blew a cloud of smoke at the sky and shifted weight from his right foot to his left. "Can he get off 'cause he's crazy, Jake?"

"So that's what's going around?"

"Oh yeah. Folks think you'll get him off like you did Carl Lee, by sayin' he's insane."

"Well, folks have to say something, don't they, Moss?"

"That they do, yes. But that ain't right, Jake." He cleared his throat and spat near the bumper as if disgusted. "Folks are gonna be upset, Jake, and I hate to see you take the blame."

"I'm just a temp, Moss. Noose has promised to find somebody else if it goes all the way to a trial."

"Is that where it's goin'?"

"Don't know. I'm pinch-hitting till there's an indictment and something gets put on a calendar, then I'll bail."

"That's good to hear. This might get nasty before it's over."

"It's already nasty."

Ozzie was back with the other deputies. He spoke to Moss Junior who opened a rear door and asked Drew to step out. They quickly escorted him inside the building and Jake followed along.

In a small conference room, Dr. Rooker was waiting and introduced herself to Jake. They had spoken on the phone several times and the introduction was brief. She was tall and slender, with bright red hair that was probably not natural, and she wore funky reading glasses of many colors that were perched on the tip of her nose. She was about fifty, older than any of the men and thoroughly unintimidated by any of them. This was her office, her show.

Once Ozzie felt the defendant was secure, he excused himself and said he and Moss Junior would be waiting down the hall. It was clear that Dr. Rooker did not like the idea of armed men waiting in her quiet little office suite, but under the circumstances she went along. It was not every day that she talked to a man, or a kid, who was charged with capital murder.

Drew looked even smaller in the oversized jumpsuit.

The rubber shower shoes looked ridiculous and were several sizes too large. They barely touched the floor as he sat with his hands folded in his lap, chin down, eyes on the floor, as if too frightened to acknowledge those around him.

Jake said, "Drew, this is Dr. Rooker, and she is here to help you."

With effort, he nodded at her, then looked back at the floor.

Jake said, "I'll be here for just a moment, then I'll disappear. I'm going to ask you to listen to her carefully and answer her questions. She's on our side, Drew. Do you understand?"

He nodded and slowly lifted his eyes to the wall above Jake's head, as if he heard something up there and didn't like it. A slow, mournful groan came out, but he said nothing. As frightening as it was, Jake wanted the kid to start his incessant humming again. Dr. Rooker needed to hear it and evaluate it, if that was possible.

"How old are you, Drew?" she asked.

"Sixteen."

"And when is your birthday?"

"February the tenth."

"So last month. Did you have a party on your birthday?"

"No."

"Did you have birthday cake?"

"No."

"Did your friends at school know it was your birthday?"

"Don't think so."

"Who is your mother?"

"Josie."

"And you have a sister, right?"

"Right. Kiera."

"And there's nobody else in your family?"

He shook his head.

"No grandparents, aunts, uncles, cousins?"

He kept shaking his head.

"How about your father?"

His eyes were suddenly wet and he wiped them on an orange sleeve. "Don't know him."

"Have you ever known your father?"

He shook his head.

She estimated his height at five feet and his weight at a hundred pounds. There was no visible muscle development. His voice was high, soft, still childlike. There was no facial hair, no acne, nothing to indicate that the middle stages of puberty had arrived.

He closed his eyes again and began rocking, slightly, leaning forward from the waist, then easing back.

She touched his knee and asked, "Drew, are you afraid of something right now?"

He began to hum in that same steady emission that at times sounded more like a soft growl. They listened to him for a moment, exchanged glances, and then she asked, "Drew, why do you make that noise?"

The only response was more of the same. She withdrew her hand, glanced at her watch, and relaxed as if they might be a while. A minute passed, then two. After five, she nodded at Jake and he quietly left the room.

THE HOSPITAL WAS not far away. Jake found Ms. Gamble in a second-floor semi-private room shared with what appeared to be a corpse but was, as it turned out, a ninety-six-year-old man who had just received a new kidney. At ninety-six?

Kiera had secured a small foldout bed and it was tucked next to her mother's. They had been there for two nights and would be leaving in the afternoon. Where they were headed was still undecided.

Josie looked awful with a swollen and bruised face, but she was in good spirits and claimed to be free of pain. The surgery had gone well, all the bones were accounted for and rearranged, and she didn't have to see a doctor for a week.

Jake settled into a chair at the foot of her bed and asked if they wanted to talk. What else did they have to do until discharged? A friendly nurse brought him a cup of hospital coffee and pulled the curtain so the corpse couldn't hear them. They spoke in low voices and Jake explained where Drew was and what was happening. For a moment Josie was hopeful she might be able to see him since he was just around the corner, but realized neither was in any condition for a visit. The sheriff wouldn't allow it and Drew was headed back to jail in short order.

Jake said, "I'm not sure how long I'll be your lawyer. As I explained, the judge gave me a temporary appointment to handle the preliminary matters, and he plans to find someone else later."

"Why can't you be our lawyer?" Josie asked. Her words were slow and difficult, but clear enough for a conversation.

"I am, for now. We'll see what happens later."

Kiera, who was shy and had trouble keeping eye contact, said, "Mr. Callison from our church said you're the best lawyer in the county, said we're lucky to have you."

Jake had not expected to be backed into a corner by his clients and forced to explain why he didn't want them. He certainly couldn't, and wouldn't, admit that Drew's case was so toxic he was worried about his own reputation. In all likelihood, he would live in Clanton for the rest of his life and try to make a decent living. The Gambles would probably be gone in a few months. But how could he explain this to two people staying in a hospital with no home, no clothing, no money, and the frightening prospect of their son and brother facing the death penalty? At the moment, he was their only protection. The church folks could provide food and comfort, but that was temporary.

He tried to duck with "Well, Mr. Callison is a very nice man, but there are a lot of good lawyers around here. The judge will probably pick someone with experience in juvenile matters."

Jake felt guilty at his own bullshit. It wasn't a juvenile matter and would never become one, and there were only a handful of lawyers in north Mississippi with capital trial experience. And Jake knew damned well that all of them would be hiding from their telephones in the days to come. No one wanted a dead-cop case in a small town. Harry Rex was right. The case had already become a liability and would only get worse.

Armed with a yellow legal pad, Jake managed to steer the conversation away from his representation and into the family's history. Without asking about Josie's past, he pried into their other addresses, other homes, other towns. How did they end up in rural Ford County? Where had they lived before, and before that?

At times Kiera remembered details, and at other times she drifted away and seemed to lose interest. One moment she was engaged, the next she was frightened and withdrawn. She was a pretty girl, tall for her age, with deep brown eyes and long dark hair. She looked nothing like her brother, and no one would have guessed that she was two years younger.

The more Jake probed, the more he became convinced that she too had been traumatized. Perhaps not by Stuart Kofer, but by other people who'd had the opportunity over the years. She had lived with relatives, in two foster homes, in an orphanage, in a camper, under an overpass, in a homeless shelter. The deeper he dug, the sadder their story became, and after an hour he'd had enough.

He said goodbye with the promise to check on Drew and to see them again as soon as possible.

13

Thursday lunch meant a quick visit to the school's cafeteria where parents were invited to grab a tray and for two dollars dine on either grilled chicken tenders or spaghetti and meatballs. It was not one of Jake's favorite meals of the week, but food was not important since he got to sit with Hanna and a gaggle of her fourth-grade girlfriends. As the weeks passed, and as they grew, he was dismayed to learn that they spent more time talking about boys. He was scheming of ways to put a stop to it but so far had thought of nothing. Carla usually dropped by for a quick chat, but her sixth graders were on a different schedule.

Mandy Baker's mother, Helen, was an occasional guest and Jake knew the family, though they would never be close. They sat across from each other on the low stools and listened with amusement as the girls all talked at once. After a few moments the girls forgot their parents were there and ramped up the chatter. When they were thoroughly preoccupied, Helen said, "I just can't believe that about Stuart Kofer, can you?"

"Such a tragedy," Jake said as he chewed on some chicken. Helen's husband's family owned a string of self-service gas stations and were rumored to be doing well. They lived at the country club and Jake avoided most of the people out there. They put on airs and enjoyed looking down and he had no patience with them.

Helen did the lunch once a month, and Jake assumed she had chosen this day to say what she was about to say. So, when she said it, he was prepared. Leaning in a bit lower, she said, "I can't believe you would represent a killer like that, Jake. I thought you were one of us."

Or, he *thought* he was prepared. The "one of us" caught him off guard and instantly brought to mind several stinging and snappy retorts that would only make things worse. He let them pass and said, "Gotta have a lawyer, Helen. You can't put the boy in the gas chamber if he doesn't have a lawyer. Surely you understand that."

"Oh, I guess. But there are so many lawyers around here. Why do you have to get involved?"

"Who would you choose, Helen?"

"Oh, I don't know. What about some of those ACLU types in Memphis or even down in Jackson. You know, the real bleeding hearts. I can't imagine doing that for a living, representing killers and child rapists and such."

"How often do you read the Constitution?" he asked, a bit sharper than he had intended.

"Oh, come on, Jake. Don't give me all that legal mess."

"No, Helen, the Constitution, as interpreted by the Supreme Court, says that a person accused of a serious crime must have a lawyer. And that's the law of the land."

"I suppose. I just don't understand why you're involved."

Jake bit his tongue to keep from reminding her that neither she nor her husband nor anyone in their families had ever sought his advice or legal services. Why, then, was she now so concerned about his practice?

She was just a gossip who could now boast to her friends that she had bumped into Jake Brigance and dressed him down in public for representing such a despicable killer. She would no doubt expand the story, lunch on it for the next month, and gain the admiration of her friends.

Thankfully, Carla appeared and eased into the child's chair next to Jake. She greeted Helen warmly and asked how her Aunt Euna was doing since her fall. The murder was instantly forgotten as the conversation moved to the upcoming fourth-grade talent show.

WITH HER JAWS wired together, Josie found it impossible to chew food, so her last lunch at the hospital was another chocolate milkshake through a straw. After which she was required to sit in a wheelchair as they rolled her out of the room and down the hallway. Eventually, she and Kiera and two orderlies exited through the front door and got into the car of Mrs. Carol Huff, who had volunteered to do the driving because she owned a four-door Pontiac. Pastor Charles McGarry and his wife, Meg, were there for the release, and they followed Mrs. Huff in their little import out of Tupelo and back to Ford County.

The Good Shepherd Bible Church had a narrow sanctuary that was pretty and timeless. Years after it was built, one of the many congregations added a two-story wing across the back, a less than handsome annex with classrooms for Sunday school upstairs and a small fellowship hall and kitchen on the first floor, next to the office where Pastor McGarry prepared his sermons and counseled his flock. He had decided that the church would offer the use of a classroom to Josie and Kiera as a short-term apartment, with access to the downstairs toilet and the kitchen. He and the deacons had met three times in extra sessions since Monday to try to find a place for the family, and a classroom in the back of the

church was the best they could do. One member owned
a rental home that might be available in a month or so,
but that member also relied upon the income from it. A
farmer had a barn/guesthouse but it needed some
work. There was the offer of a camper, but McGarry
waved it off. Josie and the kids had recently survived a
year in one.

The church had no wealthy people, the type who
owned multiple homes. Its members were retirees, small
farmers, middle-class working folks who were doing
well to scrape by themselves. Other than love and warm
food, they had little to offer.

Josie and Kiera had no other place to go and no
family to turn to. Leaving the area was out of the question because of Drew and his problems. Josie did not
have a bank account and had been surviving on limited
cash for several years. Kofer had demanded two hundred dollars a month for rent and food, and she had
always been in arrears. The original arrangement had
been based on plenty of sex and companionship in exchange for food and shelter, but the intimacy had not
lasted long. She had no credit cards and no credit history. Her last paycheck from the car wash was for $51
and a convenience store owed her $40 more. She was
not sure how to collect and not even sure if she still had
the job there, though she was assuming the worst. At
least two of her three part-time jobs were gone, and her
doctor said she could not look for work for at least two
weeks. There were relatives in south Mississippi and
Louisiana but they had stopped taking her calls years
earlier.

Charles showed them to their new quarters. The air
was thick with the smell of freshly cut wood and new
paint. Shelving had been installed above the bunk beds,
and a portable television was on a bottom shelf. There

was a rug on the floor and a fan in the window. The closet was filled with hand-me-down shirts, pants, jeans, blouses, and two jackets that the church had collected, cleaned, and pressed. There was a small refrigerator, already stocked with cold water and fruit juice. In a cheap chest of drawers there were new undergarments, socks, T-shirts, and pajamas.

Downstairs in the kitchen, Mrs. Huff showed them the larger refrigerator, filled with food and bottles of water and tea, all at their disposal. She showed them the coffeepot and filters. Charles gave Josie a key to the rear doors and invited her and Kiera to try to make themselves at home. The deacons had decided that two or three men would make the rounds each night and make sure they were safe. The ladies had put together a meal schedule for the next week. A retired schoolteacher named Mrs. Golden had volunteered to tutor Kiera in the church several hours a day until she caught up, and until they, whoever "they" might be, made the decision about her returning to school. Half the deacons thought she should return to the junior high in Clanton. The other half believed that would be too traumatic and that she should be homeschooled in the church. Josie had not yet been consulted.

Mrs. Golden used her contacts at the school to obtain a set of replacement textbooks for Kiera. The others had either been burned by Earl Kofer, as he claimed, or they were in the house and could not be retrieved. New ones would be required. Kiera was in the eighth grade, a year behind where she should be, and was still struggling to keep up with her classmates. Her teachers considered her bright, but with her chaotic family and unstable past she had missed too many days of school.

Drew was in the ninth grade, two years behind, and not gaining momentum. He loathed being the oldest kid in his class and often refused to reveal his real age. He didn't realize his luck in arriving late to puberty and looking no older than the other boys. Mrs. Golden had gone to the high school and talked to the principal about Drew's academic quandary. Obviously, he couldn't take classes from the jail, nor did the school have a tutor on its payroll. Any efforts to intervene would take a court order. They decided to let the lawyers worry about that. Mrs. Golden did notice the principal's reluctance in doing anything that might help the defendant.

As they were leaving the church, Charles and Meg promised to pick up Josie and Kiera at nine the following morning for the trip to town. They needed to fetch their car, and they were desperate to see Drew.

Josie and Kiera thanked everyone profusely and said goodbye. They walked to a picnic table next to the cemetery and sat on it. Once again their little family was separated and one step away from being homeless. But for the goodness of others, they would be hungry and sleeping in the car.

JAKE WAS SITTING at his desk, staring at a stack of pink phone messages that Portia and Bev had taken that morning. So far that week he had spent about eighteen hours working on behalf of Drew Gamble. He rarely billed by the hour because his clients were working people and indigent defendants who couldn't pay, whatever the bill, but he, like almost all lawyers, had learned the necessity of tracking his time.

Not long after Jake began to work for Lucien, a lawyer across the square, a likable guy named Mack Stafford, represented a teenager who'd been injured in an auto accident. The case wasn't complicated and Mack didn't bother recording his hours since his contract gave him a contingency of one-third. The insurance company agreed to settle for $120,000, and Mack was all set to walk off with a fee of $40,000, a rarity not only in Ford County but anywhere throughout the rural South. However, since the client was a minor the settlement had to be approved by the chancery court. Chancellor Reuben Atlee asked Mack in open court to justify such a generous fee for a rather straightforward case. Mack did not have a record of his hours and failed miserably in convincing the judge that he deserved the money. They haggled for a while and Atlee finally gave Mack a week to reconstruct his time sheets and submit them. By then, though, he was suspicious of the lawyer. Mack claimed he charged clients $100 an hour and that he had invested four hundred hours in the case. Both numbers were on the high side. Atlee cut them both in half and awarded Mack $20,000. He was so incensed he appealed to the state supreme court and lost 9–0 because the court had ruled for decades that sitting chancellors have unfettered discretion in just about everything. Mack finally took the money and never spoke to Judge Atlee again.

Five years later, in perhaps the most legendary act of criminal and ethical misconduct by a member of the local bar, Mack stole half a million dollars from four clients and skipped town. To Jake's knowledge, not a single person, including Mack's ex-wife and two daughters, had ever heard a word from him. On really bad days, Jake, as well as most lawyers in town, dreamed of being Mack and roasting on a beach somewhere with a cold drink.

At any rate, the local bar swallowed the lesson whole and most lawyers kept up with their hours. In the *Smallwood* lawsuit, Jake had worked over a thousand hours in the fourteen months since Harry Rex landed the case and associated him. That was almost half his time and he anticipated being well compensated for it. Drew's case, though, could possibly eat up huge chunks of time with little in the way of fees. Another reason to get rid of it.

The phone rang again and Jake waited for someone else to answer it. It was almost 5:00 P.M., and for a moment he thought of joining Lucien downstairs for a drink, but let it pass. Carla frowned on drinking, especially on weekdays. So his thoughts moved from hard alcohol back to Mack Stafford sipping rum drinks, studying bikinis, far away from bitching clients and cranky judges and, oh well, there you go again.

Through the intercom, Portia said, "Hey, Jake, it's Dr. Rooker in Tupelo."

"Thanks." Jake tossed the phone slips onto his desk and picked up the receiver. "Hello, Dr. Rooker. Thanks again for seeing Drew today."

"It's my job, Mr. Brigance. Are you near your fax machine?"

"I can be."

"Good, I'm sending over a letter I've addressed to Judge Noose and copies to you. Give it a look and if you agree, I'll send it to him in a moment."

"Sounds urgent."

"In my opinion, it is."

Jake hustled downstairs and found Portia standing at the fax machine. The letter read:

TO THE HONORABLE OMAR NOOSE
CIRCUIT COURT—22ND JUDICIAL DISTRICT

Dear Judge Noose:

    At the request of Mr. Jake Brigance, this afternoon I met and examined Drew Allen

Gamble, age 16. He was brought to my office in Tupelo, in handcuffs, and wearing what appeared to be a standard orange jump suit issued by the Ford County Jail. In other words, he was not properly clothed and this was not an ideal way to begin a consultation. Everything I witnessed when he arrived suggested to me that the child is being treated like an adult and is presumed to be guilty.

I observed a teenaged boy who is frightfully small for his age and could easily pass for a child several years younger. I did not, nor was I expected to, examine him physically, but I saw no signs of stage three or stage four pubescent developments.

I observed the following, all of which are highly unusual for a sixteen-year-old: (1) little growth and no muscular development; (2) no sign of any facial hair; (3) no sign of acne; (4) a childlike voice with no deepening.

For the first hour of our two-hour visit, Drew was uncooperative and said little. Mr. Brigance had briefed me on some of his background, and using this I was finally able to engage Drew in conversation that can only be described as intermittent and strained. He was unable to grasp even the simplest concepts, such as being placed in jail and not being able to leave whenever he wants. He says that at times he remembers events, at times he forgets those same happenings. He asked me at least three times if Stuart Kofer was really dead, but I did not answer him. He became irritable and on two occasions told, not asked, me to "Shut up." He was never aggressive or angry and often cried when he couldn't answer a question. Twice he said he wished he could die and admits that he often thinks of suicide.

I learned that Drew and his sister have been neglected, physically abused, psychologically abused, and subjected to domestic violence. I cannot say, and do not know, all of the people responsible for this. He was simply not that forthcoming. I strongly suspect there has been a lot of abuse and Drew, and more than likely his sister too, has suffered at the hands of several people.

The sudden and/or violent loss of a loved one can trigger traumatic stress in children. Drew and his sister had been abused by Mr. Kofer. They thought, with good reason, that he had killed their mother, and that he was about to harm them, again. This is more than sufficient to trigger traumatic stress.

Trauma in children can bring about a variety of responses, including wide swings in emotions, bouts of depression, anxiety, fear, inability to eat or sleep, nightmares, slow academic progress, and many other problems which I will detail in my full report.

If left untreated, Drew will only regress and the damage can become permanent. The last place for him right now is a jail built for adults.

I strongly recommend that Drew be sent immediately to the state mental hospital at Whitfield, where there is a secure facility for juveniles, for a thorough examination and long-term treatment.

I will finish my report and fax it to you in the morning.

Respectfully,
DR. CHRISTINA A. ROOKER, M.D.
Tupelo, Mississippi

———

AN HOUR LATER, Jake was still at his desk, ignoring the phone and wanting to go home. Portia, Lucien, and part-time Bev had already left. He heard the familiar rattle of the fax machine downstairs, and, glancing at his watch, wondered who was still working at five minutes after six on a Thursday evening. He grabbed his jacket and briefcase, turned off his light, and went down to the fax machine. It was a single sheet of paper with the official heading: *Circuit Court of Ford County Mississippi.* Just under was the style of the case: *State of Mississippi v. Drew Allen Gamble.* There was no file number because there had been no official appearance by the defendant and no indictment. Someone, probably Judge Noose himself, had typed: "The Court does hereby direct the Sheriff of Ford County to transport the above named defendant to the state mental hospital with all possible speed, preferably on Friday, March 30, 1990, and there to surrender his person to Mr. Rupert Easley, Director of Security, until further orders of this court. So Ordered, Signed, Judge Omar Noose."

Jake smiled at the outcome and placed the order on Portia's desk. He had done his job and protected the best interests of his client. He could almost hear the courthouse gossip, the rumblings at the coffee shops, the cursing among the deputies.

He told himself he didn't care anymore.

14

The weather was perfect for a funeral, though the setting left something to be desired. On Saturday, the last day of March, the sky was dark and threatening, the wind cold and biting. A week earlier, on the last day of his life, Stuart Kofer had gone fishing with friends on the lake on a beautiful, warm afternoon. They wore T-shirts and shorts and drank cold beer in the sunshine as if summer had arrived early. But so much had changed, and now, on the day of his burial, raw winds swept across the land and added more gloom.

The service was at the National Guard Armory, a bland and sterile 1950s-style block building designed for troop gatherings and community events, but not for funerals. It could hold three hundred and the family was expecting a crowd. Though unchurched, the Kofers had lived in the county for a hundred years and knew a lot of people. Stu was a popular cop with friends, acquaintances, and colleagues with families. All funerals were open to the public, and tragic deaths always attracted the curious who had little else to do and wanted to get close to the story. At 1:00 P.M., an hour before the service, the first news van arrived and was ordered to park in a reserved area. Uniformed officers were everywhere, waiting for the crowd, the press, the pomp and ceremony. The front doors of the armory opened and the parking lot began to fill. Another news van arrived and began filming. Some reporters with cameras were allowed to congregate near the flagpole.

Inside, three hundred rented chairs had been neatly arranged in a half-moon around a temporary stage and podium. The wall behind it was layered with dozens of flower arrangements, and more lined the walls. A large color photo of Stuart Kofer stood on a tripod to one side. By 1:30 the meeting hall was almost full and a few ladies were already sobbing. In the place of proper hymns favored by real Christians, someone within the family had selected a playlist of sad tunes by some country crooner, and his mournful braying echoed from a set of cheap speakers. Fortunately, the volume was not high, but it was still loud enough to add to the somber mood.

The crowd filed in and before long all chairs were taken. Additional mourners were asked to stand against the walls. By 1:45, there was no more space and those trying to get in were told the service would be broadcast outside over a PA system.

The family gathered in a small office wing and waited for the hearse from Megargel Funeral Home, the last remaining mortuary for white people in Ford County. There were two for the blacks, who were buried in their cemeteries. The whites were buried in theirs, and, even in 1990, the graveyards were tightly segregated. No one had been put to rest out of place.

Because it was a big funeral, with a crowd and the chance of cameras, Mr. Megargel had leaned on friends in the business and borrowed some nicer cars. When he pulled his sleek black hearse into the drive beside the armory there were six identical black sedans behind him. They were empty for the moment and parked in a neat row behind the building. Mr. Megargel hopped out, as did his squad of men in somber suits, and began directing things. He opened the rear door of the hearse and called for the eight pallbearers to come forward.

Slowly, they pulled the casket out and placed it on a gurney draped in velvet cloth. The family came out of the small office and stood behind the pallbearers. With Megargel leading the way, the small parade turned alongside the building and headed for the front where an impressive battalion of uniformed men awaited them.

Ozzie had worked the phones all week and his requests had been met, in fine fashion. Troops from a dozen counties, along with the state police and municipal officers from several cities, stood in formation as the casket rolled by. Cameras clicked and could be heard above the silence.

Harry Rex was in the crowd outside. He would later describe the scene to Jake by saying, "Hell, you'd've thought Kofer got killed in the line of duty, fightin' crime like a real cop. Not passed out drunk after he beat his girlfriend."

The throng parted as the pallbearers guided the casket through the front doors, into the armory, and across the small lobby. As it entered the center aisle, the pastor stood at the podium and said at full volume, "Please rise." The crowd rose noisily but then fell deathly silent as the casket inched down the aisle, with Earl and Janet Kofer in step behind it. About forty family members followed them.

They had feuded for a week over the issue of a closed casket. It was not unusual to open the casket during a funeral service so that the loved ones and friends and other mourners could glimpse a profile of the deceased. This made the situation far more dramatic and maximized the grief, which of course was the purpose though no one would ever admit it. Rural preachers preferred open caskets because they made it easier to whip up emotions and make folks worry more about their sins and their own deaths. It was not uncommon to include a few remarks directed at the deceased, as if he or she might just rise up and yell "Repent."

Earl had lost his parents and a brother, and their services had been "open," though the presiding ministers hardly knew them. But Janet Kofer knew the service would be thoroughly gut-wrenching without actually looking at her dead son. In the end she prevailed and the casket remained closed.

When the casket was in place, a large American flag was unfolded and draped over it. Later, Harry Rex would say to Jake, "Sumbitch got kicked out of the army and they carried on like it was full honors."

As the family shuffled into place in the front rows, reserved with Megargel's monogrammed velvet roping, the preacher motioned for the crowd to sit and nodded to a dude with a guitar. Wearing a burgundy suit, black cowboy hat, and matching boots, he walked to a floor mike, strummed a few chords, and waited for everyone to be seated. When things were still, he began singing the first stanza of "The Old Rugged Cross." He had a pleasant baritone and was deft with his guitar. He had once played in a bluegrass band with Cecil Kofer, though he had never met his deceased brother.

It was unlikely Stuart Kofer had ever heard the old gospel standard. Most of his grieving family members had not, but it was appropriate for the sad occasion and succeeded in heightening the emotions. When he finished the third stanza he gave a quick nod and returned to his seat.

The family had met the minister two days earlier. One of their more difficult chores during that awful week had been to locate a man of God willing to conduct the service for complete strangers. There were several country preachers who had tried to reach the

Kofers over the years, but all said no to the service. As a group, they were turned off by the hypocrisy of getting involved with people who had no use for any church. Finally, a cousin bribed an unemployed Pentecostal lay preacher with three hundred dollars to be the man of the hour. His name was Hubert Wyfong and he was from Smithfield, down in Polk County. Reverend Wyfong needed the cash, but he also saw the opportunity to perform in front of a large crowd. Perhaps he could impress someone who knew a church that was looking for a part-time preacher.

He offered a long, flowery prayer, then nodded at a pretty teenaged girl, who stepped to the mike with her Bible and read the Twenty-third Psalm.

Ozzie sat next to his wife and listened and marveled at the difference between white funerals and black ones. He and his force and their spouses sat together in three rows to the left of the family, all in their finest matching uniforms, all boots spit-shined, all badges gleaming. The section behind them was packed with officers from north Mississippi, all white men.

Counting Willie Hastings, Scooter Gifford, Elton Frye, Parnell Johnson, and himself, along with their wives, there were exactly ten black faces in the crowd. And Ozzie knew full well that they were welcome only because of his position.

Wyfong said another prayer, a shorter one, and sat down as Stuart's twelve-year-old cousin walked nervously to the mike holding a sheet of paper. He adjusted the mike, looked fearfully at the crowd, and began reciting a poem he had written about fishing with his favorite "Uncle Stu."

Ozzie listened for a moment then began to drift. The day before he had driven Drew three hours south to Whitfield, the state mental hospital, and turned him

over to the authorities there. By the time he returned
to his office the news was raging around the county.
The kid was already out of jail and was pretending to
be crazy. Jake Brigance was pulling another fast one, just
like he did five years earlier when he convinced a jury
that Carl Lee Hailey was temporarily insane. Hailey
killed two men in cold blood, in the courthouse even,
and walked. Walked free as a bird. Late Friday afternoon, Earl Kofer drove to the jail and confronted Ozzie,
who showed him a copy of the court order signed by
Judge Noose. Kofer left, cursing and vowing to get
even.

At the moment, the crowd was mourning a tragic
death, but many of those seated around him were seeth-
ing with anger.

The young poet had some talent and managed to
get a laugh. His refrain was "But not with Uncle Stu.
But not with Uncle Stu." When he finally finished, he
broke down and walked away bawling. This was conta-
gious and others sobbed.

Wyfong rose with his Bible and began his sermon.
He read from the Book of Psalms and spoke of God's
comforting words in a time of death. Ozzie listened for
a moment with interest, then began to drift again. He
had called Jake early in the morning, to pass along the
latest about the funeral and give him a heads-up that
the Kofers and their friends were upset. Jake said he'd
already talked to Harry Rex, who'd called late Friday
night and said the gossip was wild.

Ozzie would admit only to himself and to his wife
that the boy was in bad shape. During the long drive to
Whitfield, he had not said a word to either Ozzie or
Moss Junior. They initially tried to engage him in small
talk, but he said nothing. He didn't rudely ignore them.
Their words just didn't register. With his hands cuffed

in front of him, Drew was able to lie down and pull his knees to his chest. And he started that damned humming. For over two hours he hummed and groaned and at times seemed to hiss. "You okay back there?" Moss Junior had asked when he got louder. He quieted down but did not respond. Driving back to Clanton without him, Moss Junior thought it would be funny to mimic the kid and he started humming too. Ozzie told him to stop or he'd turn around and take him to Whitfield. It was good for a laugh, which they needed.

Earl Kofer's only request to the preacher was to "keep it short." And Wyfong complied with a fifteen-minute sermon that was remarkably short on emotion and long on comfort. He finished with another prayer, then nodded at the singer for a final song. It was a secular number about a lonesome cowboy and it worked. Women were bawling again and it was time to go. The pallbearers took their positions around the casket and "You'll Never Walk Alone" began to play softly over the speakers. The family followed the casket down the aisle, with Earl holding Janet steady as she wept. The procession moved slowly as someone turned up the volume.

Outside, two lines of uniformed men led to the hearse with its rear door open and waiting. The pallbearers lifted the casket and carefully placed it inside. Megargel and his men directed the family to the waiting sedans. A parade formed behind them, and when everyone was in place, the hearse inched away, followed by the family, followed by rows of officers on foot, with the Ford County contingent leading. Any and all friends, relatives, and strangers who wanted to make the trek to the cemetery fell in behind. The procession moved slowly away from the armory and down Wilson Street where barricades were in place and children stood silently by them. Townsfolk gathered on side-

walks and watched from porches and paid their respects
to the fallen hero.

JAKE HATED FUNERALS and avoided them whenever
possible. He viewed them as a serious waste of time,
money, and, especially, emotion. Nothing was gained by
having a funeral, only the satisfaction of showing up
and being seen by the grieving family. And what was
the benefit of that? After being shot at during the Hailey trial, he'd prepared himself a new will and left written instructions to be cremated as soon as possible and
buried in his hometown of Karaway with only his family present. This was a radical idea for Ford County and
Carla didn't like it. She rather enjoyed the social aspects
of a good funeral.

Saturday afternoon he left his office, drove across
town, and parked behind a city rec center. He walked
along a nature path, climbed a small hill, and veered
down a gravel trail to a clearing where he sat at a picnic
table with a view of the cemetery. Hidden among the
trees, he watched the hearse stop in a sea of aging
tombstones. The crowd worked its way to a bright purple burial tent with Megargel's logo embroidered in
bold yellow. The pallbearers labored with the casket for
at least a hundred feet, and were followed by the family.

Jake was reminded of a well-known story of a lawyer
down in Jackson who stole some clients' money, faked
his own death, and watched his own funeral while sitting in a tree. After he was caught and hauled back to
Jackson, he refused to speak to friends who did not at-
tend his funeral and burial.

How angry was the mob down there? At the moment, the prevailing emotion was one of great sorrow,
but would that quickly yield to resentment?

Harry Rex, who apparently had decided to skip the burial, was convinced that Jake had thoroughly screwed up their chances with *Smallwood*. Jake had just become the most despised lawyer in the county, and the railroad and its insurance company would probably pull back from any settlement negotiations. And what about selecting a jury now? Any pool of prospective jurors would surely have people who knew of his representation of Drew Gamble.

He was too far away to hear the words or music at the burial. After a few minutes, he left and walked back to his car.

LATE IN THE afternoon, family and friends gathered at the large metal building that housed the Pine Grove Volunteer Fire Company. No proper send-off was complete without a heavy meal, and the ladies of the community brought in platters of fried chicken, bowls of potato salad and slaw, trays of sandwiches and corn on the cob, casseroles of all varieties, and cakes and pies. The Kofer family stood at one end of the room in a receiving line and suffered through lengthy condolences from their friends. Pastor Wyfong was thanked and congratulated on such a fine service, and the young nephew received kind words about his poem. The cowboy brought his guitar and sang a few songs as the crowd filled their plates and dined at folding tables and chairs.

Earl stepped outside for a smoke and gathered with some friends near a fire truck. One man pulled out a pint of whiskey and passed it around. Half declined, half took a swig. Earl and Cecil passed.

A cousin said, "That sumbitch can't claim to be crazy, can he?"

"Already done it," Earl said. "They took him to Whitfield yesterday. Ozzie drove him down."

"He had to, didn't he?"

"I don't trust him."

"Ozzie's on our side this time."

"Somebody said the judge ordered the boy taken away."

"He did," Earl said. "I saw the court order."

"Damned lawyers and judges."

"It ain't right, I'm tellin' you."

"A lawyer told me they'll keep him locked up till he's eighteen, then turn him loose."

"Turn him loose then. We can take care of him."

"You can't trust Brigance."

"Will they even put him on trial?"

"Not if he's crazy. That's what the lawyer said."

"The system sucks, you know. It ain't right."

"Can anybody talk to Brigance?"

"Of course not. He'll fight like hell for the boy."

"That's what lawyers do. The system is designed to protect the criminal these days."

"Brigance will get him off on one of those technicalities you hear about."

"If I saw that sonofabitch on the street I'd kick his ass."

"All I want is justice," Earl said. "And we ain't gonna get it. Brigance will plead insanity and the boy will walk, just like Carl Lee Hailey."

"It ain't right, I'm tellin' you. It just ain't right."

15

Lowell Dyer was hearing the noise from down the road in Ford County. He took three calls at home Sunday afternoon, all from strangers who claimed they voted for him, and listened to their complaints about what was happening in the Gamble case. After the third, he unplugged his phone. The one at the office had a number that was advertised in every directory in the Twenty-second District, and evidently it rang all weekend. When his secretary reached for it early Monday morning she saw that there were over twenty calls and the mailbox was full. On an average weekend there were half a dozen. Zero was not unusual.

Over coffee, she and Lowell and the assistant D.A., D. R. Musgrove, listened to the messages. Some of the callers gave their names and addresses, others were more timid and seemed to think they were doing something wrong by calling the district attorney. A few hotheads used profanity, did not give their names, and implied that if the judicial system continued to go haywire they just might have to fix it themselves.

But it was unanimous—the kid was out of jail and pretending to be crazy and his damned lawyer was once again pulling a fast one. Please, Mr. Dyer, do something! Do your job!

Lowell had never had a case that attracted so much interest, and he swung into action. He called Judge Noose, who was at home "reading briefs" as he always claimed to be doing when he wasn't in court, and they agreed it was a good idea to call a special meeting of the grand jury to deal with the case. As the district attorney, Lowell controlled every aspect of "his" grand jury and needed no one's approval to call it into session. But given the sensational nature of the Gamble case, he wanted to keep the presiding judge apprised. During their brief conversation Noose said something about a "long weekend" around his house, and Lowell suspected his phone had been ringing too.

He sounded uncertain, even troubled, and when it was time for the conversation to end, Noose prolonged it by saying, "Say, Lowell, let's go off the record here and talk in the graveyard."

A pause as if it was Lowell's turn to respond. "Sure, Judge."

"Well, I'm having a devil of a time finding another lawyer to defend this boy. Nobody in the district wants the case. Pete Habbeshaw over in Oxford has three capital cases right now and just can't take on another. Rudy Thomas in Tupelo is undergoing chemo. I even had a chat with Joe Frank Jones in Jackson, and he gave me a flat no. I can't force the case on anyone outside of my jurisdiction, as you know, so all I could do was lean on these guys and I got nowhere. You have any ideas? You know our lawyers well."

Lowell indeed knew them well and wouldn't hire a single one of them if his neck were on the block. There were some fine lawyers in the district but most avoided trial work, especially of the indigent criminal variety. To stall and divert, Lowell asked, "Not sure, Judge. Who did the last capital case in the district?"

The last capital case in the Twenty-second had been three years earlier in Milburn County, in the town of

Temple. The prosecutor had been Rufus Buckley, who was still smarting from his momentous loss in the Carl Lee Hailey case. He won an easy verdict because the facts had been so horrible: A twenty-year-old drug addict murdered both of his grandparents for eighty-five dollars to buy more crack. He was now on death row at Parchman. Noose had presided and had not been impressed with the local defense lawyer he had dragged into the case.

"That won't work," he said. "That boy, what's his name, Gordy Wilson, wasn't very good and I hear he's pretty much closed shop. Who would you hire, Lowell, if you were facing these charges? Who would you hire in the Twenty-second?"

For obvious selfish reasons, Lowell wanted a pushover sitting at the defense table, but he knew that was unlikely and unwise. A weak or incompetent defense lawyer would only screw up the case and give the appeals courts plenty to chew on for the next decade.

He replied, "I'd probably go with Jake."

Without hesitation, Noose said, "So would I. But let's not tell him about this conversation."

"Of course not." Lowell got on well with Jake and did not want any friction. If Jake somehow learned that the D.A. and the judge had conspired to keep him on the clock, he would hold a grudge.

Next, Lowell called Jake and found him at the office. The purpose of the call was not to break the news that he was stuck with Gamble till the bitter end, but something more professional. Lowell said, "Jake, just calling to let you know that I'm assembling the grand jury tomorrow afternoon at the courthouse."

Jake was pleased, thought it was a courteous gesture, and said, "Thanks, Lowell. I'm sure it will be a brief meeting. Mind if I sit in?"

"You know that's not possible, Jake."

"Just kidding. Mind giving me a call when the indictment comes down?"

"You know I will."

OZZIE'S CHIEF INVESTIGATOR was his only investigator, at the moment, and he wasn't really looking for another one. His name was Kirk Rady, a veteran of the department and a well-regarded officer. Ozzie could dig for the facts better than most sheriffs, and together with Rady they handled all of the serious crimes in the county.

At straight-up four o'clock Monday afternoon, they walked into Jake's office and said hello to Portia at the front desk. She was professional as always and asked them to wait a moment.

Though he was now doing battle with Jake, Ozzie was proud to see a smart and ambitious young black woman working in one of the law offices around the square. He knew Portia and her family, and he knew she planned to be the first black female lawyer in the county, and with Jake as her mentor and supporter she would certainly succeed.

She returned and waved them over to a door down the hall. They stepped inside and the room was already occupied. Jake welcomed them with handshakes and then introduced the sheriff and Rady to Josie Gamble, Kiera Gamble, and their minister, Charles McGarry. They were on one side of the table, and Jake offered Ozzie and Rady seats on the other side. Portia closed the door and sat beside Kiera, facing Ozzie. Judging from the open legal pads, the half-empty coffee cups and water bottles, the scattered pens, and Jake's loosened tie, it was fairly obvious that the lawyer had already spent time with the witnesses.

Ozzie had not seen Josie since his quick visit to the hospital the day after the murder, a week earlier. Jake had told him that her surgery had gone well and she was mending as expected. Her left eye was still puffy, black and blue, and her left jaw was still swollen. Two band-aids were visible. She tried to be polite and smile but it didn't work.

After some awkward chitchat, Jake punched a button on a tape recorder in the center of the table and said, "Do you mind if I record this?"

Ozzie shrugged and said, "It's your office."

"True, but it's your interview. I don't know if you routinely record these things."

"Sometimes we do, sometimes we don't," Rady said like an ass. "We don't normally talk to witnesses in lawyers' offices."

"Ozzie called me," Jake fired back. "Asked me to arrange this interview. You can do it somewhere else if you like."

"We're fine," Ozzie said. "Record anything you want."

Jake spoke to the recorder, gave the date, place, and names of everyone in the room. When he finished, Ozzie said, "Now, I'd like to understand everybody's role here. We're officers investigating a crime. You two ladies are potential witnesses. And Pastor McGarry, what is your role?"

"I'm just the chauffeur," Charles said with a smile.

"That's nice." Ozzie looked at Jake and asked, "Should he be in the room?"

Jake shrugged and said, "That's your call, Ozzie. This is not my interview. I'm just making things happen."

"I'd feel better if you stepped outside," Ozzie said.

"No problem." Charles smiled and left the room.

"And what's your role here, Jake? You don't represent these ladies, do you?"

"Technically no. I have been appointed to represent Drew. Not the family. However, if we assume there will be a trial one day, Josie and Kiera will be important witnesses, perhaps called by the State, perhaps called by the defense. I may well be the defense lawyer. Their testimony might be crucial. Therefore, I have a real interest in what they tell you."

Ozzie was not a lawyer and not about to argue trial strategy and criminal procedure with Jake Brigance. "Can we interrogate them without you?"

"No. I've already advised them not to cooperate unless I'm in the room. As you know, you can't make them talk. You can subpoena them to the stand at trial, but you can't make them talk right now. They're just potential witnesses." Jake's tone was more aggressive, his words sharper. The tension was rising considerably.

Portia, taking notes, thought to herself: *I can't wait to become a lawyer.*

Everyone took a deep breath. Ozzie flashed his best politician's smile and said, "Okay, let's get on with it."

Rady opened his notebook and gave Josie a smile so drippy Jake wanted to slap him. He said, "First of all, Ms. Gamble, I'd like to ask if you are able to talk, and if so, for how long? I understand the surgery was only a few days ago."

Josie nodded nervously and said, "Thank you. I'm okay. The stitches and wires came out this morning and I can talk a little."

"Are you in pain?"

"Not too bad."

"Are you taking medication for pain?"

"Just some ibuprofen."

"Okay. Can we start with you and your background, that sort of thing?"

Jake immediately interrupted with "Let's try this. We're working on what we hope to be a complete biographical sketch of the Gamble family. Birthdates, birthplaces, homes, addresses, marriages, employers, relatives, criminal records, the good, the bad, the ugly. Some of it they remember, some is not so clear. We need it for our side. Portia is in charge of it and it has priority. When it is complete we'll give you a copy. Full disclosure. You can read it and if you then want to interrogate these witnesses again, we'll talk about it. This will save us at least an hour today and there won't be any gaps. Fair enough?"

Rady and Ozzie exchanged looks, skeptical ones. Ozzie said, "We'll try it."

Rady flipped a page and said, "Okay, let's go back to Saturday night, March 24, just over a week ago. Can you tell us what happened? Tell us your story about that night."

Josie took a sip of water through a straw and glanced nervously at Jake, who had given her strict instructions about what to cover and what to leave alone. She began with "Well, it was late, and Stu wasn't home." As instructed, she spoke slowly, and seemed to struggle with each word. The swelling didn't help. She described what it was like to wait and wait while expecting the worst. She was downstairs. The kids were upstairs in their bedrooms, awake, waiting, afraid. Stu finally came home around two, very drunk, belligerent as usual, and they had a fight. She got hit and woke up in the hospital.

"You said 'drunk as usual.' Did Stu often come home drunk?"

"Yes, he was out of control. We had lived there about a year, and his drinkin' was a real problem."

"Do you know where he had been that night?"

"No, he would never tell me that."

"But you knew he hung out in bars and such, right?"

"Oh, yes. I went with him a few times, in the earlier days, but I stopped because he would get in fights."

Rady was careful here because the sheriff's department was still looking for paperwork. On two occasions, Josie had called the dispatcher and said she was being beaten by Stuart Kofer. But when the deputies showed up, she refused to press charges. The reports were filed and then they disappeared. Jake would probably learn about this down the road, and Ozzie did not look forward to those questions. Missing paperwork, a cover-up, a sheriff's department looking the other way while one of its own spiraled out of control. Jake would make them bleed in the courtroom.

"Didn't you meet in a bar?"

"We did."

"Around here?"

"No, it was a club up around Holly Springs."

Rady paused and struggled with his notes. The wrong question could provoke the wrath of Jake. "So, you don't remember the shooting?"

"No." She shook her head and stared at the table.

"Didn't hear a thing?"

"No."

"Have you talked to your son since the shooting?"

She took a deep breath and fought to keep her composure. "We spoke by phone last night, the first time. He's down in Whitfield, but you probably know that. Said the sheriff here drove him down on Friday."

"How's he doing, if I may ask?"

She shrugged and looked away. Jake helped out with "Just so you'll know. I've talked to the counselors down there. Josie and Kiera will go to Whitfield tomorrow, the preacher is taking them, and they'll see Drew and meet with the people who are treating him. It seems to be very important that they, the doctors, talk to the family and get the background."

Ozzie and Rady nodded their approval. Rady flipped a page and read some of his notes. "Did Stu ever take Drew hunting?"

Josie shook her head. "He took him fishin' once, but it didn't go well."

A long pause. No details were coming. "What happened?" Rady asked.

"Drew was usin' one of Stu's rods and he hooked a big fish that bit hard and ran and yanked the rod out of Drew's hands. It was gone. Stu had been drinkin' beers and he flew hot, hit Drew, made him cry. That was their only fishin' trip."

"Did he take him hunting?"

"No. You gotta understand that Stu didn't want my kids to begin with, and the longer they stayed the more he resented them. The whole situation was slowly blowin' up. His drinkin', my kids, fights over money. The kids were beggin' me to leave but we had no place to go."

"To your knowledge, had Drew ever fired a gun before?"

She paused and caught her breath. "Yeah, one time Stu took him out behind the barn and they shot at targets. I don't know which gun they used. Stu had a bunch of them, you know? It didn't work out too well because Drew was afraid of guns and couldn't hit anything and Stu laughed at him."

"You said he hit Drew. Did that happen more than once?"

Josie glared at Rady and said, "Sir, it happened all the time. He hit all of us."

Jake leaned forward and said, "We're not going into the physical abuse today, guys. There was a lot of it, and we'll detail it in our summary. It might be a factor in a trial, or it might not be. But as for now, we're skipping it."

Fine with Ozzie. What was offered as proof at trial was the business of the district attorney, not the sheriff. But what a messy trial it could be.

He said, "Look, since this is the first of these visits, let's just hit the high points and move on. We've established that you, Josie, were unconscious when the shooting occurred. We didn't know that, now we do, so we're making progress. We'll ask Kiera a few questions and that'll be it, all right?"

"Sounds good," Jake said.

Rady produced another sappy smile and said to Kiera, "Okay, miss, could you tell us your story? What happened that night?"

Her story was much more involved because she remembered all of it: the dread of another Saturday night, the waiting until late, the sweep of the headlights, the commotion in the kitchen, the yelling, the sound of flesh hitting flesh, the horror of hearing his stumbling boots coming up the stairs, his heaving, his slurred words, his goofy calling of her name, their jerry-rigged brace against the door, the rattling of the doorknob, the banging, the yelling, the unrestrained fear as brother and sister clung to each other; then the silence, the sounds of his retreat down the stairs; and, worst of all, nothing from their mother. They knew he had killed her. For an eternity the house was silent, and with each passing minute they knew their mother was dead. Otherwise, she would be trying to protect them.

Kiera managed to narrate the story while wiping away tears and not slowing down. She had tissues in both hands and spoke with emotion but her voice did not crack. Jake still had no plans to be anywhere near the trial of Drew Gamble, but the courtroom lawyer in him could not help but assess her as a witness. He was impressed with her toughness, her maturity, her determination. Though two years younger, she seemed to be years ahead of her brother.

But the part about her dead mother slowed her to the point of needing water. She took a drink from a bottle, wiped her cheeks, gave Rady a hard look, and continued: They found her on the kitchen floor, nonresponsive, no pulse, and they wept. Drew eventually called the dispatcher. Hours seemed to pass. He closed the bedroom door. She heard a shot.

Rady asked, "So, did you see Stu on the bed before he was shot?"

"No."

As per Jake, answers in response to a direct question should be kept short.

"Did you see Drew with a gun?"

"No."

"Did Drew say anything to you after you heard the shot?"

Jake was quick to interrupt. "Don't answer that. It could be hearsay and inadmissible in court. I'm sure we'll fight over it later, but not now."

Ozzie had heard enough, both from the witnesses and from the lawyer. He abruptly stood and said, "That's all we need. Thank you for your time, ladies. Jake, we'll be in touch. Or not. I'm sure you'll hear from the district attorney in the near future."

Jake stood as they left the room. He sat down when they were gone, and Portia closed the door.

Josie asked, "How'd we do?"

"You were great."

16

The long day began at sunrise when Charles Mc-Garry swept his headlights across the rear of his little country church. Lights were on in the kitchen and he knew that Josie and Kiera were wide awake and ready to go. He met them at the door, exchanged hurried greetings because they had hours to talk in the car, and locked the church behind them. Kiera folded her long legs into the rear of the small McGarry family car and Josie got herself situated in the front passenger seat. Charles pointed to the digital clock on the dash and said, "Six forty-six. Remember the time. It's supposed to take three hours."

His wife, Meg, had planned to join them, but, truthfully, the car was too small for four people sitting shoulder-to-shoulder for a long ride. And a grandmother who'd promised to babysit had fallen ill.

"Meg sent some sausage biscuits," he said. "In that bag back there."

"I'm gonna be sick," Kiera said.

"She's not feelin' well," Josie said.

"I'm gonna be sick, Mom," she said again.

"Serious?" he asked.

"Pull over. Quick." They had gone less than half a mile; the church was almost visible behind them. Charles hit the brakes and stopped on the shoulder. Josie was already opening the door and pulling her daughter out. She vomited in a ditch and retched for a few minutes while Charles watched for headlights and tried not to listen. She cried and apologized to her mother and they discussed something. Both were crying when they got back in the car, and for a long time nothing was said.

Finally, Josie offered a fake laugh and said, "She's always had a problem with car sickness. Never seen anything like it. Kid can chuck it before I start the engine."

"You okay back there?" Charles asked over his shoulder.

"I'm fine," she mumbled, head back, eyes closed, arms across her stomach.

"How about some music?" he asked.

"Sure," Josie said.

"You like gospel?"

Not really, she thought. "How about it, Kiera, you want to listen to some gospel music?"

"No."

Charles turned on the radio and tuned in to the country station out of Clanton. They skirted around the edge of town and found the main highway south. At seven the news came on, weather first, then a report that the district attorney, Lowell Dyer, had confirmed that the Ford County grand jury would meet later in the day to work on its docket. And, yes, the murder of Officer Stuart Kofer would be discussed. Charles reached over and turned off the radio.

The car sickness struck again a few miles south of Clanton, this time on a highway busy with early morning traffic. Charles turned the car into someone's gravel drive and Kiera jumped out, barely averting a mess. Once she was back in the car, Josie said, "It might be the smell of those biscuits. Could we put them in the trunk?"

Charles really wanted one for breakfast, but he decided not to take chances. He unbuckled, grabbed the bag off the backseat, opened the trunk, and put away their breakfast. Meg had been up at five to fry the sausage and thaw the frozen biscuits.

On the road again, Charles glanced in his mirror every minute or so. Kiera was pale and her forehead was wet. Her eyes were closed and she was trying to nap.

Josie felt the uneasiness and knew that Charles was worrying about her daughter. To change the subject she said, "We talked to Drew last night. Thanks for allowin' us to use the church phone."

"No problem. How's he doing?"

"I don't know. It's hard to say. He's in a better place, a small room with a cellmate, a kid who's seventeen but a good boy, so far. And Drew says the people, the doctors, are nice and seem really concerned about him. They've put him on a drug, an antidepressant, and he says he's feelin' better. He met with two different doctors yesterday and they just asked him a bunch of questions, in general."

"Any idea how long they'll keep him?"

"No. That has not been discussed so far. But he'd rather stay where he is than go back to the jail in Clanton. Jake says there's no way to get him out. Says no judge in the state would set a bond in a case like this."

"I'm sure Jake knows what he's talking about."

"We like Jake a lot. Do you know him well?"

"No. Remember, Josie, I'm new around here, just like you. I grew up over in Lee County."

"Yeah, that's right. Gotta tell you, it sure is a comfort havin' a guy like Jake as our lawyer. Are we supposed to pay him?"

"I don't think so. Isn't he appointed by the court?"

She nodded and mumbled something, as if she suddenly remembered another story. Kiera managed to curl herself into a ball in the rear seat and take a nap.

After a few miles, Josie turned to look at her and whispered, "Hey, baby, you okay?"

Kiera did not respond.

IT TOOK AN hour to get processed and directed to one building and then another, where they were herded into a waiting room where two guards wore guns on their hips. One of them with a clipboard emerged from the back and approached Charles. She managed a forced smile and asked, "Are you here to see Drew Gamble?"

Charles pointed to Josie and Kiera and said, "They are. They're his family."

"Please follow me."

Every door had a buzzer that clicked, and as they moved deeper into the labyrinth the halls became wider and cleaner. They stopped at a metal door with no window and the guard said, "I'm sorry but it's family only."

"Fine with me," Charles said. He hardly knew Drew and was not eager to spend the next hour with him. Josie and Kiera walked inside and found Drew seated in the small, windowless room. All three grabbed each other with fierce embraces and began crying. Charles watched from the open door and felt enormous pity for them. The guard backed out, closed the door, and said, "A counselor would like to speak to you."

"Sure." What else was he supposed to say?

The counselor was standing in the door of a small, cluttered office in yet another wing. She introduced herself as Dr. Sadie Weaver and said she was borrowing the office for the moment. They wedged themselves inside and she closed the door.

"And you're their minister?" she began, with no

thought of preliminary chatter. She gave every impression of being incredibly busy.

"Well, sort of, let's say yes, okay? They're not officially members of my church but we've sort of adopted them. They have no place else to go. No family in the area."

"We spent a few hours with Drew yesterday. Sounds like the family has had a rough time of it. He's never seen his father. I've spoken with their lawyer, Mr. Brigance, and with Dr. Christina Rooker in Tupelo. She saw Drew last Thursday and asked the court to commit him for evaluation. So I know some of the background. Where are they living?"

"In our church. They're safe and well-fed."

"Bless you. Sounds like the mother and sister are being cared for. I, of course, am more concerned with Drew. We'll spend this afternoon and tomorrow with him and his mother and sister. I assume you're their driver."

"I am."

"How long can you leave them here?"

"I'm flexible. I have no plans."

"Good. Leave them here for twenty-four hours, pick them up tomorrow."

"Okay. How long will you keep Drew?"

"It's hard to say. Weeks, not months. As a general rule, they're better off here than in a county jail."

"Right. Keep him as long as you can. Things are pretty tense in Ford County."

"I understand."

Charles made his way out of the building and eventually found his car. He cleared the checkpoints and by noon was back on the road, headed north. At a convenience store he bought a soft drink, retrieved his biscuits from the trunk, and enjoyed the solitude with his brunch and gospel music.

THE FORD COUNTY grand jury met twice a month. Its docket was typically mundane—petty drug busts, car thefts, a knifing or two at the clubs and tonks. The last killing had been a Wild West–style shootout after a black funeral where two warring families squared off and began firing. One man was killed, but it was impossible to determine who shot who. The grand jury indicted the most likely suspect for manslaughter and his case was still pending, with no one really pushing it. He was free on bond.

There were eighteen members of the grand jury, all registered voters from the county, and they had been empaneled by Judge Noose two months earlier. They met in the small courtroom down the hall from the main one and their meetings were private. No spectators, no press, none of the usual bored courthouse gang looking for a little drama.

Typically, for the first month or so the honor of being a member of the grand jury was worth bragging about, but after a few sessions the job grew tedious. They heard only one side of the story, the one presented by law enforcement, and there was almost never any dissent. So far, they had not failed to issue any of the indictments being sought. Whether they realized it or not, they had quickly become little more than a rubber stamp for the police and prosecutors.

A special session was unusual, and by the time they gathered on Tuesday afternoon, April 3, each of the sixteen present knew exactly why they had been summoned. Two were absent but there was easily a quorum.

Lowell Dyer welcomed them back, thanked them

again as if they had a choice, and explained that they had a very serious matter in front of them. He gave the basics of the Kofer murder and asked Sheriff Walls to sit in the witness seat at the end of the table. Ozzie was sworn to tell the truth, and began his narrative: time and date, cast of characters, 911 call, the scene when Chief Deputy Moss Junior Tatum first arrived. He described the bedroom and the bloody mattress, and passed around enlarged color photos of Stuart with part of his head blown off. Several of the grand jurors took a look, reacted, then looked away. The service pistol was beside the body. The cause of death was fairly obvious. A single shot to the head, close range.

"The boy was in the living room and told Deputy Tatum that Stuart Kofer was in his bedroom and he thought he was dead. Tatum went to the bedroom, saw the body, and asked the boy, Drew, what happened but got no answer. The girl, Kiera, was in the kitchen, and when Tatum asked her what happened, she said, 'Drew shot him.' It's an open-and-shut case."

Dyer was pacing around the room and stopped to say, "Thank you, Sheriff. Any questions?"

The room was silent as the grand jurors felt the weight of such an awful crime. Finally, Miss Tabitha Green from Karaway raised her hand and asked Ozzie, "How old are these children?"

"The boy, Drew, is sixteen. His sister, Kiera, is fourteen."

"And were they home by themselves?"

"No. Their mother was with them."

"And who's their mother?"

"Josie Gamble."

"What's her relationship with the deceased?"

"Girlfriend."

"Forgive me, Sheriff, but you're not exactly forthcoming with all the facts here. I feel like I'm prying stuff out of you and that makes me very suspicious." Miss Tabitha looked around as she spoke, looking for support. So far there was none.

Ozzie glanced at Dyer as if he might need some help. He said, "Josie Gamble is the mother, and she and her two children had been living with Stuart Kofer for about a year."

"Thank you. And where was Ms. Gamble when the shooting took place?"

"In the kitchen."

"Doing what?"

"Well, according to the story, she was unconscious. When Stuart Kofer came home that night they had a fight and evidently Josie got injured and was unconscious."

"He knocked her unconscious?"

"That seems to be what happened."

"Well, Sheriff, why didn't you tell us that? What are you trying to hide from us?"

"Nothing, nothing at all. Stuart Kofer was shot and killed by Drew Gamble, plain and simple, and we're here to get him indicted for it."

"Understood, but we're not a bunch of kindergartners. You want us to indict a person for capital murder, and that of course could mean the gas chamber. Don't you think it's only natural that we might want all the facts?"

"I guess so."

"We're not guessing, Sheriff. This happened at two A.M. on a Sunday morning. Is it safe to assume that Stuart Kofer was not exactly sober when he came home and beat his girlfriend?"

Ozzie squirmed and looked about as guilty as an innocent man could look. He glanced at Dyer again and said, "Yes, it is safe to assume that."

To Miss Tabitha's rescue came Mr. Norman Brewer, a retired barber who lived in an old section of Clanton. "How drunk was he?" he asked.

A loaded question. If he had simply asked, "Was he drunk?" Ozzie could have simply answered, "Yes," while avoiding the ugly details.

"He was quite intoxicated," he said.

Mr. Brewer said, "So he came home quite drunk, as you say, and he punched her, knocked her out cold, then the suspect shot him. Is that what happened, Sheriff?"

"Basically, yes."

"Basically? Did I get something wrong?"

"No sir."

"Did he physically abuse the children?"

"They did not report that at the time."

"What condition was Kofer in when he got shot?"

"Well, we believe he was lying on his bed, asleep. Evidently, there was no struggle with Drew."

"Where was the gun?"

"We don't know exactly."

Mr. Richard Bland from down in Lake Village said, "So, Sheriff, it looks like Mr. Kofer was passed out drunk on his bed and was not awake when the kid shot him, is that right?"

"We don't know if Stu was awake or asleep when he was shot, no sir."

Lowell didn't like the direction of the questioning and said, "I'd like to remind you that the condition of either the deceased or the defendant is not an issue for this grand jury. Claims of self-defense or insanity or whatever might be raised by the defense lawyers, but they are a matter for the trial jury to consider. Not you."

"They're already claiming insanity, from what I hear," said Mr. Bland.

"Maybe so, but what you hear on the street is not important inside this room," Lowell said in a lecturing tone. "We're just dealing with the facts here. Any more questions?"

Miss Tabitha asked him, "Have you had a capital murder indictment before, Lowell? This is certainly the first one for us."

"I have not, and I'm grateful for that."

"It just seems so routine," she said. "Like all the other cases we process in here. Present a few facts, the bare necessities, limit the discussion, and we vote. We just rubber-stamp whatever you want. But this is something else. This is the first step in a case that could send a man, or a kid, to death row at Parchman. It all seems too easy, too sudden to me. Anybody else feel this way?" She looked around but found little support.

Dyer said, "I understand, Miss Green. What else would you like to know? This is a simple case. You've seen the dead body. We have the murder weapon. Besides the victim there were three other people in the house, at the scene. One was unconscious. One was a sixteen-year-old boy whose fingerprints were found on the murder weapon. The third person, his sister, told Deputy Tatum that her brother shot Stuart Kofer. That's it. Plain and simple."

Miss Tabitha took a deep breath and fell back into her chair. Lowell waited and gave them plenty of time to think. Finally, he said, "Thank you, Sheriff."

Without a word, Ozzie stood and left the room.

Benny Hamm looked across the table at Miss Tabitha

and asked, "What's the problem? There's plenty of proof. What else do you want to do?"

"Oh, nothing. It just seems so fast, you know?"

Lowell said, "Well, Miss Tabitha, I assure you there'll be plenty of time to hash out all the issues in this case. After I file the indictment, my office will investigate and prepare for a full-blown trial. The defense will do the same. Judge Noose will insist on a speedy trial, and before long you and everyone else on this grand jury can show up in the main courtroom down the hall and see how it goes."

Benny Hamm said, "Let's vote."

"Let's do it," someone said.

Miss Tabitha said, "Oh, I'll vote to indict. It just seems too perfunctory. Know what I mean?"

All sixteen voted and the indictment was unanimously returned.

17

Tensions at the Coffee Shop were lessened considerably when the deputies found another breakfast spot. For years Marshall Prather, Mike Nesbit, and other assorted deputies would arrive early to eat biscuits and stir up the gossip, but not every morning. They had other favorite spots, and their shifts changed so their routines varied. Jake, though, had been there six mornings a week for years, and he had always enjoyed mixing it up with the deputies. But they were boycotting him now. When it became apparent that Jake had no plans to alter his ritual, they went elsewhere, which was fine with Jake. He did not enjoy the forced pleasantries, the strained looks, the feeling that things were not the same. They had lost a comrade, and Jake was now on the other side.

He tried to convince himself it went with the territory. He almost believed that one day not too far away the Gamble case would be behind them and he and Ozzie and his men would be pals again. But the rift bothered him greatly, and he could not shake it.

Dell kept him abreast of the latest rumblings. Without giving names, she would report that yesterday's lunch crowd was all abuzz with the coming indictment and questions about when and where the trial might be. Or that after Jake left that morning a couple of farmers got pretty loud in their criticisms of Judge Noose and the system and Jake in particular. Or that three ladies she hadn't seen in years sat by the window for an early lunch and talked quietly about Janet Kofer and her nervous breakdown. There was a palpable fear that Jake Brigance was about to pull another insanity stunt and "get the boy off." And on it went. Dell heard everything, remembered everything, and relayed some of it to Jake when he stopped by late in the day and the café was empty. She was worried about him and his growing unpopularity.

The morning after the indictment, Jake arrived at six and joined the usual crowd of farmers, cops, some factory workers, mostly men who rose early and punched in. Jake was about the only white collar who was a regular and for this he was admired. He often dispensed free legal advice and commented on Supreme Court rulings and other oddities, and he laughed along with the crooked lawyer jokes.

Across the square at the Tea Shoppe, the white collars gathered later in the morning to discuss golf, national politics, and the stock market. At the Coffee Shop they talked about fishing, football, and local crime, what little there was of it.

After the "good mornings," a friend said, "You seen this?" He held up a copy of *The Ford County Times.* It was published every Wednesday and had managed to catch the late-breaking story from Tuesday afternoon. A bold headline screamed: **"GAMBLE INDICTED FOR CAPITAL MURDER."**

"Surprise, surprise," Jake said. However, Lowell Dyer had called him last night to confirm the news.

Dell appeared with a coffeepot and filled his cup. "Good mornin', sweetheart," Jake said.

"Keep your hands to yourself," she shot back, and scooted away. There were a dozen regulars in already, and by 6:15 the café would be packed.

Jake sipped his coffee, and reread the front-page

story, and learned nothing new. The reporter, Dumas Lee, had called his office late yesterday afternoon fishing around for comments, but got none from Portia. Mr. Brigance, she explained, was in court.

"Your name is not mentioned," Dell said. "Already checked."

"Darn. I need the publicity." Jake folded the newspaper and handed it back. Bill West, a foreman at the shoe factory, arrived and fell into his usual chair. They talked about the weather for five minutes as they waited on breakfast. It finally arrived and Jake asked Dell, "What took so long?"

"The chef's lazy. You wanna discuss it with her?"

The chef was a large rowdy woman with a short temper and the habit of throwing spatulas. They kept her in the back for a reason.

As Jake was shaking Tabasco sauce on his grits, West said, "I almost got in a fight about you yesterday. Guy I work with said he'd heard that you were braggin' about havin' that boy out by his eighteenth birthday."

"Did you punch him?"

"No. He's quite a bit bigger."

"He's also quite stupid."

"That's exactly what I called him. I said that, first of all, Jake doesn't go around poppin' off like that, and, second, you wouldn't try to game the system for a cop killer."

"Thanks."

"Would you?"

Jake spread strawberry jam on his wheat toast and took a bite. He chewed and said, "No. I wouldn't. I'm still trying to get rid of the case."

Bill said, "That's what I keep hearin' from you, Jake, but you're still on the case, right?"

"Yes, afraid so."

A crane operator named Vance walked by the table, stopped and stared at Jake. He pointed a finger and said loudly, "They're gonna fry that boy's ass, Jake, regardless of what you try to do."

"Well good mornin', Vance," Jake said. Heads were turning in the direction of the noise. "How's the family?"

Vance was a once-a-week guy and was fairly well known at the café. "Don't get smart with me. You got no business in court with that boy."

"That falls into the category of someone else's business, Vance. You take care of yours. I'll take care of mine."

"A dead officer is everybody's business, Jake. You pull a fast one and get him off on one of those 'technicalities' and there'll be hell to pay around here."

"Is that a threat?"

"No sir. It's a promise."

Dell walked in front of Vance and hissed, "Sit down or get out."

He rumbled back to his table and for a few minutes the café was quieter. Bill West finally said, "I suppose you're gettin' a lot of that these days."

Jake replied, "Oh yeah, but it's just part of the job. Since when are lawyers admired by all?"

HE LOVED THE office at 7:00 A.M., before the day began and the phone started ringing, before Portia arrived at 8:00 with a list of things for him to do and questions to answer, before Lucien rolled in mid-morning and stomped upstairs with his cup of coffee to disrupt whatever Jake was doing.

He turned on the lights downstairs and checked each room, then went to the kitchen to brew the first pot. He went upstairs to his office and took off his jacket. In the middle of his desk was a two-page motion Portia had prepared the day before. It was a request by the defense to transfer Drew Gamble's case to youth court, and when filed it would set off another round of nasty gossip.

The motion was a formality and Noose had already promised to deny it. But, as the defense lawyer of record, Jake had no choice. If the motion were granted, an impossibility, the murder charge would be tried before the youth court judge with no jury. When found guilty, Drew would be sent to a juvenile facility somewhere in the state and kept there until his eighteenth birthday, when the court surrendered jurisdiction. At that point, there was no procedural mechanism to allow the circuit court to assume jurisdiction. In other words, Drew would be allowed to go free. After less than two years behind bars. There was nothing fair about this law but Jake couldn't change it. And it was precisely for this reason that Noose would keep the case.

Jake could not imagine the backlash if his client walked after serving such a short sentence, and frankly, he was not in favor of it. He knew, though, that Noose would protect him while at the same time protecting the integrity of the system.

Portia had attached a four-page brief that Jake read with admiration. As always, she was thorough and discussed a dozen prior cases involving minors, one reaching back to the 1950s. She argued persuasively that minors are not as mature as adults and do not possess the same decision-making skills, and so on. However, each case she cited had ended with the same result—the minor was kept in circuit court. Mississippi had a long history of putting minors on trial for serious crimes.

It was an admirable effort. Jake edited the motion

and brief, and when Portia arrived they discussed the changes. At nine, he walked across the street and filed the paperwork. The assistant clerk accepted it without comment and Jake left without his customary flirting. Even the clerk's office seemed a bit cooler these days.

HARRY REX COULD always find a reason to get out of town on business, away from the turmoil of his contentious divorce practice and away from his quarrelsome wife. He sneaked out the rear door of his office late in the afternoon and enjoyed the long, quiet drive to Jackson. He went to Hal & Mal's, his favorite restaurant, took a table in a corner, ordered a beer, and began waiting. Ten minutes later he ordered another one.

During his law school days at Ole Miss, he had downed many beers with Doby Pittman, a wild man from the coast who had finished first in their class and chose the big-firm route in Jackson. He was now a partner in a fifty-lawyer group that did well representing insurance companies in major damage cases. Pittman was not involved with *Smallwood* but his firm was lead counsel. Another partner, Sean Gilder, had drawn the case.

A month earlier, over beers in the same restaurant, Pittman had whispered to his old drinking buddy that the railroad might approach Jake and discuss the possibility of a settlement. The case was frightening for both sides. Four people had been killed at a bad crossing poorly maintained by the railroad. There would be enormous sympathy for the Smallwoods. And Jake had impressed the defense with his aggressiveness and demands for a trial. He had shown no reluctance in ramming through discovery and running to Noose when he thought the defense was stalling. He and Harry Rex had hired two top railroad-crossing experts, plus an economist who would tell the jury that the four lost lives were worth millions. The railroad's biggest fear, according to bar talk from Doby, was that Jake was hungry and craving another big courtroom win.

On the other hand, the defense was confident that it could whittle away at the sympathy and prove the obvious: that Taylor Smallwood had crashed into the fourteenth boxcar without touching his brakes.

Both sides could lose big, or win big. A settlement was the safest route for both.

Harry Rex damned sure wanted a settlement. Litigation was expensive, and he and Jake had borrowed, so far, $55,000 from Security Bank to finance the lawsuit. More expenses were likely. Neither lawyer on the plaintiff's side had that kind of money lying around.

Of course, Pittman knew nothing about the loan. No one did, except for the banker and Carla Brigance. Harry Rex told his wife, his fourth one, nothing about his business.

Doby arrived thirty minutes late and didn't apologize. Harry Rex wasn't concerned with his tardiness. They drank a beer, ordered red beans and rice, and commented on the looks of some young ladies nearby. Then they got around to their jobs. Doby had never understood his friend's desire to specialize in divorces in a podunk town like Clanton, and Harry Rex was repulsed by the grind and politics of a big firm in downtown Jackson. But both were fed up with the law and wanted out. Most of their lawyer friends felt the same way.

Their orders arrived and they were starving. After a few bites, Doby said, "Looks like your boy has got himself in a mess up there."

Harry Rex knew it was coming and said, "He'll be all right once he gets rid of the case."

"That's not what I hear."

"Okay, Pitt, just go ahead and tell me what Walter Sullivan has relayed to you boys from the mean streets of Clanton. He probably calls down here every day with the latest courthouse gossip, half of which he makes up to begin with. He has never been a proven source for breaking news. I know far more and I'll correct his mistakes."

Doby laughed and shoveled in a chunk of andouille sausage. He wiped his mouth with a napkin and took a drink. "I don't talk to him, you know? Not my case. So I don't know much. What I hear comes from one of the paralegals working down the hall. Gilder keeps a lid on his files around the office."

"Got it. So what's the buzz?"

"That Brigance has got the town pretty upset because he's going the insanity route. The boy's already at Whitfield."

"Not true. He's at Whitfield, okay, but just for an initial evaluation. That's all. Insanity might be an issue down the road, at trial, but Jake won't be involved."

"Well, he's involved right now. Gilder and his gang are thinking that Jake might have trouble picking himself the right jury in the railroad case."

"So the railroad's backin' off settlement?"

"Looks like it. And they're in no hurry to go to trial. They're going into a serious delay mode, hoping Brigance gets stuck with the kid. The murder trial could get ugly."

"Delay? My gosh, I've never heard of such from a defense firm."

"It's one of our many specialties."

"But here's the problem, Pitt. Judge Noose controls

his docket with an iron fist and right now he owes Jake a big one. If Jake wants a trial real soon, then it's going to happen."

Doby worked on his food for a moment, then washed it down. "Does Jake have a number?"

"Two million," Harry Rex said with a mouthful and no hesitation.

Like a seasoned defense lawyer, Doby grimaced as if it were two billion. Both men ate in silence and thought about the numbers. The contract Harry Rex negotiated with the Smallwood relatives gave him one-third if the case was settled, and 40 percent if it went to trial. He and Jake had agreed to equally split the fee. Over beans and beers the math was easy. It would be the biggest settlement in the history of Ford County, and it was sorely needed by both lawyers for the plaintiffs. Harry Rex was not yet spending the money, but he was certainly dreaming of it. Everything Jake owned was mortgaged. Plus, there was the business of that bank loan for litigation expenses.

"How much insurance coverage?" Harry Rex asked with a smile.

Doby smiled back and said, "I can't answer that. Plenty."

"Figures. He's gonna ask the jury for a lot more than two million."

"But it's Ford County, a place that's never seen a million-dollar verdict."

"There's always the first time, Pitt. I'll bet we can find twelve people who haven't heard about the murder."

Doby laughed and Harry Rex was forced to do the same. "Hell, Harry Rex, you can't find two people who don't know about it."

"Maybe, but we'll do our research. Noose'll give us plenty of time to pick a jury."

"I'm sure he will. Look, Harry Rex, I want you to get some big bucks, some of that dirty insurance money, okay? A nice settlement that'll take the pressure off. But to do so, Brigance has got to get rid of that kid. Right now that case is a liability, at least in the minds of Sean Gilder and Walter Sullivan."

"We're working on it."

18

It was well known that the law business peaked at noon each Friday and then shut down. The lawyers who normally clogged the halls of the courthouse vanished after lunch. Most of them fibbed to their secretaries and left for the country stores where they bought cold beer and roamed the back roads in blessed solitude. With the phones silent and the bosses gone, the secretaries often sneaked away too. No self-respecting judge would be caught dead in a robe on Friday afternoon. Most went fishing or played golf. The clerks who generally milled about laden with important documents ran errands across the street and didn't come back, instead easing away to beauty parlors and grocery stores. By mid-afternoon, the wheels of justice ground to a halt.

Jake was planning to call Harry Rex to explore the possibility of a drink to catch up on things. At 3:30, he was done for the week and contemplating which excuse to feed Portia so he could leave without appearing shiftless. He still thought it was important to lead by example and she was quite impressionable. However, after working there for two years Portia knew his schedule and his lame excuses.

She buzzed him at 3:40 and said there was someone to see him. No, the person had not made an appointment. Yes, she realized it was Friday afternoon, but it was Pastor Charles McGarry and he told her the matter was urgent.

Jake welcomed him to his office and they sat in a corner, Charles on the old leather sofa, Jake in a chair that was at least a hundred years old. The preacher declined coffee or tea and was obviously troubled. He told the story of driving Josie and Kiera to Whitfield on Tuesday, leaving them there, and fetching them the following day. Jake knew all this. He had spoken twice with Dr. Sadie Weaver and knew the family had spent almost seven hours in three sessions.

Charles said, "When we were driving down early Tuesday, Kiera got sick and threw up twice. Josie said she always got car sick real easy. I didn't think much about it. When I went back to get them at Whitfield on Wednesday, one of the nurses told me that Kiera had been sick that morning, nausea, throwing up, you know? I thought it was unusual because she had not been in a car that morning. They had a room on the campus. Driving home Wednesday afternoon she was fine. Yesterday morning, Mrs. Golden, the lady who's tutoring her at church, said she got sick again and threw up. And not for the first time. I told my wife, Meg, about it and, well, you know how women are usually smarter than we are? Well, Meg and I have one child and she's due with our second in two months. We are so blessed and very excited. She had one of those home pregnancy tests left over from last year."

Jake was nodding. He had purchased several since Hanna arrived, and the results had always been negative, to their great disappointment.

"Meg agreed to have a chat with Josie. Kiera took the test and it's positive. I drove them to a doctor in Tupelo this morning. She's three months along. Wouldn't tell the doctor or his nurse anything about the father."

Jake felt like he'd been mule-kicked in the gut.

The preacher was on a roll. "Driving back this morning, she got sick again and threw up in my car. What a mess. Poor girl. We got her back to the church and Josie put her to bed. She and Meg took turns sitting with her until she felt better. She had some soup for lunch and we all just sat around in the kitchen and she started talking, you know. She said Kofer started molesting her back around Christmas, said he did it about five or six times and that he threatened to kill her if she told anyone. She didn't tell Josie and of course this near 'bout killed her mother. A lot of tears today, Jake. Mine too. Can you imagine? Fourteen years old and getting raped by a thug that she was terrified of? Too frightened to tell anyone. Not sure when it would end. She said she thought about killing herself."

"Did Drew know?" Jake asked. The answer could have enormous consequences.

"Don't know. You need to ask her that, Jake. You need to talk to her and to Josie. They're a mess, as you might guess. I mean, think about what they've been through in the past two weeks. The shooting, surgery, hospitals, Drew in jail, Whitfield and back, losing everything they had, which wasn't much, but now they're living in the back of our church. And all the talk about putting Drew in the gas chamber. They're pitiful, Jake, and they really need your help. They trust you and want your advice. I'm doing the best I can, Jake, but I'm just a rookie preacher who never made it to college." His voice cracked and his eyes watered. He looked away, shook his head, fought his emotions. "I'm sorry. It's been a long day with those two, Jake. A real long day, and they need to talk to you."

"Okay, okay."

"And there's something else, Jake. Josie's first reaction was that they would get an abortion. She feels pretty strong about it, at least for now. And I'm not in favor, for obvious reasons. I'm deadset against it. Josie seems to have some strong feelings. So do I. If Kiera gets an abortion then she's outta my church."

"Let's worry about that later, Charles. You said she saw a doctor in Tupelo?"

"Yes. Josie likes the guy who operated on her, so she called his nurse. They called someone else and the guy did a favor and got her in. Said she's healthy and all, but she's just a kid."

"And Meg knows all this?"

"Meg was in the room, Jake. Meg is right there with them."

"Okay, it's real important to keep this as quiet as possible. My head is spinning as I try to think of all of the ramifications. I know how gossip flies around in a small church."

"Right, right."

Almost as fast as it flies around in a coffee shop. Jake asked, "Is she showing?"

"I couldn't tell anything. I mean, I tried not to stare, but I don't think so. Why don't you come see for yourself, Jake? They're at the church waiting for you."

KIERA WAS NAPPING upstairs when Jake entered the rear door that opened into the kitchen. At one end of a long table was a stack of textbooks and notepads, proof that the student was getting tutored at some level. Meg and Josie were at the table working on a large jigsaw puzzle. The McGarrys' four-year-old, Justin, was playing quietly in a corner.

Josie stood and hugged Jake as if they'd been close for years. Meg went to the counter and rinsed out the coffeepot to brew a fresh one. Though the windows were up and the curtains were moving with the breeze, the room had the heavy feel and smell of a long day's drama.

It took twenty-two minutes to drive from the Clanton square to the Good Shepherd Bible Church, and in that short period Jake had tried, unsuccessfully, to first identify all the new legal issues, and then to untangle them. Assuming she was really pregnant and that Kofer was the father, how would this be presented at Drew's trial? Since she was present at the shooting, she would undoubtedly be called as a witness for the prosecution. Could her pregnancy be mentioned? What if her mother insisted on an abortion? Would the jury know about that? If Drew knew Kofer was raping his sister, wouldn't that seriously impact his defense? He killed to stop it. He killed out of retribution. Regardless of why he killed, Lowell Dyer could argue persuasively that he knew exactly what he was doing. How could they prove the child was Kofer's? What if someone else was the father? With Kiera's troubled background, wasn't it possible she had started having sex early? Could there be a boyfriend somewhere? Was Jake obliged to inform Lowell Dyer that his star witness had been impregnated by the deceased? Depending on when the trial took place, would it be wise to put her on the stand when she was obviously pregnant? By proving the rapes and physical abuse, wasn't Jake in effect putting Stuart Kofer on trial? If Kiera chose to abort, who would pay for it? If she didn't, what would happen to the child? With no home, would Kiera be allowed to keep it?

As he drove, he had decided that these issues required an entire team. Lawyer, minister, at least two psychiatrists, some counselors.

Jake looked across the table at Josie and asked, point-blank, "Did Drew know that Kofer was raping Kiera?"

The tears were instant, the emotions raw and barely contained. "She won't say," Josie said. "Which leads me to believe that he did. Otherwise, why wouldn't she just say no? I didn't know. But I cannot believe she would tell Drew and not me."

"And you had no clue?"

She shook her head and began sobbing. Meg poured Jake some coffee in a ceramic cup stained brown from decades of use. Like everything else in the room, it appeared to be well used but clean.

Josie wiped her face with a paper towel and said, "What will this do to Drew's case?"

"It helps. It hurts. Some jurors might be sympathetic to Drew for taking matters into his own hands and protecting his sister, if that's what he was thinking. We don't know yet. The prosecutors will make much of the fact that he killed Kofer to stop him, so he knew what he was doing and can't claim insanity. I honestly can't tell you how it will play out. Keep in mind, I'm just on the case temporarily. There's a good chance Judge Noose will appoint someone else for the trial."

"You can't leave us, Jake," Josie said.

Oh yes I can, he thought. Especially now. "We'll see." In search of a subject slightly less depressing, he said, "I understand you spent time with Drew."

She nodded.

"And how is he doing?"

"As well as can be expected. They put him on some meds, some antidepressants, and he says he's sleepin' better. He likes the doctors, says the food is good. He'd rather stay there than in the jail here. Why can't he get out, Jake?"

"We've had this conversation, Josie. He has been indicted for capital murder. Nobody gets bail in a case like this."

"But what about school? He's two years behind any-way, and he's just sittin' there losin' ground every day. They won't put him in a class at Whitfield because he's a security risk and only temporary. Bring him back here to wait for trial, and they ain't got no tutors at the jail here. Why can't they send him to a juvenile facility somewhere? Someplace where they at least make 'em go to class."

"Because he's not being treated like a juvenile. As of now he's an adult."

"I know, I know. Adult? What a joke. He's just a little kid who's not even shavin' yet. One of his counselors down there told me she'd never seen a sixteen-year-old boy as physically immature as Drew." A pause as she wiped her red cheeks. "His father was like that. Just a kid."

Jake glanced at Meg, who glanced at Charles. Jake decided to dig a little. "Who is his father?"

Josie laughed and shrugged and would've said "What the hell" but she was in a church. "A guy named Ray Barber. He was a boy down the road and I sorta grew up with him. When we were fourteen we started foolin' around one day, one thing led to another and we did it. Did it again and again and were havin' some fun. Didn't know a thing about birth control or basic biology, we were just a coupla stupid kids carryin' on. I got preg-nant at fifteen and Ray wanted to get married. He was afraid he might get cut off. My mother sent me to live with an aunt in Shreveport to have the baby. I don't recall any discussion about terminatin' the pregnancy. I had the baby and they wanted me to give it up, and I should have. I really should have. What I've put my kids through is nothin' but a sin."

She took a deep breath, then a sip of water from a bottle. "Anyway, I remember Ray worryin' because the other boys were shavin' and gettin' hair on their legs and he wasn't. He was afraid he was growin' up late, like his father. Evidently, other parts were workin' okay."

"What happened to Ray?" Jake asked.

"I don't know. I never went back home. When I wouldn't give up the baby, my aunt kicked me out. You know something, Jake, gettin' pregnant at fifteen was the worst mistake I've ever made. It changed my life, and not for the better. I love Drew, same as I love Kiera, but when a girl has a baby that young her whole future is shot to hell. Pardon my language. The girl probably won't finish school. She probably won't marry well. She probably won't find a good job. She'll probably do what I did—bounce from one bad man to another. That's why Kiera is not havin' this baby, you understand, Jake? If I have to rob a bank to get the money for an abortion, I'll do it. She is not messin' up her life. Hell, she didn't even want to have sex. I did. Pardon my language."

Charles shook his head and bit his lip but said nothing. It was obvious, though, that he would have plenty to say about an abortion.

Calmly, Jake said, "I understand. But this topic can be discussed at a later time. For now, I need to ask a question that has to be asked. She says Kofer is the father. Is there a chance there could be anyone else?"

Nothing fazed Josie, not even the delicate suggestion that her young daughter might have been sleeping around. She shook her head, no. "I asked her that. As you have probably noticed, she's normal for her age, a lot more mature than her brother. I know from experience what kids can do, so I asked her if there had been anybody else. She got upset at the question, said absolutely not. Said Kofer was the first to ever touch her down there."

"And this started around Christmas?"

"Yes. She said she was at the house by herself on a Saturday, right before Christmas."

Charles said, "That would've been the twenty-third of December."

"I was at work. Drew was over at a friend's. Stu came home early and decided to go to her room. He said he wanted to do it. She said no, please no. He forced himself on her, but was careful not to leave marks. When it was over, he said he'd kill her and Drew too if she ever told. He even asked her if she enjoyed it. Can you imagine? This happened several more times, five or six altogether, she thinks, and she says she was waitin' for the right time to tell me. She said she couldn't keep on like that, said she even thought about suicide. This is all my fault, Jake. See what I've done to my kids? All my fault." She was sobbing again.

Jake walked to the sink and poured out the cold coffee. He refilled his cup and walked to the door to look out. When her noises stopped, he returned to his seat and looked at her. "A few more questions?"

"Sure. I'll tell you anything, Jake."

"Do Drew and Kiera know they have different fathers?"

"No. I've never told them. I figured they'd realize it soon enough. They look nothin' alike."

"Did Kofer physically abuse Drew?"

"Yes. He slapped him around, same for Kiera, but never with his fists. He beat me several times, always when he was drunk. Sober, Stu was okay, you know? But he was a crazy drunk. Very intimidating, though, drunk or sober."

"Will you be able to take the witness stand and tell the jury about the physical abuse?"

"I suppose. I guess I'll have to, right?"

"Probably. Will Kiera?"

"I don't know, Jake. Poor thing is a total wreck right now."

On cue, Kiera appeared in the door and walked over to the table. Her eyes were puffy, her hair a mess. She wore baggy jeans and a sweatshirt, and Jake couldn't help but look at her stomach. He saw nothing suspicious. She smiled at him but didn't speak. She had a beautiful smile with perfect teeth, and Jake tried to imagine the horror of being a fourteen-year-old girl who had just learned that her body was carrying a child she wanted nothing to do with. Why does biology allow children to have children?

Charles was saying, "Back to the trial. Any idea when it will take place?"

"None whatsoever. It's still very early in the process. I know for minors who are tried as adults the courts tend to move pretty fast. Maybe this summer, but I'm not sure."

"The sooner the better," Josie said. "I want this mess behind us."

"It's not going away with a trial, Josie."

"Oh, I know that, Jake," she snapped. "It never goes away with me. Everything's a mess, always has been and I guess it always will be. I'm so sorry for this. The kids were beggin' me to leave Stu and I wanted to. If I had known about him and Kiera we would've fled in the middle of the night. Don't ask me where, but we would've left. I'm just so sorry."

There was another long pause as everyone—Jake, Charles, Meg, and even Kiera—tried to think of something to say that might be comforting.

Josie said, "I didn't mean to be short, Jake. Please understand."

"I do. It is imperative that this pregnancy be kept

absolutely quiet. I'm sure you all get this, but the question is how do we go about it. Kiera is not in school so we don't have to worry about her friends getting suspicious. What about folks around the church here?"

Charles said, "Well, we'll have to tell Mrs. Golden, the tutor. She's already suspicious."

"Can you handle that?"

"Sure."

Josie blurted, "Well, after we get the abortion we won't have to worry about it, will we?"

Charles couldn't hold his tongue any longer and snapped, "As long as you're living in this church, abortion is out of the question. If she gets one, then you'll have to leave."

"We always leave. Jake, where's the nearest abortion clinic?"

"Memphis."

"How much does one cost these days?"

"Don't know from experience, but I've heard it's something like five hundred dollars."

"Will you loan me five hundred?"

"I will not."

"Okay, we'll get us another lawyer."

"I'm not sure you can find another one."

"Oh, there are plenty out there."

Charles said, "Everybody take a deep breath. It's been a long day and nerves are frazzled." A moment passed. Jake took a last sip of coffee, rose, and walked back to the sink.

He stepped to the end of the table and said, "I need to be going, but I want you to think about a scenario that's hard to imagine. If there is an abortion, and I'm not in favor of one but that's not my decision, then you not only destroy a life, but you also destroy valuable evidence. Kiera will be called to testify at trial. If there is an abortion, she will not be permitted to mention it, nor should she because of resentment among the jurors. She can tell the jury that Stuart Kofer raped her, repeatedly, but other than her word, she cannot prove it. The police were never called. However, if she is obviously pregnant, or if she has already given birth, then the baby will be powerful evidence of Kofer's rapes. And Kiera will create enormous sympathy not only for herself, but, and more importantly, for her brother. Carrying the baby will be a huge factor in Drew's favor at trial."

"So she has the baby to save her brother?" Josie asked.

Jake replied, "She has the baby because it's the right thing to do. And, it alone will not save her brother, but it could certainly help a very desperate cause."

"She's too young to get stuck raisin' a kid," Josie said.

"There are a lot of desperate and deserving couples, Josie," Jake said. "I do three or four private adoptions a year and they're my favorite cases."

"What about its father? Not sure I'd want that gene pool."

"Since when are we allowed to pick our parents?"

But Josie was shaking her head in disgust and disagreement. As Jake drove away, he was struck by the flashes of meanness that Josie had instinctively displayed. Not that he blamed her. She had been hardened by a life of bad choices and was desperate to provide something better for her children. She had probably gone the abortion route herself and was quietly thankful that she only had two kids to worry about. Two were proving to be enough.

HE ALMOST STOPPED at a country store for a beer, one for the road, a sixteen-ounce can of something ice-cold that would take him about twenty minutes to savor. Then his car phone rang. It was Carla, reminding him in clipped tones that they were supposed to leave the house in thirty minutes for dinner at the Atcavages'. He had forgotten this. She had been calling for an hour. Where had he been?

"I can explain it all later," he said and hung up. In his sensitive cases he always struggled with how much to tell his wife. Divulging anything was technically an ethical violation, but every human, including lawyers, needed to confide in someone. Without fail, she provided a different perspective, especially when women were involved, and she never hesitated to argue a point. She would have some strong feelings about these latest developments in an already tragic story.

Crossing into Clanton and almost home, he decided he would wait a day or so, or maybe more, before he told Carla that Kiera was pregnant because she had been raped by Stuart Kofer. Just saying this to himself made his stomach churn. It was hard to imagine the raw anger that would boil in the courtroom if and when Jake detailed the sins of Stuart Kofer. A dead cop unable to defend himself.

Hanna was at a sleepover and the house was quiet. Carla was frosty because they were late, but Jake didn't care. It was Friday night, they were meeting friends, it was a casual dinner on the patio with a keg of beer. He took off his suit and changed into jeans, then sat and waited for her at the kitchen table.

As he drove, she asked, "So where have you been?"

"The Good Shepherd Bible Church, visiting with Josie and her team out there."

"That wasn't planned."

"No, it just happened. Charles McGarry came to the office at three thirty and said they needed to talk, said they were upset and needed some hand-holding. That's part of my job."

"You're getting stuck with this case, aren't you?"

"Feels like quicksand."

"We got another phone call about an hour ago. It's time to change the number."

"Did he give his name and address?"

"I doubt if he has an address, probably lives under a rock. Some bizarre, rambling nut yelling into the phone. Said that if that boy gets off he won't last forty-eight hours on the streets. Said his lawyer won't make it for twenty-four."

"So, they'll kill me first?"

"It's not funny."

"I'm not laughing. Let's change the number."

"Are you calling Ozzie?"

"Yes, not that it will do any good. We should continue that discussion about hiring private security."

"Or maybe you should just tell Noose that you've had enough."

"You want me to quit? I thought you were worried about Drew."

"I am worried about Drew. I'm also worried about Hanna, and you and me, and surviving in this very small town."

Stan Atcavage lived out by the country club in a wooded development of sprawling suburban homes built around the only golf course in the county. He ran Security Bank and held most of Jake's mortgages, as well as the brand-new line of credit for the litigation expenses of the *Smallwood* case. Stan at first had balked at such a novel loan, as had Jake and Harry Rex. But as the case progressed they realized they had no choice but to borrow. After three divorces and now with a fourth wife, Harry Rex's balance sheet was as unimpressive as Jake's, though he currently had only one mortgage on his home. At fifty-one, Harry Rex was gazing at the future and worrying about it. Jake was only thirty-seven, but it seemed as though the longer he practiced law, the more money he owed.

Stan was a close friend but Jake couldn't stomach his wife, nor could Carla. Her name was Tilda and she was from an old Jackson family she often described as wealthy, which turned off most people in Clanton. The town was far too small for her and her expensive tastes. Seeking brighter lights, she had forced Stan to join the Tupelo Country Club, a status symbol in the area, and a luxury they struggled to afford. She also drank too much, spent too much, and kept the pressure on her husband to earn more. As a banker in a small town, Stan said little, but he had confided enough in Jake to let him know the marriage was not going well. Fortunately, when they arrived half an hour late Tilda was already several drinks ahead and had moved beyond her customary stuffiness.

There were five couples, all in their late thirties and early forties, with kids ranging from three to fifteen. The women gathered at one end of the patio at a wine bar and talked about their children, while the men gathered at the keg and discussed other topics. First it was the stock market, a subject that bored Jake because he didn't have the money to play it, and even if loaded with cash he thought he knew enough to avoid it. Next, it was the rather salacious rumor that a doctor they all knew had cracked up and run off with a nurse. She was well known too because she was drop-dead gorgeous and one of the most lusted-after women in the county, single or married. Jake had not heard the rumor, never met the woman, didn't like the doctor, and tried to avoid the gossip.

It was Carla's long-standing opinion that men, contrary to popular opinion, were worse gossips than women. Jake found it hard to disagree. He was relieved when the conversation drifted to sports, and even more pleased when Stan announced dinner. No one had mentioned the Kofer killing.

They dined on smoked ribs, corn on the cob, and slaw. It was a perfect spring evening, just warm enough to eat outside on the patio and enjoy the blooming dogwoods. The fourteenth fairway was fifty yards away, and after a dessert of store-bought coconut pie, the five men fired up cigars and walked to the golf course for a smoke. The Masters was in full swing at Augusta National and this dominated the talk. Nick Faldo and Raymond Floyd were battling it out, and Stan, a serious golfer, was generous with his analysis. Since he was hosting and wouldn't be driving, he was drinking too much.

Jake had little experience with cigars and even less with golf, and as he gamely listened his mind went back to the scene at the church and the look of hopelessness and fear in young Kiera's eyes. He shook it off, and wanted to go home and crawl into bed.

Stan, though, wanted to end the night with a digestif, a fine brandy someone had sent him. Back on the patio, he poured five generous shots and the boys drifted over to bother the girls.

Carla looked at the drink in Jake's hand and whispered, "Haven't you had enough?"

"I'm okay."

One couple was paying a babysitter and needed to call it a night. Another had a new puppy that was all alone. It was almost 11:00 P.M., Friday night, and most of them were looking forward to a late morning sleeping in. Thanks and farewells were offered and accepted and the guests left.

At the car, Jake's red Saab, Carla asked, "Are you okay to drive?"

"Sure. I'm fine."

They got in and she asked, "How many drinks have you had?"

"I didn't know we were counting. Not enough."

She gritted her teeth, looked away, and said nothing else. Jake was determined to prove his sobriety and drove slowly and carefully. "So what did the girls talk about?" he asked, trying to break the ice.

"Usual stuff. Kids, school, mothers-in-law. You heard about Dr. Freddie and the nurse?"

"Oh yes. All the details. I've always avoided him."

"He's a creep, but then his wife is not much better. Watch your speed."

"I'm doing just fine, Carla, thank you." Jake fumed and concentrated on the road. He turned onto a bypass east of town and the bright lights of Clanton were just ahead. He glanced in his mirror and mumbled, "Crap! A cop."

The patrol car had materialized from nowhere and was suddenly on his bumper, with blue lights flashing and a siren that could be heard for miles. Jake knew immediately that it was a county car. The town limits of Clanton were a mile away.

Carla turned around in horror and saw the lights close behind. "Why is he stopping us?" she asked.

"Hell if I know. I was under the speed limit." Jake slowed and managed to stop on a wide shoulder.

"Do you have any gum?" he asked. Carla opened her purse, which in keeping with the current style was almost large enough to check in as luggage at the airport. Finding gum or breath mints in it, and in the dark, and under pressure, seemed unlikely. Fortunately, the officer was in no hurry. She found the gum and Jake crammed two pieces into his mouth.

It was Mike Nesbit, a deputy Jake knew well. He knew all of them, didn't he? The officer shined his light inside and asked, "Jake, can I see your license and registration, please?"

"Sure, Mike. How you doing?" Jake said as he handed them over.

"Great." Nesbit examined the cards and said, "Just a minute." He strolled back to his car and got in, just as a green Audi passed them in the center of the road. Jake wasn't positive but he believed the car was owned by the Janeways, a couple they had just enjoyed dinner with. And since Jake had the only red Saab within fifty miles, there was little doubt as to who was getting pulled over.

"Do you have any water?" he asked his wife.

"I don't normally carry water."

"Thank you."

"Did you drink too much?"

"No, I don't think so."

"How much did you drink?"

"I wasn't counting but I was not excessive. Do I seem drunk now?"

She turned away and didn't answer. The flashing lights seemed ready to burst, but thankfully the siren had been turned off. Another car passed, slowly. Jake handled at least one DUI charge each month and had been doing so for years. The great question was always: Do you agree to take a breath test, or do you refuse? Take or refuse? If you take the test and it registers too high, then you're guaranteed a conviction. Take it and slide just under the limit, and you go free. Refuse, and the cops automatically take you to jail. You post bond, get out, hire a lawyer, and slug it out in court where you have a decent chance of winning. The sage advice, always given after the fact and far too late to be of any benefit, was to take the test if you'd had only a couple of drinks. If you know you're bombed, refuse and take a trip to jail.

Take or refuse? As Jake sat there trying to act as though he had no worries, he realized his hands were shaking. Which humiliation would be greater? Getting handcuffed in front of his wife and taken away? Or dealing with the aftermath of a failed test and the embarrassment of losing his driver's license? Could there even be a bar complaint? He had represented so many drunk drivers that he'd lost any sympathy he might have for someone facing a weekend in jail. You drink and drive, you deserve the punishment.

Now, though, with the minimum level set so low, at .10, even a few drinks during the evening was too much. Take or refuse?

Nesbit was back. He approached with his flashlight shining into Jake's face. "Jake, have you been drinking?"

Another crucial question no one was ever prepared to answer. Say yes, and try to explain how little, and the officer would most certainly take the next step down the path to ruin. Say no, and lie, and face the consequences when he smelled the presence of alcohol. Say something like "Hell no! I don't drink!" and really irritate the officer with slurred words and a thick tongue.

"Yes sir," Jake said. "We're returning from a dinner party and I had some wine. Not much, though. I'm not under the influence, Mike. I'm fine. May I ask what I did wrong?"

"Swerving." Which, as Jake well knew, could mean exactly that, or it could mean anything else. Or nothing.

"Where was I swerving?"

"Will you agree to take a BAC test here on the road?"

Jake was about to say yes when more blue lights came over the hill in their direction. It was another deputy. He slowed, passed them, turned around, and parked behind Nesbit, who left to have a chat.

"I'm not believing this," Carla said.

"Nor am I, dear. Just be cool."

"Oh, I'm cool. You have no idea how cool this makes me."

"I'd rather not fight here beside the road. Can you wait till we get home?"

"Are you going home, Jake? Or somewhere else?"

"I don't know. I did not drink that much, I swear. I don't even feel a buzz."

Loss of license, time in jail, a stiff fine, increased insurance rates. Jake remembered the awful list of punishments he'd recited to a hundred clients. As a lawyer he could always game the system, at least for first-time offenders. Like himself. He could avoid jail, get some community service, cut the fine, justify his fee of $500.

Minutes dragged by as the blue lights flickered silently. Another car approached, slowed for a good look, and passed. Jake promised himself that if and when he was financially able to buy a new car, it would not be an exotic Swedish thing in a bright color. It would be either a Ford or a Chevrolet.

Nesbit approached for the third time and said, "Jake, would you please get out of the car."

Jake nodded and told himself to take careful steps and speak clearly. The field sobriety test was designed to be flunked by all drivers, after which the police could then push hard for a breath test. Jake walked to the rear of his car where the second deputy was waiting. It was Elton Frye, a veteran he had known for years.

"Evenin', Jake," Frye said.

"Hello, Elton. Sorry to trouble you."

"Mike says you been drinkin'."

"At dinner. Look at me, Elton, I'm obviously not drunk."

"So you'll take the test?"

"Of course I'll take it."

The two officers looked at each other and seemed uncertain as to their next move. Nesbit said, "Stu was a friend of mine, Jake. A great guy."

"I liked Stu too, Mike. Sorry about what happened. I know it's tough for you guys."

"It's gonna be tougher if that punk gets off, Jake. Talk about rubbin' salt into some pretty raw wounds."

Jake offered a sappy smile at such foolishness. At that moment he would say just about anything to score a few points. "He's not getting off, I can promise you that. Besides, I'm just handling his case on a temporary basis. The court will appoint another lawyer for the trial."

Mike liked this and nodded at Frye, who extended a hand that held Jake's license and registration. Mike said, "We called Ozzie. He told us to follow you home. Take it easy, okay?"

Jake's shoulders sagged as he exhaled. "Thanks, fellas. I owe you one."

"You owe Ozzie, Jake, not us."

He got in the car, latched his seat belt, cranked the engine, glanced at his mirror, and ignored his wife, who appeared to be praying. As he pulled away, she asked, "What happened?"

"Nothing. It was Mike Nesbit and Elton Frye and they both could tell I'm not drunk. They called Ozzie, told him so, and he said follow us home. Everything's fine."

The blue lights were turned off as the two patrol cars followed the red Saab into Clanton. Inside the car, nothing else was said.

THE KITCHEN PHONE showed three voice mails received during the evening. Carla was rinsing the coffeepot to prepare for the morning, as Jake poured a glass of ice water and punched a button. The first call was a wrong number, some poor soul searching for takeout pizza. The second call was from a reporter in Jackson. The third call was from Josie Gamble, and as soon as Jake hit PLAY he wished he had not. She said:

Hello Jake, it's Josie and I'm sorry to bother you at home. Really sorry. But Kiera and I have been talkin', it's been a long day as you might guess and we're sorta tired of talkin' but anyway I just want to say I'm sorry about jumpin' on you like that and askin' you for money for an abortion. I was outta line and I feel real bad. See you soon. Good night.

Carla was holding the coffeepot filled with water, her mouth open. Jake punched the CLEAR button and looked at his wife. It was difficult holding client confidences when the client left secrets in recorded voice mails.

"Abortion?" Carla asked.

Jake took a deep breath and said, "Do we have any decaf?"

"I think so."

"Let's make a pot. I'll be up all night anyway. Between a near DUI and a pregnant fourteen-year-old, I won't be sleeping much."

"Kiera?"

"Yes. Make the coffee and I'll tell you all about it."

19

The seat of Van Buren County was the backwater town of Chester. According to the 1980 census, its population was 4,100, a decline of about 1,000 from 1970, and there was no doubt the next headcount would be even smaller. It was half the size of Clanton but seemed far more desolate. Clanton had a vibrant square with cafés, restaurants, busy offices, and shops of all varieties. Next door in Chester, though, half the window fronts along Main Street were boarded up and begging for tenants. Perhaps the clearest sign of economic and social decline was the fact that all but four lawyers had fled to bigger towns, several to Clanton. Back in the day, back when young Omar Noose hung out his shingle, there had been twenty lawyers in the county.

Of the five courthouses in the Twenty-second Judicial District, Van Buren's was by far the worst. It was at least a hundred years old and its nondescript, bland design was clear proof that the county fathers could not afford an architect. It began as a sprawling, three-story edifice of white clapboard with rows of tiny offices that housed everyone from the judges to the sheriffs to the assorted clerks, even the county's crop inspector. Over the decades, and back when the county saw modest growth, various annexes and additions were attached here and there like tumors, and the Van Buren County Courthouse became somewhat notorious as the ugliest in the state. There was nothing official about this dis-

tinction, and it was so judged primarily by the lawyers
who came and went and hated the place.

The exterior was perplexing, but the interior was
downright dysfunctional. Nothing worked. The heat-
ing system barely knocked off the chill in the winter,
and in the summer the AC units gobbled electricity
but produced precious little cool air. Entire systems—
plumbing, electricity, security—collapsed with regu-
larity.

In spite of the complaining, the taxpayers had refused to pay for renovations. The most obvious remedy
would have been to simply strike a match, but arson
was still a crime.

There were a few diehards who claimed to appreciate the quirkiness and character of the building, one of
whom was the Honorable Omar Noose, senior judge
of the Twenty-second circuit. For years he had owned
the second floor where he ruled like a king in his large,
antiquated courtroom, and practically lived in his
chambers behind it. Down the hall he maintained a
smaller courtroom for quieter matters. His secretary,
court reporter, and clerk had offices near his.

Most locals believed that if not for Omar Noose and
his considerable influence, the building would have
been razed years earlier.

As he approached the age of seventy, he preferred to
travel less to his other four counties, though he didn't
actually drive at all. Either his clerk or his court reporter handled the driving, to Clanton, Smithfield,
Gretna, or Temple way over in Milburn County, almost
two hours away. He was developing the bothersome
habit of asking lawyers from those towns to come see
him if they had business on off-days. By law he had no
choice but to hold terms of court in all five counties,

but he was proving adept at finding ways to stay at home.

On Monday, Jake got the phone call asking him to see Noose at 2:00 P.M. on Tuesday, "in chambers." All five courthouses had offices for the judges, but when Noose said "in chambers" he meant get your ass over here to lovely Chester, Mississippi. Jake explained to the judge's secretary that he had appointments Tuesday afternoon, which he did, but she informed him that His Honor would expect Jake to cancel those.

And so he drove through the quiet streets of Chester early Tuesday afternoon and was once again thankful he didn't live there. Whereas Clanton had been laid out neatly by a general after the Civil War, and its streets formed a precise grid, for the most part, and the lovely courthouse sat majestically in the center of the square, Chester had somehow sprung to life in stages over the decades with little thought of symmetry or design. There was no square, no proper Main Street. Its business district was a collection of roads that met at odd angles and would have caused traffic nightmares had there been any traffic.

The oddest part of the town was that the courthouse was not to be found within its limits. It sat alone, solitary and seemingly ready to crumble, on a state highway two miles east of town. Three miles further east was the village of Sweetwater, the longtime rival of Chester. After the war, there had been precious little in the county to fight over, but the two towns managed to fester hostilities for decades, and in 1885 they could not agree on which one would be declared the county seat. There was actually some gunfire and a casualty or two, but the governor, who'd never been to Van Buren County and had no plans to visit, chose Chester. To appease the hotheads in Sweetwater, the courthouse was built beside a bayou almost halfway between the two towns. At the turn of the century, a diphtheria epidemic wiped out most of Sweetwater and now there was nothing left but a couple of dying churches.

Outside of Chester, Jake saw the courthouse sitting forlornly with cars parked around it. He could almost swear that one wing appeared to be leaning away from the central structure. He parked, went inside, and climbed the stairs to the second floor where he found the main courtroom dark and empty. He walked through it, past the ancient dusty pews for spectators, through the bar, and then stopped to take in the faded oils of dead politicians and judges, all old white men. Everything had a layer of dust, and the wastebaskets had not been emptied.

He opened a door at the back and said hello to the secretary. She managed a smile and nodded toward a door off to the side. Keep walking, he's waiting. Inside, "in chambers," Judge Noose was behind his square oak desk. Neat piles of papers covered its surface and gave the impression that, as disorganized as things appeared, he could locate any document in an instant.

"Come in, Jake," he said with a smile but without getting to his feet. An ashtray big enough for pasta held half a dozen pipes, and the air was thick with their stale aroma. Two massive windows were each cracked about eight inches.

"Good afternoon, Judge," Jake said as he made his way over, stepping around a coffee table, a magazine rack stuffed with old editions, stacks of lawbooks that belonged on shelves and not the floor, and two yellow Labs that were almost as old as their owner. Jake was certain that they had been puppies when he first visited Noose, over ten years ago. The dogs and His Honor had certainly aged, but everything else was timeless.

"Thanks for driving over, Jake. As you know, I had back surgery two months ago and I'm still recuperating. Pretty stiff down there, you know?"

Because of his gawky frame and long sloping nose, Noose had been tagged early on with the nickname of Ichabod. It seemed to fit, and when Jake started lawyering the nickname was so popular that everyone used it, behind his back, of course. But over time "Ichabod" had lost its popularity. At the moment, though, Jake remembered something Harry Rex had said years ago: "No one loves bad health like Ichabod Noose."

"No problem, Judge," Jake said.

"There are some issues we need to discuss," Noose said as he took a pipe, banged it on the edge of the ashtray, then hit it with a small flamethrower that almost singed his craggy eyebrows.

Oh really? Jake thought. Why else would you send for me? "Yes sir, a number of issues."

Noose sucked on the stem and filled his jaws. As he exhaled he said, "First of all, how's Lucien? We go way back, you know?"

"Yes sir. Lucien is, well, he's Lucien. Hasn't changed much but is hanging around the office more."

"Tell him I asked about him."

"I will." Lucien loathed Omar Noose, and Jake would never pass along the greeting.

"How's that kid doing, Mr. Gamble? Still at Whitfield?"

"Yes sir. I speak with his counselor almost every day and she says he's definitely dealing with trauma issues. She says he's improving a little, but the kid has a lot of damage, and not just because of the shooting. It'll take some time." It would take an hour to fully brief the judge on everything Dr. Sadie Weaver had told Jake, and they didn't have an hour. They would have the conversation later when a written report was received.

"I'd like to get him back in the jail in Clanton," Noose said, puffing.

Jake shrugged because he had no control over Drew's incarceration. However, he had said to Dr. Weaver that his client was much better off in a juvenile wing than in a county jail. "You can talk to them, Judge. You sent him down there and I'm sure his doctors would talk to you."

"I might do that." He put the pipe down and clasped his hands behind his head. "I gotta tell you, Jake, I can't get anyone else to take the case. God knows I've tried." He suddenly reached over, picked up a legal pad, and tossed it to the front of his desk as if Jake was supposed to have a look. "I've called seventeen lawyers, names are all right there, hell, you know most of them, seventeen lawyers with capital experience, from all over the state. I've talked to all of them on the phone, Jake, and some more than others. I've begged, pleaded, cajoled, and I would have threatened but I have no jurisdiction outside the Twenty-second. You know that. And nothing. Not a one. Nobody is willing to step up. I've called all the nonprofits—the Children's Capital Defense Fund, the Juvenile Justice Initiative, the ACLU, and others. The names are all right there. They are very sympathetic and would like to help, and may indeed help, but right now nobody can spare a trial lawyer to defend this kid. You have any ideas?"

"No, but you promised, Judge."

"I know that, and I meant it, but at the time I was desperate. I'm in charge of the judicial system in these parts, Jake, and it all fell on me to make sure this kid was taken care of, legally. You know what I went through. I had no choice. You were man enough to step up when everybody else was hiding under their desks and running from the phone. Now I'm asking you to keep it, Jake, keep this case and make sure this defendant gets a fair trial."

"Obviously, you plan to deny my motion to move it to youth court."

"Of course. I'm keeping jurisdiction for a lot of reasons, Jake. If he goes through youth court he'll be out when he's eighteen. You think that's fair?"

"No, not in theory. Not at all."

"Good, then we agree. He stays in circuit court and you're his lawyer."

"But, Judge, I'm not going to let this case bankrupt me. I practice alone and have a limited staff. So far, since your first phone call on March twenty-fifth, I have spent forty-one hours on this case and the work has just begun. As you know, the state legislature caps attorney's fees in indigent cases at one thousand dollars. Hard to believe, Judge, but a fee of one thousand dollars for a capital defense is a joke. I have to get paid, Judge."

"I'll make sure you get paid."

"But how, Judge. The statute is pretty clear."

"I know, I know, believe me I understand, Jake. It's an outrageous law and I've written letters to our lawmakers. I have an idea, something that's never been done, at least not in the Twenty-second. You keep up with your hours, and when the case is over you submit a bill to the county. When the supervisors refuse to pay, then sue them in circuit court. I'll handle the case and I'll rule in your favor. How about that?"

"It's definitely a novel idea. Never heard of it."

"It'll work because I'll make it work. We'll have a quick trial with no jury and I'll see that you get paid."

"But that's months away."

"That's the best we can do, Jake. The law is the law."

"So I'll get a thousand dollars now and pray for the rest."

"It's the best we can do."

"What about experts?"

"What about them?"

"Come on, Judge. The State will have all manner of shrinks and mental health professionals at its disposal to testify."

"Are you implying an insanity defense?"

"No, I'm not implying anything. I still can't believe I'm getting stuck with the damned case."

"And the family has no money?"

"Are you serious? They're homeless. They're wearing second- and third-hand clothing. Their relatives, wherever they are, washed their hands years ago, and they'd be starving right now if not for the generosity of a church."

"Okay, okay, just had to ask. I figured as much. I'll do what I can, Jake, to make sure you get paid."

"That's not good enough, Judge. I want a promise from you that I'll get paid a lot more than a thousand bucks."

"I promise I'll do everything within my power to see that you get paid for a proper defense."

Jake took a deep breath and told himself that it was time to accept the fact that the Gamble case belonged to him. Noose fiddled with another pipe and stuffed its bowl full of dark tobacco. He grinned at Jake with his brown teeth and said, "I'll sweeten the pot."

"*Smallwood?*"

"*Smallwood*. I'll set a trial date a week from next Monday, April twenty-third. I won't put up with Sean Gilder's nonsense and will insist that we're picking a jury bright and early that morning. I'll call Gilder and Walter Sullivan within the hour. How's that?"

"Thank you."

"Are you ready for trial, Jake?"

"I've been ready."

"Any chance of a settlement?"

"Right now that appears unlikely."

"I want you to win this case, Jake. Don't get me wrong. I will remain an unbiased referee whose job is to guarantee a fair trial. But I'd love to see you pop Gilder and Sullivan and that railroad for a big verdict."

"So would I, Judge. I need it."

Noose puffed and chewed on the stem. He said, "You and I are not very popular right now, Jake, judging by this stack of letters I've received from Ford County, and from phone calls, some anonymous, some not. They think we've already found the boy insane and let him off. Are you worried about this during jury selection?"

"Well, yes, Harry Rex and I have discussed it. He's more worried than I am because I still believe we can find twelve jurors with open minds."

"So do I. We'll take our time and screen them carefully. Let's bring the boy back from Whitfield so the hotheads will know he's back in jail, awaiting trial and not getting released on some technicality. I think that'll appease some folks. You agree?"

Jake said, "Yes," but wasn't sure he meant it. Noose had a point. If Drew was back in Ozzie's jail and awaiting trial, the locals might settle down.

Noose said, "I'll call the clerk and get the jury list released tomorrow. I think a hundred names should suffice, don't you?"

"Yes sir." One hundred was about average for a civil trial.

Noose took his time cleaning another pipe. He carefully added more tobacco, lit the pipe, savored the smoke, then stood, unfolding his lanky frame out of the chair with some effort. He walked to a window and gazed out as if taking in a beautiful landscape. Without turning around, he said, over his shoulder, "Something else, Jake, something off the record. Okay?" He seemed burdened with an unpleasant thought.

"Sure, Judge."

"I once made a living as a politician and was quite good at it. Then the voters called me home and I had to go clean and make an honest living. I've worked hard as a judge and I'd like to think I've grown into this job. Been here for eighteen years, never had a serious opponent. My reputation is pretty solid, right, Jake?" He turned around and looked down his long nose.

"I'd say it's very solid, Judge."

Noose sucked on his pipe and watched the smoke swirl near the ceiling. "I have come to despise judicial elections. Politics should be kept out of the judiciary at all levels. I know that's easy for me to say because I've been on the bench for a long time. Incumbency has its advantages. But it's sort of unseemly for judges to be forced to shake hands and kiss babies and hustle for votes, don't you agree, Jake?"

"Yes sir. It's a bad system." As bad as it seemed, the truth was that judges were rarely challenged and almost never defeated. Most ambitious lawyers considered it financial suicide to run against a sitting judge, and lose. Jake suspected Rufus Buckley was very much on Noose's mind.

He said, "It appears as though I'll have an opponent next year."

"I've heard the rumors."

"Your old pal Buckley."

"I still despise him, Judge. I guess I always will."

"He blamed me for the Hailey acquittal. Blamed

you. Blamed everyone but himself. He's been stewing for five years, plotting revenge. When he lost the D.A.'s race three years ago he became so depressed he had to seek help, at least according to my sources in Smithfield. Now he's back and he's running his mouth. Thinks the public needs him sitting on the bench in my chair. Last Friday at the Rotary Club he babbled on about the Kofer case, said you had hoodwinked the court again and convinced me to release the boy."

"I'm not worried about the Rotary Club gossip in Smithfield, Judge."

"Of course not, but your name won't be on the ballot there, now will it?"

"Judge, look, the last time Buckley ran he lost four out of five counties, and Lowell Dyer was an unknown."

"I know, I know. It wasn't close."

Jake was surprised that the conversation had shifted so quickly from business to politics. Noose had never let his guard down and become so personal. He was obviously worried about a campaign that was months away and might never happen.

Jake said, "Ford County has more voters than the other four, and your reputation there is stellar. The bar is solidly behind you for all the right reasons, and the bar utterly loathes Rufus Buckley. You'll be in good shape, Judge."

Noose returned to his desk and added the pipe to the collection in the pasta bowl. He did not sit down but rubbed his hands together as if to say, "Done."

"Thanks, Jake. Let's keep an eye on Buckley."

Jake stood and said, "Will do. I'll see you early in the morning a week from Monday."

They shook hands and Jake left in a hurry. In his car, he called Harry Rex, bluffed his way past two rude secretaries, and finally delivered the wonderful news that a trial date was set and they would know the names of the potential jurors within twenty-four hours.

Harry Rex bellowed loud enough for his entire office to hear, then cackled into the phone, "I've already got the list."

20

A sizable chunk of the funds from the litigation loan at Stan's bank had been used to pay the fee of a fancy jury consultant named Murray Silerberg. He owned a firm based in Atlanta and boasted of securing huge verdicts for the past twenty years. Jake had heard him speak at a convention of trial lawyers and was mightily impressed. Harry Rex didn't want to spend the money, and claimed he could pick a jury better than anyone else in the state. Jake had to remind his friend that he had not picked a jury in ten years because he realized back then that jurors didn't like him. They had spent a day driving to Atlanta to meet Murray Silerberg, after which Harry Rex reluctantly got on board. The fee was a flat $20,000, plus travel expenses.

Jake made the call to Stan and said hit the credit line. Stan once again told him he was crazy, to which Jake replied, in true trial lawyer fashion, "Gotta spend money to make money." It was true—litigation loans were becoming popular across the country, and trial lawyers, ever eager to brag about their verdicts, had begun bragging about how much they borrowed and spent convincing juries.

Silerberg's firm studied every civil verdict in the country, with a special interest in the Deep South and Florida. Most of their clients, and verdicts, were close to home. A partner followed verdicts in urban areas, while Silerberg was fascinated with small towns and counties where the juries were much more conservative.

When he got the green light from Jake, he immediately began polling rural voters in north Mississippi to gauge their attitudes about courts, lawyers, and lawsuits. The polling was extensive and included hypothetical cases involving parents and children killed in auto accidents.

At the same time, an investigative team working for Silerberg began digging through the backgrounds of the names on the golden list. The *Smallwood* suite had been a large, empty storage space for years, but when Jake filed suit thirteen months earlier it was converted to a war room. The investigators took it over and were soon thumbtacking sheets of paper and enlarged photos on all four walls. Photos of the homes, trailers, apartments, cars, trucks, and places of employment of the prospective jurors. They dug through land records, court filings and dockets, anything that was in the public domain. They were careful and tried not to be seen, but several prospective jurors complained later that they saw strangers with cameras in their neighborhoods.

Of the ninety-seven names, eight were soon confirmed to be dead. Jake knew only seven of those still living, and as he studied the list he once again marveled at how few names he recognized. He had lived his entire life in Ford County, population 32,000, and thought he had a lot of friends. Harry Rex claimed to know something about twenty of the potential jurors.

The early polling was less than encouraging. Not surprisingly, Murray Silerberg knew that juries in the rural South are suspicious of big verdicts and tight with money, even when it belonged to large corporations. It was extremely difficult to convince hardworking people to hand over a million dollars when they were living from paycheck to paycheck. Jake was well aware of this. He had never asked a jury for seven figures, but even so he had been burned. A year earlier, he got a bit carried away and demanded $100,000 from a jury in a case that was worth less than half of that. A split jury gave him only $26,000 and the case was on appeal. Harry Rex watched the closing arguments and thought Jake alienated some of the jurors by asking for too much.

The lawyers and their high-priced consultant knew the dangers of appearing greedy.

Privately, though, Jake and Harry Rex were delighted with the list. There were more prospects under the age of fifty than over it, and that should translate into younger parents with more sympathy. Old white jurors were the most conservative. The county was 26 percent black, and so was the list, a high number. In most white counties, blacks registered to vote in lower numbers. They were also known to be more sympathetic for the little guy battling the corporation. And Harry Rex claimed to know two "ringers," men who could be persuaded to see things the plaintiffs' way.

The mood around Jake's office changed dramatically. Gone were the worries about defending Drew Gamble and dealing with that tragedy. They were quickly replaced with the excitement of a major trial and the endless preparations for it.

BUT THE GAMBLE case was not going away. For reasons having more to do with overcrowding than proper care, Drew needed to leave Whitfield. After eighteen days, his doctor, Sadie Weaver, was ordered to ship him back to Clanton because his bed was needed by another juvenile. She telephoned Judge Noose, Jake, and Sheriff Walls. Ozzie was delighted to get the kid back in his jail, and tipped off Dumas Lee at *The Ford County*

Times. When the defendant arrived in the backseat of a patrol car driven by the sheriff himself, Dumas was waiting and clicked away. The following day, a large photo appeared on the front page under the bold headline: **"KOFER SUSPECT BACK IN CLANTON JAIL."**

Dumas reported that, according to Lowell Dyer, the district attorney, the defendant had been served with his indictment and they were awaiting a first appearance in court. No trial date had been set. Jake was quoted as offering a "No comment." Same for Judge Noose. An unnamed source (Jake) told Dumas that it was not at all unusual in serious cases to have the defendant examined at Whitfield. Another anonymous voice predicted a trial by midsummer.

AT 8:00 A.M. on Saturday, Jake met a group of people at the rear door of the courthouse, which was closed for business. Using a borrowed key, he unlocked it and herded them up a service stairway to the main courtroom where the lights were on and his team was waiting. He seated them, thirteen in all, in the jury box, and then introduced Harry Rex, Lucien Wilbanks, Portia Lang, and Murray Silerberg and one of his assistants. The courtroom was locked and, of course, there were no spectators.

He called thirteen names, thanked them for their time, and passed out thirteen checks of $300 each (another $3,900 from their litigation loan). He explained that mock juries were often used in big civil cases and he hoped the experience would be pleasant. The mock trial would consume most of the day and there would be a nice lunch in just a few hours.

Of the thirteen, seven were women, four were black,

and five were under the age of fifty. They were friends and former clients of Jake's and Harry Rex's. One of the black ladies was Portia's aunt.

Lucien assumed his place up on the bench, and for a moment seemed to enjoy being a judge. Harry Rex moved to the defense table. Jake began the trial with a scaled-down version of his opening statement. Everything would be scaled down for the sake of time. They had one day to complete the mock trial. The real one was expected to last for at least three.

On a large screen he showed color photos of Taylor and Sarah Smallwood and their three children, and talked about how close the family was. He showed photos of the crash scene, the demolished car, and the train. A state trooper had returned to the site the following day and taken a series of photos of the warning lights. Jake showed them to the jurors, and several shook their heads in disbelief at the badly maintained system.

Wrapping it up, Jake planted the seed for a big verdict by discussing money. He explained that, unfortunately, in death cases the only measure of damages was money. In other cases, the defendants could be forced to take remedial action. But not here. There was no other way to compensate the Smallwood heirs than with a money verdict.

Harry Rex, for the first and last time in his career in the role of an insurance defense lawyer, went next with his opening statement, and began dramatically with a large color photo of the fourteenth boxcar, the one struck by the Smallwoods. It was fifteen feet high and forty feet long, and it was equipped, like all railroad cars, with a set of reflective strips that when hit with headlights emitted a bright yellow glow that could be seen for three hundred yards. No one would ever know what Taylor Smallwood saw or didn't see in that final crucial second, but what he should have seen was quite obvious.

As a defense lawyer, Harry Rex was good, sufficiently dubious of the plaintiff's case, and most of the jurors followed him closely.

The first witness was Hank Grayson, played by Murray Silerberg's assistant, Nate Feathers. Eight months earlier, Mr. Grayson had been deposed in Jake's office, and he swore, under oath, that he was about a hundred yards behind the Smallwoods when the crash occurred. For a split second he wasn't sure what happened and by the time he hit his brakes he almost hit their car, which had gone airborne and spun 180 degrees. The train was still moving by. Most important, the red warning lights were not flashing.

Jake had always worried about Grayson. He believed the man was telling the truth—he had nothing to gain by lying—but he was timid, could not maintain eye contact, and had a squeaky voice. In other words, he did not project veracity. Plus, on the night in question he had been drinking.

Harry Rex pounced on this during cross-examination. Grayson stuck to his story of having only three beers at a joint down the road. He was far from drunk, knew exactly what he had seen, and spoke with several policemen in the aftermath. Not a single officer asked him if he had been drinking.

In the mock trial, Nate Feathers, the jury consultant, was a far better witness than the real Grayson would ever be.

The next witness was a railroad-crossing expert, played by Silerberg, who was holding a copy of their expert's deposition and knew his testimony well. Using the enlarged photos, Jake proved in abundant detail that Central & Southern had done a lousy job maintaining the crossing. The lenses over the red flashing lights were choked with dirt, some were broken. One pole was leaning. Paint was peeling from around the lights. On cross, Harry Rex argued a few points but didn't score.

So far, Lucien had said little and appeared to be napping, just like a real judge.

The next witness was another railroad safety expert, played by Portia Lang. She explained to the jury the various warning systems now used by railroads at their crossings. The one used by Central & Southern was at least forty years old and badly outdated. She described its shortcomings in abundant detail.

At ten o'clock, Judge Lucien woke up long enough to call for a recess. Coffee and doughnuts were passed to the jurors as everyone took a break. After the recess, Lucien told Jake to proceed. He called to the stand Dr. Robert Samson, professor of economics at Ole Miss, played by none other than Stan Atcavage, who would rather have been on the golf course, but Jake would not take no for an answer. As Jake had explained, if Stan were really worried about the litigation loan, he should do anything to help the cause. Stan was definitely worried about the loan. The real Dr. Samson was charging $15,000 for his testimony at the real trial.

The testimony was dull and filled with too many numbers. The expert's bottom line was that Taylor and Sarah Smallwood would have earned $2.2 million if they had worked for another thirty years. Harry Rex scored a few points on cross by pointing out that Sarah had always been a part-timer and that Taylor changed jobs frequently.

The next witness was Nate Feathers again, this time in the role of the state trooper who investigated the accident. After him, Portia was back as the doctor who pronounced the family dead.

Jake decided to rest the plaintiff's case at that point. At trial, he planned to call two close relatives to the stand to personalize the family and hopefully rouse up some sympathy, but that would be difficult with a mock jury.

Lucien, who by noon was thoroughly bored with life on the bench, said he was hungry and Jake broke for lunch. He led the entire group out of the courthouse and across the street to the Coffee Shop where Dell had a long table waiting with ice tea and sandwiches. Jake had asked the jurors not to discuss the case until their deliberations, but he and Harry Rex and Silerberg couldn't help themselves. They sat at one end of the table and replayed the testimony and the reactions from the jurors. Silerberg was delighted with Jake's opening statement. He had carefully watched each juror and thought all were on board. However, he was worried about the simplicity of the defense: How does an alert driver not see a moving train covered with reflective lights? Back and forth they went at their end of the table, while the mock jurors chatted among themselves over a free lunch.

His Honor went home for lunch and returned in a better mood, no doubt bolstered by a cocktail or two. He called things to order and the trial reconvened at 1:30.

For the defense, Harry Rex called the train's engineer to the stand. Portia played the role and read his sworn testimony from a deposition taken eight months earlier. He testified that he had twenty years' experience with Central & Southern and had never been involved in an accident. One of the most important rituals of his job was to monitor the warning lights at each crossing as the engine passed them. On the night in question, he was absolutely certain the red flashing lights were working properly. No, he did not see vehicles approaching on the highway. He felt a bump, knew something had happened, stopped the train, put it in reverse, saw the wreckage, then moved the train so rescue units could approach from both directions.

On cross, Jake revisited the large color photos of the poorly maintained lights, and asked the engineer if he expected the jury to believe that they worked "perfectly."

Harry Rex called an expert (Murray Silerberg again) who had not only inspected the crossing system but had tested it just days after the accident. Not surprisingly, everything worked perfectly. Regardless of its age, there was no reason for the system not to work. He showed the jury a video that explained the circuitry and wiring, and everything made sense. Sure, the lights and poles could use some work, or even replacing, but their aged condition did not mean that they didn't work. He showed another video of the crossing at night with a similar train passing. The bright reflectors practically blinded the jurors.

At the real trial, Central & Southern would be required to park a corporate officer at the defense table to represent the company. Jake couldn't wait to get his hands on the guy. Through discovery he had obtained a stack of internal memos and reports documenting forty years of near-misses at the crossing. Drivers had been complaining. Neighbors could tell stories of close calls. Miraculously, no one had been killed, but there had been at least three accidents since 1970.

Jake planned to slaughter the executive in front of the jury, and he and Harry Rex believed it would be the most crucial part of the trial. For the mock version, though, they couldn't create the right drama, so they had decided to prepare some stipulated facts that His

Honor would simply read. Lucien finally had something to do and seemed to enjoy the moment. A nighttime accident in 1970, with the car's driver claiming the warning lights were not working. Another one in 1982, with no injuries. Another in 1986, with the crash narrowly averted by an alert driver who managed to skid into a ditch and avoid the passing train. Six memos detailing complaints from other drivers. Three memos with complaints from people living near the crossing.

Even when recited in a flat monotone from the bench, the facts were damning enough. Some of the jurors shook their heads in disbelief as Lucien droned on.

In his closing argument, Jake hammered away at the railroad's antiquated system and its "grossly" negligent maintenance. He waved the internal memos and reports that proved the "arrogance" of a company that cared nothing for safety. He delicately asked the jury for money, and lots of it. It was impossible to quantify with dollars the value of a human life, but they had no choice. He suggested a million dollars for each of the Smallwoods. And he asked for five million in punitive damages to punish the railroad and force it to finally upgrade the crossing.

Harry Rex disagreed. He said nine million dollars was an outrageous sum that would do nothing to help anyone. It certainly couldn't bring back the family. The railroad had already renovated the crossing.

Jake thought Harry Rex lost some steam about halfway through his closing, and it was probably because he really wanted the nine million and felt silly trying to belittle it.

After he sat down, Judge Wilbanks read some instructions to the jurors and asked them to pay close attention to the legal concept of comparative negligence. If they were inclined to find against the railroad, then their award could be reduced because of the negligence of Taylor Smallwood, if they indeed found him to be at fault to any degree. He said that in a real trial there was no time limit on deliberations, but today they would have only one hour. Portia led them back to the jury room and made sure they had coffee.

Jake, Harry Rex, Murray Silerberg, and Nate Feathers gathered around the defense table and broke down the trial. Lucien had had enough and left. The jurors might be getting $300 for the day but he was being paid nothing.

Forty-five minutes later, Portia was back with the jury. The foreman said they were split: nine in favor of the plaintiff, two in favor of the railroad, and two on the fence. The majority would award $4 million, then reduce it by 50 percent because they felt Taylor Smallwood was also negligent. Only three of the nine would award punitive damages.

Jake invited all of the jurors to join the discussion but also said they were free to leave. They had earned their money and he was thankful. At first, no one left and they were eager to talk. He explained that in a civil case with twelve jurors only nine had to agree on a verdict. In criminal cases, a unanimous verdict was required. One juror asked if the railroad was required to produce an officer to sit through the trial. Jake said yes, one would be sitting at that very table and he would be called to the stand.

Another was confused by the economic-loss testimony of Dr. Samson. Harry Rex said he was too and got a laugh.

Another wanted to know how much of any verdict went to the attorneys. Jake tried to dodge it by saying that their contract with the family was confidential.

Another asked how much the experts were paid, and by whom?

Another asked if the railroad had insurance coverage. Jake said yes, but it could not be revealed in court.

A couple of jurors then left, but the others wanted to stay and talk. Jake had promised to turn off the lights at 5:00 P.M., and Portia finally told him it was time to go. They left down the back stairway, and once outside Jake thanked them again for their time and trouble. Almost all of them seemed to enjoy the experience.

HALF AN HOUR later, Jake walked through the rear door of Harry Rex's office building and found him in the conference room, cold beer in hand. Jake fetched one from the fridge and they fell into chairs in his library. They were thrilled with the day and the verdict.

"We got nine votes for two million dollars," Jake said, savoring the mock win.

"They liked you, Jake. I could see it in their eyes, the way they followed you around the courtroom."

"And our experts are better than theirs, in the flesh, and Sarah Smallwood's sister will make everyone cry with her testimony."

"That, plus a good mauling of the railroad officer, and we might get more than two."

"I'll take two."

"Hell, Jake, right now I'd take a lousy million."

"A lousy million. This county has never seen a million-dollar verdict."

"Don't get greedy. How much do we owe right now?"

"Sixty-nine thousand."

"Say they offer a million. The expenses come off the top. Forty percent of the rest is, what, three hundred and seventy thousand? Half for you, half for me, about one-eighty-five each. Would you take a hundred and eighty-five thousand dollars right now and walk away?"

"No, I'd sprint."

"Me too."

They had a laugh and gulped some beer. Harry Rex wiped his mouth and said, "This needs to play in Jackson. What would Sean Gilder do if he knew a mock jury in Clanton, in the same courtroom, gave us two million dollars?"

"I love it. Who do you tell?"

"Let's go through Walter Sullivan. Let him find out, because he thinks he's the man around here. Word will spread pretty fast."

"Not in this town."

21

The collision of a small car weighing three thousand pounds with the wheel unit of a loaded boxcar weighing seventy-five tons created a nasty accident scene. Once it was determined by the first responders that all four occupants were dead, some of the urgency subsided as the crews went about the grim task of prying and cutting out the bodies. Over two dozen officers and rescue personnel were at the site, along with other travelers who happened upon the scene and couldn't pass around it. A state trooper took a series of still shots, and a volunteer from a local fire brigade filled four rolls of film with the recovery and cleanup.

Early in discovery, Jake obtained sets of all the photos and had them enlarged. Over a three-month period, he meticulously collected the names of the responders and the strangers who watched them work. Identifying the firemen, police, and medics was easy. He spent time in three volunteer firehouses out in the county, as well as two from the town of Clanton. Everyone, it seemed, answered the call.

Putting names with the faces of the strangers was a far greater challenge. He was looking for witnesses, anyone who might have seen anything. Hank Grayson, the only known eyewitness, said in his deposition that he thought there was a car behind him, though he made it clear he wasn't certain. Jake went through every photograph and slowly collected the names of the people at the site. Most were from Ford County, and some admitted they showed up when they heard the chatter on their police scanners. At least a dozen were late-night travelers who got stuck on the road during the three hours it took to remove the bodies and clear the scene. Jake tracked down each one of these. Not a one had witnessed the accident; indeed, most arrived long after it happened.

But in six of the photos, there was a white man with a bald head who looked out of place. He was about fifty, wore a dark suit, white shirt, dark tie, much too nicely dressed for rural Ford County on a Friday night. He stood with other spectators and watched as the firemen cut and sawed to remove the four bodies. No one seemed to know him. Jake asked the first responders about the man, but no one had ever seen him. In Jake's world, he became the mysterious stranger, the man in the dark suit.

Melvin Cochran lived a quarter of a mile from the crossing and was awakened that night by sirens. He got dressed, went outside, saw the carnival-like scene down the hill, and grabbed his video camera. As he walked to the scene, with the switch on, he began to pass cars parked on the shoulder, all headed east. Once at the scene, he filmed for almost an hour before the battery ran low. Jake got a copy of the video and had watched it, frame by frame, for hours. The man in the dark suit was in several scenes, observing the tragedy, at times seemingly bored and wanting to move on.

As Melvin approached the site, he passed a total of eleven parked vehicles. Jake was able to identify the license plates on seven of them. The others were obscured. Five of the seven were from Ford County, one was from Tyler County, and one was from Tennessee. He doggedly tracked down each one and eventually matched the vehicles with the names and faces of their owners in the crowd.

On a wall in a workroom, Jake cut and pasted and pieced together a large composite of the scene with small nameplates for twenty-six rescue personnel and thirty-two spectators. Everyone was identified, except the man in the dark suit.

The vehicle with Tennessee plates was registered to a food brokerage firm in Nashville; thus, no individual name was available. For a month Jake considered this to be a dead end, which didn't bother him. He figured that if the mysterious man had seen anything relevant he would have spoken to an officer on the scene. But it nagged him. The man had an odd look about him, and Jake was chasing every detail. The case could be the biggest one of his career and he was determined to know everything about it.

He would later curse his curiosity.

He finally paid $250 to a private investigator in Nashville and sent him a photo of the mystery man. Two days later, the investigator faxed Jake a report, one that he at first wanted to destroy. It read:

I went to the corporate address with the photo and asked around. I was directed to the office of Mr. Neal Nickel, a district rep of some sort. He was obviously the man in the photo and I showed it to him. He was surprised that I had found him and he asked how I did so. I said I was working for some of the lawyers involved with the case but did not give any names. We talked for maybe fifteen minutes. Nice guy, with nothing to hide. He said he had been to the wedding of a relative down in Vicksburg and was on his way back home. He lives in a suburb

of Nashville. Said he was not familiar with
Highway 88 but thought it might save some
time. As he crossed into Ford County he began
to follow a pickup truck, one that was all over
the road. So he backed off and gave the guy
plenty of room, said the driver was obviously
drunk. As they went down a hill, he saw the
highway signs indicating a crossing ahead. Then
he saw the red warning lights flashing at the
foot of the hill. There was a loud noise. He
thought at first it was an explosion of some sort.
Then the truck in front of him hit the brakes
and swerved. NN stopped in the road and
hurried to the scene on foot. The train was still
passing. The crossing lights were still flashing red.
The warning bell was still ringing. The driver of
the truck was yelling at him. Steam and smoke
were coming from the wrecked car. He could
see small children crushed in the rear seat. The
train stopped, then moved backward and cleared
the crossing. By then other drivers were
stopping, and before long the first policeman
and ambulance arrived. The road was blocked
and he couldn't pass so he had no choice but to
hang around and watch. For three hours. He
said it was pretty gruesome watching the
recovery of four dead people, especially when
they pulled the little kids out. Said he had
nightmares for weeks, wished he hadn't seen it.

I made sure he was clear about the warning
lights. He said he heard the driver of the truck
tell a state trooper that the lights were not
working, and he started to say something. But
he refused to get involved. He refuses to get
involved now. Wants nothing to do with the

case. I asked him why and he said he was
involved in a bad car wreck years ago and he got
blamed for it. Had to go to trial and he has a
strong dislike for lawyers and courts. Also, NN
has a lot of sympathy for the family and doesn't
want to hurt their case.

Interesting note: He said that a few months
ago he was in the area, near Clanton, stopped by
the courthouse and asked if he could see the file
with the lawsuit. They said it was public record,
so he read some of it and was amused to see that
the witness, the driver of the pickup, Mr.
Grayson was still saying that the lights were not
working.

NN definitely wants to stay out of this.

When he was sure he wasn't going to vomit, Jake
managed to walk gingerly to the sofa and lie down. He
pinched his nose and closed his eyes and saw his fortune fly away.

Not only was Nickel a far more credible witness, he
could confirm that Hank Grayson, their star, was drinking that night.

When he could finally move, Jake folded the report
into an unmarked envelope, resisted the temptation to
burn it, and hid it in a thick lawbook where maybe it
would vanish, or maybe he would just simply forget
about it.

If Nickel wanted to avoid the trial, that was fine
with Jake. They would keep the same secret.

The fear, though, was the defense. Seven months
into the lawsuit, Sean Gilder had shown little interest in
the case and had only gone through the motions of
discovery. He had filed one set of standard interrogatories and requested the basic documents. They had

agreed to depose a few of the key witnesses. Jake estimated that he had put in three times the hours as the
defense lawyers who actually got paid by the hour.

If Neal Nickel insisted on lying low, there was a
good chance he would not be discovered by anybody
working on behalf of the railroad or its insurance company. And barring a sudden change of conscience, he
would get his wish of staying out of any lawsuit.

So why did Jake spend the next three days with a
knot in his stomach? The big question was Harry Rex.
Should he show him the report and watch him freak
out? Or should Jake simply bury it, along with any
knowledge of the mysterious eyewitness? The quandary roiled Jake's world for days, but with time he managed to shove it into another compartment and
concentrate on the rest of the case.

Two months later, on January 9, 1990, to be exact,
the issue returned with a vengeance. Sean Gilder filed a
second set of interrogatories that sought answers he already had, for the most part. Again, he appeared listless
and totally unimaginative. Jake and Harry Rex had become convinced that Gilder was not sandbagging, a
common defense tactic. Rather, it appeared as if Gilder
was overconfident because of the fact that Taylor Smallwood drove into a moving train. End of case.

But the last interrogatory, number thirty in a package of thirty, was lethal. It was one that was commonly
used, especially by lazy or busy lawyers. It read: "List the
full name, complete address, and phone number of any
and all persons with knowledge of the alleged facts of
this case."

Also known as "the Round-Up," it was a much debated, and hated, tactic that punished lawyers who
worked overtime and dug for the facts. Under the rules
of discovery, trials were supposed to be free of am-

bushes. Each side swapped all information and it was laid in a transparent fashion before the jury. That was the theory, anyway, the goal. But the new rules created unfair practices, and the Round-Up was widely despised. It said, in other words: "Work diligently to learn all the facts, then hand them to the other side on a platter."

Two days after receiving the second set of interrogatories, Jake finally placed the investigator's report on the large, messy desk in front of Harry Rex. He picked it up, read it, dropped it, and without hesitation said, "There goes the lawsuit. There goes the case. Why did you find this clown?"

"I was simply doing my job." As Jake told the story of finding Nickel, Harry Rex kicked back in his chair and stared at the ceiling. "Devastating," he mumbled more than once.

When Jake finished, he mentioned the last set of interrogatories. Without a thought, Harry Rex said, "We are not going to mention this guy. Ever. Okay?"

"Fine with me. As long as we understand the risks."

THREE MONTHS LATER, the man in the dark suit was back.

As the clerk assembled and organized the crowd of prospective jurors, and as the lawyers in their courtroom suits situated themselves around their tables and dug in for battle, and as the courthouse regulars found their places in the pews and chatted excitedly about the big trial, Sean Gilder stepped over to Jake and whispered, "We need to see the judge. It's important."

Jake was half expecting the usual last-minute maneuvering and was not alarmed. "What is it?"

"I'll explain back there."

Jake motioned for Mr. Pete, the ancient courtroom deputy, and said they needed to see Noose, who was still in chambers. Seven lawyers followed Mr. Pete out of the courtroom. They gathered before Judge Noose, who was putting on his black robe and seemed eager to start a big trial. He looked at the grim faces of Sean Gilder, Walter Sullivan, and the other lawyers, and said, "Morning, gentlemen. What's the issue?"

Gilder was holding some papers, and he sort of waved them at His Honor. "Judge, this is a motion for a continuance that we are filing right now and asking the court to grant."

"Grounds?"

"This may take a few moments, Judge. Perhaps we should sit down."

Noose gestured awkwardly at the chairs around his conference table and everybody found one.

"Proceed."

"Judge, last Friday my co-counsel, Mr. Walter Sullivan, was approached by a man who claimed to be an important witness to this accident. His name is Neal Nickel and he lives near Nashville. Mr. Sullivan?"

Walter eagerly jumped in. "Judge, the guy walked into my office and said he really needed to talk to me about the case. We had coffee and he described how he saw the Smallwood car hit the train on that terrible night. He saw it all, the perfect eyewitness."

Jake's heart and lungs were frozen and he felt ill. Harry Rex glared at Sullivan and wished he had a gun.

"A crucial issue here is whether or not the warning lights were working properly. The two railroad employees on the train swear they were flashing. One witness says they were not. Mr. Nickel is certain that they were working. However, for reasons he can explain, he did not approach an officer that night and, until now, has told no one about the incident. Obviously, he is an important witness, one that we should have the right to depose."

Noose said bluntly, "Discovery is over. The deadline was months ago. Looks like you should've found this witness before now."

Gilder took over. "True, Your Honor, but there is another problem. Back during discovery we filed, on time, some interrogatories, and one requested the names of all witnesses. When Mr. Brigance filed his responses, he did not mention Neal Nickel. Not a word. However, Mr. Nickel will tell you that he was approached last November by a private investigator working for a lawyer in Clanton, Mississippi. Didn't have his name but it was most certainly not Walter Sullivan. We quickly found the investigator and he confirmed that he was hired and paid by Jake Brigance. He submitted a two-page report summarizing what Mr. Nickel had told him."

Gilder paused, rather smugly, and looked at Jake, who was trying mightily to conjure up a believable lie that would extricate him from this catastrophe. But his brain was frozen and all efforts at creativity failed him miserably.

Gilder went on, sinking the knife deeper. "And so it's obvious, Your Honor, that Mr. Brigance found the eyewitness, Mr. Neal Nickel, and once he realized that the witness was in no way favorable, but actually quite adverse to his cause, he conveniently tried to forget about him. He violated our rules of discovery by trying to hide a crucial witness."

Harry Rex was far more crooked and devious than Jake, and turned to him and said, "I thought you supplemented those responses." It was the perfect, and perhaps only, statement to interject. Answers to interrogatories were routinely amended and supplemented as more information became available.

But Harry Rex was a divorce lawyer and thus accustomed to bluffing around judges. Jake, though, was an amateur. He managed to mumble, "I thought so too." But it was a pathetic effort and not at all believable.

Sean Gilder and Walter Sullivan both laughed, and the other three dark suits on their side of the table joined in the awful humor. Judge Noose held the motion and looked at Jake in disbelief.

Sean Gilder said, "Oh, right! I'm sure you wanted to supplement and hand us Neal Nickel, but you forgot, and you've been forgetting for five months now. Nice try, gentlemen. Judge, we have the right to depose this man."

Judge Noose raised a hand and demanded silence. For a long moment, maybe two or three, or it could have been an hour as far as Jake was concerned, he read the motion for a continuance and began to slowly shake his head. Finally, he looked at Jake and said, "This appears to be a rather obvious effort on the part of the plaintiff to hide a witness. Jake?"

Jake almost said something like "Not at all, Your Honor," but he held his tongue. If the investigator was sleazy enough to reveal the name of the lawyer who hired him, then he probably sent Sean Gilder a copy of his report. When Gilder produced it, the ax would fall. Again.

Jake shrugged and said, "Don't know, Judge. I thought we supplemented. Must've been an oversight."

Noose frowned and fired back. "That's hard to believe, Jake. An oversight for a witness this important? Don't feed me a line, Jake. You found a witness that you wished you hadn't found. Then you violated a rule of discovery. I'm appalled by this."

Not even Harry Rex could rescue him with a snappy retort. All five defense lawyers were grinning like idiots as Jake slid lower into his chair.

Noose tossed the motion onto the table and said, "Certainly, you have the right to depose this witness. Any idea where he might be?"

Quickly, Walter Sullivan said, "He left for Mexico on Saturday. For two weeks."

Harry Rex blurted, "Courtesy of Central & Southern Railroad?"

"Hell no. It's his vacation. And he said he's not giving depositions down there."

Noose waved a hand. "Enough. This complicates matters, gentlemen. I'm going to allow this witness to be deposed at a time that's convenient for everyone, so I'll grant the motion for a continuance."

Gilder pounced with "Judge, I've also prepared a motion for sanctions. This is an egregious breach of ethics on the part of the plaintiffs' lawyers, and it will cost money to reconvene somewhere to have a chat with Mr. Nickel. They should be required to pay for it and cover the expenses."

Noose shrugged and said, "But you're getting paid anyway."

"Just double-bill them," Harry Rex said. "Same as always."

Jake lost his cool and said, "Why should we be required to hand over information that you couldn't find if you'd hired the FBI? You guys sat on your asses for the first seven months and did nothing. Now you want us to feed you our work product?"

"So you admit you concealed the witness?" Gilder asked.

"No. The witness was there, at the scene and at home in Nashville. You just couldn't find him."

"And you violated the discovery rule?"

"It's a bad rule and you know it. We learned that in law school. It protects lazy lawyers."

"I resent that, Jake."

Noose raised both hands and settled things down. He rubbed his jaw and after some serious thinking said, "Well, obviously, we cannot proceed today, not with such an important witness out of the country. I'll postpone the trial and allow you gentlemen time to finish discovery. You're dismissed."

Jake said, "But, Judge, we should at—"

Noose cut him off with "No, Jake, nothing further. I've heard enough. Please, you're all dismissed."

The lawyers stood, some quicker than others, and filed out of chambers. At the door, Walter Sullivan said to Harry Rex, "What're your plans with that two-million-dollar verdict?" Sean Gilder laughed.

Jake managed to step between the two before Harry Rex could throw a punch.

22

He should've lingered and at least attempted to offer words of explanation to Steve Smallwood, Taylor's brother and the family's spokesman. He should've given instructions to Portia, who was dumbfounded. He should've huddled with Harry Rex and agreed on when to meet again to curse and throw things. He should've said goodbye, see you later to Murray Silerberg and his team scattered throughout the courtroom. He should've circled back to Noose's chambers and perhaps apologized or tried to make amends. Instead, he bolted for a side door and was out of the courthouse before most of the prospective jurors left the courtroom. He went to his car and hurried away from the square, taking the first road out of town. At the edge of Clanton he stopped at a convenience store and bought some peanuts and a soda. He had not eaten in hours. He sat by the gas pumps, ripped off his tie, then took off his coat and listened as his car phone rang. It was Portia, at the office, and he was certain she was calling about something he had no desire to deal with.

He drove south and was soon close to Lake Chatulla. He parked in a rest area on a bluff and looked at the large muddy lake. He checked the time, 9:45, and knew that Carla would be in class. He had to call her but wasn't sure what to say.

"Well, dear, I tried to hide a crucial witness whose testimony would kill our case."

Or: "Well, dear, those damned insurance lawyers outfoxed me again and caught me cheating with discovery."

Or: "Well, dear, I violated the rules and now the case has been postponed. And we're screwed!!"

He drove here and there, east and west, staying on narrow, shaded lanes that wound through the county. He finally called the office and was informed by Portia that Dumas Lee had been hanging around, smelling a story, and that Steve Smallwood had stopped by in a foul mood and was looking for answers. Lucien wasn't in, and Jake instructed her to lock the door and take the phone off the hook.

He vowed again to get rid of the red Saab because it was so conspicuous, a veritable bull's-eye, and at the moment the last thing he wanted was to be noticed. He wanted to take another turn and drive south for hours until he hit the Gulf. Then, maybe he would just keep going, off a pier and into the ocean. He could not remember a time in his life that he had so desperately wanted to run away. To disappear.

His phone startled him. It was Carla. He grabbed it and said hello.

"Jake, where are you? Are you okay? I just talked to Portia."

"I'm okay, just taking a drive, trying to avoid the office."

"She said the case has been postponed."

"That's it. Postponed."

"Can you talk?"

"Not now. It's a bad story and will take some time to go through it. I'll be home this afternoon when you get there."

"Okay. But you're fine?"

"I'm not going to kill myself, Carla, if that's what

you're worried about. Maybe I've thought about it, but I'm under control. I'll see you this afternoon and explain everything."

That was a conversation he would love to avoid. Yes, honey, I cheated, and big-time, and I got caught.

The lawyers would gather one day to depose Neal Nickel, though Sean Gilder would, as always, stall as long as possible. Now that he had the upper hand, and now that Jake would not be screaming for a trial, it would be months before that deposition took place. And Nickel would no doubt be a superb witness, well dressed and articulate and thoroughly believable. He would discredit Hank Grayson, bolster the testimony of the engineer, and lend enormous credence to the railroad's theory that Taylor Smallwood was either asleep or thoroughly distracted when he drove into the train.

The case was over, plain and simple. The case of a lifetime, or at least a career, had just gone down the toilet, flushed by the ambitions and greed of a lawyer who deliberately sidestepped the rules and arrogantly believed he wouldn't get caught.

The litigation loan was at $70,000.

He glanced at his watch—10:05. At that moment he should have been standing before the panel of prospective jurors. Eighty had arrived that morning and Jake knew all eighty names, knew where they lived, worked, worshipped. He knew where some were born, knew where some of their families were buried. He knew their ages, skin color, some of their children. He, Harry Rex, and Murray Silerberg had spent hours secluded in the workroom memorizing all the data the team had gathered.

There was not another decent case in his office and he was behind on his bills. He was arguing with the IRS.

A road sign pointed to Karaway, his hometown. He turned in the other direction, fearful that his mother might see him driving aimlessly around on a beautiful Monday morning in late April.

And now he was stuck with Drew Gamble and a losing case that would only drain away time and money, not to mention causing a lot of bad will around town.

HE DIDN'T DELIBERATELY drive through Pine Grove, but he passed the settlement anyway and was close to the Good Shepherd Bible Church before he realized it. He pulled into the gravel lot with the idea of turning around, but caught a glimpse of a woman sitting at a picnic table near the small cemetery behind the church. It was Josie Gamble, reading a book. Kiera came into view and sat near her mother.

Jake switched off his engine and decided to have a chat with two people who knew nothing of his morning's disaster, nor would they care. As he walked over, they smiled and were obviously pleased to see him. But then Jake figured they would be happy to see any visitor.

"What brings you out here?" Josie asked.

"Just passing through," he said as he sat across the table. An old maple tree shaded them. "How are you doing, Kiera?"

"I'm okay," she said and blushed. Under her loose sweatshirt there were no signs of her pregnancy.

Josie said, "I've never known anyone to just pass through Pine Grove."

"It happens. What are you reading?"

She folded a page in the paperback and said, "A history of ancient Greece. Pretty excitin' stuff. Let's just say the church's library is rather small."

"You read a lot?"

"Well, Jake, I think I told you that I spent two years in prison in Texas. Seven hundred and forty-one days. I read seven hundred and thirty books. When they released me I asked if I could stay two more weeks so I could average a book a day. They said no."

"How do you read a book a day?"

"You ever spent time in prison?"

"Not yet."

"Granted, most of them were not that thick or complicated. One day I read four Nancy Drew mysteries."

"Still a lot of books. Do you read, Kiera?"

She shook her head and looked away.

Josie said, "When I went in I could barely read, but they had a decent education program. Got my GED and started reading. The more I read, the faster I got. We saw Drew yesterday."

"How was that?"

"It was nice. They let us all three sit together in a little room, so we got to hug him and give him kisses, or at least I did. A lot of tears but we managed a few laughs too, didn't we Kiera?"

She nodded and smiled but said nothing.

"It was real sweet. They let us visit for over an hour, then ran us off. I don't like that jail, you know?"

"You're not supposed to like it."

"Guess not. Now they're talkin' death row. They can't really send him away, can they?"

"They'll certainly try. I saw him last Thursday."

"Yeah, he said you hadn't been by in a few days, said you had a big trial comin' up. How'd it go?"

"Is he taking his meds?"

"Says he is. Says he feels a lot better." Her voice cracked and she covered her eyes for a moment. "He looks so little, Jake. They got him wearin' some old faded orange coveralls, says 'County Jail' across the back and front, the smallest they had and still way too big. Got his sleeves and pants rolled up. Damned things just swallow him, and he just looks like a little boy because that's what he really is. Just a kid. And now they want to put him in the gas chamber. I can't believe this, Jake."

Jake glanced at Kiera, who was wiping her cheeks too. These poor people.

Another car pulled into the parking lot. Josie watched it and said, "That's Mrs. Golden, the tutor. She's comin' four days a week now, says Kiera is catchin' up."

Kiera stood and without a word walked to the door of the church and hugged Mrs. Golden, who waved at them. They went inside and closed the door.

"She's nice to do this," Jake said.

"I can't believe how wonderful this church is, Jake. We live here for free. They're feedin' us. Mr. Thurber, who's a foreman at the feed mill, got it worked out so I can do ten to twenty hours a week. It's only minimum wage but I've worked for that before."

"That's good news, Josie."

"If I have to work five jobs and do eighty hours a week I swear I'll do it, Jake. She is not havin' that baby and ruinin' her life."

Jake put up his hands in mock surrender. "We've had this conversation, Josie, and I really don't want to go through it again."

"I'm sorry." For a long time nothing was said. Jake gazed across the cemetery to the hills beyond it. Josie closed her eyes and seemed to meditate.

Jake finally stood and said, "I need to be going."

She opened her eyes and flashed a pretty smile. "Thanks for stoppin' by."

"I think she needs counseling, Josie."

"Hell, don't we all?"

"She's been through a lot. She was raped repeatedly, and now she's enduring another nightmare. Her situation is not going to improve."

"Improve? How can we improve, Jake? That's easy for you to say."

"Do you mind if I talk to Dr. Rooker, the psychiatrist who examined Drew over in Tupelo?"

"And talk about what?"

"About seeing Kiera."

"Who's gonna pay for it?"

"I don't know. Let me think about it."

"You do that, Jake."

THERE WAS NOTHING pleasant waiting at the office, and Jake wanted to avoid the square anyway. If he bumped into Walter Sullivan he might throw a punch. And by now every lawyer in town knew the gossip, knew that Brigance had been bounced out of court and had somehow managed to screw up *Smallwood,* the case they had all coveted. Only two or three of the thirty or so lawyers in town would truly be sad at the news. Some would be downright gleeful, and that was fine with Jake because he despised them too. Lost on the back roads, he called Lucien.

He parked in the drive behind the 1975 Porsche Carrera with a million miles on it and trudged along the sidewalk to the steps of the sweeping old porch that wrapped around the first level of the house. Lucien's grandfather had built it just before the Great Depression with the intention of having the most magnificent home in town. It sat on a hill, half a mile from the courthouse, and from the front porch where he spent his time Lucien looked down on his neighbors. He had inherited the house, along with the law firm, in 1965 when his father died suddenly.

He was waiting, rocking, always reading a thick book of nonfiction, always with a glass on the table next to him. Jake fell into a dusty wicker rocker on the other side of the table and asked, "How can you start the day with Jack Daniel's?"

"It's all about pacing, Jake. I talked to Harry Rex."

"Is he okay?"

"No. He's worried about you, thought maybe they'd find you in the woods with the motor running and a garden hose stuck in the tailpipe."

"I'm thinking about it."

"You want a drink?"

"No, I do not. But thanks."

"Sallie's grilling pork chops and we have fresh corn from the garden."

"I didn't want her to cook."

"That's her job and I eat lunch every day. What in hell were you thinking?"

"Maybe I wasn't."

Sallie appeared from around a corner and ambled toward them in her usual confident way, as if time meant nothing and she ruled the house because she'd been sleeping with the boss for over a decade. She wore one of her short white dresses that made the most of her long brown legs. She was always barefoot. Lucien had hired her as a housekeeper when she was eighteen years old, and she had soon been promoted.

"Hello, Jake," she said with a smile. No one considered her a mere house servant and she had not said the words "Mister" or "Missus" in years. "Something to drink?"

"Thanks, Sallie. Just some ice tea, no sugar."

She disappeared. "I'm listening," Lucien said.

"Maybe I don't want to talk about it."

"Well, maybe I do. Did you really think you could hide an eyewitness in such a major lawsuit?"

"It wasn't so much hiding as it was just hoping he would stay away."

Lucien nodded and put his book on the table. He lifted his glass and took a sip. He looked cold sober, no red eyes or nose. Jake was sure his innards were pickled but Lucien was a legendary drinker who could hold his liquor with anyone. He smacked his lips and said, "Harry Rex told me you guys made the decision together."

"That's awfully big of him."

"I probably would've done the same thing. It's a bad rule that lawyers have hated forever."

There wasn't the slightest doubt in Jake's mind that Lucien would have laughed at Sean Gilder's interrogatories and declined to identify any and all troublesome witnesses. The difference was that Lucien would not have located someone like Neal Nickel to begin with. Jake stumbled across him because he was being too thorough.

"You got a best-case scenario?" Lucien asked. "Harry Rex did not."

"Not really. Maybe we depose the witness and he's not as solid as we fear, then we go to trial, something like six months from now. We've paid the experts so they'll be on board. The jury guy will cost us another bundle, if we use him. The facts haven't changed, though a couple have shifted a little. The crossing is dangerous. Its warning-light system was antiquated and poorly maintained. The railroad knew it had a problem and refused to fix it. Four people were killed. We'll get to the jury and roll the dice."

"How much do you owe?"

"Seventy thousand."

"You're kiddin'? Seventy thousand dollars in litigation expenses?"

"That's not unusual these days."

"I never borrowed a dime on a lawsuit."

"That's because you inherited money, Lucien. Most of us are not so lucky."

"My office, crazy as it was, always showed a profit."

"You asked for the best-case scenario. You see a better one?"

Sallie came back with a tall glass of ice tea and some lemon. "Lunch in thirty minutes," she said as she disappeared again.

"You haven't asked for my advice yet."

"Okay, Lucien, got any advice?"

"You gotta go after this new guy. There's a reason he held back and a reason he came forward."

"He told the investigator he got sued one time and hates lawyers."

"Go after him. Find out everything about that lawsuit. Find the dirt, Jake. You gotta bury this guy in front of the jury."

"I don't want to go to court. I'd like to be trout fishing in some secluded mountain stream. That's all I want."

Lucien took another sip and returned his glass to the table. "You talked to Carla?"

"Not yet. I will when she gets home. What fun. Telling my wife, a person I adore, that I got caught cheating and tossed out of court."

"I never did well with wives."

"You think the railroad would settle?"

"Don't think like that, Jake. Don't ever show weakness. You can rebound from this by pushing hard again, squawking at Noose until he gives a new trial date, and drag these sumbitches back into court. Attack the new witness. Pick a good jury. You can handle this, Jake. No talk of settling."

For the first time in hours, Jake managed a chuckle.

THE HOCUTT HOUSE had been built a few years before Lucien's. Thankfully, old man Hocutt didn't care for yard work so he selected a small city lot for his fine new home. Jake didn't care for it either, but once a week during warm weather he pulled out the lawn mower and edger and spent a couple of hours sweating.

Monday afternoon seemed like a good time, and he was in the backyard laboring away when his girls got home from school. He was never there waiting for them, and Hanna was thrilled to see her father at home so early. He had cans of lemonade in a cooler, and they sat on the patio and talked about school until Hanna got bored with the adults and went inside.

"Are you okay?" Carla asked with great concern.

"No."

"You want to talk?"

"Only if you promise to forgive me."

"Always."

"Thanks. It might be difficult."

She smiled and said, "I'm with you, okay?"

23

Of the three jailers who came to his cell with meals and instructions, room checks and lights out, and occasionally a kind word, Mr. Zack was his favorite because he seemed to care. His voice was never harsh like the others. Sergeant Buford was the worst. He had once told Drew that he'd better enjoy the county jail because death row was a terrible place and that's where all cop killers were sent to die.

Mr. Zack arrived early with a tray of food—scrambled eggs and toast. He left it by the bunk and returned with a grocery bag and said, "Your preacher brought these by. Some clothes, real clothes that you need to put on and get dressed up."

"Why?"

"Because you're goin' to court today. Didn't your lawyer tell you?"

"Maybe. I don't remember. What am I doin' in court?"

"Hell if I know. I just handle the jail. When did you shower last?"

"I don't know, don't remember."

"I think it was two days ago. You're okay. You don't smell too bad."

"The water was ice cold. I don't want to shower."

"Then eat up and get dressed. They're comin' to get you at eight-thirty."

When the jailer was gone, Drew chewed on a piece of toast and ignored the eggs. They were always cold too. He opened the grocery sack and removed a pair of jeans, a thick plaid shirt, two pairs of white socks, and a pair of scuffed white sneakers, all obviously hand-me-downs but smelling like strong detergent. He stepped out of his orange coveralls and got dressed. Everything fit reasonably well and he liked the fact that he was wearing real clothes again. He had one change in a cardboard box under his bunk where he kept his other valuables.

He retrieved a small bag of salted peanuts his lawyer had brought him and ate them slowly, one at a time. He was supposed to read for an hour each morning, strict instructions from his mother. She had delivered two books, one a history of the state that he had used in class and found incredibly boring. The other was a novel by Charles Dickens that his English teacher sent via his preacher. He had little interest in reading either one.

Mr. Zack returned to fetch his tray and said, "You didn't eat your eggs."

Drew ignored him and stretched out on the bottom bunk for another nap. Minutes later the door burst open and a thick deputy growled, "Get up, kid."

Drew scrambled to his feet as Marshall Prather slapped cuffs on his wrists, yanked him by an elbow, and led him out of the cell, down the hall, and out the back door where a patrol car was waiting with DeWayne Looney behind the wheel. Prather shoved Drew into the rear seat and they sped away. The prisoner peeked out a window to see if anyone was watching.

Moments later they wheeled to a stop near the rear door of the courthouse where two men with cameras were waiting. With a slightly softer touch, Prather pulled Drew out and made sure he faced the cameras for full-frontal shots. Then they were inside and climbing a dark, narrow staircase.

JAKE SAT ON one side of the table, Lowell Dyer the other. Judge Noose was at the end, no robe, unlit pipe stuck between his teeth. All three men were frowning and apparently unhappy. Each for different reasons.

Noose placed some papers on the table and rubbed his eyes. Jake was irritated at even being there. The event was nothing but a first appearance for several freshly indicted defendants, and Jake had tried to waive it on behalf of Drew. However, His Honor wanted to be seen doing his job, presiding over the criminals and keeping them locked up. A crowd was expected, and Jake, cynically, believed Noose wanted to look good for the voters.

Jake, of course, wasn't worried about the voters, and he had accepted the fact that he was about to look bad regardless of what happened. He would sit next to the defendant, stand next to him, consult with him, speak for him, and so on. The clear and obvious guilt of Drew Gamble was about to rub off on his lawyer.

Jake said, "Judge, I need to hire a psychiatrist for my client. And the State cannot expect me to pay for one."

"He just came back from Whitfield. Didn't he see the experts down there?"

"He did. However, they work for the State and the State is prosecuting him. We need our own private shrink."

"I certainly do," Lowell mumbled.

"So, this is headed toward an insanity defense?"

"Probably, but how can I make that decision without consulting with our own psychiatrist? I'm sure Lowell will be able to line 'em up in court and produce several experts from Whitfield who'll say the kid knew precisely what he was doing when he pulled the trigger."

Lowell shrugged and nodded his agreement.

Noose was perplexed and said, "Let's talk about this later. I'd like to discuss our timing here and at least get a tentative trial date. Summer is approaching and it usually complicates our calendars. Jake, what are you thinking?"

Oh, lots. For one, his star witness was pregnant but still hiding it well. He was under no obligation to inform anyone of this. Indeed, it was likely that the State would call Kiera to the stand before Jake did. After long conversations with Portia and Lucien, Jake had decided that the better strategy was to push for a trial in late summer so that she would be visibly pregnant when she testified. The complicating factor was the threat of an abortion. Josie was working two minimum-wage jobs and she owned a car. Nothing prevented her from grabbing her daughter and going to Memphis for an abortion. The topic was so raw that it was not being discussed.

Second, little Drew Gamble was finally growing up. Jake was watching him carefully, as was his mother, and both had noticed some small pimples on his cheeks and a dash of new peach fuzz above his lips. His voice was changing too. He was eating more and had gained five pounds, according to the jailer.

Jake wanted a small kid sitting in the defendant's chair at trial, not a gangly teenager trying to look older. "The sooner the better. Late summer, maybe."

"Lowell?"

"There's not a lot of preparation, Judge. Not many witnesses. We should be ready to go in a couple of months."

Noose studied his docket and finally said, "Let's say Monday, August 6, and set aside the entire week."

Three months away. Kiera would be seven months along. Jake still could not envision the drama in the courtroom when she testified that she was indeed pregnant and Kofer was the father because he had repeatedly raped her.

What a nasty trial.

DREW WAS CUFFED to a wooden chair in a small dark holding room with two other criminals, both fully grown black men who were amused by the age and size of their new colleague. Their crimes seemed insignificant, unimpressive.

One said, "Say, dude, you shot that deputy?"

Drew had been lectured by his lawyer to say nothing, but in the presence of other handcuffed men he felt safe. "That's right."

"With his own gun?"

"The only gun I could find."

"He really pissed you off."

"He beat my mother. I thought she was dead."

"They gon' fry your ass in the electric chair."

"I think it's the gas chamber," the other said.

Drew shrugged as if he wasn't sure. The door opened and a bailiff said, "Bowie." One of the men stood as the bailiff took him by the elbow and led him away. When the door was closed the room was dark again and Drew asked, "What are you in for?"

"Stole a car. Wish I'd shot a cop."

SMALL PACKS OF lawyers were hovering around the courtroom as defendants were being processed. Some of the lawyers actually had business there, others were part of the courthouse crowd that never missed a show. The rumors were that the kid would finally make a public appearance and this drew them like vultures to a carcass.

When Jake emerged from Noose's chambers, he was impressed with the number of people there to witness preliminary hearings that meant little on the road to justice. Josie and Kiera were huddled in the front row with Charles and Meg McGarry, and all four looked terrified. Across the aisle, there was a pack of Kofers and friends, all angry. Dumas Lee was sniffing around with another reporter.

Judge Noose called the name of Drew Allen Gamble, and Mr. Pete left to find him. They emerged from a side door next to the jury box and paused for a moment to remove the handcuffs. Drew looked around and tried to absorb the enormity of the room, and all the people gawking at him. He saw his mother and sister sitting out there but was too stunned to smile. Mr. Pete led him to a spot in front of the bench where Jake met him and they looked up at the judge.

Jake was six feet tall. Mr. Pete was at least six-one, and both seemed at least a foot taller than the defendant.

Noose looked down and said, "You are Drew Allen Gamble."

Drew nodded and might have spoken.

"Please speak up, sir," Noose almost yelled into his microphone. Jake looked down at his client.

"Yes sir."

"And you are represented by the Honorable Jake Brigance, right?"

"Yes sir."

"And you have been indicted by the grand jury of

Ford County for the murder of Officer Stuart Kofer, right?"

In Jake's biased opinion, Noose was being far too dramatic and playing to the crowd. Hell, the entire first appearance could have been dispensed with a signature.

"Yes sir."

"And you have a copy of the indictment?"

"Yes sir."

"And you understand the charges?"

"Yes sir."

As Noose ruffled some papers, Jake wanted to say something like "Come on, Judge, how can he not understand the charges? He's been locked up for over a month." He could almost feel the stares drilling into the back of his nice gray blazer, and he knew that this day, May 8, was the day when he was unofficially crowned the most despised lawyer in town.

His Honor asked, "Do you plead guilty or not guilty?"

"Not guilty."

"Okay, you will be remanded to the custody of the sheriff's department and await trial for the murder of Stuart Kofer. Anything else, Mr. Brigance?"

Anything else? Hell, we didn't need this. "No sir."

"Take him away."

Josie was trying to control herself. Jake walked back to the defense table and tossed down a useless legal pad. He glanced at Pastor McGarry, then looked directly at the Kofer gang.

TWO WEEKS EARLIER, Lowell Dyer had informed Jake that he and his investigator would like the opportunity to meet with Josie and Kiera and ask questions. It was quite a professional move because Dyer didn't need Jake's permission to talk to anyone except the defendant. Jake represented Drew, not his family, and if anyone working for law enforcement or the prosecution wanted to chat with a potential witness they could certainly do so.

Unlike civil litigation, where all witnesses were made known and their testimonies probed long before trial, in criminal matters neither side was required to reveal much of anything. In a simple divorce case, every dollar was accounted for, in theory. But in a capital murder trial, with a human life on the line, the defense was not entitled to know what the accusing witnesses might say or what opinions the experts might put forth.

Jake agreed to arrange a meeting in his office and invited Ozzie and Detective Rady as well. He wanted a crowded room because he wanted both Josie and Kiera to experience the tension of discussing what had happened before an audience.

Noose adjourned for lunch at 11:30. Jake and Portia walked Josie and Kiera across the street, and were followed by Dyer and his investigator. They reconvened in the main conference room where Bev had laid out coffee and brownies. Jake arranged everyone around the table and sat Josie at one end, alone as if on the witness stand.

Lowell Dyer was warm and pleasant and began by thanking her for her time. He had the full report from Detective Rady and knew a lot of her background. She kept her responses brief.

The day before, Jake had spent two hours coaching her and her daughter at the church. He had even written instructions for them to review, gems such as: "Keep your answers brief. Don't volunteer anything. If you don't know, don't guess. Do not hesitate to ask Mr. Dyer to repeat the question. Say as little as possible about the physical abuse (we'll save it for trial). And, most important: Always remember that he is the enemy and he is trying to put Drew on death row."

Josie was tough and had been around the block. She got through the questions without emotion and gave only the barest of details about the beatings.

Kiera was next. For the occasion, and at Jake's request, she wore jeans and a tight blouse. At fourteen, no one would have suspected that she was four months pregnant. Jake had readily agreed to the meeting because he wanted Lowell Dyer to have the opportunity to evaluate the witness before she began showing. On her list of instructions, Portia had typed in bold letters: **"Do not mention your pregnancy. Do not mention the rapes. If asked about physical abuse, start crying and don't answer. Jake will intervene."**

Her voice broke almost immediately and Dyer didn't push. She was a frightened, fragile child who was now secretly carrying one of her own and seemed thoroughly overwhelmed.

Jake grimaced, shrugged, said to Dyer, "Maybe another time."

"Sure."

24

Jake had been careful not to get himself photographed around the courthouse. Evidently, the editor of the *Times* went to the archives and selected one of a hundred from the trial of Carl Lee Hailey, five years earlier. He plastered it on the front page next to one of Drew in handcuffs getting out of the patrol car the day before. Side by side, cop killer and lawyer. Each as guilty as the other. Jake poured a cup of coffee in his kitchen and read the report by Dumas Lee. An anonymous source said the trial was scheduled for August 6 in Clanton.

The news of the location was interesting. Jake planned to do everything in his power to change venue and have the trial as far away from Clanton as possible.

He turned back to the front page. He remembered the photo and had rather liked it back then. The caption under it read: "Defense Attorney Jake Brigance." He was all business, with a proper frown that conveyed the seriousness of the moment. Perhaps he appeared a bit thinner but he knew he weighed the same. Five years had passed and the hairline was still receding.

He heard thunder and remembered that rain was in the forecast, another wave of spring storms. He had no appointments for the day, and he had no desire to hang out in the Coffee Shop. So he said screw it and went to his bedroom, undressed, and crawled under the covers where he found the warm body of his wife.

———

GOOD NEWS CONTINUED to pour in. Judge Noose faxed copies of two letters to Jake, fifteen minutes apart. The first read:

Dear Judge Noose:

As the attorney for the Ford County Board of Supervisors, I have been asked by the Board to respond to your request for attorney's fees for Jake Brigance in the Stuart Kofer matter. As you well know, Section 99-15-17 of the Mississippi Code clearly states that the maximum to be paid by the county for the representation of indigents charged with capital murder is $1000. There is no language in that statute that gives the Board the discretion to pay more. There should be and we both know that the limit is not sufficient. However, I've discussed this matter with the Board, all five members, and it is their position that the maximum compensation will be $1000.

I know Jake well and am happy to discuss this with him.

Sincerely,
TODD TANNEHILL
Attorney at Law

The second letter was from Sean Gilder, attorney for the railroad, and it read:

Dear Judge Noose:

It is with a heavy heart that I write to inform you that one of our experts, Dr. Crowe Ledford, died suddenly last week just moments after completing the Key West Marathon. The cause is suspected to be cardiac arrest. Dr. Ledford was a professor at Emory University and an esteemed expert in the field of highway and railroad safety. His testimony was to be the cornerstone of our defense.

Though no trial date has been set, we will obviously need additional time to find and hire an expert to replace Dr. Ledford.

Our apologies to the court. I will contact Mr. Brigance and tell him this awful news.

Sincerely,
SEAN GILDER

Jake tossed the letter onto his desk and looked at Portia. "A dead expert will buy them another six months."

She said, "Boss, we need to talk."

Jake glanced at his door and said, "It's closed. What's up?"

"Well, I've been working here for almost two years."

"And you're ready to become a partner?"

"No, not yet, but I plan to take over after law school."

"You can have it."

"Anyway, I'm worried about this place. I've looked at the phone records for the first three months of this year and compared them to the last six weeks. Boss, the phone isn't ringing."

"I know that, Portia."

"And worse, the foot traffic has really slowed. On average we open one new file each day, five a week, twenty a month, and we keep about fifty active. In the past six weeks we've opened seven new files, most for small stuff like shoplifters and no-fault divorces."

"That's my practice."

"Seriously, Jake, I'm worried."

"Thank you, Portia, but I don't want you worrying. That's my job. You learn quick in this business that it's feast or famine."

"When's the feast?"

"We'll get a thousand bucks for Gamble."

"Seriously Jake."

"I appreciate your concern, but let me handle it. You have your sights set on law school in August and that's enough to keep you busy."

She took a deep breath and tried to smile. "I think the town has turned against you, Jake."

He paused long enough to acknowledge it, then said, "It's temporary. I'll survive Gamble, then I'll settle *Smallwood*. A year will pass and everybody will be clamoring for my services. I promise you, Portia, when you finish law school I'll still be here, suing people."

"Thanks."

"Please, go worry about something else."

WITH HER MOTHER working sporadic hours at both the feed mill and a chicken-processing plant, Kiera got bored in the afternoons and hung around the parsonage tending to Justin, the McGarrys' four-year-old. Meg, now eight months pregnant, was taking classes at a junior college and appreciated the babysitting. Often, when she was home, they went for long walks down a gravel road behind the church, with Justin ahead of them on his little bike. They liked to stop at a bridge over Carter's Creek and watch him play in the shallow water.

Kiera adored Meg and talked to her about things her mother wouldn't understand. The abortion had been off-limits for some time, but Meg and Charles were watching the calendar and knew the timing was becoming crucial. Kiera was mid-term and a decision had to be made.

Sitting on the edge of the bridge with their feet hanging down, Meg said, "Does Josie still want you to get an abortion?"

"She says she does, but we can't pay for one."

"What do you want, Kiera?"

"I don't want to have a baby, that's for certain. But I really don't want to go through an abortion. Mom says it's not a big deal. Can I tell you a secret?"

"You can tell me anything."

"I know. Mom says she got an abortion one time, after Drew and I were born, says there's nothing to it."

Meg tried to hide her shock that a mother would tell her fourteen-year-old daughter such a secret. "That's not true, Kiera, not at all. Having an abortion is a horrible thing to do and the damage lasts for many years. As Christians, we believe that life begins at conception. The two children you and I are carrying right now are living beings, little gifts from God. Having an abortion terminates a life."

"So you think it's murder?"

"I do. I know it is."

"I don't want to do it."

"Is she pressuring you?"

"All the time. She's afraid she'll get stuck raising another kid. Can she make me get an abortion?"

"No. Can I tell you a secret?"

"Sure, that's what we're doing, right?"

"It is. I talked to Jake, off the record, and asked him what would happen if Josie took you to a clinic in Memphis and you objected. He said that no clinic, no doctor, will perform an abortion if the mother doesn't want it. Don't let her make you do it, Kiera."

Kiera took her hand and squeezed it. Justin yelled

and pointed to a frog at the edge of the water. Meg said, "You're too young to worry about raising a child, Kiera, that's why adoption is the best route. There are plenty of young couples out there who desperately want a child. Charles knows other ministers and he'll have no problem finding the perfect home for your baby."

"How about a home for us? I'm tired of living in a church."

"We'll find something. And speaking of church, there is another issue we need to chat about, with your mom too. You're starting to show and we're trying to keep this a secret, right?"

"That's what Jake said."

"It may be time to stop attending services."

"But I enjoy the services. Everyone is so nice."

"They are, and they like to talk, same as any small church. If they realize you're pregnant, word will spread like crazy."

"What am I supposed to do for the next four months? Hide in the church kitchen?"

"Let's discuss it with your mother."

"She'll just say get an abortion."

"That's not happening, Kiera. You're gonna have a healthy baby and make some young couple very happy."

AFTER HANNA WAS asleep, Jake went to his car, grabbed a bottle of red wine, uncorked it at the kitchen counter, found two seldom-used wineglasses, stepped into the den, and said to his wife, "Meet me on the patio."

Outside, she saw the bottle on the table and asked, "What's the occasion?"

"Nothing good." He poured two glasses, gave one to

her, they clinked and sat down. "Here's to our pending bankruptcy."

"Cheers, I guess."

Jake took a big gulp, Carla a much more reasonable sip.

He said, "*Smallwood* just got delayed by months. The county refuses to pay me more than a thousand dollars for a capital murder defense. The phone has stopped ringing at the office. Josie needs three hundred dollars a month to rent a place. And the backbreaker is that Stan Atcavage called today and his boss wants a payment on our litigation loan."

"How much of a payment?"

"Something like half would make them happy. Half of seventy thousand dollars. It is, of course, unsecured and the bank didn't want to make the loan in the first place. Stan says they've never been in the litigation business and are afraid of it. Can't blame 'em for that."

"I thought they agreed to wait until the case settled."

"Stan did, verbally, but his boss is leaning on him. Remember, they sold out three years ago to a bigger bank in Jackson. Stan gets frustrated with some of the decisions down there."

Carla took another sip and breathed deeply. "Okay. I thought Judge Noose had a plan to make sure you got paid."

"He does but it's a lousy plan. I'm supposed to wait until the trial is over and then sue the county for my time and expenses. He promises to rule in my favor and force the county to pay."

"What's wrong with that?"

"Everything. It means I get nothing for months, nothing to pay the overhead while the practice dries up and the town boycotts me. When I'm forced to sue the county, that'll make the newspaper, so more bad press.

And there is really no way Noose can force the county to pay more than a thousand bucks. If the supervisors dig in, and they will, we're screwed."

She nodded as if she understood, took another sip, and eventually said, "Lovely."

"Yes. Noose thinks it's really clever, but then he's desperate for a lawyer to represent the kid."

"Dare I ask how much cash we have right now?"

"Not much. Five thousand in the office account. Eight thousand in our money market. Ten-plus in savings." He slurped some more wine. "Pretty pathetic, if you think about it. Twelve years as a lawyer and only eighteen thousand dollars socked away."

"We have a good life, Jake. We both work. We live better than most. There is equity in the house, right?"

"A little. We'll have to squeeze out every penny of it to pay Stan."

"A second mortgage?"

"There's no way around it."

"What did Harry Rex say?"

"Well, when he stopped cussing me we called Stan and they got into it. Harry Rex maintains it's a line of credit with no due date so the bank will just have to wait. Stan cussed right back and said he would call the entire loan. When I hung up they were still cussing."

"That's unfortunate."

A moment passed as they listened to the crickets. The street was quiet except for the buzz of insects and the distant barking of a dog. Carla asked, "Did Josie ask for money?"

"No, but she needs to get away from the church. They're tired of living there and you can't blame them. Kiera is mid-term and starting to show. She won't be able to hide it much longer. You can imagine how much fun the busybodies will have when they realize she's pregnant."

"And Josie's found a place?"

"She says she's looking, but she's also working part-time jobs now. She can squeeze together a hundred bucks a month for rent. Plus, they don't have a stick of furniture."

"So we're paying rent, too?"

"Not yet, but I'm sure we'll have to help. And, she has a pile of medical bills that she'll have to bankrupt."

"What about medical care for Kiera?"

"Oh, that too."

After another long pause, Carla said, "I have a question."

"Okay."

"Did you buy more than one bottle of wine?"

25

Three days after classes ended, and Hanna and Carla were set free for the summer, the Brigances loaded themselves and the dog into the car and headed for the beach, their annual vacation. Carla's parents had semi-retired to the Wilmington area and owned a spacious condo on the water in Wrightsville Beach. Hanna and Carla loved the sand and the sun. Jake appreciated the rent-free accommodations.

Her father, still "Mr. McCullough" to Jake, liked to refer to himself as an "investor" and could bore anyone with the latest earnings reports. He also wrote a column for a minor financial magazine that Jake had once, long ago, subscribed to in a vain effort to understand what the guy was up to. His real motive for the subscription had been to figure out if his father-in-law had serious money. So far, Mr. McCullough's net worth was a mystery, but it was obvious he and his wife were quite comfortable. Mrs. McCullough was a pleasant lady in her mid-sixties who was active in all manner of garden clubs, turtle savers, and hospital volunteers.

The summer before, and the summer before that, the Brigances had flown from Memphis to Raleigh where they rented a car for the vacation. Hanna wanted to fly again and was disappointed when she first learned of the family road trip. Twelve hours of it. She was too young to know of their belt-tightening, and her parents were careful with their words and actions. They planned the trip as a grand adventure and mentioned a few sites they might visit along the way. The truth was that they would take turns driving and hoped their daughter would get plenty of sleep.

The Saab stayed home. Carla's car was of a more recent vintage and had far fewer miles. Jake bought new tires and got it serviced properly.

Off they went, at seven in the morning, with Hanna barely awake under the covers in the backseat and cuddled up with the dog. Jake found a '60s station out of Memphis and he and Carla hummed along with the oldies as the sun rose before them. They had vowed to keep things light, not only for their benefit but for Hanna's. The law practice was crumbling around them. The bank wanted money. *Smallwood,* their pot of gold, had become another kind of train wreck. The Gamble trial was two months away and loomed like its own execution date. As their income fell, their debts climbed and seemed insurmountable.

But they were determined to survive. They were not yet forty years old, in good health, with a lovely home and plenty of friends and a law office that Jake still believed he could build into something bigger. This would be a difficult year financially, but they would get through it and emerge stronger.

Hanna announced she was hungry and Carla challenged her to select the right breakfast place. She chose a fast-food restaurant beside the interstate and they went through the drive-thru. They were making good time and Jake wanted to arrive before dark. Mrs. McCullough promised to have dinner on the table.

They played car games, card games, pick-the-billboard games, count-the-cows games, any kind of game Hanna could think of, and they sang along with the radio. When Hanna drifted off, Carla pulled out a paperback and everything was quiet. Lunch was a burger at another drive-thru, another place selected by Hanna, and before they drove away they changed drivers. Carla drove for an hour before getting sleepy. Jake wasn't fond of her driving anyway, so they swapped again. Once in the passenger's seat, she came to life and couldn't nap. It was almost 2:00 P.M. and they had hours to go.

Carla looked to make sure Hanna was sound asleep, and said, "Okay, I know we're not talking about this, at least in front of her, but I can't get it off my mind."

Jake smiled and said, "Neither can I."

"Good. So here's a big question. A year from now, where will Drew Gamble be?"

A mile passed as he considered this. "There are three possible answers, all dictated by what happens at trial. One, he's found guilty of capital murder, which is likely because there's no doubt about what happened, and he's sent to Parchman to await an execution. It might be possible to pull strings and get him placed in some type of protective custody because of his age and size, but it will still be a horrible place. They'll probably place him on the actual death row, where he might be safer because he'll be in solitary confinement."

"And his appeals?"

"They'll go on forever. If he's convicted, I suspect I'll still be writing briefs for him when Hanna's in college. Number two, he's found not guilty by reason of insanity, which is unlikely. If so, he'll probably be put in a treatment facility for an undetermined length of time and eventually released. I'm sure the Gambles will flee the area, and we might be right behind them."

"That doesn't really seem fair either. Great for them. Terrible for the Kofers. We're caught in the middle."

"True."

"I don't want the kid to go to prison for the rest of

his life, but to walk away after what he did is not fair. There should be something in between, some lesser form of punishment."

"I agree, but what is it?" Jake asked.

"I'm not sure, but I do know something about the insanity defense because of Carl Lee. He wasn't insane and he got off. Drew seems far more traumatized and detached from reality than Carl Lee."

"I agree again. Carl Lee knew exactly what he was doing when he killed those two. He planned it carefully and carried it out perfectly. His defense was not about his mental state, it was about sympathy from the jury. It will all come down to the jury, as always."

"And how do you make the jurors sympathetic?"

Jake glanced over his shoulder. Hanna and Mully were fast asleep. Softly, he said, "The pregnant sister."

"And the dead mother?"

"The dead mother will be a powerful element and we'll use it continually. However, she wasn't dead. She was still breathing, with a pulse, and the prosecution will make much of that. The kids should've known that Josie wasn't dead."

"Come on, Jake. Two kids absolutely terrified, probably hysterical because their mother was unconscious and not responsive, once again beaten by a brute. It seems to me that was quite reasonable to believe she was dead."

"That's what I'll tell the jury."

"Okay, what's the third scenario? A hung jury?"

"Yes. A few of the jurors are sympathetic and refuse to go along with capital murder. They want something less, but the majority digs in and wants the gas chamber. Deliberations could be a free-for-all as the jury completely deadlocks and hangs itself. After a few days Noose has no choice but to declare a mistrial and sends everybody home. Drew goes back to his cell and waits for the retrial."

"And how likely is that?"

"You tell me. Put yourself on the jury. You already know the facts. There aren't many of them."

"Why do you always put me on the jury?"

Jake chuckled. He was guilty, again. "A hung jury would be a big win. A guilty verdict is more likely. A not-guilty-by-reason-of-insanity is a long shot."

Carla watched the hills pass. They were on an interstate, somewhere in Georgia, and she wasn't finished. She turned around again and checked on Hanna, then said, softly, "Josie promised you there will not be an abortion, right?"

"She did, reluctantly. Plus, it's too late."

"So there'll be a baby in September, assuming nature cooperates. And Kiera seems to be doing well and seeing a doctor."

"Yes, we're paying for some of that."

"And she has agreed to an adoption."

"You were there when she did. Josie is demanding it. She knows who'd end up raising the kid and right now she can barely feed Kiera and herself."

Carla took a deep breath and looked at her husband. "Have you thought about adopting the child?"

"As a lawyer?"

"No, as a father."

Jake almost gasped, and there was a slight jerk on the wheel. He looked at her in utter amazement, shook his head, and said, "Well, no, I have not thought about it. Obviously you have."

"Can we talk about it?"

"What don't we talk about?"

Both turned to check on Hanna.

"Well," Carla said, in that tone that meant that the

discussion they were about to have would be complicated. Jake stared straight ahead and ran through his own quick list of complications. "We talked about adoption years ago and then, for some reason I can't really remember, we just stopped talking. Hanna was a toddler. The doctors had told us that we were lucky to get pregnant with her, after some false starts, and that it would not happen again. We wanted at least one more, maybe two."

"I remember. I was there."

"I guess we just got busy with life and became content with an only child."

"Very content."

"But the baby will need a good home, Jake."

"I'm sure they'll find one. I do several private adoptions a year and there's always a demand for babies."

"We would have the inside track, Jake, don't you think?"

"I think there are at least two big issues here. Most important, are we as a family ready to expand? Do you, at the age of thirty-seven, want another baby?"

"I think so."

"What about Hanna? How will she react?"

"She'll absolutely adore a little brother."

"Brother?"

"Yes. Kiera told Meg two days ago that it's a boy."

"And why wasn't I informed?"

"It's girl talk, Jake, and you're always too busy. Think about it, Jake, a little boy with a big sister almost ten years older."

"Why am I suddenly thinking about diapers and walking the floor at night?"

"They outgrow that. The worst part of having a child is giving birth."

"I rather enjoyed it."

"Easy for you to say. Now we can avoid all that."

They were quiet for several miles as both plotted their next moves. Jake was reeling and trying to organize his thoughts. Carla had planned the attack and was prepared for any resistance.

He seemed to relax, and then he smiled at his adorable wife. "When exactly did you start thinking about this?"

"I don't know. I've been mulling it over for some time. At first I thought it was a ridiculous idea, and I thought of all the reasons to let it go. You're the de facto attorney for the family. How would it look for you to use your inside position to get the baby? How would the town react?"

"That's the least of my worries."

"What type of relationship, if any, would the child have with Kiera and Josie? What about the Kofers? I'm sure they'll be horrified when they learn that Stuart left a grandchild behind. I doubt if they'll want anything to do with the child, but you never know. I've thought of a lot of issues and a lot of reasons not to do it. But then I keep thinking about the child. Someone, some lucky couple somewhere, will get the magical phone call. They'll drive to the hospital and leave with a little baby boy. It will be all theirs. Why can't it be us, Jake? We're just as qualified as anyone else."

From the rear seat a sweet, sleepy little voice said, "Anybody thinking about a potty break?"

Jake quickly said, "We are now," and began looking at exit signs.

THEY WERE ON the beach at dusk, ambling along in the surf with Hanna splashing and chattering nonstop as she held hands with both grandparents. Jake and

Carla held hands too and fell behind, happy at the sight of their little girl being smothered in love. Carla wanted to talk but Jake was not ready for another discussion about expanding the family.

"I have an idea," she said.

"I'm sure you're about to share it."

Ignoring him, she said, "Drew is sitting in jail every day, falling further behind in his education. He's been there since the end of March with no tutoring. Josie said he's already two years behind."

"At least."

"Could you arrange for me to go to the jail two or three days a week and tutor the kid?"

"Do you have the time?"

"I have the summer, Jake, and I can always find the time. We can ask your mother to keep Hanna, she never says no, and we can also find a babysitter to help."

"Or I can babysit. The way my practice is drying up I'll have plenty of time."

"Seriously. I can get the textbooks from the school and at least get him on some type of schedule."

"I don't know. Ozzie would have to approve it and he's not too cooperative these days. Maybe I can ask Judge Noose."

"Would it be safe? I've never been to the jail."

"You're lucky. I'm not sure I like the idea. You'd be close to some rough characters and you'd be around some cops who are not my best friends these days. Ozzie would have to take some precautions and he'd probably balk."

"Will you talk to him?"

"Sure, if that's what you want."

"No chance he could leave the jail for a few hours each week to meet somewhere else?"

"Not a chance."

Hanna and her grandparents had turned around and were getting close. Mrs. McCullough said, "How about a glass of wine while I get dinner ready?"

"Sounds delightful," Jake said. "We've eaten two meals in the car today and I'm ready for some real food."

26

After five days of walking the beach, swimming, reading, sleeping late and napping, and getting slaughtered in chess by Mr. McCullough, Jake was ready for a break. Early on the morning of May 31 he hugged Carla, said goodbye to his in-laws, and happily drove away, eager to spend the next five hours in blissful solitude.

The Kids Advocacy Foundation had an office on M Street near Farragut Square in central Washington. The building was a 1970s-style block of gray brick with five floors and far too few windows. The directory in the lobby listed the names of dozens of associations, nonprofits, coalitions, federations, brotherhoods, and so on, everything from AMERICAN RAISIN GROWERS to the DISABLED RURAL MAIL CARRIERS.

Jake got off the elevator on the fourth floor and found the right door. He stepped inside to a cramped reception room where a small dapper gentleman of about seventy sat behind a neat desk and greeted him with a smile. "You must be Mr. Brigance, all the way from Mississippi."

"I am, yes," Jake said, stepping forward with an outstretched hand.

"I'm Roswell, the boss around here," he said, standing. He wore a tiny red bowtie and a crisp white shirt. "A pleasure to meet you." They shook hands.

Jake, in khakis and a button-down, no tie, no socks, said, "And nice to meet you."

"You drove up from the beach, right?"

"Yes." Jake glanced around and took in the decor. The walls were covered with framed portraits of young people in prison whites and jail coveralls, some looking out from behind bars, others in handcuffs.

"Welcome to our headquarters," Roswell said with another cheerful smile. "That's quite a case you have down there. I've read your summaries. Libby expects us to read everything." He waved at a door as he spoke. "She's waiting."

Jake followed him into a hallway and they stopped at the first door. Roswell said, "Libby, Mr. Brigance is here. Mr. Brigance, meet the real boss, Libby Provine."

Ms. Provine was waiting in front of her desk and quickly offered a hand. "A pleasure, Mr. Brigance. Mind if I call you Jake? We're quite informal around here." The accent was thick Scottish. The first time they had spoken on the phone, Jake struggled to handle the brogue.

"Jake's fine. Nice to meet you."

Roswell disappeared and she pointed to a small conference table in the corner of her office. "I thought you might want some lunch."

On the table were two deli sandwiches on paper plates and bottles of water. "Lunch is served," she said. They took their places at the table but neither made a move for the food.

"An easy drive?" she asked.

"Uneventful. I was happy to get away from the beach and the in-laws."

Libby Provine was about fifty, with red curly hair that was graying, and she wore sleek designer frames that made her almost attractive. From his research he knew she had founded the nonprofit twenty years earlier, not long after she finished law school at Georgetown. KAF, as it was known, had a staff of paralegals and four lawyers, all in-house. Its mission was to assist in the defense of teenagers on trial for serious crimes, and, more specifically, to try and rescue them during the sentencing phase after they had been convicted.

After a few minutes of chitchat, with neither reaching for the sandwiches, though Jake was starving, Libby asked, "And you expect the State to proceed with capital murder?"

"Oh yes. We have a hearing in two weeks on the issue, but I do not expect to win. The State is going full speed ahead."

"Even though Kofer was not actually on duty?"

"That's the issue. As you know, the statute was changed two years ago and the new one is hard to ignore."

"I know. Such a needless change of law. What's it called, the Death Penalty Enhancement Act? As if the State needed more muscle in its quest to fill up death row. Total rubbish."

She knew everything. Jake had spoken to her twice on the phone and sent a forty-page review that he and Portia had put together. He had talked to two other lawyers, one in Georgia, one in Texas, who had relied on KAF at trial and their opinions were glowing.

She said, "Only Mississippi and Texas allow the death penalty for the killing of an officer regardless of whether he was on duty. It makes no sense."

"We're still fighting the war down there. I'm starving."

"Chicken salad or turkey-and-Swiss?"

"I'll take the chicken salad."

They unwrapped the sandwiches and took a bite, hers much smaller than his. She said, "We dug up some newspaper reports about the Hailey trial. Sounds like a real show."

"You could call it that."

"Looks like the insanity defense worked for a man who wasn't insane."

"It was all about race, something that will not be a factor with Gamble."

"And your expert, Dr. Bass?"

"I wouldn't dare use him again. He's a drunk and a liar and I used him only because he was free. We got lucky. Have you found us the right expert?"

She nibbled on the crust of her sandwich and nodded. "You'll need at least two experts. One for the insanity defense, which I believe is all you have, and one for sentencing, assuming he's convicted. That's where we can help. Virtually all of our clients are guilty, and some of their crimes are pretty horrific. We just try to keep them alive and out of prison for the rest of their lives."

Jake had a mouthful so he just nodded. Libby apparently was a light eater.

She continued, "One day in this great land the Supreme Court will rule that sending juveniles to death row is cruel and unusual punishment, but we're not there yet. The Court may also see the light and rule that sentencing kids to prison for life without parole is nothing but a death sentence. Again, we're not there yet. So we soldier on."

She finally took another bite.

Jake had asked for money and manpower. Money for expert testimony and litigation expenses. And he wanted the assistance of another seasoned lawyer in the "second chair" during the trial. The law required a second defense lawyer but Noose was having trouble finding one.

Jake had made these requests in writing and they had discussed them over the phone. KAF lawyers were overworked. Its funds were tight. He had driven five hours for the meeting to say hello and impress upon Libby Provine the urgency of Drew's case. Perhaps a face-to-face meeting would lead to her cooperation.

Two other requests to similar organizations were pending but did not look promising.

She said, "We've used a child psychiatrist from Michigan in a number of cases, a Dr. Emile Jamblah. He's the best so far. A Syrian, slightly darker skin, speaks with an accent. Might this be a problem down there?"

"Oh yes. Could be a real problem. Anybody else?"

"Our second choice would be a doctor out of New York."

"Got anybody with the right accent?"

"Maybe. There's one who's on the faculty at Baylor."

"Now you're talking. You know how experts work in courtrooms, Libby. He or she needs to be from another state because the farther he or she has traveled to get there, the smarter he or she is perceived to be by the jury. On the other hand, people down there react strongly to strange accents, especially Northern ones."

"I know. I tried a case in Alabama ten years ago. Can you imagine me talking to a jury in Tuscaloosa? It was not a good outcome. The kid was seventeen. Now he's twenty-seven and still on death row."

"I think I read that case."

"What will your jury look like?"

"Frightening. A regular posse. It's rural north Mississippi, and I'll try to change venue to another county simply because of the notoriety. But wherever we go the demographics are much the same. Seventy-five percent white. Average household income of thirty thousand. I expect nine or ten whites, two or three blacks, seven women, five men, ages thirty to sixty, all Christians or claiming to be. Of the twelve, maybe four made it to college. Four didn't finish high school. One person earning fifty thousand a year. Two or three unemployed. God-fearing souls who believe in law and order."

"I've seen that jury. Is the trial still set for August the sixth?"

"It is and I don't see a delay."

"Why so soon?"

"Why not? And I have a good reason for wanting the trial on August sixth. I'll explain in a moment."

"Okay. How do you see it unfolding?"

"Fairly cut-and-dried, to a point. The State will go first, of course. The prosecutor is competent but inexperienced. He'll begin with the investigators, crime scene photos, cause of death, autopsy, and so on. The facts are plain, unambiguous, the photos are horrendous, so he'll have the jury in his pocket at the opening bell. The victim was an army veteran, a fine peace officer, a local boy, all that. The case is really not that complicated. Within minutes the jury will know the victim and his killer and see the murder weapon. During cross-examination, I'll ask about the autopsy and drag out the truth that at the time of his death Mr. Kofer was blind drunk. That will begin the ugly process of putting him on trial, and it'll get worse. Some of the jurors will resent this. Others will be shocked. At some point the State will probably call the sister, Kiera, to the stand. She is an important witness and she'll be expected to say that she heard the gunshot and her brother admitted to killing Kofer. The D.A. will attempt to prove that his actions and movements before the shooting show that the kid knew what he was doing. It was revenge. He thought his mother was dead and he wanted revenge."

"Sounds believable."

"Indeed it does. But Kiera's testimony could be even more dramatic. When she takes the stand, the jury and everybody else in the courtroom will know immediately that she is pregnant. Over seven months along. And guess who the father is?"

"Not Kofer."

"Yes. I'll ask her to identify the father and she'll testify, rather emotionally I suspect, that he was raping her on a regular basis. Five or six times, beginning around Christmas. Whenever they were alone he raped her, and after each assault he threatened to kill her and her brother if she told anyone."

Libby was speechless. She shoved her sandwich a few inches away and closed her eyes. After a moment, she asked, "Why would the State put her on the stand if she's pregnant?"

"Because the State doesn't know it."

She took a deep breath, moved her chair back, stood, and walked to the other end of her office. From behind her desk, she asked, "Don't you have an obligation to inform the prosecutor?"

"No. She's not my witness. She's not my client."

"I'm sorry, Jake, but I'm having some trouble processing this. Are you trying to hide the fact that she's pregnant?"

"Let's just say I don't want the other side to know it."

"But won't the D.A. and his investigators meet with their witnesses before trial?"

"Normally, yes. It's up to them. They can meet with her whenever they want. They talked to her two weeks ago in my office."

"Is the girl in hiding? Does she have friends?"

"Not many, and, yes, she's basically in hiding. I explained to Kiera and Josie that it would be best if no one knows she's pregnant, but there's always the chance that she'll be discovered. There's also the chance that the D.A. will find out. But she's going to testify at trial, either for the prosecution or the defense, and if the trial's in August she'll be seven months pregnant."

"Is she, uh, showing?"

"Barely. Her mother has told her to wear nothing but oversized clothing. They're still living in the church but I'm trying to find them a place, an apartment in another town. They stopped attending church services a couple of weeks ago and are trying to avoid everyone."

"At your recommendation, I'm sure."

Jake smiled and nodded. Libby paced back to the table and sat down. She drank from her bottle and said, "Wow."

"I thought you'd like it. A defense lawyer's dream. A total ambush of the prosecution's witness."

"I know discovery is limited down there, but this seems a bit extreme."

"As I said in my memo, there is virtually no discovery in criminal cases. Same for most of the country."

She knew this. She took a bite of her sandwich and chewed slowly, her mind racing. "What about a mistrial? Surely the State will scream about the surprise and want a new trial."

"The State rarely gets a mistrial. We've gone back eighty years and researched hundreds of cases involving mistrials. Only three were granted to the prosecution, and all involved important witnesses who didn't show up for court. And I'll argue that a mistrial is unnecessary because the girl will testify at trial regardless of which side calls her as a witness."

"Any chance Kofer is not the father?"

"Doubtful. She's fourteen and swears he was the first and only."

Libby shook her head and looked away. When she looked back, Jake noticed moisture in her eyes. "She's just a baby," she said softly.

"A sweet girl who's had a tough life."

"You know, Jake, these are terrible trials. I've been through dozens of them in many states. Kids who commit murder are not like adults who commit murder. Their brains have not fully formed. They are easily influenced. They are often abused and mistreated and cannot escape bad environments. Yet they're able to pull the trigger, same as an adult, and the victims are just as dead. Their survivors are just as angry. This is your first, right?"

"Yes, and I didn't ask for it."

"I know. As bad as these trials are, this is my work, my calling, and I'm still challenged by it. I love the courtroom, Jake, and I really don't want to miss the moment when Kiera takes the stand. Talk about drama of the highest order."

"Does this mean—"

"I want to be there. I have a trial in Kentucky in early August but we'll push for a continuance. Our other lawyers are booked. Maybe, just maybe, I can clear my schedule and step in."

"That would help considerably." Jake could not suppress a smile. "What about the money?"

"We're broke, same as always. We'll cover my time and expenses and we'll provide the expert if and when we get to the sentencing. I'm afraid you're on your own to hire the right insanity person."

"Any ideas?"

"Oh sure," she said. "I know plenty of them. White,

black, brown, male, female, young or old. Take your pick. I'll find the right one, just let me think about it."

"Definitely white, probably female, don't you think? Our best chance for a little mercy might come from women. Someone who's been slapped around by a drunk. Someone carrying a dark secret about being sexually assaulted. Someone with a teenage daughter."

"We keep a thick file on the best experts."

"Don't forget about the accent."

"Of course not. In fact there's a shrink in New Orleans we used about three years ago. I wasn't in the courtroom but our lawyers were impressed. So was the jury."

"How much might this expert cost me?"

"Twenty thousand, give or take."

"I don't have twenty thousand."

"I'll see what I can do."

Jake offered a hand to shake and said, "Welcome to Ford County, though let's hope the trial is somewhere else."

She shook his hand and said, "Deal."

27

The investigator for the district attorney was a former Tyler County deputy named Jerry Snook. On a Monday morning, he arrived for work at the D.A.'s office in the courthouse in Gretna and began planning his week. Fifteen minutes later he was summoned to Lowell Dyer's office next door.

His boss was already in a foul mood. Dyer said, "Just got off the phone with Earl Kofer, who calls me at least three times a week. Wanted to know what he always wants to know. When's the trial? I said August the sixth, same as the last time you called. The date is set and will not be moved. Wanted to know if the trial will be in Ford County. I said I don't know because Brigance wants to move it. Why, he asked? Because he thinks there's too much notoriety around Clanton and is looking for a friendlier venue. He wants a jury that's not familiar with the case. This upset Earl and he started cussing, said the system is always rigged to protect the criminal. I explained that we will resist any effort to move the case but the decision will be left to Judge Noose. He ranted about Brigance and the Carl Lee Hailey trial and said the system wasn't fair because he got off by claiming to be insane and that's what Brigance will do again. I reminded him that Judge Noose refused to change venue in that trial and it's been a long time since he agreed to move one. I explained that it's rare in Mississippi for a judge to change venue, and so on. But he doesn't listen and is really bitter, which I understand. He wants me to guarantee that the kid will be convicted and sent to death row, and he wanted to know when there will be an execution. He said he read somewhere that Mississippi has plenty of men on death row but can't seem to get them to the gas chamber. Said the average time on death row is eighteen years. Said he can't wait that long, that his family is devastated, and on and on. The same conversation we had last Friday."

"Sorry, boss," Snook said.

Dyer moved some papers around on his desk. "Oh well, just part of the job, I guess."

"You wanted to talk about the mother and sister."

"Yes, primarily the sister. We need to talk to them, now. We have a general idea of what Josie will say at trial, but we will not call her as a witness. The girl, though, has to testify. We have to assume that the defendant will not take the stand, so we have to call his sister. What do you know about them as of today?"

"They're still living in the church. Josie is working at least two part-time jobs. Don't know what the girl is doing. She's a kid and school's out."

"We can't talk to her unless her mother is present. I mean, we could, in theory, but it would cause problems. Brigance would get involved and raise hell. It looks like they're doing whatever he says."

"I don't mind knocking on the door when Josie is gone."

Dyer was shaking his head. "She'll freak out and call her mother. It's too risky. I'll call Brigance and arrange a meeting."

"Good luck with that."

"The trial's in two months. Are you ready?"

"I will be."

"When are you headed to Ford County?"

"Tomorrow."

"Stop by and say hello to Earl Kofer. The family needs to be reassured."

"Would love to."

JAKE AND CARLA parked in front of the jail and walked in the front door. He had his briefcase. She was carrying a large cloth bag filled with textbooks and notepads. Inside, Jake spoke to two deputies he knew but did not introduce his wife. The mood was immediately tense and the greetings were strained. He led Carla through a door to the jail and stopped at the counter where Sergeant Buford was waiting on them.

Jake said, "Ozzie told us to be here at nine. Judge Noose's orders."

Buford glanced at his watch as if Jake couldn't tell time. "I need to look at that," he said, pointing to Jake's briefcase. Jake opened it for a quick inspection. Satisfied but not pleased with the encounter, Buford looked at Carla's bag and asked, "What's in there?"

She opened it and said, "Textbooks and notepads."

He poked around without removing anything and growled, "Follow me."

Though Jake had reassured her, Carla's stomach was in knots. She had never been inside the jail and half-expected to see real criminals leering at her through the bars. But there were no cells, only a dank, narrow hallway with worn carpet and doors on both sides. They stopped at one and Buford unlocked it with one of the many keys on his ring.

"Ozzie said two hours. I'll be back at eleven."

"I'd like to leave in an hour," Jake said.

Buford shrugged as if he could not care less and opened the door. With a jerk of the head, he motioned

for them to step inside and then locked the door behind them.

Drew was sitting at a small table in the same faded
coveralls he wore every day. He did not stand or say
hello. His hands were free and he'd been playing with a
deck of cards.

Jake said, "Drew, this is my wife, Ms. Brigance, but
you can call her Miss Carla."

Drew smiled, because it was impossible not to smile
at Carla. They sat in metal chairs across the narrow
table.

Carla smiled and said, "Nice to meet you, Drew."

Jake said, "Now, Drew, as I explained yesterday, Miss
Carla will visit you twice a week and organize a plan
for your schoolwork."

"Okay."

Carla said, "Jake tells me you were in the ninth grade
last year, right?"

"Uh-huh."

With a smile, Jake said, "Drew, I want you to get in
the habit of saying 'Yes ma'am' and 'No ma'am.' 'Yes sir'
and 'no sir' would be a good thing too. Can you practice this?"

"Yes sir."

"Attaboy."

Carla said, "I checked with your teachers and they
told me your subjects were Mississippi history, Algebra
One, English, and general science. Does that sound
right?"

"I guess so."

"Do you have a favorite subject?"

"Not really. I didn't like any of them. I hate school."

The teachers had verified this. They were unanimous in their assessment that he was indifferent to his
studies, barely made passing grades, had few friends,

kept to himself, and in general seemed miserable at school.

Carla's first impression was similar to Jake's. It was difficult to believe that the kid was sixteen years old. Thirteen would have been a good guess. He was frail, skinny, with a mop of blond hair that badly needed trimming. He was awkward, timid, and avoided eye contact. The thought that he had committed such a heinous murder was hard to fathom.

She said, "Okay, a lot of kids hate school, but you can't drop out. Let's just say that this is not school. Let's call it private tutoring. What I want to do is take about thirty minutes with each subject and then leave you with some homework."

"Homework sounds like school," Drew said and they laughed. For Jake, it was a minor breakthrough, the first attempt at humor he had seen by his client.

"I guess it does. Where would you like to start?"

He shrugged and said, "I don't care. You're the teacher."

"Okay. Let's start with math."

Drew frowned and Jake mumbled, "Not my favorite either."

Carla reached into her bag, pulled out a notebook, and placed it on the table. She opened it and removed a single sheet of paper. "Here are ten basic math problems I want you to do for me." She handed him a pencil. The problems were simple sums that any fifth grader could handle in a matter of minutes.

To ease the pressure, Jake removed a file from his briefcase and was soon lost in something lawyerly. Carla pulled out a history textbook and thumbed through it. Drew went to work and did not appear to struggle.

His academic progress had been uneven, to say the least. In his young life he had attended at least seven schools in different districts and states. He had dropped out at least twice and transferred numerous times. He had lived in three foster homes, one orphanage, with two relatives, in a borrowed camper, spent four months in a juvenile jail for stealing bikes, and there had been stretches of homelessness in which there had been no school at all. His most stable period had been from the ages of eleven to thirteen when his mother was in prison and he and Kiera were sent to a Baptist orphanage in Arkansas where they found structure and security. Once paroled, Josie reclaimed her children, and the family continued its chaotic journey to somewhere.

With Josie's written consent, Portia had doggedly tracked down his school records, and Kiera's as well, and put together their sad little biographies.

Jake, while pretending to read with a frown, was thinking of how far his client had come in the past eleven weeks. From his catatonic state in their first meetings, through his first words, his two weeks at Whitfield, his forced acceptance of solitary confinement, and the dreariness of life in a cell, to a point now where he could maintain a decent conversation and ask about his future. There was little doubt the antidepressants were working. It also helped that Mr. Zack, another jailer, liked him and spent time with him. He brought the kid chocolate brownies baked by his wife, and comic books, and he gave Drew a deck of cards and taught him gin rummy, poker, and blackjack. When things were slow, Mr. Zack went down to his little room for a hand or two. Human contact was crucial for everyone, and Mr. Zack loathed the notion of solitary confinement.

Jake was stopping by almost every day. They often played cards and talked about the weather, girls, friends, games that Drew once played. Anything but the killing and the trial.

Jake was still not ready to ask his client the most important question: "Did you know Kofer was raping Kiera?" And that was because Jake was not ready for the answer. If it was "Yes," then revenge was in play, and revenge meant that Drew acted with forethought to protect her. Forethought equaled premeditation, and that meant the death penalty.

Perhaps he would never ask the question. He still had serious reservations about putting Drew on the stand to face a withering cross-examination by the district attorney.

As Jake watched him do the math, he could not imagine allowing the kid to be sacrificed in front of the jury. It was a decision any defense lawyer had the right to reserve until the last moment. Mississippi did not require the defense to divulge before the trial whether or not the accused would testify. Jake had hinted to Judge Noose and Lowell Dyer that Drew would not, but that was part of a ploy to force the prosecution to call Kiera as a witness. Other than her brother, she was the only possible eyewitness.

Drew said, "Here," and handed Carla the sheet of paper. She smiled, handed him another, and said, "Okay, now try these." It was another series of slightly more difficult sums.

As he worked, Carla graded the first set. He'd missed four out of ten. She had her work cut out for her.

BUFORD WAS BACK after an hour and Jake was ready to leave. He asked Drew to stand, shake hands firmly, and say goodbye. Carla was preparing a brief lesson on the Native Americans who once lived in their state.

Jake left the jail on foot and walked three blocks to the square for a meeting he wanted to avoid. He entered Security Bank, waited five minutes in the lobby, and soon saw Stan Atcavage waving him into his spacious office. They exchanged greetings like the good friends they were, but both were dreading what they were about to discuss.

"Let's cut to the chase, Stan," Jake finally said.

"Right, look Jake, as I've said before, this is not the same bank it was two years ago. Back then we were locally owned and Ed gave me plenty of wiggle room. I could do almost anything I wanted. But, as you know, Ed sold out and he's gone now, and the new guys down in Jackson run a different show."

"We've had this discussion."

"And we're having it again. We've been good friends for many years and I'd do anything within my power to help you. But I'm not calling all the shots anymore."

"How much do they want?"

"They don't like this loan, Jake. Lending money for litigation. They refer to it as 'Tort Sport' money and they said no at first. I convinced them that you knew what you're doing and you were certain *Smallwood* would be a gold mine. Now that the case has blown up, they feel vindicated. They want half of the seventy thousand and they want it real soon."

"And so that leads us to my request for a refinancing. If the bank will redo the mortgage on my home, extend more credit, I'll have some cash to work with. I can pay down the litigation loan and stay in business."

"Well, your business model worries them. They've gone through your financials and are not impressed."

The idea of a bunch of big-shot bankers poking through his financials and frowning at his income made his blood boil. He hated banks, and once again vowed to somehow get them out of his life. At the moment, though, that seemed impossible.

Stan continued, "Last year you grossed ninety thousand and netted fifty before taxes."

"I know this. Believe me I do. But the year before I grossed one-forty. You know what it's like hustling clients in a small town. With the exception of the Sullivans, every lawyer around the square is up and down."

"True, but the year before you were sitting fat because of fees from the Hubbard will contest."

"I really don't want to argue with you, Stan. I bought the house two years ago from Willie Trainer for two-fifty, a lot for Clanton, but then it's a lot of house."

"And I approved the loan, without hesitation. But the guys in Jackson are skeptical of your appraisal."

"You and I both know the appraisal is on the high side. I'll bet those sumbitches down in Jackson live in homes that cost a lot more than three hundred thousand."

"That's beside the point, Jake. They're saying no to a new mortgage. I'm sorry, Jake. If it were up to me I would approve the loan to you with just your signature, no collateral."

"Let's not get carried away here, Stan. You are, after all, a banker."

"I'm your friend, Jake, and it pains me to pass along the bad news. Zero. No new mortgage. I'm sorry, Jake."

Jake sighed in defeat and almost felt sorry for his friend. They watched each other for a moment. Jake finally said, "Okay, I'll shop it around. When do they want their money?"

"Two weeks."

Jake shook his head as if in disbelief. "I guess I can dip into the rather shallow pool of my savings."

"I'm sorry, Jake."

"I know you are, Stan, and I know this is not what you want. Don't beat yourself up over it. I'll survive. Somehow."

They shook hands, and Jake couldn't wait to get out of the bank.

HE USED THE back alleys to avoid people and minutes later eased into his office. More bad news was waiting.

Josie was sitting with Portia at the front desk. Both were drinking coffee and seemed engaged in a pleasant conversation. She had not bothered to make an appointment and Jake was not in the mood for more hand-holding, but he couldn't say no. She followed him upstairs to his office and sat across from him at his cluttered desk. They talked about Drew for a moment and Jake reported that Carla was over at the jail going through their initial tutoring session. He exaggerated a little and said Drew seemed to be enjoying the attention. They talked about Kiera for a moment and Josie described her as lonely, bored, and frightened. Mrs. Golden from the church visited three times a week for lessons. She was piling on the homework and this kept Kiera somewhat engaged. Charles and Meg McGarry stopped by every other day to check on her. Josie had stopped going to church because Kiera couldn't go with her anymore. She was finally showing a little and their secret had to be protected.

Josie pulled some letters out of her purse and handed them over. She said, "Two from the hospitals, here and in Tupelo, and one from the doctor over there. A total of sixteen thousand dollars and change, and, of course, they're makin' threats. What am I supposed to do, Jake?"

Jake quickly scanned the numbers and once again marveled at the cost of health care.

She said, "I'm working three part-time jobs now, all minimum wage, and we're barely gettin' by, but I can't pay these bills. Plus my car needs a new transmission. If it croaks we're just screwed, plain and simple."

Jake said, "We can bankrupt these." He avoided bankruptcy work with as much enthusiasm as he avoided divorces, but occasionally he waded into the pit with a client in dire need.

"But I need my doctor, Jake. I can't bankrupt him. Plus, I filed two years ago down in Louisiana, for the second time. Isn't there a limit on how many times you can file?"

"I'm afraid so." With her financial problems, criminal convictions, and divorces, he figured she knew more about the law than most lawyers. While he admired her spunk and determination to survive and protect her children, he fought the urge to judge her harshly for her mistakes.

"So, I can't file again. What do you suggest?"

He wanted to suggest that she go hire herself another lawyer. He had his hands full with her son, and that would probably drive himself into bankruptcy. He had never agreed to represent her. On the contrary, he had been strong-armed into defending Drew. But he was the family's lawyer and there was no way out of it.

Harry Rex would run her off, shoo her out of the office, and show little sympathy. Lucien would take her in and then dump her problems on the desk of some lowly associate while he mounted a noisy defense of her son. Jake didn't have that luxury. And the truth was that he rarely said no to an indigent client in need. At times it seemed that half of his work was pro bono, either agreed on up front or realized months later when his fees were written off.

Complicating matters was the ticking clock. Kiera would have a baby in about three months. His conversations with Carla were still fresh.

"Okay, I'll call the hospitals and doctors and have a chat."

She was wiping her eyes. "You ever had your paycheck garnished, Jake?"

What paycheck? "No, I haven't."

"It's awful. You work hard at a crap job and when you finally get paid there's a yellow notice in the envelope. Some credit card company or finance company or crooked used car dealer has snagged your paycheck and cut it in half. It's just awful. That's the way I live, Jake. Always climbin' a mountain, tryin' to keep food on the table, and there's always somebody after me. Writin' mean letters. Hirin' collection lawyers. Threatenin', somebody's always threatenin'. I don't mind workin' hard but I'm just tryin' to stay afloat, to survive. I can't even think about gettin' ahead."

It was easy to think that her problems were all self-imposed, the damage self-inflicted, but Jake wondered if she had ever really had a chance. She had lived for thirty-two hard years. If given the chance she could be attractive, and this had no doubt led to serious problems with bad men. Perhaps she had been abused. Or perhaps she had always made wrong decisions.

"I'll make the calls and buy some time," he said, because he could think of nothing else and needed to do some work, hopefully something that paid.

She blurted, "I need eight hundred dollars for a transmission, Jake, a used one. Can you make me a loan?"

In the life of a small-town lawyer, this was not an

unusual request. Jake had learned the hard way to avoid lending money to broke clients. The standard and trusted response was *Sorry, but it's unethical for me to loan money to you.*

Why?

Why? Because the chances of getting repaid are rather slim. Why? Because the ethics people down at the state bar association realized decades ago that most of its members, the majority of whom are small-town lawyers, need to be protected from such requests.

At the moment, he had about $4,000 in his firm account, money that would be sorely needed in the forthcoming months to keep his doors open. But, what the hell? She needed the money far more than he did, and if her car quit he would inherit even more problems he didn't want to deal with. He could work longer hours, hustle more clients, ask Noose to give him indigent appointments that he could ramp up and obtain plea bargains. He was proud to be a street lawyer, as opposed to those stiff suits in the big firms, and he had always been able to hustle for extra work when in a pinch.

He smiled and nodded and said, "I can swing that. I'll ask you to sign a promissory note with a due date a year from now. It's sort of a formality, for ethical reasons."

She wept for a while as Jake pretended to take notes. When the crying finally stopped she said, "I'm sorry, Jake. So sorry."

He waited until she was somewhat composed and said, "Josie, I have an idea. You're tired of living in the church. Pastor McGarry and his flock have been amazing in their support for you and Kiera, but you can't stay there. They'll soon realize she's pregnant and the gossip will begin. You can't pay these bills, and it's unrealistic to think the hospitals and doctors will back off. I want you to disappear, to move, to simply vanish from this area."

"I can't leave, not with Drew in jail and facin' trial."

"You can't help Drew right now. Move somewhere not far away and lay low until the trial."

"Where?"

"Oxford. It's only an hour away. It's a college town with lots of cheap apartments. We'll find one that's furnished. Summer is here and the students are gone. I have a couple of lawyer friends there and I'll lean on them to help find a job or two. Forget these bills. The debt collectors can't find you."

"That's the story of my life, Jake. Always runnin'."

"There's no reason to stay here, no family, no real friends."

"What about Kiera's doctor?"

"They have a nice hospital in Oxford, a regional, with plenty of good doctors. We'll make sure she's taken care of. That's a priority."

Her tears were gone, her eyes clear. "I'll need another loan to get set up."

"There's another reason, Josie. She'll have the baby sometime in September, after the trial and after everyone in Clanton knows about her pregnancy. If she has the baby in Oxford, few people here will know anything about it. Very few. Including the Kofers. They'll be shocked when they learn about their grandchild and they'll probably want nothing to do with it. However, as I've learned, it's impossible to predict what people will do. There's the chance that they might want some contact with the child. That cannot happen."

"That will not happen."

"We'll do the adoption over there, in another judicial district. Kiera will be in another school and her new friends will know nothing about her pregnancy. Moving away is the best move for her, and for you too."

"I don't know what to do, Jake."

"You're a survivor, Josie. Get away from this place. Nothing good will happen to you and your daughter if you stay in this county. Trust me on this."

She bit her lip and fought back more tears. Softly, she said, "Okay."

CHANCELLOR REUBEN ATLEE's fine old home was two blocks from Jake's in central Clanton. It was old enough to have its own name, Maple Run, and the judge had lived there for decades. Late in the afternoon, Jake parked behind a large Buick and knocked on the screen door. Atlee was a notorious tightwad who still refused to install air-conditioning.

A voice called him inside and Jake stepped into the humid and sticky foyer. Judge Atlee appeared with two tumblers filled with brown liquid, his standard whiskey-sour toddy to end another hard day. He handed one to Jake and said, "Let's sit on the porch." They went outside where the air was noticeably lighter and settled into rockers.

Judge Atlee had ruled the chancery court for a long time and quietly kept his nose in most of the county's business. His jurisdiction was family law, all the divorces, adoptions, plus will contests, land disputes, zoning matters, a long list of legal matters that almost never included jury trials. He was wise, fair, heavy-handed, and had no patience with windy or lazy lawyers.

He said, "I see you got stuck with the Gamble case."

"Afraid so." Jake sipped the whiskey, not his favorite, and wondered how he would explain this to Carla. It wouldn't be that difficult. If Judge Atlee handed you a drink and said sit on the front porch, no lawyer could say no.

"Noose called me for advice. I said there was no other lawyer in the county who could handle the case."

"Thanks for nothing."

"It's part of being a lawyer, Jake. You don't always get to choose your clients."

And why not? Why couldn't he and every other lawyer say no to a client? "Well, I'm stuck with it."

"I suppose you're going with insanity."

"Probably, but he shot him in cold blood."

"Such a shame. It's all so tragic. What a waste of life, for the deputy and the kid."

"I doubt there will be much sympathy for the kid."

Atlee took a sip and gazed at the rooftops down the hill. The roof of the Hocutt House was visible in the distance. "What's a fair punishment, Jake? I don't like the idea of putting children on trial for capital murder, but the deputy is just as dead regardless of who pulled the trigger. The killer has to be punished, and severely."

"That's the great question, isn't it? But it doesn't really matter. The town wants a death verdict and the gas chamber. My job is to fight it."

Atlee nodded and took another sip. "You said you needed a favor."

"Yes sir. I don't think it's fair to try the kid in this county. It will be impossible to pick an impartial jury. Do you agree?"

"I don't deal with juries, Jake. You know that."

Jake also knew that Judge Atlee knew more about the case than all but a handful of people. "But you know the county, Judge, better than anyone. I plan to ask for a change of venue, and I need your help."

"In what way?"

"Talk to Noose. You guys have a way of communicating that few people know about. You just said that he called you looking for advice on who to appoint. Lean on him to change venue."

"To where?"

"Anywhere but here. He'll keep jurisdiction because it's his case and it's high-profile. Doesn't want to miss the fun. Plus, he might have an opponent next year and he wants to look good."

"Buckley?"

"That's the rumor. Buckley's making noises down there."

"Buckley's a fool and he got slaughtered in his last election."

"True, but no sitting judge wants an election."

"I've never had one," he said a bit too smugly. No lawyer with half a brain would challenge Reuben Atlee. Jake said, "Noose refused to change venue in Carl Lee Hailey's trial, and his reasoning was that it was so notorious that everybody in the state knew the details. He was probably right. This is different. A dead cop is a big story. Tragic and all, but it happens. The headlines go away. I'll bet the folks up in Milburn County aren't talking about it."

"I was there last week. Not a word."

"It's different here. The Kofers have lots of friends. Ozzie and his boys are pissed. They'll keep things stirred up."

His Honor was nodding. He took another sip and said, "I'll talk to Noose."

28

After another round of verbal abuse from Harry Rex, Stan managed to convince his boss down in Jackson to reduce the payment to $25,000. Jake raided his savings and wrote a check for half. Harry Rex found some money and wrote his own, along with a handwritten note vowing to never speak to Stan again. He stopped just short of threatening to punch him the next time he saw him on the square.

Harry Rex was still confident they would get *something* out of the *Smallwood* case, if only a nuisance settlement to save the railroad the costs of defending a big trial. When that trial might take place no one knew. Sean Gilder and the railroad boys were up to their patented stall game and claimed to still be searching for just the right expert. Noose had pushed them hard for over a year, but since Jake's debacle in discovery he had lost interest in a speedy trial. Gilder's partner, Doby Pittman, had intimated that the railroad might consider a nuisance settlement to make the case go away. "Something like a hundred grand," he whispered over more drinks in Jackson.

In the unlikely event that the railroad and its insurance company did in fact write a check, the litigation expenses—now at $72,000 and change—would be reimbursed first. Whatever was left would be divided, with two-thirds going to Grace Smallwood and one-third to Jake and Harry Rex. The fee would be paltry but at least they would have dodged a bullet with their ill-fated "Tort Sport" loan.

However, Doby Pittman wasn't calling the shots and had been wrong before. Sean Gilder showed no signs of backing off and seemed confident of a glorious courtroom victory.

ON FRIDAY, June 8, Lowell Dyer and Jerry Snook, along with Ozzie and his investigator, Kirk Rady, settled into the main conference room of Jake's office suite. Across the table, Jake sat with Josie on one side and Kiera on the other.

For the meeting, the girl was wearing a pair of loose-fitting jeans and a bulky sweatshirt. Though the temperature was close to ninety, no one seemed to notice that the sweatshirt seemed out of place. Jake and Josie assumed that everyone in the room knew that the family was wearing secondhand clothing that had been donated. She was six months pregnant with a small baby bump that was well concealed.

After an attempt at a few awkward pleasantries, Dyer began by explaining to Kiera that since she was a witness to the crime, she might be called by the State to testify. "Do you understand this?" he asked, somewhat delicately.

She nodded and softly said, "Yes, I do."

"Has Mr. Brigance explained to you what will happen in court?"

"Yes, we've talked about it."

"Has he told you what to say?"

She shrugged and looked confused. "I guess."

"So what did Mr. Brigance tell you to say?"

Jake, itching for a fight, interrupted with "Why don't you just ask her what happened?"

"Okay, Kiera, what happened that night?"

Avoiding eye contact, she focused on a legal pad in the center of the table and told her story: awake at 2:00 A.M., waiting for Stuart Kofer to return home; hiding in her bedroom with Drew while their mother waited downstairs; unable to sleep because of the fear; sitting on her bed in the dark with her brother with the door locked; seeing the headlights; hearing the car; hearing the kitchen door open and slam; hearing the voices of her mother and Kofer as they argued; then louder voices as he called her a whore and a liar; the sound of her mother getting slapped around again; then the silence for a few minutes as they waited; the heavy footsteps of Kofer climbing the stairs, calling her name as he got closer; the rattling of her doorknob; the banging on the door as they cried and held their breath and prayed for help; the silence for a moment as he decided to leave them alone; the sounds of him going back down the stairs; the horror of knowing their mother was injured or else she would have been fighting to protect them; the long awful silence as they waited.

Her voice cracked and she wiped her cheeks with a tissue.

Dyer said, "I realize this is difficult, but please try to finish. This is very important."

She nodded and clenched her jaws in determination. She looked at Jake and he nodded. Finish it.

Drew eased downstairs and found their mother unconscious. He ran back upstairs and, in tears, said she was dead. They went to the kitchen where Kiera begged her mother to wake up, then she sat down and took her mother's head in her lap. One of them, she couldn't remember who, said to call 911. Drew made the call as Kiera held her mother, who wasn't breathing. They knew she was dead. She held her mother's head and stroked her hair and whispered to her. Drew was moving around but she wasn't sure what he was doing. He said that Kofer was passed out on his bed. Drew closed the bedroom door and Kiera heard the gunshot.

She began sobbing and the adults in the room avoided eye contact. After a minute or two, she wiped her cheeks again and looked at Dyer.

He asked, "What did Drew say after the gunshot?"

"He said he shot Stu."

"So, you did not actually see him shoot Stuart?"

"No."

"But you heard the gunshot?"

"Yes."

"Did Drew say anything else?"

She paused and thought about this and finally said, "I don't remember anything else he said."

"Okay, what happened next?"

Another pause. "I don't know. I was just holding my mother and I couldn't believe she was dead."

"Do you remember a deputy arriving on the scene?"

"Yes."

"And where were you when you saw the deputy?"

"I was still on the floor, holding my mother."

"Do you remember the deputy asking you what happened?"

"I think so. Yes."

"And what did you say?"

"I said something like, 'Drew shot Stuart.'"

Dyer offered a sappy smile and said, "Thank you, Kiera. I know this is not easy. While you were holding your mother, was she breathing?"

"No, I didn't think so. I held her for a long time and I just knew she was dead."

"Did you try to check her pulse?"

"I don't think so. I was too scared. It's kinda hard to think when something like that happens."

"I understand." Dyer looked at some notes and paused before proceeding. "Now, I believe you used the word 'again' when you said that you heard Stuart Kofer and your mother arguing and fighting downstairs. Is this correct?"

"Yes sir."

"So this had happened before?"

"Yes sir. Many times."

"Did you ever actually see these fights?"

"Yes, but I wouldn't call them fights. My mother was just trying to protect herself when he beat her."

"And you saw this?"

"One time, yes. He came home late and drunk, as usual."

"Did he ever hit you or Drew?"

Jake interrupted with "She's not answering that."

"Why not?" Dyer shot across the table.

"Because on direct examination you're not going to ask that question. She'll be *your* witness then."

"I have the right to know what her testimony will be."

"On direct, when she's your witness. You have no right to know what she might say on cross."

Dyer ignored Jake, looked at Kiera, and asked the question again. "Did Stuart Kofer ever hit you or Drew?"

Jake said, "Don't answer that."

"You're not her lawyer, Jake."

"But she'll be my witness on cross. Let's just say that her testimony on cross will not be helpful to the State."

"You're wrong about this, Jake."

"Then we'll have a chat with Judge Noose."

"You're out of line here."

"We'll see, but she's not answering that question until the judge orders her to. You got what you want, now let it go."

"I will not. I'll file a motion to compel her to answer my questions."

"Fine. And we'll argue your motion before the judge."

Dyer made a production of putting the cap back onto his pen and gathering his notes. Meeting over. He said, "Thank you, Kiera, for your time."

Jake, Kiera, and Josie didn't move as the rest of them stood and filed out of the room. When the door was closed, Jake patted Kiera on the arm and said, "Nice job."

It was a splendid performance by a fourteen-year-old girl.

BROKE AS HE was, Jake wanted to host a backyard barbecue. Late Friday afternoon, he fired up his grill on the patio, marinated chicken breasts and thighs, and roasted hot dogs and corn on the cob while Carla mixed a large pitcher of lemonade.

The Hailey clan arrived first: Carl Lee and Gwen with their four children, Tonya, now seventeen and going on twenty, and the three boys, Ernie, Jarvis, and Micah. They always arrived a bit reticent because they were guests at a fine home in the white section of town, a rarity in Clanton. Jake had never been to a barbecue or a cocktail party or even a wedding to which blacks were invited. Since Carl Lee's trial five years earlier, he and Carla had been determined to change this. They had hosted the Haileys, along with Ozzie and his family, many times on the patio. And they had been to the Haileys' home for cookouts and sprawling family gatherings where they were the only white folks. Among the blacks in Ford County, Jake Brigance could do no wrong. He was their lawyer. The problem was they had little to pay in the way of fees, and most of their legal issues fit in the pro bono category, Jake's specialty.

Ozzie had been invited but found an excuse to stay away.

Josie and Kiera arrived with Charles and Meg Mc-Garry. Meg was nine months pregnant and due any moment. Kiera was four months behind and was still wearing the same bulky sweatshirt, in spite of the heat.

Harry Rex was always invited, along with his current wife, but he usually declined because beer was not permitted. Lucien was an occasional guest, and had even brought Sallie once, the only time the two were seen together about town. But he, like Harry Rex, couldn't enjoy a barbecue without booze. That, and he took pride in being fiercely antisocial.

Stan Atcavage had once been on the list but rarely made an appearance. His wife, Tilda, didn't like to mingle with the lower classes.

As the kids played badminton and the women huddled on the patio and fussed over Meg and her due date, Jake and Carl Lee sipped lemonade in lawn chairs in the shade and caught up with the gossip. Lester was always a topic. He was Carl Lee's younger brother and lived in Chicago where he earned big wages as a union ironworker. His troubles with women were always the source of tall stories and endless humor.

When everyone else was preoccupied, Carl Lee said, "Looks like you've got yourself in another mess."

"You could say that," Jake agreed with a smile.

"When's the trial?"

"August, two months away."

"Why don't you put me on the jury?"

"Carl Lee, you're the last person they would put on my jury."

They enjoyed the light moment. Carl Lee still worked at a lumber mill and was now a foreman. He owned his home and five acres around it, and he and Gwen raised their children in a strict environment with many rules. Church every Sunday, plenty of chores for the kids, homework and good grades, respect for elders. His mother lived half a mile down the road and saw her grandchildren every day.

"Willie didn't care for Kofer," Carl Lee said. Willie Hastings was Gwen's second cousin and the first black deputy Ozzie hired.

"I'm not surprised."

"He had no use for blacks. He sucked up to Ozzie for obvious reasons, but he had a dark side. Real dark. Willie thinks the boy got messed up in the army. They kicked him out, you know?"

"I know. A dishonorable discharge. But Ozzie liked him and he was a good cop."

"Willie says Ozzie knew more than he's lettin' on. Says all the deputies knew that Kofer was outta control, drinkin', druggin', fightin' in the clubs."

"That's the rumor."

"Ain't no rumor, Jake. You ever hear of 'clearin' a bar'?"

"No."

"It's a fool's game where a bunch of drunk thugs walk into a tonk that ain't one of theirs. On cue, they start a brawl, start punchin' folks and just beat the shit out of everybody there, then they hit the door and make their escape. Sort of an extreme version of the Friday Night Fights. It's supposed to be great fun because you never know what you're gonna find inside the tonk. Maybe a bunch of old men who can't fight, maybe some real badasses who break bottles and pool sticks."

"And Kofer was into it?"

"Oh yeah. He and his crowd were known for clearin' bars, usually joints outside of the county. A few months back, not long before his demise, they hit a black tonk down in Polk County, just over the line. I guess Kofer, bein' an upstandin' officer of the law, didn't want to get caught in Ford County."

"They raided a black honky-tonk?"

"Yep, accordin' to Willie. Joint called the Moondog."

"I've heard of it. I had a client years ago who was charged in a knife fight down there. Rough place."

"That's it. Always a big dice game on Saturday night. Kofer and four other white guys came through the door throwin' punches and kickin' people. Broke up the dice game. Helluva brawl. Some tough guys, Jake."

"And they made it out alive?"

"Barely. Some dude pulled a piece and shot the walls. White boys scrambled out and got away."

"That's crazy, Carl Lee."

"Crazy as hell. Lucky they all didn't get cut or shot."

"And Willie knew this?"

"Yep, but he's a cop and he ain't one to rat on another cop. I don't think Ozzie heard about it."

"That's insane."

"Well, Kofer was crazy like that and he ran with a tough crowd. You gonna use that at trial?"

"I don't know. Hang on." Jake jumped to his feet and walked to the grill where he flipped the chicken and added more sauce. Pastor McGarry met him there and, eager to get away from the women, followed Jake back to the shade with Carl Lee. The conversation shifted from Stuart Kofer to the badminton game where Hanna and Tonya, on one side of the net, were having a bad go of it against the three Hailey boys on the other side. Finally, Tonya yelled at her father to come play and even things out. Carl Lee happily picked up a racket and joined the fun.

At dusk, they gathered around a picnic table and dined on chicken, hot dogs, and potato salad. The talk was of summer things—trips to the lake, fishing, baseball and softball games, family gatherings.

The looming murder trial seemed far away.

29

Four days later, June 12, Meg McGarry gave birth to a healthy baby at the Ford County Hospital. After work, Jake and Carla drove over for a quick visit. They took flowers and a box of chocolates, though food was not needed. The flock at the Good Shepherd Bible Church descended upon the hospital halfway through labor and the waiting room was filling up with casseroles and cakes.

After a brief visit with Meg and a glimpse of the newborn in her mother's arms, Jake and Carla were obliged to have cake and coffee with the ladies of the church. They stayed longer than they had planned, primarily because Jake was among people who liked him.

THE FOLLOWING DAY, Libby Provine of the Kids Advocacy Foundation arrived from Washington and brought with her an ace psychiatrist from Baylor University. Dr. Thane Sedgwick worked in the field of adolescent criminal behavior and had a résumé an inch thick. Credentials aside, he grew up in rural Texas, near Lufkin, and spoke with a twangy drawl that would never draw attention in north Mississippi. His task was to first spend a few hours with Drew, then prepare a profile. At trial, he would be held in the bullpen until the sentencing phase and brought to the stand in the likely event Drew was found guilty and the defense was fighting for his life.

According to his résumé, Dr. Sedgwick had testified in twenty trials over the past thirty years, always in last-ditch efforts to keep the client off death row. Jake liked him immediately. He was jovial, even comical, laid-back, and his accent was a thing of beauty. Jake marveled at the fact that somehow, while picking up four college degrees and spending a long career in academia, the Texas drawl had not been flattened out.

With Portia tagging along, they went to the jail and met Drew in what was now his classroom. After thirty minutes of small talk, Jake, Portia, and Libby left the room and Dr. Sedgwick set about his work.

At 2:00 P.M., they walked across the street and entered the main courtroom. Lowell Dyer and his assistant were already there with papers strewn over the State's table. Jake introduced Libby to the other lawyers. Dyer was cordial, though he had resisted Jake's petition to allow Libby to assist him at trial. It had been a silly objection, in Jake's opinion, because Judge Noose, along with every other trial judge in the state, permitted out-of-state counsel on a onetime basis when properly associated with a local lawyer.

As they chatted, Jake checked out the courtroom and was surprised at the number of spectators. One group, sitting behind the prosecution, was the Kofer clan and a number of friends. Jake recognized Earl Kofer from a newspaper photo Dumas Lee had run not long after the murder. Next to him was a lady who looked as though she had been crying for a year. No doubt it was the mother, Janet Kofer.

Earl glared at him with pure hatred, and Jake pretended not to notice them. But he glanced again, and again, because he wanted to register the faces of the Kofer boys and cousins.

Judge Noose took the bench at 2:30 and motioned

for everyone to keep their seats. He cleared his throat, pulled his mike closer, and announced, "We are here to discuss several motions, but first a pleasant matter. Mr. Brigance, I believe you have an introduction."

Jake stood and said, "Yes, Your Honor, Ms. Libby Provine of the Kids Advocacy Foundation will be joining the defense efforts. She is licensed to D.C., Virginia, and Maryland."

Libby stood with a smile and nodded at His Honor, who said, "Welcome to the fray, Ms. Provine. I've reviewed your application and résumé, and I'm satisfied that you are more than qualified to sit in the second chair."

"Thank you, Your Honor." She sat down, and Noose picked up some papers. "Let's get right into the defense's motion for a change of venue. Mr. Brigance."

Jake moved to the podium and addressed the judge. "Yes, Your Honor, in our motion I included affidavits from several people, all of the opinion that it will be difficult if not impossible to find twelve people in this county who are impartial. Four are local lawyers, all well known to the court. One is the former mayor of the town of Karaway. One is the minister of the Methodist church here in town. One is a retired school superintendent down in Lake Village. One is a farmer in the Box Hill community. The other is a community organizer."

"I've read the affidavits," Noose said, rather curtly.

Of the non-lawyers, all were former clients Jake had leaned on heavily, and all agreed to the affidavits with the stipulation that they would not have to appear in court. Many of the people Jake had approached had flatly refused to get involved, and he couldn't blame them. There was a great reluctance to do anything that might be perceived as helping the defense.

The affidavits all read the same: The witnesses had lived in the county a long time, knew a lot of people, knew a lot about the case, had discussed it with family and friends, most of whom had already formed opinions, and doubted that a fair, impartial, and uninformed jury could be found in Ford County.

"Do you plan to call these people to the stand today?" Noose asked.

"No sir. Their affidavits are straightforward and state everything they might say in court."

"I've also read your rather lengthy brief. Anything to add to it?"

"No sir. It's all there."

Noose, like Judge Atlee, detested wasting time with lawyers who felt the need to repeat during arguments everything they had submitted in writing. Jake knew better than to cover the same territory. The brief was a thirty-page masterpiece Portia had worked on for weeks. In it, she traced the history of venue changes not only in Mississippi but also in more progressive states. Moving a case rarely happened, and she argued that it wasn't done enough, resulting in trials that were not fair. However, the state supreme court almost never second-guessed trial judges.

Lowell Dyer felt otherwise. In response to Jake's motion, he had submitted his own stack of affidavits, eighteen in all, and they included a veritable roll call of hardcore law-and-order types whose tone was more in favor of a guilty verdict than an impartial jury. His six-page brief stuck to precedents and included nothing creative. The law was on his side and he made it plain.

"Do you plan to call any witnesses, Mr. Dyer?" Noose asked.

"Only if the defense does."

"It's not necessary. I'll take the matter under advisement and issue a ruling in the near future. Let's move on to the next motion, Mr. Brigance."

Dyer took his seat as Jake returned to the podium. "Your Honor, we have moved to dismiss the capital murder indictment on the grounds that it violates the Eighth Amendment's prohibition against cruel and unusual punishment. Until two years ago, this indictment would not be possible because Stuart Kofer was not killed in the line of duty. As you know, in 1988 our esteemed legislature, in a misguided effort to get even tougher on crime and to expedite more executions, passed the Death Penalty Enhancement Act. Until then, the murder of a law enforcement official was a capital offense only if he or she was on duty. Thirty-six states have the death penalty, and in thirty-four of them the officer must be on duty to allow such a charge. Mississippi, in an effort to imitate Texas and increase executions, decided to broaden the scope of death penalty crimes. Not only is murder required, but murder plus something. Murder plus rape, or robbery, or kidnapping. Murder of a child. Murder for hire. And now, under this new and misguided statute, murder of an officer off duty. An officer not on duty has the same standing as every other citizen. To expand, like Mississippi has now done, violates the Eighth Amendment."

"But the U.S. Supreme Court has yet to rule on this," Noose said.

"True, but a case like this could well lead the Court to strike down the new law."

"I'm not sure I'm in a position to strike it down, Mr. Brigance."

"I understand this, Your Honor, but you can certainly see that it is an unfair law and you have the power to quash the indictment on these grounds. The State will then be required to re-indict on a lesser charge."

"Mr. Dyer?"

Lowell stood at his table and said, "The law is the law and it's on the books, Your Honor. Plain and simple. The legislature has the power to pass whatever it chooses and it's our responsibility to follow its dictates. Until the law is amended or struck down by a higher court, we have no choice."

"You chose the wording of the indictment and the statute you're prosecuting under," Jake said. "No one made you indict for capital murder."

"It's capital, Mr. Brigance. Cold-blooded murder."

"The term 'cold-blooded murder' appears nowhere in the statute, Mr. Dyer. There's no need to sensationalize it."

"Gentlemen," Noose said loudly. "I've read the briefs on this issue and I'm not inclined to quash the indictment. It follows the statute, whether we agree with it or not. Motion denied."

Jake was not surprised. But to argue this point on appeal, after a conviction, he was required to raise it now. He had long since accepted the reality that he would be litigating appeals for Drew for years to come, and much of the groundwork had to be laid before the trial. The statute's validity had not been tested before the U.S. Supreme Court and it seemed destined to go there.

Noose shuffled some papers and said to Jake, "What's next?"

Portia handed Jake a brief and he returned to the podium. "Your Honor, we are asking the court to move the defendant to a juvenile facility until the trial. He is now and has for the past two and a half months been locked up here in the county jail, which is no place for a sixteen-year-old. In a juvenile facility he will at least be housed with other minors and given limited contact.

More importantly, he will have access to some level of educational instruction. He is at least two years behind in his schoolwork."

"I thought I had approved a private tutor," Noose said, peering over the reading glasses that were perpetually lodged at the very tip of his long, sloping nose.

"A few hours a week, Your Honor, and that's not enough. I know the tutor very well and she says he needs daily instruction. He is barely keeping up and will only fall further behind. I've spoken to the director of the facility down in Starkville and he assures me the defendant will be secured and confined. There is no chance of escape."

Noose was frowning. He looked at the district attorney and said, "Mr. Dyer."

Lowell rose at his table and said, "Your Honor, I've checked with the directors of all three juvenile facilities in this state and there's not a single capital murder defendant in any of them. Our system simply doesn't work that way. For a crime like this, the defendant is always held in the county where the crime took place. Mr. Gamble will be tried as an adult."

Jake said, "Adults are finished with their education, Your Honor. The ones in jail may need more of it, but it's behind them. That's not true for this defendant. If he gets sent to Parchman he'll have access to some level of instruction, though I'm sure it's inadequate."

Dyer said, "And he'll be held in maximum security. That's where capital murderers are housed."

"He hasn't been convicted yet. Why not place him with other juveniles and at least give him the chance to be in a classroom? There's nothing on the books to prevent this. It's true that these defendants are customarily held in their home counties, but that's not the law. The court has discretion."

"It's never been done," Dyer argued. "So why make an exception now?"

"Gentlemen," Noose said again, cutting off the debate. "I'm not inclined to move the defendant. He's charged as an adult and will be tried as one. And he'll be treated as one. Motion overruled."

Again, Jake was not surprised. He fully expected Judge Noose to preside over a fair trial and favor neither side, so asking for favors at this point was a waste of time.

"What's next, Mr. Brigance?"

"That's all the defense has for now, Your Honor. Mr. Dyer has a motion in limine, and I suggest that we take it up in chambers."

Dyer said, "Agreed, Your Honor. It's of a sensitive nature and should not be discussed in open court, at least not now."

"Very well. We will adjourn and reconvene in chambers."

Stepping over to his table, Jake couldn't help but steal a glance at the Kofers. If Earl had a gun, he would have opened fire.

NOOSE REMOVED HIS robe and fell into his throne at the end of the table. Jake, Libby, and Portia sat along one side. Opposite were Lowell Dyer and his assistant, D. R. Musgrove, a veteran prosecutor. The court reporter sat to the side with her stenograph and recorder.

Noose fired up his pipe without thinking to open a window. He sucked in a mouthful of smoke as he scanned a brief in front of him. He exhaled and said, "This is very troubling."

It was Dyer's motion so he spoke first. "Your Honor, we want to limit some of the testimony at trial. Evidently, this killing took place after a nasty fight between Josie Gamble and Stuart Kofer. We will not call her as a witness but the defense certainly will. Therefore, she will be asked questions about the fight, prior fights, and perhaps other physical abuse by the deceased. This could turn into a real circus as the defense, in effect, puts Stuart Kofer on trial. He will not be around to defend himself. This is simply not fair. The State seeks a ruling by the court, pretrial, that testimony about any alleged physical abuse be severely restricted."

Noose was flipping through the motion and supporting brief filed by Dyer, though he had already read it. "Mr. Brigance."

Libby cleared her throat and said, "Your Honor, may I?"

"Of course."

"The reputation of the deceased is always fair game, especially in situations like this where violence was in play." She was precise, with perfect diction, her Scottish brogue conveying authority. "In our brief, we trace the history of this issue in this state for many decades. Rarely has testimony about the deceased's violent reputation been excluded, especially when the defendant was also the subject of abuse."

"The kid was abused?" Noose asked.

"Yes, but we did not include this in our brief because it would then be public record. On at least four occasions, Mr. Kofer slapped Drew in the face, in addition to threatening him many times. He lived in fear of the man, as did Josie and Kiera."

"How extensive was the physical abuse?"

Libby quickly slid across the table an eight-by-ten color photo of Josie in the hospital with her face bandaged. She continued, "Well, we can start with Josie on the night in question. He slapped her in the face, then knocked her out with a broken jaw that required surgery."

Noose gawked at the photo. Dyer frowned at his copy.

Libby said, "Josie will testify that the beatings were common and were happening with more frequency. She wanted to leave and was threatening to do so but had no place to go. The family, Your Honor, was living in a state of well-earned fear. Drew was being slapped around and threatened. And, Kiera was being sexually abused."

"Come on!" Dyer hissed.

"I didn't expect you to like it, Mr. Dyer, but it's the truth and it needs to be discussed at trial."

Dyer said angrily, "That's the problem here, Judge, and this is why I filed a motion to compel testimony from the girl. Jake wouldn't allow her to answer my questions. I have the right to know what she'll say at trial."

"A motion to compel in a criminal case?" Noose asked.

"Yes, Judge. It's only fair. We're getting ambushed here."

Jake loved the word "ambush." *Just wait until you see her belly.*

Noose said, "But if you call her to the stand, she's your witness. I'm not sure how you can compel the testimony of your own witness."

Dyer replied, "I'll be forced to call her. There were three witnesses at the scene. The mother was unconscious and did not hear the gunshot. It's unlikely the defendant will testify. That leaves the girl. Now I learn that she was sexually abused. This isn't fair, Your Honor."

"I'm not inclined to grant your motion to compel her to talk now."

"Fine, then we won't call her to the stand."

"Then we will," Jake said.

Dyer glared at him, fell back into his chair, and crossed his arms over his chest. Defeated. He stewed for a moment as the tension rose, then said, "This just isn't fair. You cannot allow this trial to descend into a one-sided slander-fest against a dead police officer."

Jake said, "The facts are the facts, Mr. Dyer. We can't change them."

"No, but the court can certainly restrict some of this testimony."

"That's an excellent idea, Mr. Dyer. I'll take your motion under advisement and rule at trial when I see where things are going. You can renew them at that time and you can certainly object to any testimony."

"It'll be too late," Dyer said.

Damned right it will be, Jake thought to himself.

CARLA BAKED A pan of chicken thighs with cherry tomatoes and morel mushrooms, and they ate on the patio after dark. A thunderstorm had moved through and taken most of the humidity with it.

Avoiding all talk of murder and trials of teenage killers, they tried their best to stick to more pleasant matters. Libby told stories of growing up in Scotland, in a small town near Glasgow. Her father was a well-known barrister and had encouraged her to follow the law. Her mother taught literature at a nearby college and wanted her to become a doctor. An American teacher inspired her to study in the States, and she had never left. As a law student at Georgetown she had sat through a gut-wrenching trial of a seventeen-year-old boy with a low IQ and a heartbreaking history. He had been given life without parole, a death sentence. Enough of that. Her next story was about her first husband, who was now on everybody's short list to be nominated to the Supreme Court.

Dr. Thane Sedgwick had spent three hours with Drew in his cell and preferred to talk about something else. They would meet for two more hours in the morning, and Sedgwick would prepare a lengthy profile. Sedgwick was quite the raconteur. His father had been a rancher in rural Texas and he'd spent his childhood in a saddle. His great-grandfather had once shot two cattle rustlers, loaded their bodies into his wagon, and delivered them to the sheriff two hours away. The sheriff thanked him.

Late in the evening, Libby said to Sedgwick, "I doubt you'll be needed in this trial."

"Oh really. Feeling pretty confident, huh?"

"No," Jake quipped. "We have no grounds for confidence."

Libby said, "I see a trial that will be difficult for either side to win."

"You don't know these jurors," Jake said. "In spite of what you heard today, there will be a lot of sympathy for the deceased, and no small amount of resentment for the way he'll be portrayed at trial. We have to be careful."

Carla said, "Enough of that. Who wants peach cobbler?"

30

The following Saturday, Jake and Carla dropped off Hanna in Karaway to spend the day with her grandparents. She saw Jake's parents every week but it was never enough. After a quick cup of coffee and a brief visit, they left her there and it was impossible to tell who was more excited, Hanna or Mr. and Mrs. Brigance.

They headed to Oxford, a town they would always love because of their college days. They had met at a fraternity party when they were juniors and had been together ever since. One of their favorite day trips was to spend a Saturday at an Ole Miss football game and tailgate with old college friends. Several times a year they made the hour drive for no reason other than to get out of town, to park on the picturesque square, visit the bookstore, and have a long lunch in one of the many good restaurants before returning to Clanton.

In the backseat were the housewarming gifts—a toaster and a platter of Carla's chocolate chip cookies. She had wanted to bring baby gifts because Kiera would have nothing, but Jake said no. As a lawyer, he had witnessed firsthand the damage that could be done once a young mother saw her baby, held it, and immediately got attached to it. They often changed their minds and refused to go forward with the adoption. He knew that Josie would not let that happen. Nonetheless, Jake insisted that they do nothing that might arouse the powerful feelings of motherhood.

Two years earlier he had spent an entire day at the hospital in Clanton, waiting with the paperwork as a fifteen-year-old mother agonized over her final signature. His clients, a childless couple in their early forties, sat in his office and stared at the phone. Late in the day, the hospital administrator informed Jake that, with such indecision, she could not sign off. The administrator felt as though the mother was being coerced by her mother, the new grandmother, and any decision was not being freely made. As Jake lingered, he was eventually told that a decision had been made and the child would not be given up for adoption.

He drove to his office and broke the news to his clients. The scene was still painful to recall.

He and Carla were not yet committed to an addition to their family. They had discussed it for hours and had agreed to keep talking about it. They had a doctor friend in town whose phone rang at four o'clock one morning. He and his wife hustled over to Tupelo and returned home at noon with a three-day-old baby, their second adoption. Their decision had been instant, but then they had been searching for a long time. They knew what they wanted and were committed. Jake and Carla weren't there yet. Before Kiera, they had not thought about adopting for many years.

The idea was laden with complications. Though Jake claimed not to worry about the town and any appearance of impropriety, he knew that they would be criticized by some for seizing the opportunity to take a baby from a client. To this, Carla pushed back with her belief that any criticism would be temporary and would go away as the years passed and the child prospered in a good home. Besides, wasn't Jake being condemned enough already? Let 'em talk. Their families and friends would be thrilled for them and would circle the wagons. Who else really mattered?

Jake worried about raising a child in a community where his DNA might become known. He would be the product of a rape. His real father had been murdered. His real mother was just a kid herself. Carla pushed back with the argument that the child would never know it. "No one gets to pick their parents," she liked to say. The child would be sheltered and loved as much as any lucky kid, and with time folks would accept him for what he was. The DNA couldn't be changed.

Jake didn't like the fact that the Kofers would always be close by. He doubted they would have any interest in the child, but that was not a certainty. Carla believed they would not. Besides, neither she nor Jake had ever met the Kofers. They lived in another part of the county and their paths had never crossed. The private adoption would take place in Oxford, in a different judicial district, and in a closed proceeding where the file could be sealed, and there was a good chance that most of the townsfolk, the very people Jake claimed to now care nothing for, would never know the details.

Though he avoided discussing it, Jake was concerned about the expense. Hanna was nine and they had not yet started saving for her college. Indeed, their meager savings had just been raided and their financial future looked grim. Adding a child would require Carla to stay at home for at least the next year or two, and they needed her salary.

The Gambles could damn well bankrupt him. Notwithstanding Noose's rather screwball scheme to get him compensated for the trial, he expected to be paid very little. The first loan to Josie was for $800 and a new transmission. The second was $600 to cover the deposit on the apartment, the first month's rent, and hooking up the utilities. The landlord wanted a six-month lease, which Jake signed in his name. Same for the phone, gas, and electricity. Nothing was in Josie's name, and he advised her to find a job as a waitress and work for cash and tips. The bill collectors would have trouble finding her. There was nothing illegal about this arrangement but he didn't feel entirely comfortable with it. Under the circumstances, though, he had no choice.

When Josie left Ford County two weeks earlier, she was working three part-time jobs and had proven adept at hustling for low wages. She promised to repay every dime, but Jake had his doubts. Her rent was $300 a month and she was determined to pay at least half of it.

The next loan would be to cover Kiera's medical care. She was almost seven months along and so far there had been no complications. Jake had no idea what it would cost.

On a troubling note, Josie had mentioned, on the phone, the issue of money for the adoption. Jake had explained that the adopting parents always cover the costs of the delivery and the lawyer's fees. Josie would be expected to pay nothing. She then beat around the bush for a few minutes and asked, "Is there anything in the deal for the mother?" In other words, exchanging money for the baby.

Jake had anticipated this and quickly replied, "No, that's not permissible."

Although it was. He had handled an adoption years earlier in which the prospective parents agreed to pay an additional $5,000 to the young mother, which was not unheard of in private adoptions. Agencies charged a fee and some of the money was quietly routed to the mother. However, the last thing he wanted was for Josie to get wild ideas and dream of making a profit. He had assured her that he and Pastor McGarry would find a nice home for the baby. No need for her to go shopping around.

THEY PARKED ON the square and did a loop, checking the windows of the shops they had known in college. They browsed through Square Books and had coffee upstairs on the porch while gazing at the courthouse lawn where Mr. Faulkner once sat alone and watched the town. At noon they went to a deli and bought sandwiches for lunch.

The apartment building was a few blocks off the square, on a side street crammed with cheap student housing. Jake had lived nearby for three years during law school.

Josie answered the door with a huge smile, obviously delighted to see someone she knew. She invited them in and proudly showed off her new coffee machine, one given to her by the ladies of Good Shepherd. When Charles McGarry informed them that Josie and Kiera would be moving away and into their own apartment, the entire church gathered a collection of used bedsheets, towels, dishes, more clothing, and a few small appliances. The apartment was furnished with the bare basics—sofas, chairs, beds, and tables that had been abused by long-forgotten college students.

As they sat at the kitchen table and had coffee, Kiera appeared and gave them hugs. In a T-shirt and shorts, her pregnancy was becoming obvious, though Carla later said she was showing little to be that far along. She said she felt fine, was bored with no television, but was reading a lot of paperbacks donated by the church.

Not surprisingly, Josie had already landed a job waiting tables at a diner north of town. Twenty hours a week, cash and tips.

Carla had spent four hours with Drew that week and gave a glowing account of his progress. After a slow start, he was showing an interest in science and Mississippi history, though he had no use for math. Talk of him saddened Josie and her eyes watered. She planned to drive to the jail on Sunday for a long visit.

All four agreed that they were hungry. Kiera changed into jeans and put on sandals, and they drove to the Ole Miss campus, which on a Saturday in June was deserted. They parked near the Grove, the shaded, park-like expanse that was the heart of the school. They found a picnic table under an ancient oak, and Carla unpacked sandwiches, chips, and soft drinks. As they ate, Jake pointed to the law school over there, the Student Union not far away, and described the Grove on game day, when it was packed with tens of thousands of tailgaters. And over there, under that tree near the stage, was where he surprised his girlfriend with an engagement ring and asked her to marry him. Luckily, she said yes.

Kiera loved the story and wanted all the details. It was obvious that she was enthralled with the idea of such a future, of going to college, of having some handsome boy propose to her, of having a life far different from what she had known. She got prettier each time Carla saw her. The unwanted pregnancy agreed with her, at least on the surface. Carla wondered if she had ever set foot on a college campus before. She adored Kiera, and her heart ached at what the girl was facing. The fear of giving birth, of letting go of her child, the stigma of being raped and pregnant at fourteen. She needed counseling, and plenty of it, but it wasn't happening. The best scenario was that she would give birth in late September, then enroll as a freshman at Oxford

High School as if nothing had happened. A law school buddy of Jake's was the city attorney and would facilitate matters.

After lunch, they took a long walk through the campus. Jake and Carla alternated as tour guides. They passed the football stadium, the Lyceum, the chapel, and they bought ice cream in the Student Union. On a sidewalk along Sorority Row, Carla pointed out the Phi Mu House where she had lived as a sophomore and junior. Kiera whispered to her, "What's a sorority?"

Several times during the languid walk, Carla wondered what would happen if they adopted the baby. Would they be forced to forget about Kiera and Josie? Jake felt strongly that they would. He believed the safest adoptions were those where all contact with the real mother was cut off. At the same time, though, he feared that the Gambles would be a part of their lives for years to come. If Drew got convicted, Jake would be tied up with appeals forever. A hung jury, and there would be another trial, then perhaps another. Only an acquittal would rid them of the family, and that was highly unlikely.

It was all so complicated, and unpredictable.

ON SUNDAY MORNING, the Brigance family dressed in their finest and left for church. At the edge of town, Hanna asked from the backseat, "Hey, where are we going?"

Jake said, "We're visiting another church today."

"Why?"

"Because you always say that the sermons are boring. Half the time you fall asleep. There are at least a thousand churches around here and we thought we'd try another one."

"But I didn't say I wanted to go somewhere else. What about my friends in Sunday school?"

"Oh, you'll see them again," Carla said. "Where's your sense of adventure?"

"Going to church is an adventure?"

"Just hang on. I think you'll like this place."

"Where is it?"

"You'll see."

Hanna said nothing more and sulked as they drove through the countryside. When they parked in the gravel lot next to Good Shepherd, she said, "This is it? It's so small."

"It's a country church," Carla said. "They're always smaller."

"I don't think I like it."

Jake said, "If you'll be sweet, we'll take you to lunch at Nana's."

"Lunch at Nana's? All right!"

Jake's mother had called that morning with the invitation they were always anticipating. She had picked fresh corn and tomatoes from her garden and was in the mood to cook.

Some men were finishing their cigarettes under a shade tree to one side. Some women were chatting at the front door. The Brigances were met in the vestibule by an usher, a woman who greeted them warmly and gave each a bulletin for the service. Inside the handsome sanctuary, the pianist was playing as they found a seat in a padded pew halfway to the front. Charles McGarry quickly spotted them and walked over with a warm hello. Meg was at home with the baby, who had a cold but was otherwise doing fine. He thanked them for coming and was genuinely happy to see them.

As city folks, they immediately felt overdressed, but

no one seemed to care. Jake noticed only one other dark suit among the pews. He couldn't help but notice the stares. Word was out—Mr. Brigance was in the house—and others began stopping by for friendly welcomes.

At eleven, a small choir in blue robes filed in from a side door and Pastor McGarry stepped to the pulpit for his opening announcements. He offered a short prayer, then yielded to the choir director who asked them to stand. After three stanzas they sat and listened to a solo.

When the sermon began, Hanna moved to a cozier spot between her parents and seemed ready for a nap, determined to prove she could sleep through any service. For a preacher so young and without a lot of training, Charles was at home in the pulpit. His sermon came from Paul's letter to Philemon and his theme was forgiveness. Our ability to forgive others, even those who are undeserving, is indicative of the forgiveness we received from God through Christ.

Jake enjoyed sermons and all other types of speeches. He invariably timed them. Lucien had taught him that anything beyond twenty minutes, especially final summations to juries, and you risked losing your audience. In Jake's first jury trial, an armed robbery, his closing argument lasted all of eleven minutes. And it had worked. His minister at the Presbyterian Church, like most preachers, tended to run long, and Jake had suffered through too many sermons that ran out of gas and became boring.

Charles was finished in eighteen minutes and closed nicely. When he sat down, a children's choir lit up the place with a lively song. Hanna perked up and enjoyed the music. Then Charles was back as he asked the worshippers to share their joys and concerns.

It was definitely a different type of service, far less stuffy, much warmer, and with a lot more humor. After the benediction, Jake and Carla were surrounded by the members, who wanted to make sure they felt sufficiently welcomed.

31

In what felt like a never-ending string of bad days, Monday promised to be one of the worst. Unable to concentrate, Jake watched the clock until 9:55, then left his office for a quick stroll to the other side of the square.

There were three banks in Clanton. Stan, at Security, had already said no. The Sullivans ran not only the largest law firm in the county, but some cousins held a majority interest in the biggest bank. Jake would not subject himself to the indignity of asking them for money. They would say no anyway, and gleefully. He walked past their law firm and cursed them, then cursed them again as he walked past their bank.

The third, Peoples Trust, was run by Herb Cutler, a chubby old curmudgeon Jake had always avoided. He wasn't a bad guy, just a tightfisted banker who demanded more than enough collateral for any loan. The nerve. To get money from Herb, one had to show enough collateral to prove that one didn't really need a loan to begin with.

Jake entered the lobby as if someone was holding a gun to his head. The receptionist pointed to a corner and he entered a huge, messy office at exactly ten o'clock. Herb, in his standard bright red suspenders, was waiting behind his desk and did not stand up. They shook hands and went through the usual preliminaries, though Herb didn't waste many words and was known for his bluntness.

He was already shaking his head as he got down to business. "Jake, I just don't know about the loan, this idea of refinancing your mortgage. This appraisal seems awfully high, I mean, three hundred thousand? I know you paid two-fifty for the place two years ago, but it looks to me like Willie Trainer clipped you on it."

"Naw, Herb, I got a good deal. Plus, my wife really wanted the place. I can handle a new mortgage."

"Really? Three hundred thousand for thirty years at ten percent? That's a monthly nut of twenty-five hundred bucks."

"I know that and it's no problem."

"The house ain't worth it, Jake. You're in Clanton, not north Jackson."

He knew that too.

"Plus taxes and insurance and you're looking at three thousand. I mean, hell, Jake, that's a big mortgage for anybody in this town."

"Herb, I know that, and I can swing it." Such a number made him nauseous and he suspected he wasn't faking it very well. For the month of May his quiet little office had grossed less than $2,000. June was on track to see even less.

"Well, I need to see some proof. Financials, tax returns, the like. Not sure I can trust them because I damned sure don't trust your appraisal. What's your gross gonna be this year?"

The indignity was overwhelming. Suffering at the whim of another banker who wanted to poke through his books. "You know how it is, Herb, in this business. You can't predict what'll walk in the door. I'll probably do a hundred and fifty."

Half of that would be a bonanza at the current rate.

"Well, I don't know. Put together some financials and I'll take a look. What's in the pipeline now?"

"What do you mean?"

"Look, Jake, I deal with lawyers all the time. What's the best case in your office?"

"The *Smallwood* wrongful deaths, against the railroad."

"Oh really? I heard that one blew up in your face."

"Not at all. Judge Noose will give us a new trial date later in the fall. We're on track, so to speak."

"Ha, ha. What's the next-best case?"

There wasn't one. Jesse Turnipseed's mother slipped on some pickle juice on the floor at the grocery store and broke her arm. It healed perfectly. The insurance company was offering $7,000. Jake couldn't threaten it with a trial because she had a habit of falling in well-insured stores when no one was around. "The usual assortment of car wrecks and such," he said with a discernible lack of conviction.

"Junk. Anything of value?"

"Not really. Not now anyway."

"What about other assets. I mean, anything worth a shit?"

Oh, how he hated bankers. His paltry savings account had been demolished to pay Stan. "Some savings, couple of cars, you know?"

"I know, I know. What about other debts? You in hock up to your ears like most lawyers around here?"

Credit cards, the monthly note on Carla's vehicle. He wouldn't dare mention the litigation loan because Herb would blow a gasket. The very idea of borrowing that much money to fund a lawsuit. At that moment, it did indeed seem foolish. "The usual, nothing serious, nothing I'm not taking care of."

"Look, let's cut to the chase here, Jake. Get some numbers together and I'll take a look, but I gotta tell you, three hundred won't work. Hell, I'm not sure two-fifty ain't too much."

"Will do. Thanks, Herb. See you around."

"Don't mention it."

Jake bolted from the office, his hatred of banks refortified. He left thoroughly defeated and slinked back to his office.

THE NEXT MEETING would be even more painful. Three hours later, Harry Rex stomped up his stairs, cracked the door, and said, "Let's go."

They made the same walk Jake had made earlier in the day, but stopped at the Sullivan law firm. A pretty secretary led them to a large, majestic conference room with people waiting. On one side of the table, Walter Sullivan sat with Sean Gilder and one of his many associates. The two railroad lawyers were with them. The handshaking took a while and everybody was polite. A court reporter sat at one end, next to the chair reserved for the witness.

On cue, Mr. Neal Nickel walked in and said hello. The court reporter swore him to tell the truth and he took his seat. It was Gilder's deposition and he quickly took charge with instructions for the witness and a long list of preliminary questions. Since he worked by the hour, he was slow and meticulous.

Jake studied Nickel's face and felt as though he knew him well. He had seen him so many times in the photos at the accident scene. He was still wearing a dark suit and was articulate, educated, and not the least bit intimidated.

The ugly truth came out soon enough. On the night of the crash, he was following an old pickup truck that was barely staying on the road. Swerving from one

shoulder to the other. Nickel gave it plenty of room. As
he topped a hill, he saw the red crossing lights flashing
at the bottom. A train was passing. The headlights from
the pickup and the car in front of it reflected off the
bright yellow warning strips attached to each boxcar.
Suddenly there was an explosion. The pickup hit the
brakes, as did Nickel. He got out and raced to the crossing and saw the small car had flipped 180 degrees and
was facing him, its front crumpled into an ugly mess.
The train was still passing, clicking along at a reasonable
speed as if nothing had happened. The driver of the
truck, a Mr. Grayson, was yelling and flailing his arms as
he ran around the car. Inside there was a mess. The
driver—a man—and his woman passenger were
crushed, mangled, bleeding. A little boy and little girl
were crushed in the rear seat and apparently dead.
Nickel walked to some weeds and vomited as the train
finally cleared. Another car stopped, then another, and
as they crowded around the wreck they realized they
could do nothing. The train stopped and began to
slowly come back, in reverse. "They're dead, they're all
dead," Grayson kept saying as he circled the wreck. The
other drivers were as horrified as Nickel. Then there
were sirens, and plenty of them. The responders quickly
realized there was no urgency—all four were dead.
Nickel wanted to leave but the highway was blocked.
He wasn't from the area and didn't know the back
roads, so he waited and watched with the crowd. For
three hours he stood off to the side and watched as the
firemen cut and sawed and removed the bodies. It was
a horrible scene, one he would never forget. He'd had
nightmares.

With this beautiful gift in hand, Sean Gilder slowly
and meticulously walked Nickel through his testimony
again, nailing down every detail. He handed him large

photos of the crossing lights, but Nickel said he didn't think to observe them in the chaos. They were flashing away at the time of the collision and that was all that mattered.

Sadly, at least for the plaintiffs, Nickel was far more credible than Hank Grayson, who still maintained that the lights were not flashing and he himself didn't see the train until he almost crashed into the Smallwood vehicle.

Having far too much fun, Gilder then moved to events that took place months after the accident. In particular, the meeting with a private investigator at Nickel's office in Nashville. Nickel had been surprised that someone had found him. The investigator said he was working for a lawyer in Clanton but did not give his name. Nickel cooperated fully and told the investigator the same story he had just testified to under oath, leaving out no details. The investigator thanked him and went away, never to be heard from again. Back in February, he had been traveling near Clanton and decided to stop by the courthouse. He asked about the lawsuit and was told that the file was a public record. He spent two hours with it and realized that Hank Grayson was sticking to his original story. Nickel was bothered by this but still did not want to get involved because he had sympathy for the Smallwoods. However, over time he felt compelled to come forward.

In the deposition game, some lawyers played all their cards and flushed out every detail. Their goal was to win the deposition. Gilder was in that camp. Better lawyers held back and didn't reveal their strategies. They saved their best shots for trial. Great lawyers often skipped the depositions altogether and plotted brutal cross-examinations.

Jake had no questions for the witness. He could have

asked Nickel why, as an eyewitness, he said nothing to the police. The scene was crawling with deputies and there were two state troopers working the crowd, but Nickel had offered nothing. He stood silently by and kept his mouth shut. His name appeared in none of the reports.

Jake could have asked him a question that was so obvious, yet had so far been missed by Gilder and his team. The train cleared the crossing, stopped, and backed up because the engineer had heard a thud. On the track, trains ran both ways. Why, then, did the lights not work when the train approached from the other direction, in reverse? Jake had statements from a dozen witnesses who swore the lights were not flashing while the train sat nearby and the rescue was underway. Gilder, either overconfident or just lazy, had not spoken to these witnesses.

Jake could have asked him about his past. Nickel was forty-seven years old. At the age of twenty-two he had been involved in a terrible auto accident in which three teenagers were killed. They were drinking beer, joyriding, racing down a county road on a Friday night when they ran head-on into a car driven by Nickel. As it turned out, everybody was drunk. Nickel registered .10 and was arrested for drunk driving. There was talk of an indictment for manslaughter, but the authorities eventually decided the accident was not his fault. The three families sued anyway and the case dragged on for four years before his insurance company negotiated a nuisance settlement. Thus, his reluctance to get involved.

This valuable background had been discovered by a private investigator who charged Jake $3,500, another ding to the old Tort Sport loan sitting in Stan's office. Jake had the dirt. Sean Gilder probably did not because he didn't mention it during the deposition. Jake relished the moment when he sprung it on Nickel before the jury and slaughtered him with it. His credibility would be tarnished, but his past would not change the facts of the *Smallwood* accident.

Jake and Harry Rex had argued over strategy. Harry Rex wanted a full-frontal assault in the deposition to spook the defense and soften up Gilder for, just maybe, some settlement talk. They were desperate for cash, but Jake still dreamed of a big verdict in his courtroom. And he would not push for a trial. A year needed to pass for things to settle down. The Gamble trial needed to come and go and take the baggage with it.

Harry Rex thought this was a foolish dream. Hanging on for a year seemed impossible.

32

Jake worked late on Monday and left the office after dark. Preoccupied, he was almost home when he remembered Carla wanted milk, eggs, two cans of tomato sauce, and coffee from the grocery store. He turned around and went to a Kroger east of town. He parked his red Saab in the lot that was almost empty, went in, filled his basket, checked out, sacked his own items, and was almost to his car when things took a sudden turn for the worse. An unfriendly voice behind him said, "Hey Brigance." Jake turned and for a split second saw a face that was vaguely familiar. Holding the grocery bag, he couldn't duck in time to miss the sucker punch. It landed flush on his nose, cracked it, and knocked him to the asphalt beside his car. For a second he could see nothing. A heavy boot landed on his right ear as he scrambled around. He felt a can of tomato sauce and quickly hurled it at the man, hitting him in the face. The man yelled, "You son of a bitch!" and kicked him again. Jake was almost to his feet when a second man tackled him from behind. He landed hard on the asphalt again and managed to grab the hair of his tackler. The same heavy boot landed again on his forehead, and Jake was too stunned to fight back. He released his grip on the hair and tried to get up, but he was pinned on his back. The second assailant, a thick heavy guy, pounded away at his face, cursing and growling, while the first one kicked his ribs and gut and anywhere else he could land a boot. When he kicked him in the testicles Jake screamed and blacked out.

Two loud gunshots cracked through the air and someone yelled, "Stop it!"

The two thugs were startled and bolted from the scene. They were last seen sprinting around the corner of the store. Mr. William Bradley ran over with his pistol and said, "Oh my God."

Jake was unconscious and his face was a bloody mess.

WHEN CARLA ARRIVED at the ER, Jake was being X-rayed. A nurse told her, "He's breathing on his own and somewhat alert. That's all I know right now." His parents arrived half an hour later and she met them in the waiting room. Mr. William Bradley was in a corner talking to a Clanton city policeman, giving his story.

A doctor, Mays McKee, a friend from church, stopped by for the second time and gave them the latest. "It's a pretty nasty beating," he said gravely. "But Jake is awake and stable and in no danger. Some cuts and bruises, a broken nose. We're still doing X-rays and giving him morphine. A lot of pain. I'll be back in a minute." He eased away and Carla sat with Jake's parents.

A county deputy, Parnell Johnson, arrived and spent a moment with them. He huddled with Mr. Bradley and the city policeman, then sat on a coffee table in front of Carla and said, "Looks like there were two of them. They jumped Jake as he was about to get into his car outside Kroger. Mr. Bradley over there had just parked and saw the beating and grabbed his .38. He fired twice, ran them off. He saw a green GMC pickup race away on a side street behind the store. No idea of who it was, not now anyway."

"Thank you," Carla said.

A long hour passed before Dr. McKee returned. He told them Jake had been moved to a private room and wanted to see Carla. His parents would not be allowed in at the moment but could visit tomorrow. Dr. McKee and Carla went to the third floor and stopped outside a closed door. The doctor whispered, "He looks terrible and he's pretty groggy. Broken nose, two broken ribs, two missing teeth, three cuts on his face that required forty-one stitches, but I got Dr. Pendergrast to sew him up. He's the best and he doesn't expect significant scarring."

She took a deep breath and closed her eyes. At least he was alive. "Can I stay here tonight?"

"Sure. They'll send in a foldaway bed."

He pushed the door open and they eased inside. Carla almost fainted when she saw her husband. From his eyebrows up, everything was wrapped in heavy gauze. Another bandage covered most of his chin. A line of small black stitches ran across his nose. His eyes were hideous, swollen shut with bulging masses as large as boiled eggs. His lips were thick, puffy, and red. A tube snaked its way into his mouth while two IVs hung from above. She swallowed hard and took his hand. "Jake, honey, I'm here." She kissed him softly on the cheek, on a small patch of open skin.

He grunted and tried to smile. "Hey, babe. You okay?"

She had to smile too, although he could see nothing. "Let's not worry about me right now. I'm here and you're going to be okay."

He mumbled something incomprehensible, then moved a leg and groaned.

Dr. McKee said, "He took a nasty shot to the crotch

and his testicles are quite swollen. And the swelling will continue."

Jake heard them and said, with remarkable clarity, "Hey, babe, you wanna fool around?"

"No I don't. We'll have to wait a couple of days."

"Dammit."

A long moment passed as she squeezed his hand and stared at his bandages. The tears began and were soon running down her cheeks. Jake appeared to doze off, and Dr. McKee nodded at the door. In the hallway he said, "He has a concussion I want to monitor, so he'll be here for a couple of days. I don't think it's serious but we need to watch it. Stay if you like, but there's really no need. There's nothing you can do and I think he'll soon drift off and go to sleep."

"I'm staying. His parents will keep Hanna."

"As you wish. I'm really sorry about this, Carla."

"Thank you, Dr. McKee."

"He's gonna be okay. Really sore for the next week or so, but he's in one piece."

"Thank you."

HARRY REX SHOWED up and cursed a nurse when she turned him away. On the way out the door he threatened to sue her.

BY MIDNIGHT, JAKE had not made a sound in over an hour. Carla, barefoot and still in jeans, sat propped up on pillows in her flimsy foldaway and flipped through magazines under a dim table lamp. She tried not to think about who the thugs were, but she knew the beating was related to Kofer. Five years earlier, the Klan had burned their home and taken a shot at Jake outside the courthouse during the Hailey affair. For three years they had lived with guns and extra security because the threats continued. She could not believe the violence was back.

What kind of life were they living? No other lawyer faced such intimidation. Why them? Why did her husband get involved with dangerous cases that paid nothing? For twelve years they had worked hard and tried to save and dreamed of building something for the future. Jake had an enormous capacity for work and was determined to succeed as a noted trial lawyer. He was ambitious to a fault and dreamed of wowing juries and winning big verdicts. The money would come by the truckload, one day, he was certain of it.

And look at them now. Her husband beaten to a pulp. His law practice drying up, their debts mounting by the week.

At the beach last month, her father had once again, quietly and when Jake wasn't around, mentioned that he could find a place for Jake in money management. He had several friends who were investors, most of them semiretired, but they were contemplating putting together a fund to invest in hospitals and medical device startups. She wasn't sure what that meant and she had not said a word to Jake about it. But it meant a move to the Wilmington area and a complete change of his career. Her father even mentioned a loan to make things easier. If he only knew how deep their debts were.

Things would certainly be safer at the beach.

At times they had talked about the drudgery of small-town living. The same routines, same friends, the lack of a meaningful social life. For arts and athletics they had to drive an hour to either Tupelo or Oxford. She enjoyed her friends but there was the constant game of who had the bigger house, the nicer cars, the sexier vacations. In a small town everyone was eager to help, but then everyone also knew your business. Two years ago they had paid too much for the Hocutt House, and she had noticed a definite coolness from a couple of her girlfriends. It was as if the Brigances were moving up too quickly and leaving the others behind. If they only knew.

The nurses came and went, making sleep impossible. The monitors glowed and blinked. The opioids seemed to be working fine.

Could this be the pivotal moment in their lives? The final straw that freed Jake from the grind of a ham-and-eggs lawyer struggling to pay the bills each month? They were not yet forty. There was plenty of time and it was the perfect moment to change course and move on to something better, to get out of Mississippi and find an easier place. She could always get a job as a schoolteacher.

She put down the magazines and closed her eyes. Why not get through the Gamble mess in August, adopt Kiera's baby in September, and leave Clanton? Drew's future, as uncertain as it was, would be dumped on another lawyer, but there were always plenty of them. Wouldn't it be safer and wiser to move a thousand miles away? They would be near her parents, who would be eager to help with the babysitting. Jake could start a new career, one that included a guaranteed paycheck each month, and they would live at the beach year-round.

She was wide-eyed when a nurse eased in at 1:30 and gave her a sleeping pill.

FOR BREAKFAST, JAKE sipped apple juice from a carton through a straw. His entire body ached and he complained of pain everywhere. A nurse cranked up the morphine and he slipped away.

At seven, Dr. McKee appeared and told Carla that he wanted to do a brain scan and more X-rays. He suggested that she leave for a few hours, check on the house and Hanna, and take care of herself.

At home, she called Jake's parents with an update and asked them to bring Hanna home. She called Harry Rex and told him what little she knew. No, she had not asked Jake if he knew who beat him. She called Portia, Lucien, Stan Atcavage, and Judge Noose, all of whom had questions but she kept the conversations brief. She would call again later. She fed the dog, cleaned the kitchen, washed a load of clothes, and sat on the patio with a cup of coffee and tried to collect herself. One concern was what to tell Hanna. They couldn't hide Jake from his daughter and he would look awful for days to come. The child would be horrified when she saw her father and there was no way she could begin to understand. She would be terrified to learn that there were bad people out there who wanted to hurt her dad.

The coffee didn't help her nerves and she finally called her mother and told her what was going on.

At eleven, Mr. and Mrs. Brigance arrived with Hanna, who ran to her mother in tears and asked her how Daddy was doing. Carla hugged her, said he was at the hospital but doing fine, and that she would spend the day at Becky's house. She needed to get a quick bath and change clothes. She reluctantly left the kitchen, and Carla asked Mrs. Brigance, "What did you tell her?"

"Not much, just that her dad had been injured, was at the hospital, but would be home soon and everything was okay."

Mr. Brigance said, "We weren't sure what to say but she knows something is up."

Carla said, "She can't see him for a few days. It would be too much of a shock."

"When can we see him?" Mrs. Brigance asked.

"Today. We'll go in a minute."

The waiting room was getting crowded. When they arrived, they met Portia, Harry Rex, Stan and his wife, and their minister, Dr. Eli Proctor. Carla hugged them all and said she would see Jake and report back. Dr. McKee appeared and motioned for her to join him. They went to Jake's room and found him sitting up and arguing with a nurse who wanted to treat his face with cold packs. Carla spoke to him, took his hand, and he said, "Let's get outta here."

Dr. McKee said, "Not so fast, Jake. The scans and X-rays look good, but you're not going anywhere for a few days."

"Days? Are you kidding me?" He moved a leg and flinched sharply in pain.

"Does it hurt?" Carla asked.

"Only when I breathe."

"Where is the pain?"

"Pick a spot. My nuts feel like grapefruits."

"Don't be crude, Jake. Your mother will be here in a minute."

"Aw come on. Keep them away for now, okay? I can't even see them. I can't see anything."

Carla smiled and looked at Dr. McKee. "I think he's doing better already."

"He'll be fine. The concussion is mild. Everything else will mend, but it will take some time."

"So no additional brain damage?" she asked.

"None whatsoever."

"Thanks, dear," Jake said. "Where's Hanna?"

"At the Palmers', playing with Becky."

"Good. Keep her there. I don't want her spooked by a zombie."

"I'll get your parents, okay?"

"I don't want to see anybody."

"Relax, Jake. They're worried sick and they'll just stay a minute or so."

"Whatever."

Carla and Dr. McKee left the room as the nurse eased forward with the cold packs. "Let's try this again," she said sweetly.

"Touch me and I'll sue you."

LATE IN THE afternoon, Jake was napping when Dr. McKee gently shook his arm and said, "Jake, you have some visitors."

He tried to sit up, flinched again, and mumbled, "I'm tired of visitors."

"It's Sheriff Walls. I'll step outside." He left them and closed the door.

Ozzie and Moss Junior stepped to his bedside and tried to ignore the shock of his face. Ozzie said, "Hello, Jake."

Jake grunted and said, "Ozzie. What brings you here?"

"Hello, Jake," Moss Junior said.

"Howdy. I can't see anything but I'm sure you guys look as stupid as always."

Ozzie said, "Well, probably so, but we won't comment on your looks right now."

"Pretty good ass-kicking, wouldn't you say?"

"One of the best I've seen in a long time," Ozzie said with a laugh. "So, the obvious question is: Who did it? Did you get a look?"

"There were at least two of them. I never saw the second guy, but the first was one of the Kofer boys. Either Cecil or Barry. I'm not sure which one because I don't know them. Just saw them in court last week."

Ozzie glanced at Moss Junior, who was nodding. No surprise.

"And you're sure?" Ozzie asked.

"Why would I lie?"

"Okay. We'll pay 'em a visit."

"Sooner rather than later. I nailed the Kofer guy in the face with a fourteen-ounce can of tomato sauce. Square in the face, probably left a mark, but it'll heal in a few days."

"Attaboy."

"They jumped me, Ozzie. I didn't have much of a chance."

"Of course you didn't."

"They would've killed me if somebody hadn't started shooting."

"Mr. William Bradley pulled up, saw it, and whipped out his pistol."

Jake shook his head as a moment passed. "He saved my life. Tell him I'll say thanks when I can."

"I'll do that."

"And ask him why he didn't take a few shots at them."

"We'll go see the Kofers."

33

As uncomfortable as they were, the cold packs were working and Jake eventually stopped complaining about them. By Wednesday morning, the swelling had gone down enough so that he could open his eyes and see blurred images. The first was the pretty face of his wife, who, though unclear, looked better than ever. Jake kissed her for the first time in forever and said, "I'm going home."

"Oh no you're not. You have appointments this morning. First the eye doctor, then a dentist, then some more doctors, then a rehab specialist."

"I'm more concerned about my testicles."

"So am I, but there's little to do but ride it out. I took a peek last night when you were snoring and they're quite impressive. Dr. McKee says there's nothing to do down there but take pain pills and pray that you'll one day walk like a man again."

"Which specialist works on testicles?"

"That would be the urologist. He stopped by when you were out of it and took some pictures."

"You're lying."

"No I'm not. I held the sheet up and he clicked away."

"Why does he need photos?"

"Said he likes to enlarge them and hang 'em on the wall of his reception room."

Jake managed a laugh, one that was cut short when a surge like a hot knife ripped through his ribs and he grimaced. The pain would be a way of life for days and he was determined not to show it, at least not in front of his wife. "How's Hanna?"

"She's fine. She's with your parents and they're having a big time."

"That's nice. What have you told her?"

"Well, not the whole truth. I told her you were involved in an accident, didn't say what type, and that you were injured and need to spend a few days in the hospital. She's very upset and wants to see you."

"Not in here. I want to see her too but I don't want to scare her to death. I'll be home tomorrow and we'll have a little family meeting."

"Who said you're going home tomorrow?"

"I did. I've had enough of this place. The bones are set and cuts are closed. I can convalesce at home with you as my full-time nurse."

"Can't wait. Look, Jake, there are a lot of people who are worried about you. Lucien wants to come by but I told him to wait. Harry Rex calls all the time."

"I've seen Harry Rex and all he did was laugh at me for getting my ass kicked. Lucien can wait. I've talked to Portia and she's stalling our clients. I think we have maybe three left."

"Judge Noose has called."

"He should. He got me into this mess."

"He's very concerned. Dell called. Judge Atlee. Dr. Proctor. Pastor McGarry. A lot of folks."

"They can wait. I'm in no mood to see anyone if I can avoid them. Let's get home and lock the doors and let me get on my feet. Some folks are just nosy, you know?"

"And some are very concerned."

"I'm alive, Carla. I'll mend quickly enough. I don't need anyone stopping by to hold my hand."

———

CECIL KOFER WAS the foreman of a dirt crew working on a channel near the lake. Late in the morning, Moss Junior and Mick Swayze parked next to his truck and walked into the construction trailer. Cecil was standing and talking on the phone, his hard hat on his desk. Nearby a secretary looked up said, "Good mornin'."

Moss Junior glared at her and said, "Beat it."

"I beg your pardon."

"I said, 'Beat it.' We need to chat with your boss."

"You don't have to be so rude."

"You got about five seconds to step outside."

She stood and huffed out of the trailer. Cecil hung up the phone as the deputies confronted him. Moss Junior said, "Hello, Cecil. This is Mick Swayze. Ozzie sent us."

"A real pleasure, gentlemen."

Cecil was thirty-one, stocky, with at least fifty pounds he didn't need. For some reason he'd stopped shaving and wore a scruffy red beard that did nothing to improve his looks.

Moss Junior stepped to within striking distance and asked, "You go to town Monday night?"

"I don't remember."

"It was a long time ago. That green GMC out there is yours, right?"

"Probably."

"Tag number 442ECS. Someone saw it speed away from the Kroger at about nine Monday night. Someone else was probably drivin' it, right?"

"Maybe I loaned it to a friend."

"What's his name?"

"Can't remember."

"That's a nasty knot on your forehead. What's under the band-aid? Some stitches?"

"That's right."

"How'd it happen?"

"I walked into a shelf in my garage."

"Damned shelves, always in the way. Mick, that look like another shelf injury?"

Swayze took a step closer and stared at Cecil's forehead. "No, I'd say that looks like one of those knots from a fourteen-ounce can of tomato sauce. We see it all the time."

Moss Junior said, "No doubt about it." Slowly, he unsnapped a pair of handcuffs from his belt and rattled them, making as much noise as possible. Cecil took a deep breath and stared at the cuffs.

Moss Junior said, "There's a fine line between simple assault and aggravated. Simple gets up to two years in the slammer, aggravated carries twenty years."

"That's good to know."

"Write it down 'cause your memory sucks. Two-on-one with the intent to do serious body damage qualifies as aggravated. At Parchman. Who'll take care of your wife and three kids while you're away?"

"I'm not goin' anywhere."

"That, son, is now out of your control. Jake identified you, and the man with the gun saw your truck flee the scene."

His shoulders sagged a bit and he looked around for something. "He don't even know me."

"He saw you in court, said it was the Kofer boy with the mangy red beard. We talked to Barry and his mangy beard is black, not red. Why don't you guys buy some razor blades?"

"I'll write that down."

Moss Junior hammered away. "The sentencin' judge

will be Omar Noose. He's quite fond of Jake and he's very upset that one of his lawyers got the shit beat out of him because of a case pending in his court. He'll throw the book at you."

"Don't know what you're talkin' about."

"We'll report back to Ozzie and he'll send us out tomorrow to make the arrest. You want to do it here or at your house, in front of your kids?"

"I'll get a lawyer."

"Not in this county you won't. You can't find one who'll risk pissin' off Judge Noose. Here or at home?"

His shoulders dropped even further and the tough guy act was over. "For what now?"

"For your arrest. We'll take you to jail, book you, put you in a cell, bail will be somethin' like ten grand so round up a thousand in cash and you can bond out. Here or at home?"

"Here, I guess."

"See you tomorrow."

THE PHYSICAL THERAPIST was a strong bossy woman named Marlene who first wanted to take a peek at Jake's balls. He flatly refused. She found it funny and Jake wondered if the entire hospital staff was snickering at his expense. Was anything private in a hospital?

With Carla gently tugging on one side, he managed to delicately pivot and hang his feet off the bed.

"You ain't leavin' here until you can walk to that door and back," Marlene said, challenging him. She cupped her hand under one armpit and Carla took the other. Jake slid down until his bare feet touched the cold linoleum floor, and grimaced as spears of pain shot through his groin, ribs, and all the way up through his neck and skull. He felt dizzy and hesitated for a second as he closed his eyes and gritted his teeth. He took a small step, then another, then said, "Let go." They released him and he began to shuffle. His enormous testicles ached and prevented anything resembling a normal gait or even normal posture, and he waddled like a bowlegged duck to the door and slapped the handle. He proudly turned around and took eight steps back to his bed. "There. Now check me out of here."

"Not so fast, cowboy. Do it again."

His legs were weak and unsteady, but he walked to the door and back. As painful as walking was, he was invigorated to be off his back and doing something that was close to normal. After the fourth little trip, Marlene asked, "Why don't you take a pee?"

"I don't need to pee."

"Do it anyway. Let's see if you can go to the toilet by yourself."

"You wanna come watch?"

"Not really."

Jake waddled to the bathroom door, stepped inside, and closed it behind him. He pulled up his gown and tucked the hem under his chin. Slowly, he looked down at his monstrous privates and laughed in sheer disbelief. A painful, gleeful howl that caused Carla to knock on the door.

LATE WEDNESDAY AFTERNOON, Jake was sitting up in his hospital bed with Carla at his feet. They were watching cable news when there was a tap on the door. It was opening when Jake said, "Come in." Ozzie and Moss Junior were back. Carla muted the television.

"Doc says you're leavin' in the mornin'," Ozzie said.

"Not soon enough," Jake said.

"That's good to hear. You feelin' better?"

"A hundred percent."

"You still look like hell," Moss Junior said.

"Thanks. It'll take some time."

"Come on, guys," Carla said. She moved to the other side of the bed and faced the men. Ozzie nodded at Moss Junior who said, "We paid a visit to Cecil Kofer this mornin', found him at work. He's got a real knot and cut on his forehead. Of course he denies everything but he's the man. We'll pick him up tomorrow."

"I'm not pressing charges," Jake said.

Ozzie looked at Carla and she was nodding her head. They had obviously discussed this and made their decision.

"Come on, Jake," Ozzie said. "We can't let this go unpunished. They could've killed you."

"But they didn't. I'm not pressing charges."

"Why not?"

"I don't want the hassle, Ozzie. I have plenty on my mind right now as it is. Plus, that family has been through enough. I'll heal just fine and forget about this."

"I doubt that. I got jumped once in Memphis, got knocked around pretty good by some bad dudes. I still remember every punch."

"I've made my decision, Ozzie. No charges."

"I can arrest him anyway, you know?"

"Don't do that. Besides, you can't convict if I don't testify. Just tell the Kofers to leave me alone. No more phone calls, no more threats, no more intimidation. If they as much as frown at me, then I'll file an affidavit for this and press charges. Let's keep it hanging over their heads. Okay?"

Ozzie shrugged. No sense arguing with Jake. "If that's what you want."

"It is. And tell the family that I carry guns and have

permits. They won't catch me out again like that, but if they get too close they'll pay."

"Come on, Jake," Carla mumbled.

FOR HIS THIRD and final night, he slept alone. Carla was tired of the backbreaking foldaway, and Jake convinced her to go fetch their daughter and have a quiet night at home. They called at nine and said goodnight.

But the sleeping pills didn't work, nor did the pain relievers. He asked a nurse for something stronger but she said he'd had enough. The second sleeping pill backfired and at 2:00 A.M. he was wide awake. The physical shock was wearing off and the swelling was decreasing, but he would be stiff, fragile, and racked with pain for a long time. His bones and muscles, though, would heal. He wasn't so sure about the fear, the horror of being so violated. One moment he was his usual self, fit and busy with his mind on pressing matters; the next moment he was on his back, stunned, bleeding, and taking blow after blow to the face while getting mauled. Forty-eight hours later, it still seemed surreal. He'd had the same nightmare twice, a horrific recall of seeing the hate-filled face of the man on top of him pounding away. He could still feel the hard asphalt under his head, blow after blow.

He thought of Josie again and wondered how any human could tolerate the reality of constant physical danger. Jake was six feet tall, weighed 180, and if he'd had the chance he could have traded a few punches before going down. Josie weighed all of 120 and didn't stand a chance against a brute like Kofer. And imagine the horror the kids endured hearing their mother getting knocked around, again.

34

When Dr. McKee arrived early on his rounds, Jake was standing in the center of his room with his hands raised halfway above his head. His gown was lying across his bed and he wore a T-shirt and bulky sweatpants, the largest pair Carla could find. And he was wearing running shoes, as if ready for a morning jog.

"What are you doing?" McKee asked.

"Stretching. I'm leaving. Sign the papers."

"Sit down, Jake."

He backed onto the bed and sat on the edge. The doctor gently unwrapped the gauze around his head, probed his stitches, and said, "We'll get these out in a week or so. Not much else to do with your nose but let it heal. It reset nicely and won't have much of a bend to it."

"I really don't want a crooked nose, Doc."

"You'll have more of a rugged look," McKee replied like a smart-ass as he pulled off the last of the gauze. "How are your ribs?"

"Still there."

"Stand up and drop your pants." Jake did so and gritted his teeth as the doctor examined, quite delicately, his testicles. "Still growing," he mumbled.

"When can I have sex?"

"Wait till you get home."

"Seriously."

"Coupla years maybe. I'll release you, Jake, but you must take it easy. This will not be a quick recovery."

"Take it easy? What else can I do? I can barely walk with these things."

Carla eased into the room as Jake was pulling up his sweatpants. "I'm outta here," he said proudly.

"Take him home," McKee said to her. "But he stays in bed for the next three days, and I mean it. No physical activity at all. And we're cutting back on the Vicodin. That stuff's addictive. I want to see you Monday."

He left and Carla handed Jake a newspaper, the *Times* from the day before. A bold headline announced: **"BRIGANCE ATTACKED, HOSPITALIZED."**

"Front page again," she said. "Just where you want to be."

Jake sat on the edge of the bed and read Dumas Lee's sensational account of the beating. No suspects had been identified. No comments from the victim or his family or anyone in his office. Ozzie said only that it was still under investigation. There was a stock photo of Jake entering the courthouse during the Hailey trial.

A nurse brought some paperwork and a bottle of Vicodin. "Only two a day for the next five days, and then that's it," she said as she gave the bottle to Carla. She left and returned with a fruit shake and a straw, his usual breakfast. An hour later an orderly pushed a wheelchair through the door and asked Jake to have a seat. He declined, said he wanted to walk out. The orderly said no, hospital procedure required all patients to leave in a chair. What if a patient fell and hurt himself again? He'd probably sue, you know? Especially a lawyer.

"Just sit, Jake," Carla snapped. She handed him a cap and his sunglasses and said, "I'll get the car." As the orderly pushed him out of the room and along the hallway, Jake said goodbye to the nurses and thanked them for their help. He rode the elevator down and was at the front entrance when he spotted Dumas Lee lurking near the door with a camera. Dumas approached him with a smile and said, "Hello, Jake, got time for a comment?"

Jake kept his cool and said, "Dumas, if you take a photo of me right now I swear I'll never speak to you again."

Dumas didn't touch his camera but asked, "Any idea who did it, Jake?"

"Did what?"

"Attack you."

"Oh that. No, no idea and no comment. Get lost, Dumas."

"You think it's related to the Kofer case?"

"No comment. Get lost. And don't touch that camera."

A security guard appeared from nowhere and walked between Jake and the reporter. The wheelchair was rolled through the wide front doors and Carla was waiting at the curb. She and the orderly eased Jake into the front seat, closed the door, and as they drove away Jake flipped Dumas the bird.

"Was that really necessary?" Carla asked.

Jake did not reply. She said, "Look, I know you're in a lot of pain, but you're being rude to people and I don't like it. We're about to be cooped up in the house together and you're going to be nice to me. And to Hanna."

"Where is this coming from?"

"Me. The boss. Just chill out and be nice."

"Yes ma'am," Jake said as he chuckled.

"What's so funny?"

"Nothing. I'm not sure you're cut out to be a nurse."

"I am most certainly not."

"Just keep the bedpan warm and the pain pills coming and I'll be super nice." They rode in silence as they approached the square. "Who's at the house?" he asked.

"Your parents are there with Hanna. No one else."

"Is she ready for this?"

"Probably not."

"I made the mistake of looking at myself in the mirror this morning. My little girl will be horrified when she sees her father. Purple, puffy eyes. Cuts and bruises. A nose the size of a potato."

"Just keep your pants on."

Jake started laughing and felt like crying at the same time as his ribs screamed. When he managed to stop, he said, "Most nurses have great compassion. I'm not feeling it here."

"I'm not a nurse. I'm the boss and you'll do what I say."

"Yes ma'am."

She parked in the drive and helped him get out. As he waddled across the patio, the rear door opened and Hanna ran out. He wanted to grab her and squeeze her and whirl her around, but he bent low for a peck on the cheek. She had been warned and didn't try to hug him.

"How's my girl?" he asked.

"Great, Daddy. How are you?"

"Much better. In a week I'll be as good as new."

She took his hand and led him inside where his parents were waiting in the kitchen. He was already exhausted and lowered himself into a chair at the breakfast nook, where the small table was covered with cakes, pies, platters of cookies, and flowers of all varieties. Hanna pulled a chair close to him and held his hand. He chatted with his parents for a few minutes as Carla poured coffee.

Hanna said, "Are you going to take off those sunglasses?"

"No, not today. Maybe tomorrow."

"But how can you see in here?"

"I can see your beautiful face just fine and that's all that matters."

"Those stitches are gross. How many do you have? Tim Bostick cut his arm last year and got eleven stitches. He was so proud."

"Well, I've got forty-one, so I beat him."

"Mom says you lost two teeth. Let me see."

Carla scolded, "Hanna, that's enough. I said we're not going to talk about this stuff."

JUDGE NOOSE WAS up in Tyler County, in the courthouse at Gretna, going through another dreary Civil Docket call, staring at a list of active cases that no judge anywhere would want to preside over. The plaintiffs' lawyers were half-heartedly pushing for trials while the defense lawyers were using their standard delay tactics. He called for recess and retired to his chambers, where Lowell Dyer was waiting with a copy of *The Ford County Times*.

Noose took off his robe and poured a cup of stale coffee. He read the article and asked, "Have you talked to Jake?"

"No. Have you?"

"No. I'll call him this afternoon. I've spoken to his wife, and I chatted with his law clerk, Portia Lang, at his office. Any idea who's behind it?"

"I talked to Ozzie. He swore me to secrecy, said it's some of the Kofers, but Jake refuses to press charges."

"Sounds like Jake."

"Me, I'd want the death penalty."

"But you're a prosecutor. What does this do to venue?"

"You're asking me? You're the judge."

"I know, and I'm trying to decide. I think Jake has a point. My sources in Clanton tell me it's a hot topic and picking a jury might get complicated. Why run the risk on appeal? Does it really matter to the State where we have the trial?"

"I don't know. Where would you move it?"

"Well, I'd certainly keep it in the Twenty-second. You could pick the same jury in the other four counties. But Ford County worries me."

"Bring it here."

Noose laughed and said, "What a surprise. You'd like it in your own backyard, wouldn't you?"

Dyer thought about this and took a sip of coffee. "What about the Kofers? They'll be upset if you move it."

"They're not in charge, are they? And they're gonna be upset by everything that happens. I gotta tell you, Lowell, I'm really bothered by what happened to Jake. I forced the case on him and now he's been beaten to within an inch of his life. If we tolerate this, then the whole system starts to break down."

With Ford and Tyler out of the running, that left Polk, Milburn, and Van Buren counties. The last place Dyer wanted to try a big case was in the old courthouse in Chester, Noose's home. He had a hunch, though, that that was where it was headed.

He said, "Jake will be on the sidelines for a while, Judge. You think he'll ask for more time, want a continuance? The trial is seven weeks away."

"I'll ask him this afternoon. Will you object if he asks for more time?"

"No, not under these circumstances. But the trial

will not be that complicated. I mean, there's no question about who pulled the trigger. The only sticky part is the insanity issue. If that's where Jake is headed I need to know soon so I can send the boy back to Whitfield for an evaluation. Jake needs to make a decision."

"Agreed. I'll bring it up."

"Just curious about something, Judge. How did Jake convince the jury that Hailey was insane?"

"I don't think he did. Hailey wasn't insane, not under our definition. He carefully planned those killings and knew exactly what he was doing. It was nothing but retribution, plain and simple. Jake won by convincing the jurors that they would have done what Hailey did if given the chance. It was masterful."

"He may have trouble doing it this time."

"Indeed. Every case is different."

AFTER TWO HOURS at home, Jake was bored. Carla pulled the shades in the living room, unplugged the phone, closed the door, and ordered him to rest. He had a stack of pink sheets, as they were commonly known—advance copies of the state supreme court rulings that every lawyer claimed to dutifully read immediately upon publication—but his eyes wouldn't focus and his head ached. Everything ached, and the Vicodin was proving less effective. He napped periodically but it wasn't the deep sleep he needed. When his nurse peeked in to check on him, he demanded the right to go to the den to watch television. She reluctantly agreed and he changed sofas. When Hanna passed through and saw his face without the sunglasses, she bent low for a better look and started crying.

Soon he was starving and insisted on a bowl of ice cream for lunch. Hanna shared one with him, and as they were watching a western the doorbell rang. Carla took care of it and reported that it was a neighbor, one they barely knew and rarely saw, who wanted to say hello to Jake.

A lot of people wanted to stop by but Jake was adamant. The swelling around his eyes would last for days and the colors would go from purple to black and blue. He had seen this in football locker rooms and he had seen it several times with clients charged in honkytonk brawls. A depressing range of dark and ominous colors was creeping through his face, and the show would go on for a couple of weeks.

Once Hanna was over the shock, she cuddled with her father under his quilt and they watched television for hours.

AFTER MUCH DISCUSSION, it was finally decided, by Ozzie, that the meeting would best be handled by two white guys. He sent Moss Junior and Marshall Prather, Stuart's closest friend in uniform. They called ahead, and Earl Kofer was waiting for them outside under the sourwood tree late on Thursday afternoon. After each lit a cigarette, Earl said, "So what's up?"

"Cecil," Moss Junior said. "Jake identified him. Pretty stupid move, Earl, and it complicates matters for you and the family."

"Don't know what you're talkin' about. Brigance ain't the brightest guy in town so obviously he's mistaken."

Prather smiled and looked away. Moss Junior would do the talking and continued, "Okay. Whatever you say. Aggravated assault carries twenty years in prison, not sure if they can make it stick, but hell, even simple assault can get the boy a year in the county jail. Judge

Noose is really pissed about this and would probably throw the book."

"Throw it at who?"

"Right. Jake's not pressin' charges, not now anyway, but he can always do it later. Statute of limitations is somethin' like five years. Plus he can sue in a civil court, Judge Noose again, and collect money to cover his medical expenses, money I'm sure Cecil doesn't have."

"Am I supposed to be gettin' nervous?"

"I would be. If Jake decides to pull the trigger then Cecil is off to jail and bankrupt to boot. It ain't smart to fool with a lawyer like that, Earl."

"You boys want a drink?"

"We're on duty. Please pass this along to your son, both sons, cousins, all the clan. No more mischief, Earl, you got it?"

"I got nothin' for you."

They turned and walked back to their patrol car.

35

For lunch Friday, Jake managed to choke down a bowl of mushy pea soup. Chewing was still uncomfortable and solid foods were out of the question. Afterward, Carla and Hanna left to spend the afternoon shopping and doing girl stuff, and as soon as they disappeared Jake called Portia and asked her to stop by. Immediately. She arrived forty-five minutes later and, once over the shock of his battered face, followed him to the dining room where they spread out a stack of files she had brought. They covered his current cases and upcoming court appearances and made plans to deal with his brief absence.

"Anything new?" he asked, almost afraid of her answer.

"Not really, boss. The phone's been ringing but it's primarily friends and old law school buddies checking on you. You have some nice friends, Jake. A lot of them want to drive over and say hello."

"Not now. They can wait. Most of them just want to see how bad I got my butt kicked."

"Pretty bad, I'd say."

"Yes, it wasn't much of a fight."

"And you're not pressing charges?"

"No. That decision has been made."

"Why not? I mean, I've talked to Lucien and Harry Rex, at length, and we agree that you should go after these thugs, teach 'em a lesson."

"Look, Portia, that decision is behind me. I don't

have the mental or physical energy to pursue Cecil Kofer right now. Have you been to the jail?"

"No, not this week."

"I'd like for you to stop by every other day and spend an hour with Drew. He likes you and needs a friend. Don't talk about the case, just play cards and games with him and encourage him to do his homework. Carla says he's studying more."

"Will do. When are you coming back to the office?"

"Real soon, I hope. My nurse is a Nazi and my doctor's a hard-ass, but I think he'll release me next week when he takes out the stitches. I had a long chat with Noose yesterday and he's pushing me to make a decision on insanity. I'm inclined to notify him and Dyer that we plan to go with M'Naghten and argue our client did not appreciate the nature of his actions. Your thoughts?"

"That's been the plan all along, right?"

"Sort of. One problem, however, is money for an expert. I talked to that guy in New Orleans this morning and really like him. He's testified a lot and knows his stuff. His fee is fifteen thousand dollars and I said no way. This is an indigent case and the county will not pay that much for a defense expert. So it comes out of my pocket up front and I doubt if I'll get reimbursed for all of it. He said he would do it for ten. Still too much. I thanked him and said we'll think about it."

"What about Libby Provine? I thought KAF was trying to find some money."

"She is and she knows a lot of doctors. I'm leaning on her. Noose asked about a continuance, said we could have more time if needed, said Dyer would not object. I said no thanks."

"Because of Kiera?"

"Because of Kiera. She'll be seven-and-a-half

months along by August the sixth and I want her pregnant when she takes the stand."

Portia tossed a legal pad on the table and shook her head. "I gotta tell you, Jake, I don't like this. It doesn't seem fair to hide the fact that she's pregnant. Don't you think Judge Noose will throw a fit when he, along with everybody else, realizes that she's pregnant and Kofer is the daddy?"

"She's not my client. Drew is. If the State calls her, then she's their witness."

"You keep saying that, but Dyer will howl and the entire courtroom might blow up. Think about the Kofers and their reaction to the fact that their son left behind a child they knew nothing about."

"Oddly enough, I don't care about the Kofers right now, and I don't care if Noose has a fit and Dyer has a stroke. Think about the jurors, Portia. Nothing matters but the jurors. How many of them will be shocked and angry when the truth comes out?"

"All twelve."

"Maybe. I doubt we'll get all twelve, but three or four will be enough. A hung jury will be a victory."

"Is it about winning, Jake, or is it about truth and justice?"

"What is justice in this case, Portia? You're about to go off to law school where you'll spend the next three years being told that trials should be about truth and justice. And they should be. But you're also old enough to serve on a jury. What would you do with this kid?"

She considered this for a moment and said, "I don't know. I think about it all the time and I swear I don't have the answer. That boy did what he thought was right. He thought his mother was dead and—"

"And he thought they were still in danger. He thought Kofer might get up and continue with his rampage. Hell, he'd beaten them and threatened to kill them before. Drew figured he was drunk but he didn't know Kofer was so saturated with booze that he was in a coma. At that moment, Drew believed he was protecting his sister and himself."

"So it was justified?"

Jake tried to smile. He pointed at her and said, "Exactly. Forget insanity. It was justifiable homicide."

"Then why go through the motions of a M'Naghten hearing?"

"We won't. I'll ask for one and make Dyer do some work. They'll send Drew to Whitfield to be examined by their doctors and they'll find one who'll testify that the kid knew exactly what he was doing. Then, before the hearing I'll withdraw the motion. Just mess with them a little."

"This is a game?"

"No, it's a chess match, but one where the rules are not always binding."

"I think I like it. I'm not sure a jury will buy into the idea that a sixteen-year-old kid was insane. I know that insanity is not a medical diagnosis and all that, and I know that kids can have all sorts of mental problems, but it just doesn't sound right to claim that a teenaged boy was insane."

"Well, that's good to hear. I might change my mind tomorrow. I'm on pain pills and not always thinking that clearly. Let's finish up these files and get you out of here before my nurse gets back. I'm not supposed to be working and if she catches us she'll cut off my ice cream. How much money is in the bank?"

"Not much. A little less than two thousand bucks."

Jake shifted and grimaced and fought a wave of pain in his ribs and groin.

"You okay, boss?"

"Great. When I talked to Noose yesterday he said he'd assign me some new court appointments in all five counties. Not much in the way of fees, but at least they'll bring in a few bucks."

"Look, Jake, I want you to forget about paying me for now. I'm living at home and I can afford a little furlough."

He grimaced again, shifted his weight. "Thank you, Portia, but I'll make sure you get paid. You need all the money you can earn for law school."

"We can afford law school, Jake, thanks to you and old man Hubbard. My mom is set and she's forever grateful to you for that."

"Nonsense, Portia. You're doing great work and you'll get paid."

"Lucien said to forget the rent for a few months."

Jake tried to smile and tried to laugh. He looked at the ceiling and tried to shake his head. "After the Hailey trial, for which I was paid the fat fee of nine hundred dollars, I was as broke as I am now, and Lucien told me to forget about the rent for a few months."

"He's worried about you, Jake. He told me that in his prime he was the most hated lawyer in Mississippi, got death threats, had few friends, judges despised him, lawyers avoided him, and he loved it, relished being the radical lawyer, but he never got beat up."

"My first and last, I hope. I've talked to Lucien and I know he's concerned. We're gonna survive, Portia. You bust your butt till the trial is over, then you're off to law school."

JAKE WAS WADDLING around the patio late Friday afternoon, in an old T-shirt and a pair of baggy gym shorts, barefoot, trying his best to stay mobile and active and stretch his legs, as per the physical therapist, when he heard a car door slam in the front drive. His first impulse was to hustle back inside so no one would see him. He was almost to the door when a familiar voice said, "Hey, Jake."

Carl Lee Hailey appeared from around the hedge and said, "Hey, Jake. It's me, Carl Lee."

Jake tried to smile and said, "What're you doing here?"

They shook hands and Carl Lee said, "Just checkin' on you."

Jake waved at the wicker table and said, "Have a seat." They settled into chairs and Carl Lee said, "You look awful."

"Yes, I do, but at least I look worse than I feel. An old-fashioned ass-kicking."

"That's what I hear. You gonna be okay?"

"Sure, Carl Lee, already on the mend. What brings you into town?"

"I heard the news and I'm worried about you."

Jake was touched and wasn't sure what to say. So many friends had called and sent flowers and cakes and wanted to stop by, but he had not expected to hear from Carl Lee.

"I'll be fine, Carl Lee. Thanks for being concerned."

"Is Carla here?"

"She's inside, with Hanna. Why?"

"Say, look, Jake, I'll get right to it. When I heard about this I got really upset, still am, ain't slept much this week."

"That makes two of us."

"Rumor is you know who did it but you ain't gonna press charges. That right?"

"Come on, Carl Lee. We're not going there."

"Here's the deal, Jake. I owe you my life and I've

never been able to do much in the way of sayin' thanks. But this really pisses me off. I got some friends, and we can even things out."

Jake was shaking his head. He remembered the many hours he'd spent with Carl Lee in jail as his trial approached, and the awe and intimidation he'd felt at being in the presence of a man capable of such raw violence. Carl Lee had shot and killed the two rednecks who'd raped his daughter, then walked through their blood and drove home to wait for Ozzie to come get him. Fifteen years earlier he'd been decorated in Vietnam.

"It's not going to happen, Carl Lee. The last thing we need is more violence."

"Jake, I won't get caught and I swear I won't kill anybody. We'll just give the dude a little of his own medicine, make sure it don't happen again."

"It's not going to happen again, Carl Lee, and you're not getting involved. Believe me, it would only complicate matters."

"Give me his name and he'll never know what hit him."

"No, Carl Lee. The answer is no."

Carl Lee clenched his jaws, nodded his disapproval, and was about to press on when Carla opened the door and said hello.

ON SUNDAY, THE old Mazda with a rebuilt transmission parked in the lot beside the jail and Josie got out. As bad as Kiera wanted to see her brother, she knew she could not go inside. She rolled down the windows and stuck her nose in a paperback Mrs. Golden had given her two days earlier.

Josie checked in at the desk where Mr. Zack welcomed her back. She followed him down the hall and he unlocked the door to Drew's cell. She stepped inside and he locked the door behind her. The defendant was sitting at his small table, his textbooks stacked neatly in the center of it. He jumped to his feet and hugged his mother. They sat down, and Josie opened a paper bag and pulled out a bag of cookies and a soft drink.

"Where's Kiera?" he asked.

"Outside, in the car. She can't come in anymore."

"Because she's pregnant?"

"That's right. Jake doesn't want anyone to know."

He popped the top and chewed on a cookie. "I can't believe she's gonna have a baby, Mom. She's only fourteen."

"I know. I had you when I was sixteen and that was way too young, believe me."

"What'll happen to the baby?"

"We're putting him up for adoption. Some nice couple will get a beautiful little baby boy and he'll be raised in a fine home."

"Lucky him."

"Yes, lucky him. It's about time somebody in this family caught a lucky break."

"He's not really part of the family, is he, Mom?"

"I guess not. It's best if we just forget about him. Kiera will heal up nicely, be as good as new, and start school over in Oxford. No one there will ever know she had a baby."

"Will I ever get to see him?"

"I don't think so. Jake knows a lot about adoptions and he thinks it's best if we never see the baby, says it only complicates things."

He took a sip and thought about this. "You want a cookie?"

"No thanks."

"You know, Mom, I'm not sure I want to see that kid. What if he looks like Stuart?"

"He won't. He'll be as beautiful as Kiera."

Another sip, another long pause. "You know, Mom, I'm still not sorry I shot him."

"Well, I'm certainly sorry you did. Otherwise you wouldn't be in here."

"And otherwise we might all be dead."

"I want to ask you a question, Drew, one that's been on my mind for a long time. Jake wants to know the answer too but he hasn't asked you, not yet anyway. Kiera says you did not know that Stuart was raping her. Is that true?"

He shook his head and said, "I didn't know. She didn't tell anybody. Lookin' back, I think Stuart waited until there was nobody else around the house. If I had known I'd've shot him sooner."

"Don't say that."

"It's true, Mom. Somebody had to protect us. Stuart was gonna kill all of us. Hell, I thought you were dead that night, and I guess I just went crazy. I didn't have a choice, Mom." His lip quivered and his eyes watered.

Josie began wiping her eyes as she looked at her pitiful little son. What a tragedy, what a mess, what a screwed-up life she had led her children into. She carried the burdens of a hundred bad decisions and ached with the guilt of being such a rotten mother.

He finally said, "Don't cry, Mom. I'll get out of here one day and we'll be together again, just the three of us."

"I hope so, Drew. I pray every day for a miracle."

36

Eight days after the beating, Jake spent a long afternoon held captive in the chair of an oral surgeon who hammered and drilled and poured what felt like concrete to fix his teeth. He was groggy and in pain, with temporary caps, and would return in three weeks for the permanent crowns. The following day, Dr. Pendergrast removed the stitches and admired his handiwork. The scars would be tiny and would add "character" to Jake's face. His nose had shrunk to near normal size, but the puffiness around his eyes had turned a hideous shade of dark yellow. Because his nurse had tortured him with constant cold packs on everything swollen, most of his body parts had returned to normal size. The urologist, prodding gently, was impressed with the shrinkage.

He planned the return to his office so that he could park in a back alley and enter through a rear door. The last thing he wanted was to be spotted shuffling along a sidewalk and hiding under a cap and behind oversized sunglasses. He made it safely inside, gave Portia a quick hug, said hello to Bev, the chain-smoker, in her little nicotine den behind the kitchen, and walked gingerly up the stairs to his office. By the time he sat down he was winded. Portia brought him a cup of fresh coffee, gave him a long list of lawyers, judges, and clients he needed to call, and left him alone.

It was June 28, five weeks before the capital murder trial of Drew Allen Gamble. Normally, by now he would have had a discussion with the district attorney about the possibility of a plea bargain, a deal that would negate a trial and all the preparations one would entail. But that conversation was not going to happen. Lowell Dyer could offer nothing but a full guilty plea, and no defense lawyer would allow his client to risk pleading to a death sentence. If Drew did so, his sentencing would be left to the discretion of Judge Omar Noose, who could send him to the gas chamber, or to prison for life without parole, or to a lesser term. Jake had yet to discuss this with Noose and wasn't sure he would do so. The judge did not want the added pressure of having to hand down the sentence. Leave that for the twelve jurors, good folks who did not worry about getting reelected. Add politics to the mix, and Jake doubted Noose would show much sympathy for a cop killer. Leniency would be out of the question, regardless of the facts.

And what would Jake suggest? Thirty years? Forty years? No sixteen-year-old kid could think in those terms. Jake doubted Drew and Josie would agree to a guilty plea. How would he advise his client? Roll the dice and take your chances with the jury? It took only one determined holdout to hang it up. Could he find such a person? A hung jury meant another trial, and another. A depressing scenario.

He frowned at the list and picked up the phone.

AFTER PORTIA LEFT for the day, Lucien entered, without knocking, and fell into a leather chair opposite Jake. Surprisingly, he was drinking only coffee, though it was almost five. Always sarcastic and acerbic, he was in a good mood and almost sympathetic. They had spoken twice on the phone during the convalescence. After some light chatter he said, "Look, Jake, I've been here every day for the past week, and it's obvious the phone is not ringing as it should be. I'm worried about your practice."

Jake shrugged and tried to smile. "You're not the only one. Portia has opened four new files in the month of June. This place is drying up."

"I'm afraid the town's turned against you."

"That, and, as you know, it takes a certain amount of hustling to stay in business. I haven't been doing much of that."

"Jake, you've never asked me for money."

"Never thought about it."

"Let me tell you a secret. My grandfather founded First National Bank in 1880 and built it into the biggest bank in the county. He liked banking, didn't care for the law. When my father died in 1965, I inherited most of the stock. I hated the bank and the men who ran it, and so I sold out as soon as I could. Sold it to Commerce over in Tupelo. I'm no businessman but I did a smart thing, one that still surprises me. I didn't take cash because I didn't need it. The law office was hitting on all cylinders and I was busy, right here at this desk. Typical bank, Commerce got itself sold and merged and all that, and I hung onto the stock. It's now called Third Federal and I'm the second largest stockholder. The dividends roll in every quarter and they keep me afloat. I have no debts and don't spend much. I heard you saying something about refinancing your mortgage to get some cash. That still in the works?"

"Not really. The banks here said no. I haven't ventured outside the county."

"How much?"

"I have an appraisal, one of those friendly ones from Bob Skinner, at three hundred thousand."

"How much do you owe?"

"Two twenty."

"That's a lot for Clanton."

"It sure is. I paid too much for the house but then we really wanted it. I could put it on the market now but I doubt it would sell. I don't suppose Carla would be too happy about that."

"No, she wouldn't. Don't sell, Jake. I'll call the folks at Third Federal and get it refinanced."

"Just like that?"

"It's easy. Hell, I'm the second largest stockholder, Jake. They'll do the favor for me."

"I don't know what to say, Lucien."

"Say nothing. But that's an even bigger loan, Jake. Can you handle it?"

"Probably not, but I'm out of options."

"You're not going out of business, Jake. You're the son I never had, and at times I feel as though I live vicariously through you. This office will not close."

A wave of emotion swept over Jake and he couldn't speak. A long moment passed as both men looked away. Finally, Lucien said, "Let's go sit on the porch and have a drink. We need to talk."

With a scratchy voice, Jake said, "Okay, but I'll stick with coffee."

Lucien left and Jake shuffled to the door and stepped onto the veranda with a grand view of the square and the courthouse. Lucien returned with a whiskey on the rocks and sat next to him. They watched the late afternoon traffic and the same old men whittling and spitting tobacco juice under an ancient oak next to the gazebo.

Jake said, "You called it a 'secret.' Why?"

"How many times have I told you not to do your banking in this town? Too many people see what you do and know your balances. You settle a nice case, rake in a nice fee, and someone will see a big deposit at the bank. People talk, especially around here. You have a few bad months and your accounts get low, and too many people know it. I've advised you to bank out of town."

"I really had no choice. I get loans from Security because I know the banker."

"I'm not going to argue. But one day, when you're back on your feet, get the hell away from these banks."

Jake was not in the mood to argue either. Lucien was troubled and wanted to discuss something important. They watched the traffic for a moment, then Lucien said, "Sallie left me, Jake. She's gone."

Jake was surprised but then he wasn't. "I'm sorry, Lucien."

"It was sort of a mutual breakup. She's thirty years old and I've encouraged her to find another man, a husband, and start a family. Wasn't much of a life living with me, you know? She moved in when she was eighteen years old, started off as a housekeeper, and one thing led to another. I grew very fond of her, as you know."

"I'm sorry, Lucien. I like Sallie, figured she would always be around."

"I bought her a car, wrote her a nice check, and waved goodbye. Damned place is awfully quiet these days. But I'll probably find someone else."

"Sure you will. Where did she go?"

"She wouldn't say, but I was suspicious. I think she's already found someone else and I'm trying to convince myself that's a good thing. She needs a family, a real husband, kids. I couldn't stand the thought of her taking care of me in my decline. Driving me to the doctor, doling out pills, catheters, bedpans."

"Come on, Lucien, you're not ready for the end. You have some good years left."

"For what? I loved the law and I miss the glory days, but I'm too old and too set in my ways to make a comeback. Can you imagine an old geezer like me trying to pass the bar exam? I'd flunk it and that would kill me."

"You could at least try," Jake said but without conviction. The last thing he needed was Lucien with a new law degree causing trouble around the office.

Lucien raised his glass and said, "Too much of this, Jake, and the brain is not what it used to be. Two years ago I hit the books and was determined to pass the exam, but the memory is not working. I couldn't remember statutes from one week to the next. You know how taxing it is."

"Yes I do," Jake said, recalling, with horror, the pressures of the bar exam. His best friend from law school flunked it twice and moved to Florida to sell condos. A great career move.

"My life has no purpose, Jake. All I do is putter around here and spend most of my time on the front porch reading and drinking."

In the twelve years he had known Lucien, Jake had never heard such self-pity. Indeed, Lucien never complained about his own problems. He might rage for hours about injustice and the state bar association and his neighbors and the shortcomings of lawyers and judges, and he would on occasion suffer a bout of nostalgia and wish he could sue people again, but he never let his guard down and revealed his feelings. Jake had always believed Lucien's inheritance had grounded him well; that he considered himself luckier than most.

"You're always welcome around the office, Lucien. You're a great sounding board and I value your insights." Which was only partially true. Two years earlier when Lucien was making noise about getting reinstated, Jake had been unhappy with that prospect. With time, though, as the studying became too rigorous, Lucien stopped talking about the bar exam and fell into a routine of stopping by for a few hours on most days.

"You don't need me, Jake. You have a long career ahead of you."

"Portia has come to respect you, Lucien." After a rough start, the two had settled into an uneasy truce, but in the past six months had actually enjoyed working together. Already, and without the benefit of law school, she was an excellent researcher, and Lucien was teaching her how to write like a lawyer. He was delighted by her dream of becoming the first black female lawyer in town and he wanted her in his old office.

"Respect might be too strong a word. Plus, she's leaving in two months."

"She'll be back."

He rattled his ice and took a drink. "You know what I miss the most, Jake? The courtroom. I loved the courtroom, with a jury in the box and a witness on the stand and a good lawyer on the other side and, hopefully, a seasoned judge refereeing a fair fight. I loved the drama of the courtroom. People discuss things in open court they wouldn't talk about anywhere else. They have to. They don't always want to, but they have to because they are witnesses. I loved the pressure of swaying a jury, of convincing good skeptical people that you're on the right side of the law and they should follow you. You know who they'll follow, Jake?"

At that moment, Jake couldn't count the number of times he'd heard this little lecture. He nodded and listened as if for the first time.

"Jurors will not follow a fancy Dan in a designer

suit. They will not follow a silver-tongued orator. They will not follow a smart boy with all the rules memorized at his fingertips. No sir. They will follow the lawyer who tells them the truth."

Word for word, same as always.

"So, what's the truth with Drew Gamble?" Jake asked.

"Same as Carl Lee Hailey. Some people need killing."

"That's not what I told the jury."

"No, not in those words. But you convinced them that Hailey did exactly what they would do if given the chance. It was brilliant."

"I'm not feeling so brilliant these days. I have no choice but to put a dead man on trial, a guy who can't defend himself. It will be an ugly trial, Lucien, but I see no way around it."

"There is no way around it. I want to be in that courtroom when that girl takes the stand. Almost eight months pregnant and Kofer is the father. Talk about drama, Jake. I've never seen anything like it."

"I expect Dyer will howl for a mistrial."

"I'm sure he will."

"What will Noose do?"

"He won't be happy, but it's rare for the State to get a mistrial. I doubt if he'll do it. She's not your client and if Dyer calls her first then the mistake will be his, not yours."

Jake took a sip of cold coffee and watched the traffic. "Carla wants to adopt the baby, Lucien."

He rattled his ice and thought about it. "And you want this too?"

"I don't know. She's convinced it's the right thing to do, but she worries that it will appear to be, what's the right word, opportunistic?"

"Somebody will get the kid, right?"

"Yes. Kiera and Josie are going the adoption route."

"And you're worried about how this will look."

"I am."

"That's your problem, Jake. You worry too much about this town and all the gossipmongers. To hell with them. Where are they now? Where are all these wonderful people when you need them? All your friends at church. All your buddies in your little civic clubs. All those important people at the Coffee Shop who once thought you were the golden boy but don't care for you now. They're all fickle and uninformed and none of them realize what it takes to be a real lawyer, Jake. You've been here for twelve years and you're broke because you worry about what these people might say. None of them matter."

"So what matters?"

"Being fearless, unafraid to take unpopular cases, fighting like hell for the little people who have no one to protect them. When you get the reputation as a lawyer who'll take on anybody and anything—the government, the corporations, the power structure—then you'll be in demand. You have to reach a level of confidence, Jake, where you walk into a courtroom thoroughly unintimidated by any judge, any prosecutor, any big-firm defense lawyer, and completely oblivious to what people might say about you."

Another mini-lecture he'd heard a hundred times.

"I don't turn away too many clients, Lucien."

"Oh really. You didn't want the Gamble case, tried your best to get rid of it. I remember you whining when Noose dragged you into it. Everybody else in town ran and hid and you were pissed because you got stuck with it. This is exactly the kind of case I'm talking about, Jake. This is where a real lawyer steps up and says to hell with what people are whispering and walks into the courtroom proud to be defending a client no one else wanted. And there are cases like this all over the state."

"Well, I can't afford to volunteer for many of them." Once again, Jake was struck by the reality that Lucien had the means to be a radical lawyer. No one else owned half of a bank.

Lucien drained his glass and said, "I need to go. It's Wednesday and Sallie always roasted a hen on Wednesdays. I'll miss that. I guess I'll miss a lot of things."

"I'm sorry, Lucien."

Lucien stood and stretched his legs. "I'll call the guy at Third Federal. Get your paperwork together."

"Thanks, Lucien. You'll never know what this means."

"It means a lot more debt, Jake, but you'll bounce back."

"I will. I have no choice."

37

In 1843, an unstable Scottish woodturner named Daniel M'Naghten believed that the British prime minister Robert Peel and his Tories were following and persecuting him. He saw Peel walking along a London street and shot him in the back of the head, killing him. He got the wrong man. His victim was Edward Drummond, Peel's private secretary and longtime civil servant. At his trial for murder, both sides agreed that M'Naghten suffered from delusions and other mental problems. The jury found him not guilty by reason of insanity. His case became famous and led to an insanity defense that was widely accepted in England, Canada, Australia, Ireland, and in most of the United States, including Mississippi.

The M'Naghten Rule states: *To establish a defense on the ground of insanity it must be clearly proved, that, at the time of committing the act, the party accused was laboring under such a defect of reason from disease of the mind, as not to know the nature and quality of the act he was doing, or if he did know it, that he did not know that what he was doing was wrong.*

For decades the M'Naghten Rule ignited fierce debates among legal scholars, and it was modified and rejected outright in some jurisdictions. But in 1990 it was still the standard in most of the states, including Mississippi.

Jake filed a M'Naghten notice and attached a thirty-page brief in support that he and Portia, and Lucien, worked on for two weeks. On July 3, Drew was again taken to the state mental hospital at Whitfield to be examined by its doctors, one of whom would be selected to testify against him at trial. The defense had little doubt that Lowell Dyer would find one if not more psychiatrists willing to say that Drew was not mentally ill, did not suffer from mental disease, and knew what he was doing when he pulled the trigger.

And the defense would not argue otherwise. So far, there was nothing in Drew's profile to suggest he suffered from mental illness. Jake and Portia had obtained copies of his youth court abstracts, intake and discharge summaries, incarceration records, school reports, and evaluations from Dr. Christina Rooker in Tupelo and Dr. Sadie Weaver at Whitfield. Taken as a whole, they portrayed an adolescent physically, emotionally, and mentally immature and whose first sixteen years had been shockingly chaotic. He had been traumatized by Stuart Kofer and threatened repeatedly, and on the night in question was certain that his mother had been killed. But, he was not mentally ill.

Jake knew it was possible to find and hire an expert who would say otherwise, but he did not want a courtroom fight over insanity that he could not win. Portraying Drew as deranged and unaccountable would backfire with the jury. He planned to pursue the ruse of M'Naghten for the next few weeks, then drop it before trial. It was, after all, a chess match, and there was nothing wrong with sending Lowell Dyer off in the wrong direction.

STAN ATCAVAGE WAS at his desk when Jake interrupted with "Hey, got a minute?"

Stan was genuinely glad to see him. He had stopped

by the house a week earlier, as soon as Carla would allow it, and had a glass of lemonade on the patio.

"Good to see you out and about," he said.

Seventeen days after the beating, Jake was almost back to normal. The scars were small but visible, and his eyes were clear with only a trace of bruising under them.

"Glad to be out," he said as he handed over some papers. "A little gift for you and the boys in Jackson."

"What is it?"

"My mortgage cancellation. Security Bank is paid in full."

Stan looked at the sheet on top. It was stamped CAN-CELED.

"Congratulations," Stan said, shocked. "Who's the lucky bank?"

"Third Federal in Tupelo."

"Great. How much did they loan?"

"That's really none of your business, now is it? And I'm moving all my accounts over there too. Meager as they are."

"Come on, Jake."

"No, seriously, they're really nice folks and I didn't have to beg. They recognized the full value of my lovely home and they have confidence in my ability to pay. How refreshing."

"Come on, Jake. If it was left up to me, you know?"

"But it's not, not anymore. All you have to worry about now is the litigation loan. Tell your boys down there to relax and it'll get paid soon enough."

"Sure it will. I have no doubts. But you don't have to move your business. Hell, Jake, we've handled your accounts and loans since the beginning."

"Sorry, Stan, but this bank couldn't help me when I really needed it."

Stan tossed the paperwork onto his desk and cracked his knuckles. "Okay, okay. Are we still pals?"

"Always."

ON FRIDAY, July 6, Jake awoke in the dark from a nightmare and realized he was soaked with sweat. The dream was the same—his head stuck on the hot asphalt as a hulking, faceless thug battered his face. His heart was pounding and he was breathing heavily, but he managed to settle himself without moving and waking Carla. He glanced at the clock—4:14. Slowly he calmed himself and his breathing returned to normal. For a long time he was still, afraid to move a muscle because they all still ached, and he stared at the black ceiling and tried to shake off the nightmare.

The trial was one month away, and once he started thinking about it there would be no more sleep. At 5:00, he managed to gently pull down the sheets and swing his stiff legs to the side of the bed. As he stood, Carla said, "And where do you think you're going?"

"I need coffee. Go back to sleep."

"Are you okay?"

"Why wouldn't I be okay? I'm fine, Carla, go back to sleep."

He went quietly into the kitchen, made the coffee, and stepped onto the patio where the air was still warm from the day before and would only grow hotter with the hours. He was still wet with sweat and the coffee did little to cool things, but he needed it because it was an old friend and starting the day without it was un-thinkable. Thinking—that was the curse these days. Too much to think about. He dwelt on Cecil Kofer and the beating and how badly he wanted to press charges and sue for civil damages, to at least get some measure of justice, not to mention a few bucks to cover his medical expenses. He thought of Janet and Earl Kofer and their tragic loss, and as a parent he tried mightily to feel sympathy. But the sins of their son had caused heartbreak that could not be measured and would last for decades. Sympathy was an emotion he could not feel. He tried to imagine them sitting in the courtroom and absorbing blow after blow as Jake put their son on trial, but the facts could not be changed. He thought of Drew and for the thousandth time tried to define justice, but it was not within his grasp. Murder must be punished, but murder can also be justified. He engaged himself in his daily debate about putting Drew on the witness stand. To prove the crime was justified it would be necessary to hear from the defendant, to re-create the horror of the moment, to visualize for the jury the unmitigated fear in the house as his mother lay unresponsive and Kofer roamed the house looking for the kids. Jake was almost convinced that he could adequately prep his client with hours of practice before he took the stand.

He needed a long hot shower to wash away the dried sweat and soothe the aches. He went to the basement to take one without making noise. When he returned to the kitchen in his bathrobe, Carla was at the breakfast table in her pajamas, sipping coffee, and waiting. He kissed her on the cheek, told her he loved her, and sat across the table.

"Rough night?" she asked.

"I'm okay. Some bad dreams."

"How do you feel?"

"Better than yesterday. Did you sleep well?"

"The usual. Jake, I want to go to Oxford tomorrow, a Saturday day trip, just the two of us. We can picnic with Josie and Kiera, and I want to ask them for the baby."

It sounded odd, as if asking for a favor, for advice, for a recipe or even something more tangible like a book to borrow. Her eyes were moist and Jake looked at them for a long time. "You've made up your mind?"

"Yes. Have you?"

"I'm not sure."

"Jake, it's time to make a decision because I can't keep on like this. We either say yes or forget about it. I think about it every day, every hour, and I'm convinced it's the right thing to do. Look down the road, one year, two years, five years, when all this is behind us, when Drew is wherever Drew will be, when the gossip has died down and people have accepted it, when this mess is over, and we'll have a beautiful little boy that will be ours forever. Somebody gets him, Jake, and I want him to grow up in this house."

"If we still have the house."

"Come on. Let's make the decision tonight."

The decision had been made and Jake knew it.

6:00 A.M. SHARP, Jake walked into the Coffee Shop for the first time in weeks. Dell greeted him at the front with a sassy "Well, good morning, handsome. What have you been up to?"

Jake gave her a quick hug and nodded to the regulars. He took his old seat where Bill West was reading the Tupelo paper and drinking coffee. Bill said, "Well, well, look what the dogs drug up. Good to see you."

"Good morning," Jake said.

"We heard you were dead," Bill said.

"You can't believe anything around here. The gossip is terrible."

Bill gawked at him and said, "Looks like your nose is a bit crooked."

"You should've seen it last week."

Dell poured him coffee and asked, "The usual?"

"Why would I change after ten years?"

"Just tryin' to be nice."

"Give it up. It doesn't suit you. And tell the chef to hurry up. I'm starving."

"You want your butt kicked again?"

"No, as a matter of fact, I do not."

One table over, a farmer named Dunlap asked, "Say, Jake, we heard you got a good look at those boys. Any idea who it was?"

"Professionals, sent in by the CIA to silence me."

"Seriously, Jake. Tell us who it is and I'll send Willis here out for a little payback."

Willis was eighty years old with one lung and one leg. "Damned right," he said, tapping his cane. "I'll get those bastards."

"Watch your language," Dell yelled from across the café as she refilled coffee.

"Thanks, fellas, but I have no idea," Jake said.

"That ain't what I heard," Dunlap said.

"Well, if you heard it here it can't be right."

The day before, Jake had sneaked down to the café late in the day to catch up with Dell. He had talked to her twice on the phone when he was being held hostage at home by his nurse, and so he knew what his breakfast regulars were saying about him. At first they were shocked and angry, and then concerned. There was a general belief that it was related to the Kofer case, and that was confirmed four days after the attack when the rumor surfaced that it was one of Earl's boys. The following day, the gossip was that Jake was refusing to press charges. Roughly half the crowd admired him for this while the others wanted justice.

His grits and wheat toast arrived and the talk moved to football. The pre-season magazines were out and Ole Miss was ranked higher than expected. This pleased some and upset others, and Jake was relieved that things were returning to normal. The grits slid down with ease, but the toast needed chewing. He did so slowly, careful not to indicate that his jaw still ached and he was avoiding the temporary crowns. A week earlier he'd been dining on fruit shakes through a straw.

Late in the afternoon, Harry Rex called to check on him. He asked, "You see the legals in the *Times*?"

Every lawyer in town checked the weekly legal notices to see who had been arrested, who had filed for divorce or bankruptcy, which dead person's estate had been opened for probate, and whose land was being foreclosed. The notices were in the back with the classifieds, all in fine print.

Jake was behind with his reading and said, "No. What's up?"

"Take a look. They're probating Kofer's estate. He died with no will and they need to transfer his land to his heirs."

"Thanks. I'll check it out."

Harry Rex studied the legals with a magnifying glass to keep abreast of the news and gossip. Jake usually just scanned them, but he had not ignored Stuart Kofer's property. The county assessed the house and ten acres at $115,000, and there were no mortgages or liens. The title was free and clear, and all potential creditors had ninety days from July 2 to file claims against the estate. Kofer had been dead for over three months and Jake wondered what took so long, though such a delay was not unusual. State law provided no deadline to open probate.

He thought of at least two possible lawsuits. One filed on behalf of Josie for her medical bills, now in excess of $20,000—but the debt collectors couldn't find her. The second could be filed on behalf of Kiera for child support. And he could not forget his own lawsuit against Cecil Kofer for the beating and the bills it created, only half of which were covered by Jake's no-frills health insurance policy.

But suing the Kofers at this point could be counterproductive. His sympathy for the family had dissipated in the Kroger parking lot, but they had suffered enough. For now. He would wait until after Drew's trial and reassess the situation. The last thing he needed was more bad press. Lucien be damned.

38

Beginning in early July, as soon as Jake was physically able, Judge Noose began appointing him to indigent criminal cases throughout the Twenty-second district. It was not unusual for a lawyer from one county to handle cases next door, and Jake had done so throughout his career. The local lawyers did not complain because most of them did not want the work to begin with. The pay was not great—$50 an hour—but at least it was guaranteed. And, it was common practice throughout the state to pad the indigent files with a few extra hours to cover time spent driving from one courthouse to another. Noose even bunched Jake's cases together so that the ninety-minute trip to the town of Temple in Milburn County would be somewhat profitable when four new defendants were hauled into court for their initial appearances. Jake was soon running down to Smithfield in Polk County, and to the crumbling Van Buren County courthouse outside the town of Chester, Noose's home. He was appointed to every indigent case in Ford County.

He suspected, but of course could never prove, that Chancellor Reuben Atlee had intervened with one of his judges-only chats and whispered to Noose something to the effect of "You stuck him with Gamble, now help him out."

Two weeks before the Gamble trial, Jake was in Gretna, seat of Tyler County, handling the first appearances of three freshly indicted car thieves, with Lowell

Dyer representing the State. After a long morning grinding the wheels of justice, Judge Noose called them both to the bench and said, "Gentlemen, let's have lunch together in chambers. We have things to discuss."

Since Dyer's office was just down the hall, he asked his secretary to order sandwiches. Jake asked for egg salad, the easiest to chew. When the food arrived, they took off their jackets, loosened their ties, and started eating.

"In the Gamble matter, gentlemen, what's pending?" Noose knew exactly what matters needed to be decided before trial, but the meeting was informal and off the record so he let the lawyers choose the impromptu agenda.

Jake said, "Well, venue, for one."

Noose said, "Yes, and I'm inclined to agree with you, Jake. It might be difficult to pick an impartial jury in Clanton. I'm changing venue. Lowell?"

"Judge, we've filed our objection and supporting affidavits. There's nothing else to say."

"Good. I've been fully briefed and I've thought about it for a long time."

And you've also had an earful from Judge Atlee, Jake thought.

"We'll try the case in Chester," Noose declared.

For the defense, any venue other than Clanton was a win. But trying the case in the dilapidated Van Buren County Courthouse was not much better. Jake nodded and tried to appear pleased. An August trial in that dusty old courtroom, with a packed house, would be like slugging it out in a sauna. He almost wished he hadn't howled for a change of venue. Polk County had a modern courthouse with toilets that actually flushed. Why not there? And Milburn County Courthouse had just been renovated.

"It may not be your favorite courtroom," Noose said, stating the obvious. "But I'll get it spruced up. I've already ordered some new window units to keep things cool."

The only way to improve Noose's favorite courtroom was to burn it. What a challenge it would be to examine witnesses over the din of straining AC units.

Noose went on, trying to justify a decision based more on the comfort of the judge than the convenience of the litigants. "The trial is two weeks away and I'll have the place ready." Jake suspected His Honor wanted to shine in front of his home folks. Whatever. The slight advantage was Jake's, but the State could try the case anywhere and still have the upper hand.

"We'll be ready," Dyer said. "I'm concerned about the psychiatric expert for the defense, Your Honor. We've asked twice for his name and résumé and have received nothing."

Jake said, "I'm not going with insanity, and I'm withdrawing the M'Naghten notice."

Dyer was startled and blurted, "Couldn't find an expert?"

"Oh, there are plenty of experts, Lowell," Jake said coolly. "Just a change in strategy."

Noose was surprised too. "When did you decide this?"

"Within the past few days." They ate for a moment and considered this.

"Well, that should make the trial even shorter," Noose said, obviously pleased. Neither side wanted a war over expert testimony that few jurors could grasp. Insanity was used in less than 1 percent of all criminal trials, and though it rarely worked for the defense it never failed to stir strong emotions and confuse juries.

"Any more surprises, Jake?" Lowell asked.

"Not at this time."

"I don't like surprises, gentlemen," Noose said.

Dyer said, "Well, Judge, there's an important matter still hanging in the air, and it's no surprise to anyone. It seems patently unfair to the State to allow this trial to turn into a slander campaign against the victim, a fine officer of the law who cannot be there to defend himself. There will be allegations of physical abuse, even sexual abuse, and we have no way of knowing the truth about these claims. The only three witnesses are Josie Gamble and her two children, assuming Drew will be a witness, which I doubt, but these three will have the opportunity to say virtually anything about Stuart Kofer. How am I supposed to get to the truth?"

"They'll be under oath," Noose said.

"Sure they will, but they'll have every motive known to man to exaggerate, even lie and fabricate. Drew will be on trial for his very life, and I don't doubt for a second that he and his mother and sister will paint a nasty portrait of the victim. It is simply not fair."

Jake deftly opened a file and withdrew two enlarged color photos of Josie lying in the hospital bed with her face swollen and bandaged. He slid one across the table to Dyer and handed the other to His Honor. "Why lie?" he asked. "This speaks for itself."

Dyer had already seen the photographs. "You plan to offer this as evidence?"

"I certainly do, when she testifies."

"I'll object to the jury seeing this one and the others."

"Object all you want, but you know they'll be admitted."

"I'll make that decision at trial," Noose said, reminding them of who was in charge.

"And what about the girl?" Dyer asked. "I assume she'll testify that she was sexually assaulted by Kofer."

"Correct. She was repeatedly raped."

"But how do we know? Did she tell her mother? Did she tell anyone? We know she didn't call the authorities."

"That was because Kofer threatened to kill her if she did."

Dyer threw up his hands and said, "See, Judge, how do we know she was raped?"

Just wait, thought Jake. You'll find out soon enough.

Dyer went on, "It's just not fair, Judge. They can say anything they want about Stuart Kofer and we have no way to counter."

"The facts are the facts, Lowell," Jake said. "They were living a nightmare and were afraid to tell anyone. That's the truth and we can't hide it or change it."

"I want to talk to the girl," Dyer said. "I have the right to know what she'll say on the stand, assuming I'm forced to call her as a witness."

"If you don't call her I will."

"Where is she?"

"I'm not at liberty to say."

"Come on, Jake. Are you hiding another witness?"

Jake took a deep breath and held his tongue. Noose showed them his palms and said, "We're not going to bicker, gentlemen. Jake, do you know where they are?"

Jake glared at Dyer and said, "Cheap shot." He looked at Noose and said, "I do and I'm sworn to secrecy, Your Honor. They're not far away and they'll be in court when the trial starts."

"Are they hiding?"

"You could say that, yes. After I was attacked they were rattled and left the area. Who can blame them? That, plus Josie has bill collectors hounding her, so she's gone underground. Nothing new for her, really, because she's been running most of her life. She's moved around more than the three of us combined. They'll be in the courtroom when the trial starts, I guarantee it. They will be witnesses and they have to be there for Drew."

"I'd still like to talk to her," Dyer said.

"You've done that twice already, both times in my office. You asked me to make them available and I did."

"Are you going to put the defendant on the stand?" Dyer asked.

"Don't know yet," Jake said with a sappy smile, because he didn't have to answer the question. "I'll wait and see how the trial goes."

Noose took a bite of his sandwich and chewed for a while. "I don't like the idea of putting the deceased on trial. However, there was obviously a violent encounter with the mother just moments before he died. There are allegations of abuse of the children, and threats to keep them silent. Taken as a whole, I see no way to keep this from the jury. I'd like you to submit briefs on this issue and we'll talk again before the trial."

They had already submitted briefs and had nothing to add. Noose was stalling and looking for a way to avoid a tough decision. "Anything else?" he asked.

"What about the list of potential jurors?" Jake asked.

"It will be faxed to your respective offices at nine A.M. next Monday. I'm working on it now. We purged our voter registration rolls last year, at my direction, and this county is in good shape. We'll summon about a hundred for jury selection. And I'm warning both of you to stay away from the pool. Jake, as I recall, there were a lot of rumors about contact with the pool in the Hailey trial."

"Not by me, Your Honor. Rufus Buckley was out of control and the prosecution was stalking people."

"Whatever. This is a small county and I know most of the people. If anyone is contacted I'll hear about it."

"But we can conduct our basic investigations, right, Judge?" Dyer asked. "We have the right to gather as much background as possible."

"Yes, but no direct contact."

Jake was already thinking about Harry Rex and wondering who he might know in Van Buren County. And Gwen Hailey, Carl Lee's wife, was from Chester and had grown up not far from the courthouse. And years ago Jake had handled a land dispute for a nice family out in the county, and won it. And Morris Finley, one of the few lawyers left in Chester, was an old friend.

Across the table, Lowell Dyer was having similar thoughts. In the race to dig up dirt on the potential jurors, he would have the upper hand because Ozzie would lean on the local sheriff, an old-timer who knew everybody. The race was on.

LEAVING THE COURTHOUSE in Gretna, Jake called Harry Rex and told him the trial would be in Chester. Harry Rex cursed and said, "Why that dump?"

"That's the question of the day. Probably because Noose wants the trial in his backyard so he can go home for lunch. Get busy."

He had just crossed into Ford County when a red warning light next to his odometer began flashing. His engine was losing power and he stopped in front of a country church without another car in sight. It had finally happened. He and his beloved 1983 Saab had traveled 270,000 miles together and their journey had finally come to an end. He called the office and asked

Portia to send a tow truck. He sat on the shaded steps of the church for an hour and stared at his most cherished possession.

It had been the coolest in town when he bought it new, in Memphis, after settling a workers' comp case. The fee went for the down payment but the monthly notes had stretched on for five years. He should have traded it in two years earlier when he had cash from the Hubbard will contest, but he didn't want to spend the money. Nor did he want to part with the only red Saab in the county. But the repair bills had become outrageous because no mechanic in Clanton would touch the damned thing. Service required an all-day trip to Memphis, something he would not miss. The car attracted too much attention. He had been easy to spot driving away from Stan's that night when Mike Nesbit pulled him over and almost charged him with DUI. And he had no doubt that his beating at Kroger had been facilitated by the fact that the red Saab was easy to follow.

The tow truck driver's name was B.C., and Jake sat in the cab with him after he hitched up his car and they drove away. Jake had never been a passenger in a tow truck before.

"Mind if I ask what B.C. stands for?" he asked, loosening his tie.

B.C. had a mouth full of tobacco, and he spat in an old Pepsi bottle. "Battery Charger."

"I like it. How'd you get tagged with Battery Charger?"

"Well, when I was a kid I liked to steal batteries out of cars. I'd take 'em to Mr. Orville Gray's service station, sneak in at night, charge 'em real good, then sell 'em for ten bucks. Clear profit, no overhead."

"You ever get caught?"

"Nope, I was too slick. But my buddies knew about it and that's where the name came from. That's a weird car back there, if I say so."

"It certainly is."

"Where do you get it fixed?"

"Not around here. Let's take it to the Chevrolet place."

At Goff Motors, Jake paid B.C. a hundred dollars in cash and gave him several business cards. With a grin Jake said, "Pass these out at the next car wreck."

B.C. knew the game and asked, "What's my cut?"

"Ten percent of the settlement."

"I like it." He stuffed the cash and cards in his pocket and drove away. Jake looked down a row of shiny new Impalas and eyed a gray one, with four doors. By the time he looked at the sticker a smiling salesman appeared from nowhere and stuck out a friendly hand. They went through the usual ritual and Jake said, "I'd like to trade in my old car." He nodded at the Saab.

"What is it?" asked the salesman.

"1983 Saab with a lot of miles."

"I think I've seen that around town. What's the trade-in value?"

"Five thousand and change."

He frowned and said, "That may be a bit high."

"Can I get this financed through General Motors?"

"I'm sure we can work something out."

"I'd like to stay away from the banks around here."

"No problem."

Laden with even more debt, Jake drove away an hour later in a leased Impala, gray in color and one that blended in nicely with the traffic. It was a good time for him to be inconspicuous.

39

At 9:00 A.M. Monday, Jake and Portia were standing at the fax machine drinking coffee and waiting anxiously for the jury list from Judge Noose. Ten
minutes later it arrived—three sheets of paper with
ninety-seven names in alphabetical order. Name, address, age, race, gender, nothing else. There was no standard form for the publication of the jury pools and it
varied throughout the state.

Not surprisingly, Jake did not recognize a single
name. Van Buren County had 17,000 people, the smallest population of any of the five in the Twenty-second
Judicial District, and in his twelve years as a lawyer Jake
had spent almost no time there. There had been no
reason to. Not for the first time, he asked himself if he
had made a mistake in insisting on a change of venue.
At least in Ford County he would recognize a few of
the names. Harry Rex would know even more.

Portia made ten copies, took one with her, said
goodbye, and headed for the courthouse in Chester
where she would spend the next three days poring over
the public records for land transactions, divorces, wills,
vehicle loans, and criminal charges. Jake faxed one copy
to Harry Rex and one to Hal Fremont, a lawyer buddy
across the square who had moved to Clanton a few
years back when his practice in Chester dried up. He
faxed another copy to Morris Finley, the only lawyer he
knew in Van Buren County.

At ten, he met with Darrel and Rusty, two brothers

who worked as Clanton city policemen and moonlit as private investigators. As was typical in small jurisdictions, the city police played second fiddle to the county sheriff's department and there was no love lost between the two forces. Darrel knew Stuart Kofer in passing; Rusty did not. It didn't matter—for $50 an hour each, they were happy to get the work. Jake gave them the list and firm instructions not to get noticed as they snooped around Van Buren County. They were expected to find and photograph, if possible, the homes, vehicles, and neighborhoods of the potential jurors. When they left, Jake mumbled to himself, "They'll probably make more off this case than me."

The *Smallwood* war room downstairs had been converted to the makeshift headquarters for the Gamble jury. On one wall there was a large map of the county, and on it Jake and Portia had marked every church, school, highway, county road, and country store. Another large map laid out the city streets of Chester. Working from the list, Jake began locating as many of the addresses as possible and memorizing names.

He could almost envision the jury. White with maybe two or three blacks. Hopefully more women than men. Average age of fifty-five. Rural, conservative, religious.

Booze could be a big factor in the trial. Van Buren was still a dry county, and fiercely so. Its last liquor vote was in 1947 and the drinkers lost in a landslide. Since then the Baptists had squelched any efforts to have another election. Each county controlled its liquor laws and half the state was still dry. As always, the bootleggers did a brisk business in the parched areas, but Van Buren had a reputation as the home of serious teetotalers.

How would these sober folks react to the testimony that Stuart Kofer was a raging drunk the night he died?

That there was enough alcohol in his blood to practically kill him? That he'd spent the afternoon drinking beer and then topped it off with illegal moonshine as he and his friends blacked out?

The jurors would certainly be shocked and disapproving, but they would also be conservative enough to love the men in uniform. Killing an officer called for the death penalty, a punishment revered in those parts.

At noon, Jake left town and drove twenty minutes to a lumber mill deep in the county. He saw Carl Lee Hailey eating a sandwich with his men in the shade of a small pavilion and waited in his new car, which was not recognizable. When they finished lunch, Jake walked over and said hello. Carl Lee was surprised to see him and at first thought there might be some trouble. Jake explained what he was after. He gave Carl Lee a list of the jurors and asked him and Gwen to study the names and quietly ask around. Most of her large family still lived in Van Buren County and not far from Chester.

"This ain't illegal, is it?" he asked, flipping a page.

"Would I ask you to do something illegal, Carl Lee?"

"Probably not."

"This is pretty typical stuff in a jury trial. You sure can believe we did it for yours."

"Something worked," Carl Lee said with a laugh. He flipped another page and stopped laughing. "Jake, this guy here is married to Gwen's cousin on her daddy's side."

"His name?"

"Rodney Cote. Know him pretty well. He was in the courtroom for my trial."

Jake was thrilled but tried not to show it. "Is he a reasonable man?"

"What does that mean?"

"It means—can you talk to him? On the sly, you know, off the record, over a beer."

Carl Lee smiled and said, "I get it."

They were walking to Jake's car. "What's this?" Carl Lee asked.

"A new set of wheels."

"What happened to that funky little red thang?"

"It quit."

"About time."

JAKE WAS ELATED as he drove back to town. With luck, and perhaps a bit of coaching from Carl Lee, Rodney Cote could survive the barrage of qualifying questions to be thrown at the pool during selection. Was he related to Drew Gamble? Obviously not. Did he know anyone in the defendant's family? No. No one knew the Gambles. Did he know the deceased? No. Did he know any of the lawyers for either the prosecution or defense? Here, Rodney would have to be careful. Though he'd never met Jake, he certainly knew who he was, which in itself would not disqualify him. In small towns it was inevitable that potential jurors knew some of the lawyers. Rodney should remain silent here. Mr. Brigance over there is involved in the private practice of law: He ever do any business for you or anyone in your family? Again, Rodney should not raise his hand. Jake had represented Carl Lee, not Gwen. Being married to a non-blood relative was not close enough to warrant further examination, at least not in Jake's opinion.

Jake was suddenly obsessed with getting Rodney Cote on the jury, but he would need some luck. Next Monday, when they first arrived in the courtroom, the jurors would be seated at random, not alphabetically.

Each would get a number pulled from a hat. If Rodney was in the first forty or so, he stood a good chance of making the final twelve, with some skillful manipulation by Jake. A high number meant he would not make it.

The problem would be Willie Hastings, Gwen's cousin, on her mother's side, and the first black deputy hired by Sheriff Walls. Ozzie was undoubtedly already working for the prosecution, polling his deputies, and if Willie spoke up about Rodney Cote, then he would be struck for good cause.

Perhaps Ozzie might not quiz Hastings. Perhaps Hastings didn't know Cote, but that was unlikely.

Jake almost turned around for another chat with Carl Lee, but decided to do it later. Soon, though.

BY WEDNESDAY, THE walls of the jury room were covered with more maps and more names stuck to the maps with colored push-pins. Dozens of enlarged photos were tacked to the maps, photos of cars and old pickups, tidy homes in towns and trailers in the country, farmhouses, churches, gravel driveways with no homes in sight, small stores where people worked, and low-wage factories that produced shoes and lamps. The average household in the county earned $31,000 a year, barely enough to survive, and the photos told the tale. Prosperity had bypassed Van Buren County and its population was declining, a sad trend that was not unusual in rural Mississippi.

Harry Rex had tracked down seven names. Morris Finley added another ten. Hal Fremont recognized only a few names on the list. As small as the county was, trying to pinpoint ninety-seven names out of 17,000 was still an uphill battle. Darrel and Rusty had managed to procure eleven church directories, and these revealed the names of twenty-one prospective jurors. There were at least a hundred churches, though, and most were too small to print the names of their members. Portia was still digging through the public records but had found little of value. Four of the prospects had divorced in the last ten years. One bought a 200-acre tract of land the year before. Two had been arrested for drunk driving. How this gossip was supposed to help was lost on the team.

By Thursday, Jake and Portia were playing the name game as they worked. He picked a name from the list, announced it, and from memory she either rattled off what little info they had or admitted they had nothing. Then she picked a name and from memory he spouted the person's age, race, gender, and anything else they had learned. They worked late into the nights, combing their data, nicknaming the jurors, and memorizing everything. The selection process could be slow and tedious, but there would also be moments when Jake would need to react quickly, saying yes or no after only a moment's reflection, before moving on to the next prospect. Because it was a capital case, Noose would be in no hurry. He might even allow the lawyers to meet privately with a person on the list to probe even deeper. Each side would have twelve peremptory challenges, or rejections for no cause at all. If Jake didn't like the sneer on a person's face, he could cut her for no reason. These, though, were valuable, and had to be used with great discretion.

Any juror could be challenged for cause. If your husband was a police officer, so long. If you were related to the victim, hit the door. If you could not consider a death verdict, bye-bye. If you had been the victim of domestic violence, it was best if you didn't serve. The fiercest fights were always over who to cut for cause. If the judge agreed that a person might not be impartial for a reason, then he dismissed him or her without burning either side's peremptory challenges.

It had been Jake's experience that most people, once they were subpoenaed and had gone to the trouble of showing up for selection, actually wanted to serve on the jury. This was especially true in the more rural areas where trials were rare and offered a little drama. However, when the death penalty was in play, virtually no one wanted to get near the jury box.

The longer he looked at the list, the more he became convinced that he could throw darts at it and take any twelve. As long as he got Rodney Cote.

Harry Rex thundered in Friday afternoon and said they needed a break. Portia was exhausted and Jake sent her home. He locked his office and insisted on driving. He and Harry Rex climbed into his shiny new Impala and, without stopping for beer, drove to Chester for a bit of recon. Along the way they argued trial strategy and scenarios. Harry Rex had become convinced that Noose would probably declare a mistrial when Kiera told the jury who had impregnated her, assuming that Dyer was caught off guard. Jake disagreed, though he was not completely confident he could pull off the ambush. At some point Monday morning, probably before they began jury selection, Dyer would want to meet with Kiera to go over her testimony once again. She was over seven months pregnant and that would be impossible to conceal.

They discussed putting Drew on the witness stand. Jake had spent hours with him and was still not sure the kid could withstand a brutal cross-examination. Harry Rex was adamant in his belief that the defendant should never testify.

It was Friday, and the courthouse was clearing out. They removed their coats and ties and made it upstairs to the courtroom without being noticed. Inside, they were surprised to feel cool air. Noose's new window units were running at full speed and not making much noise. They would probably work overtime through the weekend. The courtroom had been cleaned thoroughly, not a speck of dust or dirt anywhere. Two painters were hard at work adding a fresh coat of white enamel while another was on his knees brushing the woodwork around the bench with a new finish.

"Well, I'll be damned," Harry Rex mumbled. "This place has never looked so good."

The faded oil portraits of dead judges and politicians had been removed, no doubt sent to the basement where they belonged, and the bare walls gleamed with shiny new paint. The ancient pews had been refinished. Twelve new chairs with comfortable cushions were in the jury box. The large overhanging balcony had been cleared of neglected filing cabinets and storage boxes, replaced with two rows of rented chairs.

"Noose is spending some money on the place," Jake whispered.

"About time. I guess it's his big moment, too. Looks like he's expecting a crowd." They had no desire to see the judge and after a few minutes headed for the door. Jake stopped for another look and realized that his stomach was in knots.

Before his first jury trial, Lucien had said, "If you're not nervous as hell when you walk into that court-room, then you're not ready." Before the Hailey trial, Jake had locked himself in a toilet next to the jury room and vomited.

Down the hallway, Harry Rex stepped into a rest-room. He emerged moments later and said, "Well, I'll be damned. The commodes are actually flushing. Looks like old Ichabod has really cracked the whip around here."

They left the town and headed east, in no hurry to go anywhere. When they crossed into Ford County, Jake stopped at the first country store and Harry Rex went in to buy a six-pack. They drove to Lake Chatulla and found a picnic table under a shade tree on a bluff, a hiding place both had visited in the past, together and alone.

40

Monday, August 6. Jake slept in short little naps interrupted by long stretches of wide-eyed worries about all the things that could go wrong. His dream was to become a great trial lawyer, but, as always on the first morning, he asked himself why anyone would want the stress. The meticulous pretrial preparation was tedious and nerve-racking, but nothing compared to the actual battle. In the courtroom, and in front of the jury, a lawyer has at least ten things on his mind, all crucial. He must concentrate on the witness, either his or an opponent's, and hear every word of the testimony. Should he object, and why? Has he covered all of the facts? Are the jurors listening, and if so do they believe the witness? Do they like the witness? If they're not paying attention, is this beneficial or not? He must observe every move made by his opponent and predict where he is going. What is his strategy? Has he changed midcourse, or is he laying a trap? Who was the next witness? And where was she or he? If the next witness was adverse, how effective would she be? If he was a defense witness, was he ready? Actually in the courthouse? And prepared? The absence of discovery in criminal trials only heightened the stress because the lawyers were not always certain what the witness might say. And the judge—was he on top of his game? Listening? Napping? Hostile or friendly or neutral? Were the exhibits properly prepared and ready? Would there be a fight over their admission into evidence, and if so did the lawyer know the rules of evidence inside and out?

Lucien had lectured him on the importance of being relaxed, cool, calm, unflappable, regardless of how the trial was progressing. The jurors missed nothing, and every move made by the lawyer was noticed. Acting was important: feigning disbelief at damaging testimony, showing compassion where needed, occasionally flashing anger when appropriate. But overacting could be devastating if it verged on phoniness. Humor could be lethal because in tense situations everyone needed a good laugh, but it was to be used rarely. A man's life was on the line and a comment made too lightly could backfire. Watch the jurors constantly but don't overdo it, don't let them catch you trying to read them.

Have all motions been properly filed? Were the jury instructions ready? The final summation was often the most dramatic moment, but preparing it ahead of time was difficult because the witnesses had not yet been heard. He'd won the Hailey acquittal with a stunning closing argument. Could he do it again? What magic words or phrases could he conjure up to save his client?

His greatest moment would be ambushing the State with Kiera's pregnancy, and he had lost hours of sleep thinking about it. How could he protect the secret that very morning, in just a few hours, as all the players gathered in the crowded courtroom?

He drifted away again and woke up from a moment of deep sleep to the distant aroma of frying bacon. It was 4:45 and Carla was at the stove. He said good morning, kissed her, poured coffee, and said he was taking a quick shower.

They ate quietly at the breakfast nook—bacon and scrambled eggs with toast. Jake had eaten little over the weekend and had no appetite.

She said, "I'd like to run through my plan again, if you don't mind."

"Sure. You're basically babysitting."

"Nice to be so necessary."

"I assure you your role is crucial. Let's hear it."

"I'll meet Josie and Kiera outside the courthouse at ten and keep them in the hallway on the first floor. We'll wait there while the selection process begins. What am I supposed to do if Dyer wants to talk to them?"

"Not sure. Dyer will have plenty on his mind first thing this morning. Like me, he'll be consumed with worry about the jury pool, but if he asks about Kiera and Josie I'll tell him they're on the way. Selection will drag on through the morning and probably the entire day, and I'll send instructions to you. If I get a break, I'll come find you. They're under subpoena so they have to be close by."

"And if Dyer finds us?"

"He has the right to talk to Kiera, not Josie. He'll probably realize she's pregnant but I doubt he'll have the guts to ask who's the father. Keep in mind the only thing Dyer wants from her is the testimony that Drew shot Kofer. He has to have that, and I doubt he'll go much further."

"I can do this," she said nervously.

"Sure you can. There will be a crowd swarming around the courthouse so just try to get lost in it. At some point I'll want you in the courtroom as we narrow the pool and start picking the twelve."

"And what am I supposed to do in the courtroom, exactly?"

"Study the jurors, especially those on the first four rows. Especially the women."

After a few bites, he said, "Gotta go. I'll see you over there."

"You need to eat, Jake."

"I know, but I'll probably lose it anyway."

He kissed her on the cheek and left the house. In his car, he removed a pistol from his briefcase and hid it under the seat. He parked in front of his office, unlocked the door, and turned on the lights. Portia arrived half an hour later, and at seven Libby Provine made her entrance in a tight pink designer dress, high heels, and a loud paisley scarf. She had arrived in Clanton late Sunday afternoon and they had worked until eleven.

"You look rather smashing," Jake observed, with reservations.

"You like it?" she shot back.

"I don't know. It's pretty bold. I doubt if we'll see another pink dress in the courtroom today."

"I like to be noticed, Jake," she sang in her best Scottish brogue. "I know it's rather nontraditional, but I've found that jurors, especially the men, like a bit of fashion amongst all the dark suits. You look quite handsome."

"Thanks, I guess. My newest lawyer suit."

Portia kept staring at the pink dress.

Libby said, "Just wait till they hear me talk."

"They probably won't understand a word."

She wouldn't be talking much, not at first. Her role was to assist Jake during the guilt, or second, phase of the trial, and say little until then. If Drew were convicted of capital murder, she would play a bigger role in the war over his sentencing. Dr. Thane Sedgwick was on standby at Baylor in case he was needed to sprint over to try and save the kid's life. Jake was praying that would not be necessary, but he expected it. He didn't have time to worry about it that morning.

Jake looked at her and said, "Tell me about Luther Redford."

Libby shot back, "White male, age sixty-two, lives in the country on Pleasant Valley Road, raises organic chickens and sells them to the best restaurants in Memphis. Married for forty years to the same woman, three adult children, scattered, a bunch of grandchildren. Church of Christ."

"And what does 'Church of Christ' mean?"

"Devout, clannish, conservative, fundamental, strong on law and order with a dim view of violent crime. Almost certainly a teetotaler with no use at all for alcohol and drunkenness."

"Would you take him?"

"Probably not, but he might be on the cusp. We defended a seventeen-year-old two years ago in Oklahoma and the defense lawyer avoided all Church of Christ members, as well as a lot of Baptists and Pentecostals."

"And?"

"Guilty. It was an awful crime, but we hung the jury on sentencing and got life without parole, which is supposed to be a win, I guess."

"Would you take him, Portia?"

"No."

"We can play this game driving over. How many jurors are complete mysteries?"

"Seventeen," Portia said.

"That's a lot. Look, I'll load the car while the two of you go through the hit-list of all jurors we will challenge for cause."

"We've already done that, at least twice," Portia said. "I have the list memorized."

"Memorize it again."

Jake left his office, went downstairs, and loaded three

large document boxes into the trunk of his Impala, which had far more space than the old Saab. At 7:30, the defense team left Clanton with Portia behind the wheel and Jake in the backseat calling off the names of people they had never seen but were about to meet.

JOSIE PARKED AT the jail and told Kiera to stay in the car. Lying neatly on the rear seat was a navy blazer, white shirt, clip-on tie, and gray slacks, all arranged carefully on a hanger. Josie retrieved the outfit, which she had put together in the past week browsing through discount stores in and around Oxford. Jake had given her strict instructions on what to buy, and she had spent the previous day washing and ironing Drew's trial ensemble. The shoes didn't matter, Jake had said. He wanted his client to look nice and respectful but not too preppy. Drew's secondhand sneakers would do just fine.

Mr. Zack was waiting at the jail desk and he led her down the hall to the juvenile cell. "He's had his shower, but he didn't want to," he said quietly as he unlocked the door. Josie stepped in and he closed the door behind them.

The defendant was sitting at his table playing solitaire. He stood and hugged his mother and noticed her red eyes. "Are you cryin' again, Mom?" he asked.

She did not reply but laid his outfit on the bottom bunk. On the top bunk she noticed an untouched tray of eggs and bacon and asked, "Why haven't you eaten?"

"Not hungry, Mom. I guess this is my big day, huh?"

"It is. Let's get dressed."

"I gotta wear all that?"

"Yes sir. You're goin' to court and you gotta look nice, like Jake said. Let me have the overalls." No sixteen-year-old boy wanted to strip in front of his mother, regardless of the circumstances, but Drew knew he couldn't complain. He stepped out of the orange jail garb as she handed him the slacks first.

"Where'd you get this stuff?" he asked, taking them and quickly pulling them on.

"Here and there. You gotta wear this every day, Jake's orders."

"How many days, Mom? How long will this take?"

"Most of the week, I think." She helped him into his shirt and buttoned it for him. He stuffed in the shirttail and said, "It feels a little too big."

"Sorry, it's the best we can do." She picked up the tie, clipped it over the top button, fussed with it, and said, "When's the last time you wore a tie?"

He shook his head and wanted to complain, but why bother? "I've never worn one."

"Didn't think so. You're gonna be in the courtroom with lots of lawyers and important people and you need to look nice, okay? Jake said the jury will look you over and appearances are important."

"He wants me to look like a lawyer?"

"No, he wants you to look like a fine young man. And don't stare at the jurors."

"I know, I know. I've read his instructions a hundred times. Sit straight, pay attention, don't show emotion. If I get bored, scribble something on some paper."

The entire family had pages of written instructions from their lawyer.

She helped him into the navy blazer, another first, and stepped back to admire him. "You look great, Drew."

"Where's Kiera?"

"Outside in the car. She's doin' fine."

She was not. She was a wreck, same as her mother.

Three lost souls about to enter a lions' den with no idea what was about to happen to any of them. She tousled his mop of blond hair and wished she had a pair of scissors. Then she grabbed him and squeezed him fiercely and said, "I'm so sorry, baby, I'm so sorry. I got us into this mess. It's all my fault. All my fault."

He stood stiff as a board and waited for the moment to pass. When she finally released him he looked at her moist eyes and said, "We've already talked about this, Mom. I did what I did and I don't regret it."

"Don't say that, Drew. Don't say it now and don't say it in court. Don't ever say that to anyone, you understand?"

"I'm not stupid."

"I know you're not."

"What about my shoes?"

"Jake said to wear your sneakers."

"Well, they don't really go with the rest of my outfit, do they?"

"Just do as he says. Always, Drew, just do what he says. You look nice."

"And you'll be there, right, Mom?"

"Of course I'll be there. On the front row, right behind you."

41

The prospective jurors began arriving at the old courthouse at 8:30, and they were greeted by the sight of three brightly painted news vans, one from the station in Tupelo, one from an affiliate in Jackson, one from Memphis. Crews were setting up lights and cameras as close to the front door as a deputy would allow them. The hamlet of Chester had never felt so important.

The jurors, each holding a summons to validate their presence, were met at the front door by a polite clerk who checked their paperwork, made an entry of some sort on the master list, and asked them to continue on up the stairs to the courtroom on the second floor where they would receive further instructions. The courtroom was locked and guarded by men in uniform who asked them to wait a few minutes. A crowd soon gathered in the hallway as the nervous and curious jurors mingled and whispered. The summonses did not mention the matter at hand, but suspicions ran wild. Word soon spread that it was a criminal case involving a murdered deputy from over in Ford County.

Harry Rex, wearing a John Deere cap and dressed like a rustic good ol' boy from the hollows, and holding a sheet of paper that could pass for his own summons, mixed with the locals and listened to the gossip. He knew virtually no one from the area and none of the jurors had ever laid eyes on him, but he nonetheless kept his guard up in case Lowell Dyer or anyone working for him ventured into the hallway. He chatted with a woman who said she had no time for jury duty and was needed at home to care for her aging mother. He overheard an older man say something to the effect that he had no qualms with the death penalty. He asked a younger woman if it was true that it was the case from Clanton where a deputy was murdered back in March. She said she didn't know but seemed horrified at the prospect of sitting in judgment for such an awful matter. As the crowd thickened, he stopped talking and just listened, waiting for a stray word here or there that would reveal something crucial, something that might not be admitted in open court during the selection process.

Spectators joined the jurors, and when Harry Rex saw the Kofers arrive he eased into a restroom and lost the cap.

At 8:45, the door was opened and a clerk asked those summoned to step into the courtroom and have a seat on the left side. They filed down the aisle, gawking at the vastness of the large, freshly painted room, a place few of them had ever seen. Another clerk pointed to the pews on the left. The right side would remain vacant for a while longer.

Evidently, Noose had ordered the air-conditioners to run at full speed throughout the weekend and there was a noticeable chill in the air. August 6, with a high of ninety-five expected, but oddly enough the spruced-up courtroom was pleasant.

Jake, Portia, and Libby stood around the defense table, whispering about important matters as they sized up the prospects. A few feet away, Lowell Dyer and D. R. Musgrove chatted with their investigator, Jerry Snook, as clerks and bailiffs milled about in front of the bench.

Dyer stepped over and said to Jake, "I assume Mrs. Gamble and her daughter are here."

"They'll be here, Lowell, I gave you my word."

"Did you give them their subpoenas?"

"I did."

"I'd like to chat with Kiera at some point this morning."

"No problem."

Dyer was nervous and fidgety, obviously feeling the strain of his first big trial. Jake worked hard at appearing to be the seasoned veteran, but though he had more courtroom experience than his opponent, his stomach was in knots. Dyer didn't have a belt notched with big convictions, but he still had all the advantages handed to the State—good over evil, law enforcement over the criminal, plenty of resources over an indigent defense.

WITH OZZIE BEHIND the wheel, the defendant arrived in the rear seat of the sheriff's clean and shiny patrol car. For the benefit of the press, it was parked in front of the courthouse where Ozzie and Moss Junior, grim-faced and all business, yanked open a rear door and removed the alleged killer, handcuffed and ankle-chained but reasonably well dressed. They grabbed his skinny arms and walked him slowly in an old-fashioned perp march to the front door of the courthouse as the cameras clicked and rolled. Inside, they hustled him through a door that led to one of the building's many appendages and soon found the meeting room of the Van Buren County Board of Supervisors. A local deputy opened it for them while saying to Ozzie, "Got this place secured for you, Sheriff."

The room had no windows and not much in the way of air-conditioning. Drew was told to sit in a certain chair, then left there as Ozzie and Moss Junior stepped outside and closed the door.

Three hours would pass before it opened again.

BY 9:15 THE POOL was seated on one side; the other was still empty as the spectators waited in the hallway. A bailiff called court to order and asked everyone to rise. As they did, the Honorable Omar Noose appeared from a door behind the bench. The lawyers settled around their tables and the clerks took their positions.

Noose stepped down and walked to the bar dividing the courtroom, his long black robe flowing behind him. Jake, seated only a few feet away, whispered to Libby, "Oh no, it's the Flowing Robe Routine." She gave him a blank look.

Occasionally, and especially when elections were looming, state trial judges liked to get closer to the masses, the voters, and greeted them not from a lofty perch on the bench but down on the floor, at their level, from just behind the bar.

Noose introduced himself to his home crowd and gave them a friendly welcome, thanking them for being there. As if they had a choice. He spent a moment rambling on about the importance of jury service to the orderly flow of justice. He hoped it would not be burdensome. Without going into detail, he described the nature of the case and explained that much of the day would be spent selecting a jury. He looked at a sheet of paper and said, "I have been informed by the clerk that three members of this pool have failed to show. Mr. Robert Giles, Mr. Henry Grant, and Mrs. Inez Bowen. All received proper subpoenas but have not bothered to check in this morning. I'll ask the sheriff to round 'em up." He looked gravely at the sheriff seated near the jury box and nodded, as if prison might just be an option here.

"Now, we have ninety-four people here in the pool, and our first order of business is to see who might be exempt. If you're sixty-five or older, state law allows you to pass on jury service. Any volunteers for?"

Noose and the clerk had already culled the seniors chosen from the voter registration records, but there were eight in the pool between the ages of sixty-five and seventy. He knew from experience that not all of those would claim the exemption.

A man on the front row sprung up, waving his hand.

"And you are?"

"Harlan Winslow. I'm sixty-eight and I got better things to do."

"You're excused, sir."

Winslow almost sprinted down the aisle. He lived deep in the country and had an NRA sticker on the bumper of his pickup. Jake happily struck his name. Good riddance.

Three others begged off and left the courtroom. Down to ninety.

Noose said, "Next, we'll consider those with medical issues. If you have a note from your doctor, please step forward." The pews creaked and rustled as a number of jurors stood and made their way forward, forming a line in the aisle in front of the judge. Eleven in all. The first one, a slothful younger man who was morbidly obese, looked as though he might collapse at any moment. He handed over a note that Noose studied carefully before smiling and saying, "You are excused. Mr. Larry Sims." He smiled and lumbered toward the door.

As Noose methodically worked through the hardships, the lawyers studied their notes, scratched off names, and looked at the remaining members of the pool.

Two of the eleven with doctors' notes were on Jake's list of complete mysteries, and he was pleased when they left. After forty minutes of tedium, all eleven were gone. Down to seventy-nine.

Noose said, "Now, the rest of you are qualified to be examined during the selection process. We will do this by calling names at random. When you're called, please have a seat over on this side, beginning with the front row." He waved to his left, to the empty pews. A clerk stepped forward and handed him a small cardboard box, which he set on the defense table.

This little lottery was the most crucial part of the selection process. The final twelve would likely come from the first four rows, the first forty names pulled from the box.

The lawyers quickly moved their chairs to the other side of their tables, facing the pool, their backs to the bench. Noose removed a folded strip of paper and called out, "Mr. Mark Maylor." A man stood with great uncertainty and shuffled down the row to the aisle.

Maylor. White male, age forty-eight, longtime algebra teacher at the only high school in the county. Two years at a junior college, degree in math from Southern Miss. Still married to his first wife, three children, the youngest still at home. Nice blazer and one of the few neckties in the pool. First Baptist Church of Chester. Jake wanted him.

As he sat at the far end of the front row, Noose called the name of Reba Dulaney. White female, age fifty-five, a housewife who lived in town and played the organ at the Methodist church. She took a seat next to Mark Maylor.

Number three was Don Coben, a sixty-year-old

farmer whose son was a policeman in Tupelo. Jake would challenge him for cause, and if that didn't work he would burn a peremptory challenge to get rid of him.

Number four was May Taggart, the first black chosen. She was forty-four and worked at the Ford dealership. It was the collective wisdom of the defense team, including Harry Rex and Lucien, that blacks were preferred because they were more likely to have less sympathy for white officers. Dyer, though, would be able to challenge them without the usual racial issues because both the defendant and the victim were white.

After an hour on his feet, His Honor was feeling some strain in his lower back. When the first row was seated, he retired to the bench, to his comfortable chair with thick cushions.

Jake studied the first ten. Two he would definitely take, three he would not. The others would be argued over later. Noose reached into his box and pulled out the first name for the second row.

CARLA ENTERED THE courthouse at ten and found the lobby filled with men in uniform. She said hello to Moss Junior and Mike Nesbit, and she recognized a few of the others. Jake had subpoenaed Ozzie's entire force.

She eased away from them and walked to a first-floor annex where the county tax assessor had her office. Inside, sitting in plastic chairs and appearing to be completely overwhelmed, were Josie and Kiera. They were delighted to see a friendly face and quick to hug her. They followed her out of the building and to her car. Once inside, she asked, "Have you talked to Jake this morning?"

No, they had not. "Haven't talked to anyone," Josie said. "What's going on?"

"Just jury selection. Probably last all day. How about some coffee?"

"Can we leave?"

"Sure. Jake said it's okay. Have you seen Mr. Dyer or anyone working for him?"

Josie shook her head. They drove away and minutes later stopped on Main Street in Chester. "Have you had breakfast?" Carla asked.

"I'm starving," Kiera blurted. "I'm sorry."

"Jake says this is the only café in town. Let's go."

On the sidewalk, Carla got her first good look at Kiera. She was wearing a simple cotton summer dress that was tight around the middle and clearly revealed her pregnancy. But it was concealed somewhat by a light, fluffy, oversized vest that, when pulled together, would probably hide things. Carla doubted Jake had selected the garment, but she had no doubt that he had discussed the outfit with Josie.

THE CRACK OF NOON was heard louder in a court-room than perhaps anywhere else. After three hours of tension, everyone was watching the clock and in need of a break. Hunger pains were overwhelming, and few judges ventured long into the afternoon. Noose had seated the seventy-nine in the first eight rows, and he had listened to three of them plead for relief. One was a grandmother who kept her daughter's children every day. One was a woman who was sixty-two but looked twenty years older and was her dying husband's full-time caregiver. One was a gentleman in a coat and tie who claimed he might lose his job. Noose listened thoughtfully but seemed unmoved. He said he would consider their requests during lunch. He learned years ago not to grant such exemptions in open court with the entire panel watching. If he showed too much sympathy, too many of the prospective jurors would soon be waving their hands and claiming all manner of hardship.

He would quietly dismiss the three after lunch.

The defense team, along with Harry Rex, went to Morris Finley's office on Main Street, their headquarters for the duration of the trial. Finley had sandwiches and soft drinks waiting and they ate quickly.

Rodney Cote, Gwen Hailey's cousin, was juror number twenty-seven, and certainly within reach. Jake knew for a fact that Carl Lee had met with him and discussed the case. Jake was still obsessed with the fact that Cote had been in the courtroom during the Hailey trial. What Jake didn't know was whether Willie Hastings had told Ozzie about the connection. Several times during the morning, Jake had made clear eye contact with Cote, who appeared intrigued but noncommittal. And what exactly was he supposed to do? Wink at Jake? Give him a thumbs-up?

Finley, who'd been two years ahead of Jake in law school at Ole Miss, wiped his mouth with a paper napkin and said, proudly, "Ladies and gentlemen, we have ourselves a ringer."

"I love it," Harry Rex said.

"Let's hear it," Jake said.

"As you requested, Jake, I sent the jury list to about ten lawyer friends in nearby counties, just part of the fishing process, never works but what the hell, we all do it. Might get lucky with a name or two. Well, folks, we're lucky. Juror number fifteen is Della Fancher, white, age forty, lives on a farm near the Polk County line, with husband either number two or three. They have two kids and appear to be stable, though virtually unknown. A buddy of mine—Jake, do you know Skip Salter over in Fulton?"

"No."

"Anyway, Skip scanned the list and for some reason stopped at the name of Della Fancher. Della is not a common first name, not around here anyway, so he got curious, checked an old file, and made a few calls. When he met her about fifteen years ago she was Della Mc-Bride, married to David McBride, a man she desperately wanted to get away from. Skip filed the divorce on behalf of Della and when the deputy served papers on Mr. McBride, he beat the hell out of her, and not for the first time. Put her in the hospital. It turned into a really ugly divorce, not much money to fight over but he became violent, abusive, and threatening. There were all kinds of restraining orders and such. He stalked her and harassed her at work. Skip finally got the divorce and she fled the area. Found her way here and started a new life."

"I'm surprised she registered to vote," Jake said.

"This could be huge," Harry Rex said. "A bona fide victim of domestic abuse sitting on the jury."

"Maybe," Jake said, obviously stunned by the story. "But she's not there yet. Let's think about this. The panel is about to be examined extensively—by me, Dyer, probably even by Noose. It'll go on and on and take up the afternoon. At some point the questions will get around to domestic violence. I certainly plan to go there if the others don't. If Della raises her hand and tells her story, then she'll be challenged for cause and sent home. I'll object and all that, but she'll be off the jury, no question about it. However, what if she doesn't speak up? Just sits there and thinks that no one in this county knows her past?"

Morris said, "It means she has an ax to grind, a score to settle, pick your cliché."

Libby said, "Excuse me, but when will the pool learn more about the case?"

"Now, just after lunch, when we reconvene," Jake said.

"So, Della will know before the questions start that there are allegations of domestic violence."

"Yes."

The four lawyers pondered the scenarios, each choosing to think for a moment and not speak. Then Portia said, "Excuse me, I'm just a lowly law clerk, soon to be first-year law student, but doesn't she have the duty to speak up?"

The four nodded in unison. "Yes," Jake said, "she certainly has the duty, but it's no crime to stay quiet. Happens all the time. You can't make people come forward and tell their secrets and reveal their biases during jury selection."

"But that seems wrong."

"It is, but it's rare for a juror to be exposed after the trial. Keep in mind, Portia, she may have other motives. She may be hiding from her past and doesn't want folks around here to know about it. It takes courage to admit being a victim of abuse. Guts. But if she doesn't speak up, then maybe she wants to serve, and that's where it gets interesting. Could it be a bad thing for us?"

"No way," Libby said. "If she wants on that jury it's because she'll have no sympathy for Stuart Kofer."

Another long pause as they considered what might happen. Finally, Jake said, "Well, we won't know until we get there. She might jump out of her seat and flee the courtroom if given half a chance."

"I doubt it," Libby said. "We looked at each other a couple of times. I'll bet she's with us."

42

By 1:30 the jurors were back in their seats, seventy-six in all now that the last three hardships had been quietly informed by a bailiff that they were free to go. Once the pool was in place, the doors opened to the public and a crowd swarmed in. Several reporters rushed to the front row on the left side behind the defense. The Kofer family and friends filed in, after having spent hours loitering in the humid hallway. Dozens of others jockeyed for seats. Harry Rex sat near the back, as far away from the Kofers as possible. Lucien eased into a middle row to observe the pool. There was rustling and creaking from above as the balcony opened up and spectators found their places in folding chairs.

Carla found a seat near the front, not far from Jake. She had taken Josie and Kiera to Finley's office where they would spend the afternoon, waiting. If Dyer wanted to talk to Kiera, she was a phone call away.

When the lawyers were in place, Judge Noose reappeared and settled himself at the bench. He frowned around the room to make sure all was in order, then pulled his mike closer. "I see we have a number of spectators who've joined us in the gallery. Welcome. We will maintain order and decorum throughout these proceedings and anyone who becomes disruptive will be taken away."

There had not been a disruptive squeak before the warning.

He looked at a bailiff and said, "Bring in the defendant."

A door by the jury box opened and a deputy walked out, with Drew behind him, free of cuffs and shackles. At first he seemed overwhelmed by the size of the room, and the crowd, and so many people staring at him; then he looked down and watched the floor as he was led to the defense table. He sat in a chair between Jake and Miss Libby, with Portia behind them by the bar.

Noose cleared his throat and began, "Now, for the next few hours we will attempt to select a jury, twelve jurors and two alternates. This will not be that exciting and there will be no live testimony until tomorrow, assuming we have a jury chosen by then. This is a criminal case from Ford County. It's styled *The State of Mississippi v. Drew Allen Gamble*. Mr. Gamble, would you please stand and face the jury pool."

Jake said this would happen. Drew stood, turned and faced the courtroom with a serious face, no smile at all, then nodded and sat down. Jake leaned over and whispered, "I like that coat and tie."

Drew nodded but was afraid to smile.

Noose continued, "We will not dwell on the facts at this time, but I will read to you a quick summary of the indictment, the formal charge against the defendant. It reads: 'That on March 25, 1990, in Ford County, Mississippi, the defendant, one Drew Allen Gamble, age sixteen, did willfully and deliberately and with full criminal intent, shoot and kill the deceased, Stuart Lee Kofer, an officer of the law. Pursuant to section 97-3-19 of the Mississippi Code, the murder of an officer of the law, whether on duty or not, is a capital offense, punishable by death.' Therefore, ladies and gentlemen, this is a capital case, and the State is seeking the death penalty."

Apparently, Noose had squeezed the county for even more money, for a new PA system. His words were clear and loud, and "death penalty" rattled around the ceiling for a few seconds, then landed hard on the jurors.

Noose introduced the lawyers and rambled on a bit too long about each. Humorless and dull by nature, he was trying mightily to show some personality and make everyone feel right at home in his courtroom. It was a noble effort, but tension was high, there was work to be done, so everyone wanted to get on with it.

He explained to the courtroom that the selection process would be done in phases. Initially, he would examine the panel, and many of his questions were required by law. He urged the prospects to be forthcoming, not afraid to speak up, not afraid to let everyone know what was on their minds. Only by an honest and open give-and-take could they hope to find a fair and impartial jury. He then launched into a series of inquiries designed not so much to provoke discussion as to put people to sleep. Many of them were about jury service and qualifications, and Noose lost territory already gained. Age, physical limits, medications, doctors' orders, dietary restrictions, addictions. After half an hour of this, Noose had managed not only to not raise a single hand, but he was boring them to death.

As the jurors watched and listened to the judge, the lawyers studied the jurors. On the front row there were nine whites and one black woman, May Taggart. On the second row there were seven white women, including Della Fancher at number fifteen, and three black men. Four blacks in the first twenty, not a bad percentage, and Jake asked himself for the hundredth time if he was correct in his assumption that blacks would be more sympathetic. Lucien thought so because a white cop was involved. Harry Rex had his doubts because the crime was white on white and race was not a factor. Jake had argued that in Mississippi race was always a factor. Looking at the faces, he still preferred younger female jurors of any color. And, he was assuming that Lowell Dyer wanted older white men.

On the third row there was one black, Mr. Rodney Cote, at number twenty-seven.

As Noose plodded on, Jake occasionally glanced at the spectators. His lovely wife was by far the most attractive person in the room. Harry Rex, in a plaid shirt, sat low in the back. For a second, his eyes met those of Cecil Kofer, who couldn't help himself and offered a smirk behind his scraggly red beard. As if to say, "I kicked your ass once and I'd love to do it again." Jake shook it off and returned to his notes.

When His Honor finished with the required questions, he shuffled papers and readjusted his posture. "Now, the deceased, the victim in this case, was a county deputy named Stuart Kofer, age thirty-three at the time of his death. He was born in Ford County and still has family there. Did any of you know him?"

No volunteers.

"Do any of you know anyone in his family?"

A hand went up on the fourth row. Finally, after an hour, a response from the pool. Number thirty-eight was Mr. Kenny Banahand.

"Yes sir, please stand, give us your name, and explain your relationship with the family."

Banahand stood slowly, somewhat embarrassed, and said, "Well, Judge, I don't really know the family, but my son once worked with Barry Kofer at the distribution plant near Karaway." Jake looked at Barry, who was seated next to his mother.

"Thank you, Mr. Banahand. Did you ever meet Barry Kofer?"

"No sir."

"Thank you. Please be seated. Anyone else?"

"Okay. Now, you've already been introduced to the defendant, Mr. Drew Allen Gamble. Has anyone ever met him?"

Of course not. The trip from the jail was Drew's first excursion into Van Buren County.

"His mother is Josie Gamble and his sister is Kiera. Anyone ever met them?"

No one.

Noose waited for a moment, then continued. "There are four lawyers involved in this trial and you've already met them. I'll start with Mr. Jake Brigance. Has anyone ever met him?"

No volunteers. Jake had memorized the list and knew the sad truth that his struggling practice and meager reputation had not stretched far beyond Ford County. There was a chance that a few in the pool might recognize his name from the Hailey trial, but the question was: Had they ever met Jake? No they had not. That trial had been five years ago.

"Have you or anyone in your immediate family ever been involved in a case in which Mr. Brigance was one of the lawyers?"

No hands. Rodney Cote sat motionless, even stoic, with no expression whatsoever. If quizzed later, he could claim that the word "immediate" confused him. Gwen Hailey, Carl Lee's wife, was a distant cousin, one of many Rodney didn't consider to be "immediate." He looked directly at Jake and their eyes met.

Noose moved on to Libby Provine, a Scottish woman from D.C. who had first traveled to their county

that very morning. Not surprisingly, no one in the pool
had ever heard of her.

Lowell Dyer was an elected official who lived in
Gretna, up in Tyler County. Noose was saying, "Now,
I'm sure many of you folks met Mr. Dyer when he was
campaigning here three years ago, probably at a rally or
a barbecue. He received sixty percent of the vote in this
county, but let's assume for right now he got most of
your votes."

"A hundred percent, Judge," Lowell said with perfect timing and everyone laughed. Humor was desperately needed.

"Let's go with a hundred percent. Now, the question
is not whether you've met Mr. Dyer, but do you know
him personally, in some way?"

Mrs. Gayle Oswalt, number forty-six, stood and said
proudly, "My daughter and his wife were sorority sisters
at Mississippi State. We've known Lowell for many
years."

"Okay. Would the fact that you know him well influence your ability to remain fair and impartial?"

"I don't know, Judge. I'm not sure."

"Do you think you'd tend to believe him over Mr.
Brigance?"

"Well, don't know about that, but I'd believe anything Lowell said."

"Thank you, Mrs. Oswalt."

Over her name Jake scratched, "PC." Peremptory
challenge.

Dyer's assistant, D. R. Musgrove, was a career prosecutor from Polk County and proved to be unknown
that far from home.

"Mr. Dyer, you may examine the pool," Noose announced and tried to relax in his chair. Lowell stood,
stepped to the bar, and smiled at the crowd. He said,

"Well, first of all, I want to thank each and every one of you for voting for me." More laughs, another break in the tension. With all eyes on the prosecutor, Jake was able to study the faces and body language of those on the front four rows.

With the ice broken somewhat, Dyer began with questions about prior jury service and a few hands went up. He asked the volunteers about their experiences. Criminal case, or civil? If criminal, was there a conviction? How did you vote? All had found the defendants guilty. Do you trust the jury system? Do you understand its importance? Law school textbook stuff. Nothing creative but then jury selection rarely yielded much in the way of drama.

Ever been the victim of a crime? A few hands—house burglaries, a stolen car, not much crime in Van Buren County. Anyone in your family ever been the victim of a violent crime? Number sixty-two, Lance Bolivar, slowly got to his feet and said, "Yes sir. My nephew was murdered eight years ago over in the Delta." Well, well, a bit of drama after all.

Dyer zeroed in and, feigning too much sympathy, followed up nicely. He stayed away from the details of the crime and asked about its investigation and aftermath. The killer was found guilty and was serving a life sentence. The experience was terrible, devastating, and the family would be forever scarred. No, Mr. Bolivar did not believe he could be an impartial juror.

Jake wasn't worried about him because he was too deep in the pool.

Dyer moved on to questions about "peace officers," as he called them, and wanted to know if anyone had ever worn a uniform or was related to a cop. One lady had a brother who was a state trooper. She was number fifty-one and Jake made another "PC" by her name, though he doubted he would have to use it. Number three, Don Coben, reluctantly admitted that his son was a policeman in Tupelo. His reluctance was a clear sign, at least to Jake, that he wanted to serve on the jury. He had already reached a verdict.

Dyer did not ask if anyone had a criminal record. It was a potentially embarrassing question and not worth the risk. Most convicted felons could not vote, and of those whose records had been expunged, few bothered with registering. However, number forty-four, Joey Kepner, had been convicted of a drug offense twenty years earlier. He served two years in prison before getting clean and having his record erased. Portia had found the old indictment and had a file on him. The question was: Did Dyer know about it? Probably not, because of the expungement. Jake desperately wanted him on the jury. He had served hard time for possessing a small quantity of marijuana and probably had a dim view of law enforcement.

Stuart Kofer's bad habits would not be discussed during jury selection. Jake doubted Dyer would go there because he did not want to weaken his case so early. Nor would Jake drag out the dirt. It would come soon enough, and he did not want to be seen as an overzealous defense lawyer too eager to blame the victim.

Dyer was methodical but good on his feet. He smiled a lot as he warmed to the task and seemed to connect with the jurors. He stuck to his script, stayed on point, and did not belabor the obvious. When he finished he thanked them again and sat down.

Jake took his spot at the bar and fought to settle his nerves. He introduced himself and said that he had been practicing law next door in Ford County for twelve years. He introduced Libby and described her work with a nonprofit organization in Washington. He introduced Portia as his law clerk, just so the jurors would know why she was sitting with the defense.

He said that he had never been accused of a crime but had represented many people who had. It was frightening and unsettling, especially when a person believed he or she was not guilty or had acted in a reasonable manner. He then asked if anyone in the pool had ever been accused of a serious crime.

Joey Kepner did not raise his hand. Jake was relieved and assumed that Kepner felt as though his record had been thoroughly erased. That, and he probably believed that possessing ten ounces of pot was not that "serious."

Jake explained that the trial would include allegations of domestic abuse by Stuart Kofer. He cautioned that he wasn't about to go into the details—that's what the witnesses would attempt to do. However, it was important to know if any of the prospective jurors had ever been the victim of domestic abuse. He did not look at Della Fancher, but Libby and Portia were watching her every move. Nothing. No reaction other than a slight glance to her right. She was on board, or so they thought.

Jake moved to an even heavier issue. He talked about killing, and its various forms. Manslaughter, negligent homicide, self-defense, and outright premeditated murder, the charge against his client. But did anyone on the panel believe that killing could ever be justified? Dyer shifted in his chair and seemed ready to object.

The question was too vague to elicit responses. Without knowing the details, it was difficult for any juror to speak up and initiate a conversation. Several squirmed and looked around, and before anyone could answer, Jake said he knew it was a tough one. He didn't want a response. The seed was planted.

He said Drew's mother was Josie Gamble, a woman with a colorful past. Without going into it, he explained that she would testify, and when she did the jurors would learn that she had a criminal record. That is always revealed, for any witness. Would that fact lessen her credibility? Her past had nothing to do with the events surrounding the death of Stuart Kofer, but, in the spirit of full disclosure, he wanted the jurors to know that she had served time.

There was no response from the pool.

Full disclosure? Since when was selecting a jury the time to be completely transparent?

Jake kept his questions brief and sat down after thirty minutes. He and Dyer would soon get the chance to quiz the jurors individually.

Next, Noose asked the first twelve to move to the jury box. With the clerk directing them to their assigned seats, they settled in as if already chosen to hear testimony. Not so fast. Not nearly so fast. Noose explained that they would begin the process of privately interviewing the first forty or so jurors. Those with numbers higher than fifty were free to leave the courtroom for one hour.

The jury room was more spacious and far less cluttered than his chambers, so he instructed the lawyers to retire there. The court reporter followed them, and they gathered around a long table where the jury would eventually decide the case. When Noose was settled at one end, with the defense on one side, the State on the other, he said to a bailiff, "Bring in number one."

Jake said, "Judge, if I may, could I offer a suggestion?"

"What is it?" Noose was grimacing with lower back pain as he chewed on the stem of an unlit pipe.

"It's almost three and it's pretty clear we won't start

testimony today. Can we release the witnesses we have under subpoena until tomorrow?"

"Good idea. Mr. Dyer?"

"Fine with me, Judge."

A small victory for the defense. Get Kiera out of town for now.

Mark Maylor settled into an old wooden chair looking as though he was guilty of something. The Judge took charge: "Now, Mr. Maylor, I remind you that you're under oath." His tone was almost accusatory.

"I realize that, Your Honor."

"This won't take long. Just a few questions from me and the lawyers. Okay?"

"Yes sir."

"As I said, this is a capital case, and if the State proves its allegations, you will be called upon to consider voting to impose the death penalty. Will you be able to do this?"

"I don't know. I've never been asked to do this before."

"How do you feel, personally, about the death penalty?"

Maylor looked at Jake and looked at Dyer and finally said, "I guess I'm for it, but believing in it is one thing. Being asked to send a guy to the gas chamber is something else. And he's just a kid."

Jake's heart skipped a beat.

"Mr. Dyer?"

Lowell smiled and said, "Thank you, Mr. Maylor. The death penalty, whether you, or I, or we, like it or not, is the law in this state. Do you believe that you can follow the laws of Mississippi?"

"Sure, I suppose so."

"You seem to be hedging a bit."

"I'm a little off guard, Mr. Dyer. I'm not prepared to

say one way or the other what I might do. But, yes, I will try my best to follow the law."

"Thank you. And you don't know anything about this case?"

"Only what I've heard this morning. I mean, I remember the newspaper stories when it happened. We get the Tupelo paper and I think it was on the front page, but it died down pretty fast. I haven't kept up."

Noose looked at Jake and said, "Mr. Brigance."

"Mr. Maylor, when you saw the news back in March, did you say to yourself something like, 'Well, he's probably guilty'?"

"Sure. Don't we all do that when someone gets arrested?"

"I'm afraid so. But you understand the presumption of innocence, don't you?"

"Sure."

"And so as of right now do you believe that Drew Gamble is innocent until proven guilty?"

"I guess so."

Jake had more questions, but he knew Maylor would not serve on the jury because of his reticence about capital punishment. Dyer wanted a dozen death penalty supporters and the courtroom was full of them.

Noose said, "Thank you, Mr. Maylor. You are excused for one hour."

Maylor stood quickly and disappeared. Waiting outside the door with a clerk was Mrs. Reba Dulaney, the organist at the Methodist Church. She was all smiles and seemed to appreciate the importance of the moment. Noose asked a few questions about the notoriety of the case and she claimed to know nothing. Then he asked if she could impose the death penalty.

She was taken aback by the question and blurted, "For that kid out there? I don't think so."

Jake was pleased to hear it but knew immediately that she, too, was as close to being on the jury as she would ever get. He asked a few questions but didn't dig.

Noose thanked her and called for number three, Don Coben, a tough old farmer who claimed to know nothing about the case and believed firmly in the death penalty.

Number four was May Taggart, the first black, and she had misgivings about capital punishment but was convincing in her belief that she could follow the law.

The parade continued with steady efficiency as Noose limited his questions and those from the lawyers. His two concerns were readily obvious—knowledge of the case and reservations about the death penalty. As each juror was excused and asked to leave the jury room, another was pulled from the pool and placed in the jury box in the courtroom. After the first forty, Noose decided to take those on the fifth row. Jake suspected this was because there were several who had misgivings about the death penalty and would be challenged for cause.

In the courtroom, the spectators came and went and killed time. The only person who didn't move was Drew Gamble, who sat at the defense table with two deputies nearby just in case he decided to make a dash for it.

At 4:45, Noose needed his next round of pills. He told the lawyers that he was determined to pick a jury before dinner and start the testimony first thing in the morning. "Let's meet at 5:15 sharp in chambers and go through the list."

Morris Finley commandeered a room in Land Records on the first floor, and the defense team met there. Carla, Harry Rex, and Lucien joined Portia, Jake, and Libby, and they hurriedly went through the names.

Lucien didn't like any of them. Harry Rex said, "Dyer will probably cut all the blacks, don't you think?"

Jake said, "That's our assumption. And since there are only eleven blacks in the first five rows, we're looking at an all-white jury."

"Can he do that?" Carla asked. "Just on the basis of race?"

"Yes, he certainly can, and he will. Both the victim and the accused are white, so *Batson* doesn't apply."

Because she was married to a criminal defense lawyer, Carla knew that the *Batson* decision prohibited the exclusion of potential jurors solely on the basis of race. "Still doesn't seem right," she said.

"What's your take on Della Fancher?" Jake asked Libby.

"I'd stick with her."

"She should've raised her hand," Portia said. "I think she wants to be on the jury."

"Then I'd be worried," Lucien said. "I'm suspicious of anyone who wants to serve on a capital jury."

"Morris?" Jake asked.

"She's our ringer, right? I sort of agree with Lucien, but, dammit, we have a battered wife who refused to speak up. She has to have sympathy for Josie and her kids."

"I don't like her," Carla said. "She has a hard look, bad body language, doesn't want to be here. Plus, she's hiding something."

Jake frowned at Carla but didn't respond. He reminded himself that his wife was usually right about most things, especially when sizing up other women.

"Portia?"

"I don't know. My first impulse is to take her, but something in my gut says no."

"Great. We'll lose Rodney Cote and Della Fancher,

two of our three ringers. That leaves Joey Kepner with his drug conviction."

"And you're assuming Dyer doesn't know about it?" Lucien asked.

"Yes, and I freely admit that all of our assumptions could be wrong."

"Good luck, ole boy," Lucien said. "It's always a crap-shoot."

WITH HIS ROBE off, his tie loosened, and his pill bottles put away, His Honor fired a torch into the bowl of his pipe, sucked hard on the stem, let loose a lethal cloud of smoke, and said, "Any challenges for cause, Mr. Dyer?"

Lowell had three names he wanted to get rid of. For twenty minutes they went back and forth and it was obvious the prosecutor considered them unfit because they seemed soft on capital punishment. Jake argued forcefully to keep them and preserve his peremptory challenges, which could be used to strike any juror but not to keep one. Noose finally said, "We'll strike the organ player, Mrs. Reba Dulaney, because it was obvious that she would struggle with the death penalty. Mr. Brigance?"

Jake wanted to strike Mrs. Gayle Oswalt because she was a friend of Dyer's, and Noose agreed. He asked to strike Don Coben, number three, because his son was a policeman, and Noose agreed. He asked to strike number sixty-three, Mr. Lance Bolivar, because his nephew had been murdered, and Noose agreed. He asked to strike Calvin Banahand, because his son once worked with Barry Kofer, but Noose said no.

With no more challenges for cause, Dyer used seven of his peremptories and submitted a list of twelve—ten older men, two older women, all white. Jake's assumptions were correct. He huddled with Libby and Portia on their side of the table, and challenged six of them, including Della Fancher. It was tense work, reviewing the names they had memorized, trying to remember their faces, their body language, trying to guess Dyer's next move, and anticipating how deep into the pool the selection might go. And the clock was ticking as His Honor waited and Dyer schemed and pored over his own well-worn lists. Jake used six of his prized challenges and kicked the ball across the table.

The prosecutor submitted his second list of twelve and stuck with his game plan of excluding blacks and preferring older white men. Ten of his peremptory challenges were gone, but he had used one for Rodney Cote. Jake cut three of them. Dyer saved his last two for two younger women, one white, one black, and in doing so revealed that he did not know of Joey Kepner's drug conviction. To get to Kepner, Jake was forced to exclude two women he really wanted. Kepner was the last juror chosen.

Twelve whites—seven men and five women, ages ranging from twenty-four to sixty-one.

They haggled over the selection of two alternates, two white women, but doubted that they would be needed. The trial, once it began, would not last more than three days.

43

Tuesday morning arrived with dark skies, a line of storms, and eventually a tornado watch for Van Buren and the surrounding counties. Heavy rains and winds began pounding the old courthouse an hour before the trial was to resume, and Judge Noose stood at his window with his pipe and wondered if he should delay matters.

As the courtroom filled, the jurors were guided to the box and given a round tin badge with the word JUROR stamped in bold red letters across it. In other words: No contact, keep your distance. Jake, Libby, and Portia deliberately waited until 8:55 to enter the courtroom and begin unpacking their briefcases. Jake said good morning to Lowell Dyer and complimented him on such a nice white jury. The prosecutor had a hundred things on his mind and did not take the bait. Sheriff Ozzie Walls and his entire uniformed force were seated in the front two rows behind the State's table, an impressive show of police muscle. Jake, who had subpoenaed all of them, ignored his former friends and tried to ignore everyone else in the crowd. The Kofers were packed together behind the deputies and ready for battle. Harry Rex, dressed casually, was three rows behind the defense table and watching everything. Lucien, clear-eyed and pretending to read a newspaper, was in the back row on the State's side. Carla arrived in jeans and sat in the third row behind the defense. Jake wanted all the eyes he could trust to observe the jurors.

At nine o'clock Drew was led into the courtroom from a side door with enough police protection to save the governor. He smiled at his mother and sister seated on the front row less than ten feet behind him.

Lowell Dyer looked at the crowd, noticed Kiera, walked over to Jake, and said, "Is that girl pregnant?"

"Yes, she is."

"She's only fourteen," he said, rattled.

"Basic biology."

"Any idea who the father is?"

"Some things are private, Lowell."

"I still want to talk to her during the first recess."

Jake sort of waved at the front row as if to say, "Talk to whoever you want. You're the prosecutor."

Lightning cracked near the courthouse and the lights flickered. Thunder shook the old building and for a second the trial was forgotten. Dyer asked Jake, "You think we ought to ask Noose to delay this a bit?"

"Noose'll do whatever he wants."

Rain began pecking at the windows as the lights flickered again. A bailiff stood and called the court to order. Everyone rose respectfully as His Honor lurched to the bench and took his seat. He pulled his mike closer and said, "Please be seated." Chairs and pews cracked and floors squeaked as everyone resettled themselves. He began, "Good morning. Assuming the weather cooperates, we will get on with this trial. I'd like to repeat my admonition to the jurors to refrain from discussing anything to do with the trial while you are in recess. If anyone approaches you or in any way tries to engage you, I want to know about it immediately. Mr. Brigance and Mr. Dyer, I assume you want to invoke the Rule."

Both nodded. The Rule required all potential witnesses to be absent from the courtroom until after they had testified, and either side could invoke it. The Judge said, "All right. If you have been subpoenaed to testify in this trial, I'll ask that you leave the courtroom and wait outside in the hallway or some other place in the building. A bailiff will find you when we need you." Confusion reigned as both Jake and Dyer instructed their witnesses to leave the room. Earl Kofer did not want to do so and stormed out angrily. Because Jake had subpoenaed Ozzie and his thirteen deputies, he insisted they all leave. He whispered to Josie and Kiera and they left to hide in Land Records on the first floor. Bailiffs and clerks pointed here and there and escorted the witnesses from the courtroom.

When things settled down, His Honor looked at the jury and said, "Now, we will begin this trial by allowing the attorneys to make brief opening remarks. And since the State of Mississippi has the burden of proving its case, it will always go first. Mr. Dyer."

The rain stopped and the thunder was moving on as Lowell walked to the podium and looked at the jurors. A large white screen hung on a bare wall opposite the jury, and with the push of a button Dyer displayed the handsome smiling face of the late Stuart Kofer, in his full deputy's uniform. He gazed at it for a second, then addressed the jurors.

"Ladies and gentlemen, this was Stuart Kofer. Age thirty-three years old when he was murdered by the defendant, Drew Gamble. Stuart was a local boy, born and bred in Ford County, graduate of Clanton High School, a veteran, two tours in Asia, a distinguished career as a law enforcement officer, protecting the public. In the early hours of March twenty-fifth, as he was sleeping in his own bed, in his own home, he was shot and killed by the defendant, Drew Gamble, sitting right there."

He pointed as dramatically as possible to the defendant, who was sitting low between Jake and Libby, as if the jurors were not sure who exactly was on trial.

"The defendant got his hands on Stuart's own service gun, a nine-millimeter Glock pistol." Dyer stepped to the table where the court reporter was taking it all down, picked up State's exhibit number one, and showed it to the jury. He placed the weapon back on the table and continued, "He took it, and with deliberate will and premeditated intentions, pointed it at Stuart's left temple, and from a distance of about an inch, he pulled the trigger." Dyer pointed to his own left temple for even more drama. "Killing him instantly."

Dyer flipped a page of his notes and seemed to study something. Then he tossed it on the podium and took a step closer to the jury box. "Now, Stuart had some problems. The defense will attempt to prove—"

Jake was itching to interrupt. He jumped to his feet and said, "Objection, Your Honor. This is the State's opening, not mine. The district attorney cannot comment on what we might attempt to prove."

"Sustained. Mr. Dyer, just stick to your case. This is an opening statement, ladies and gentlemen, and I caution you that nothing either lawyer says at this point is in evidence."

Dyer smiled and nodded as if the judge had somehow vindicated him. He continued, "Stuart was drinking too much, and too often, and he had been drinking during the night before he was murdered. And he was not a pleasant drunk, prone to violence and bad behavior. His friends were worried about him and were discussing ways to help him, to intervene. Stuart was no choirboy and he was struggling with his demons. But he answered the bell every morning for work and never missed a day, and when he was on duty he was one of the finest deputies in Ford County. Sheriff Ozzie Walls will testify to that.

"Now, the defendant was living in Stuart's home, along with his mother and his younger sister. Josie Gamble, his mother, and Stuart had been together for about a year, and, to say the least, their relationship was rather chaotic. Josie Gamble's entire life has been chaotic. But Stuart provided her and her kids with a good home, a roof, plenty to eat, warm beds, protection. He gave them security, something they had known little of. He took them in and he took care of them. He really didn't want any kids, but he welcomed them and didn't mind the added financial burden. Stuart Kofer was a good, honest man whose family has lived in Ford County for generations. And his murder was senseless. Murdered, ladies and gentlemen, Stuart Kofer was killed by his own gun while sleeping in his own bed."

Dyer paced a bit and the jurors absorbed every word. "As the witnesses come forward, you will hear some awful testimony. I ask that you hear it, consider it, but also consider where it is coming from. Stuart is not here to defend himself, and those who attempt to disgrace his good name have every reason to portray him as a monster. At times it might be difficult not to be suspicious of their motives. You may even feel sympathy for them. But, I ask you to do one thing as you consider their testimony. Ask yourself, over and over, the same question, and it's simply this: At that crucial moment, did the defendant have to pull the trigger?"

Dyer backed away from the jury box and took a step closer to the defense table. He pointed at Drew and asked, "Did he have to pull the trigger?"

He walked to the State's table and sat down. Brief, to the point, and very effective.

His Honor said, "Mr. Brigance."

Jake stood, walked to the podium, picked up the remote, punched it, and the smiling face of Stuart Kofer disappeared from the wall. Jake said, "Your Honor, I will defer until the State has rested."

Noose was surprised, as was Dyer. The defense had the option of opening now or later, but it was rare that a lawyer passed up the opportunity to sow seeds of doubt at the very beginning. Jake sat down and Dyer gawked at him, confused, wondering what trick he was trying to pull.

"Very well," Noose said. "That's up to you. Mr. Dyer, please call your first witness."

"Your Honor, the State calls Mr. Earl Kofer."

A bailiff at the door stepped into the hallway to find the witness, and Earl soon appeared. He was led to the witness stand where he raised his right hand and swore to tell the truth. He gave his name and address and said he had lived in Ford County his entire life. He was sixty-three years old, married to Janet for almost forty years, and had three sons and a daughter.

Dyer pressed a button and a large image of a teenage boy appeared. "Is this your son?"

Earl glanced at it and said, "That was Stuart when he was fourteen." He paused for a second and added, "That's my boy, my oldest son." His voice cracked and he looked down at his feet.

Dyer took his time and finally pressed the button again. The next image was of Stuart in a high school football uniform. "How old was Stuart in this photo, Mr. Kofer?"

"Seventeen. He played for two years before he messed up his knee." He groaned loudly into the mike and wiped his eyes. The jurors watched him with tremendous sympathy. Dyer pressed the button and the third photo of Stuart appeared, this one of a smiling twenty-year-old in a crisp army uniform. Dyer asked, "How long did Stuart serve his country?"

Earl gritted his teeth, wiped his eyes again, and tried to collect himself. He struggled to say, "Six years. He liked the army and talked of making it a career."

"What did he do after the army?"

Earl shifted uncomfortably and in measured words said, "Came home, worked a couple of jobs in the county, then decided to go into law enforcement."

The army shot was replaced by the familiar one of a smiling Stuart decked out in a full deputy's uniform.

"When was the last time you saw your son, Mr. Kofer?"

He bent forward and collapsed as tears ran down his cheeks. After a long awkward gap, he tightened his jaws and said, loudly, clearly, bitterly, "At the funeral home, in his casket."

Dyer studied him for a moment, to prolong the drama, and said, "I tender the witness."

Jake had offered to admit in pretrial filings that Stuart Kofer was indeed dead, but Dyer refused. Noose believed that a proper murder trial should begin with some tears from the victim's family, and he was not alone. Virtually every trial judge in the state allowed such needless testimony, and the Supreme Court had approved it decades earlier.

Jake stood and walked to the podium to begin the ugly task of tarnishing the reputation of a dead man. He had no choice.

"Mr. Kofer, was your son married at the time of his death?"

Earl glared at him with unbridled hatred and said, simply, "No."

"Was he divorced?"

"Yes."

"How many times?"

"Twice."

"When did he get married the first time?"

"I don't know."

Jake walked to the defense table and grabbed some papers. He returned to the podium and asked, "Is it true that he married one Cindy Rutherford in May of 1982?"

"If you say so. That sounds right."

"And they divorced thirteen months later, in June of 1983?"

"If you say so."

"And in September of 1985 he married one Samantha Pace?"

"If you say so."

"And eight months later they were divorced?"

"If you say so." He was snarling, spewing venom, obviously disgusted with Mr. Brigance. His cheeks, wet only moments earlier, were fiery red, and his anger was costing him sympathy.

"Now, you said that your son talked about a career in the army. Why did he change his mind?"

"I don't know, don't really remember."

"Could it have been because he was kicked out of the army?"

"That's not true."

"I have a copy of his dishonorable discharge. Would you like to see it?"

"No."

"Nothing further, Your Honor."

"You are excused, Mr. Kofer," His Honor said. "You may take a seat out there. Mr. Dyer, call your next witness."

"The State calls Deputy Moss Junior Tatum."

The witness was retrieved from the hallway, entered

a packed but silent courtroom, nodded at Jake as he passed him, and stopped by the court reporter. He was armed and in full uniform, and Judge Noose said, "Deputy Tatum, state law prohibits a witness from taking the stand with a gun. Please put it right there on the table." As if coached, Tatum placed his Glock next to the one used in the murder, in plain view of the jurors. He swore to tell the truth, took his seat, and answered Dyer's preliminary questions.

On to the night in question. The 911 call came in at 2:29 A.M. and he was dispatched to the scene. He knew it was the home of Stuart Kofer, his friend on the force. The front door was unlocked and slightly open. He entered cautiously and saw Drew Gamble sitting in a chair in the den, looking out the window. He spoke to him and Drew said, "My mother's dead. Stuart killed her." Tatum asked, "Where is she?" He said, "In the kitchen." Tatum asked, "Where's Stuart?" He said, "He's dead too, back there in his bedroom." Tatum eased through the house, saw a light on in the kitchen, saw the woman lying on the floor with the girl holding her head. Behind him, at the end of the hall, he could see feet hanging off the bed. He walked to the bedroom and found Stuart lying across his bed, his pistol a few inches from his head, and blood everywhere.

He returned to the kitchen and asked the girl what happened. She said, "He killed my mother." Tatum asked, "Who shot Stuart?"

Dyer paused and looked at Jake, who was getting to his feet. As if rehearsed, he said, "Your Honor, I object to this testimony on the grounds that it is hearsay."

His Honor was waiting for this. "Your objection is noted, Mr. Brigance. For the record, the defense filed a motion to limit this portion of the testimony. The State responded, and on July the sixteenth I held a hearing on the motion. After full and spirited argument from both sides, and being fully briefed, the court ruled that this testimony is admissible."

"Thank you, Your Honor," Jake said and sat down.

"You may proceed, Mr. Dyer."

"Now, Deputy Tatum, when you asked the girl, Miss Kiera Gamble, who shot Stuart, what did she say?"

"She said, 'Drew shot him.'"

"What else did she say?"

"Nothing. She was holding her mother, crying."

"What did you do then?"

"I went to the den and asked the boy, I mean, the defendant, if he shot Stuart. He did not respond. He just sat there looking out the window. When it became obvious he wasn't talking, I left the house, went to my patrol car, and called for backup."

Jake watched and listened to his friend, a guy he'd known throughout his career, a regular at the Coffee Shop, an old buddy who would do anything he asked, and he wondered, briefly, if his life would ever be the same. Surely, as the months and years passed, it would return to normal and he would not be viewed by the cops as a defender of the guilty, a coddler of criminals.

Jake shook it off and told himself to worry about the future next month.

Dyer said, "Thank you, Deputy Tatum. I have no more questions."

"Mr. Brigance?"

Jake stood and walked to the podium. He glanced at some notes on a legal pad and took in the witness. "Now, Deputy Tatum, when you first entered the house you asked Drew what happened."

"That's what I said."

"And where, exactly, was he?"

"As I said, he was in the den, sitting in a chair, looking out the front window."

"As if waiting for the police?"

"I guess. Not sure what he was waiting for. He was just sitting there."

"Did he look at you when he said his mother and Stuart were dead?"

"No. He just kept looking out the window."

"Was he in a daze? Was he frightened?"

"I don't know. I didn't stop to analyze him."

"Was he crying, emotional?"

"No."

"Was he in shock?"

Dyer rose and said, "Objection, Your Honor. I'm not sure this witness is competent to give an opinion as to the defendant's mental state."

"Sustained."

Jake continued, "And you then found both bodies, Josie Gamble's and Stuart Kofer's, and you spoke to the girl. Then you walked back to the den, and where was the defendant?"

"As I said, he was still sitting at the window, looking out."

"And you asked him a question and he didn't respond, correct?"

"That's what I said."

"Did he look at you, acknowledge your question, your presence?"

"No. He just sat there, like I said."

"No further questions, Your Honor."

"Mr. Dyer?"

"Nothing, Your Honor."

"Deputy Tatum, you are excused. Please get your gun and have a seat in the courtroom. Who's next?"

Dyer said, "Sheriff Ozzie Walls."

A moment passed as the courtroom waited. Jake whispered to Libby and ignored the stares from the jurors. Ozzie, with the swagger of a former professional football player, strode down the aisle, through the bar, and to the witness stand where he was disarmed and sworn to tell the truth.

Dyer began with the routine questions about his background, election and reelection, his training. Like all good prosecutors, he was methodical, almost tedious. No one was expecting a long trial and there was no hurry.

Dyer asked, "Now, Sheriff, when did you hire Stuart Kofer?"

"May of '85."

"Were you concerned about his dishonorable discharge from the army?"

"Not at all. We discussed it and I was satisfied that he got a raw deal. He was really excited about law enforcement and I needed a deputy."

"And his training?"

"I sent him to the police academy down in Jackson for its two-month program."

"How'd he perform?"

"Outstanding. Stuart finished second in his class, got really high marks in everything, especially firearms and weaponry."

Dyer ignored his notes, looked at the jurors, and said, "So, he was on your force for about four years before his death, correct?"

"That's right."

"And how would you rate his work as a deputy?"

"Stuart was exceptional. He quickly became one of the favorites, a tough cop who never shied away from danger, always ready to take the worst assignments. About three years ago we got a tip that a drug gang out

of Memphis was making a delivery that night at a remote spot not far from the lake. Stuart was on duty and
volunteered to have a look. We weren't expecting
much—the informant was not that reliable—but when
he got there he was ambushed and took fire from some
pretty nasty guys. Within minutes, three were dead, and
a fourth surrendered. Stuart was slightly wounded but
never missed a day of work."

A dramatic story, which Jake knew was coming. He
wanted to object on the grounds of relevance, but
Noose would probably not stop the action. The defense
team had discussed it at length and had finally agreed
that the heroic story could benefit Drew. Let Dyer portray Stuart as a total badass, deadly with firearms, a dangerous man to be feared, especially by his girlfriend and
her kids who were helpless when he got drunk and
slapped them around.

Ozzie told the jury that he arrived at the scene
about twenty minutes after the call from Deputy Tatum,
who was waiting at the front door. An ambulance was
already there and the woman, Josie Gamble, was on the
stretcher and being readied for the trip to the hospital.
Both of her children were seated, side by side, on the
sofa in the den. Ozzie was briefed by Tatum, then
walked into the bedroom and saw Stuart.

Dyer paused, glanced at Jake, and said, "Your Honor,
at this time the State would like to show the jury three
photographs of the crime scene."

Jake stood and said, "Your Honor, the defense will
renew its objection to these photographs on the
grounds that they are inflammatory, grossly prejudicial,
and unnecessary."

Noose said, "Your objection is noted. For the record,
a timely objection was filed by the defense and on July
sixteenth the court held a hearing on this matter. After

being fully briefed, the court ruled that three of the photos are admissible. Your objection, Mr. Brigance, is overruled. As a word of caution, to the jurors and the spectators, the photos are graphic. Ladies and gentlemen of the jury, you have no choice but to examine the photographs. As for anyone else, please use your own discretion. Proceed, Mr. Dyer."

Regardless of how shocking and horrible they were, crime scene photos were rarely excluded in murder trials. Dyer handed a color eight-by-ten to Ozzie and said, "Sheriff Walls, this is State's exhibit number two. Can you identify it?"

Ozzie looked, grimaced, said, "This is a photo of Stuart Kofer, taken from the doorway of his bedroom."

"And does it accurately portray what you saw?"

"Afraid so." Ozzie lowered the photograph and looked away.

Dyer said, "Your Honor, I'd like permission to hand the jurors three copies of the same photo, and to put the image on the screen."

"Proceed."

Jake had objected to blasting the blood and gore on the big screen. Noose had overruled him. Suddenly, there was Stuart, lying across his bed, his feet hanging off the side, pistol beside his head, with a pool of dark red blood soaking the sheets and mattress.

There were groans and gasps from the spectators. Jake stole a few glances at the jurors, several of whom looked away from the photos and the screen. Several others glared at Drew with pure contempt.

The second photo was taken from a spot near Stuart's feet, a much closer view of his head and shattered skull, brains, lots of blood.

A woman behind Jake was sobbing, and he knew it was Janet Kofer.

Dyer took his time. He was playing his strongest hand and making the most of it. The third photo was a wider shot and clearly revealed the sprayed blood and matter across the pillows, headboard, and wall.

Most of the jurors had seen enough and were preoccupied with their feet. The entire courtroom was stunned and felt as though it had been assaulted. Noose, sensing that everyone had seen enough, said, "That'll do, Mr. Dyer. Please remove the image. And let's take a fifteen-minute break at this time. Please take the jurors to the jury room for a little recess." He rapped his gavel and disappeared.

Portia had found only two cases in the last fifty years in which the Supreme Court had reversed a murder conviction because of gruesome and hideous crime scene photos. She had argued that Jake should object, but only for the record and not too strenuously. An overabundance of blood and gore might actually save their client on appeal. Jake, however, was not convinced. The damage was done, and the damage, at that moment, seemed insurmountable.

JAKE BEGAN THE cross-examination of his former friend with "Now, Sheriff Walls, does your department have a protocol for internal affairs?"

"Sure we do."

"And if a citizen has a complaint against one of your men, what do you do about it?"

"The complaint has to be in writing. I review it first and have a private conversation with the officer. Then we have a three-person review panel—one current deputy, two former ones. We take complaints seriously, Mr. Brigance."

"How many complaints were filed against Stuart Kofer during his time as your deputy?"

"Zero. None."

"Were you aware of any problems he was having?"

"I have—had—fourteen deputies, Mr. Brigance. I can't get involved in all of their problems."

"Were you aware that Josie Gamble, Drew's mother, had called 911 on two prior occasions and asked for help?"

"Well, I was not aware of it at the time."

"And why not?"

"Because she did not press charges."

"Okay. When a deputy is dispatched after a 911 call to the scene of a domestic disturbance, does he file an incident report afterwards?"

"Supposed to, yes."

"On February the twenty-fourth of this year, did officers Pirtle and McCarver answer a 911 call at the Kofer residence, a call made by Josie Gamble, who told the dispatcher that Stuart Kofer was drunk and threatening her and her kids?"

Dyer jumped to his feet and said, "Objection, Your Honor, calls for hearsay."

"Overruled. Continue."

"Sheriff Walls?"

"Not sure about that."

"Well, I have the 911 recording. You want to hear it?"

"I'll take your word for it."

"Thank you. And Josie Gamble will testify about it."

"I said I'd take your word for it."

"So, Sheriff, where is the incident report?"

"Well, I'll have to go through the records."

Jake walked to three large storage boxes stacked together beside the defense table. He pointed to them and said, "Here they are, Sheriff. I've got copies of all of the incident reports from your office for the past twelve months. And there's not one here filed by Officers Pirtle and McCarver for February twenty-fourth in response to a call by Josie Gamble."

"Well, I guess it was misplaced. Keep in mind, Mr. Brigance, if no charges are filed by the complaining party, then it's really no big deal. Not much we can do. Oftentimes we'll answer a domestic call, settle things down without taking any official action. The paperwork is not always that important."

"I guess not. That's why it's missing."

"Objection," Dyer said.

"Sustained. Mr. Brigance, please refrain from testifying."

"Yes, Your Honor. Now, Sheriff, on December the third of last year, was Deputy Swayze dispatched to the same house after a 911 call from Josie Gamble? Another domestic disturbance?"

"You have the records, sir."

"But do *you* have the records? Where is the incident report filed by Deputy Swayze?"

"It's supposed to be in the file."

"But it's not."

Dyer stood and said, "Objection, Your Honor. Does Mr. Brigance intend to introduce into evidence all of the records?" He waved at the boxes.

Jake said, "Certainly, if necessary."

Noose removed his reading glasses, rubbed his eyes, and asked, "Where are you going with this, Mr. Brigance?"

The perfect opening. Jake said, "Your Honor, we will prove that there was a pattern of domestic abuse and violence perpetrated by Stuart Kofer against Josie

Gamble and her children, and that it was covered up by the sheriff's office to protect one of its own."

Dyer responded, "Your Honor, Mr. Kofer is not on trial and he's not here to defend himself."

"I'll stop you at this time," Noose said. "I'm not sure if you've established the relevance."

"Fine, Judge," Jake said. "I'll just call the sheriff back to the stand during our defense. No further questions."

Noose said, "Sheriff Walls, you are excused but you are still under subpoena, so you need to leave the court-room. After you get your gun."

Ozzie glared at Jake as he walked by.

"Mr. Dyer, please call your next witness."

"The State calls Captain Hollis Brazeale of the Mississippi Highway Patrol."

Brazeale looked out of place in a sharp navy suit with a white shirt and red tie. He zipped through his qualifications and many years of experience, proudly informing the jury that he had investigated over one hundred murders. He talked about his arrival at the crime scene and wanted to dwell on the photos, but Noose, along with everyone else, had seen enough blood. Brazeale described how his forensic team from the state crime lab pored over the scene, taking photographs and videos, collecting samples of blood and brain matter. The Glock's magazine held fifteen bullets when fully loaded. Only one was missing, and they found it buried deep in the mattress near the head-board. Their tests matched it to the pistol.

Dyer handed him a small plastic zip-bag holding a bullet and explained that it was the one found in the mattress, and it came from the pistol. And asked him to identify it. No doubt about it. Dyer then pressed a button, and enlarged photos of the gun and bullet appeared. Brazeale launched into a mini-lecture about what happens when a bullet is fired: Primer and the powder explode within the cartridge, forcing the bullet down the barrel. The explosion produces gases that escape and land on the shooter's hands and, often, his clothing. Gases and gunpowder particles follow the bullet and can provide evidence of the distance between the barrel and the entry wound.

In this case, their tests revealed that the bullet traveled only a short distance. In Brazeale's opinion, "Less than two inches."

He was cocksure of his opinions and the jurors listened intently. Jake, though, thought the testimony was dragging as it went on and on. He stole glances at the jurors, one of whom glanced around as if to say, "All right, all right. We get it. It's pretty obvious what happened."

But Dyer plowed onward, trying to cover everything. Brazeale said that after the body was removed, they took the sheets, two blankets, and two pillows. The investigation was routine and not complicated. The cause of death was obvious. The murder weapon was secure. A suspect had confessed to the murder to another credible witness. Later that Sunday morning, Brazeale and two technicians went to the jail and fingerprinted the suspect. They also swabbed the suspect's hands, arms, and clothing to collect gunshot residue.

Next was a symposium on fingerprints, with Brazeale working through a series of slides and explaining that four latent prints were removed from the Glock and matched to partials taken from the defendant. Every person's prints are unique, and, pointing to a thumbprint with "tented arches," he said there was no doubt the four prints—three fingers and one thumb—were left on the gun by the defendant.

Next was a windy, technical analysis of chemical

tests used to find and measure GSR—gunshot residue. No one was surprised when Brazeale finally reached the conclusion that Drew had fired the weapon.

When Dyer tendered the witness at 11:50, Jake stood, shrugged, and said, "The defense has no questions, Your Honor."

Noose, along with everyone else, needed a break. He looked at a bailiff and said, "We'll be in recess. Is the lunch prepared for the jurors?"

The bailiff nodded.

"Okay, we're in recess until one-thirty."

44

When the courtroom was empty, Drew sat alone at the table, twiddling his thumbs under the languid gaze of a crippled bailiff. Moss Junior and Mr. Zack appeared and said it was time for lunch. They led him through a side door, up a rickety set of ancient stairs to a third-floor room that had once housed the county law library. It, too, had seen its better days, and gave the impression that legal research was not a priority in Van Buren County. Shelves of dusty books sat at odd angles, with some leaning precariously, much like the courthouse itself. In an open area there was a card table with two folding chairs. "Over there," Moss Junior said, pointing, and Drew took a seat. Mr. Zack produced a brown bag and a bottle of water. Drew removed a sandwich wrapped in foil and a bag of chips.

Moss Junior said to Mr. Zack, "He should be safe here. I'll be downstairs." He left and they listened as he lumbered down the stairs.

Mr. Zack sat across from Drew and asked, "What do you think of your trial so far?"

Drew shrugged. Jake had lectured him about talking to anyone in a uniform. "Things don't look so good."

Mr. Zack grunted and smiled. "You can say that again."

"What's weird is how they make Stuart out to be such a nice guy."

"He was a nice guy."

"Yeah, to you. It was a different story livin' with him."

"You gonna eat?"

"Not hungry."

"Come on, Drew. You barely touched your breakfast. You gotta eat something."

"You know, you've been sayin' that ever since I met you."

Mr. Zack opened his own bag and took a bite from a turkey sandwich.

Drew asked, "You bring any cards?"

"I did."

"Great. Blackjack?"

"Sure. After you eat."

"You owe me a buck-thirty, right?"

TWO MILES AWAY, in downtown Chester, the defense team ate sandwiches in Morris Finley's conference room. Morris, a busy lawyer himself, was away tending to matters in federal court. He didn't have the luxury of spending entire days watching another lawyer's trial. Nor did Harry Rex, whose stressful office was being completely ignored by the only lawyer in his firm, but he wouldn't miss the Gamble trial for anything. He, Lucien, Portia, Libby, Jake, and Carla ate quickly and went through the State's case so far. The only surprise had been Noose's refusal to allow Brazeale to revisit the ghastly crime scene photos.

Ozzie had done a passable job, though he had looked bad trying to cover for the missing paperwork. It was a small win for the defense, but one that would be forgotten soon enough. The fact that county deputies were not exactly thorough with their mundane reports would not be important when the jury debated guilt or innocence.

Overall, the morning had been a huge win for the State, but that was no surprise. The case was simple, straightforward, and had no missing clues. Dyer's opening was effective and captured the attention of every juror. Taking one name at a time, they talked about all twelve. The first six men were convinced and ready to vote guilty. Joey Kepner had revealed nothing in his facial expressions and body language. The five women did not appear to be any more sympathetic.

Most of their lunch was consumed with Kiera. Dyer had proven that Drew had committed the murder beyond a reasonable doubt. The State didn't need Kiera as a witness to bolster its case. Her statement to Tatum that Drew shot Stuart was already in evidence.

"But he's a prosecutor," Lucien argued. "And as a breed they're known to pile on. She's the only person who can testify that she heard the gunshot and heard her brother admit to the shooting. Of course, Drew could admit this himself, but only if he takes the stand. Josie was there but unconscious. If Dyer doesn't call Kiera to the stand, the jurors will wonder why not? And what about the appeal? What if the Supremes rule that Tatum's testimony should have been excluded as hearsay? It'll be a close call, right?"

"Maybe, maybe not," Jake said.

"Okay, let's say we win on hearsay. Dyer might be worried about that, and he might be thinking he needs to double down and get the girl to testify to it."

"Do they really need it?" Libby asked. "Isn't there an abundance of physical evidence already in the record?"

"It sure feels like it," Jake said.

Harry Rex said, "Dyer's a dumbass if he puts her on.

Plain and simple. He's got his case made, why not just rest and wait on the defense?"

Jake said, "He'll put her on, get her statement, then fight like hell when we start with the abuse."

"But the abuse is coming in, right?" Libby asked. "There's no way to keep it out."

"It'll be up to Noose," Jake said. "He has our brief and we've argued, convincingly, at least in my opinion, that the abuse is relevant. To keep it out will be reversible error."

"Are we trying to win the trial or the appeal?" Carla asked.

"Both."

And so they debated as they ate bad deli sandwiches to ward off hunger.

THE STATE'S NEXT witness was Dr. Ed Majeski, the pathologist hired to perform the autopsy. Dyer led him through the usual list of dry questions to establish his expertise and made much of the fact he had performed, over a thirty-year career, two thousand autopsies, including approximately three hundred involving gunshot wounds. When offered the opportunity to question his credentials, Jake declined and said, "Your Honor, we accept Dr. Majeski's qualifications."

Dyer then approached the bench, with Jake, and whispered to the judge that the State would like to introduce four photos taken during the autopsy. This was no surprise because Dyer had produced the photos in a pretrial hearing. Noose, as usual, deferred a ruling until that moment. He looked at the photos again, shook his head, and said, away from the mike, "I don't think so. This jury has seen enough of the blood and gore. The defense's objection is sustained."

It was obvious that His Honor was troubled by the crime scene photos and their gruesomeness.

Dyer switched to a rather cartoonish diagram of a generic corpse and put it on the screen. For an hour, Dr. Majeski belabored the obvious. Using far too many medical terms and jargon, he bored the courtroom with testimony that proved, beyond any doubt, that the deceased died of a single bullet wound to the head, one that blew away most of the right side of his skull.

As he droned on, Jake couldn't help but think of Earl and Janet Kofer, seated not far away, and their pain at hearing such details about their son's fatal injury. And as always when he thought of the parents, he reminded himself that he was fighting to keep a kid away from the gas chamber. Now was not the time for sympathy.

When Dyer mercifully tendered the witness, Jake jumped to his feet and stepped to the podium. "Dr. Majeski, did you draw a sample of blood from the deceased?"

"Of course. That is standard practice."

"And did this sample reveal anything significant?"

"Such as?"

"Such as the level of alcohol in his system?"

"It did."

"Now, for the benefit of the jury, and for me as well, could you please explain how one's alcohol level is measured."

"Certainly. The blood alcohol concentration, better known as BAC, is the amount of alcohol in the bloodstream, or in urine, or on one's breath. It is expressed as the weight of ethanol, or alcohol, in grams, the metric unit, in one hundred milliliters of blood."

"Let's keep this simple, Doctor. The legal limit for drunk driving in Mississippi is point-one-zero BAC. What does that mean?"

"Sure, it means point-one-zero grams of alcohol per one hundred milliliters of blood."

"Okay. Thank you. Now what was Stuart Kofer's BAC?"

"It was quite significant. Point-three-six grams per hundred."

"Point-three-six?"

"That's correct."

"So, the deceased was three and a half times over the legal limit for driving?"

"Yes sir."

Juror number four, a white man of fifty-five, glanced at juror number five, a white man of fifty-eight. Juror number eight, a white woman, appeared shocked. Joey Kepner shook his head slightly in disbelief.

"Now, Dr. Majeski, for how long had Mr. Kofer been dead before you drew a sample of his blood?"

"Approximately twelve hours."

"And, is it possible that during that twelve-hour period the alcohol level could have actually decreased?"

"Unlikely."

"But it's possible?"

"That's unlikely, but no one really knows. It's rather hard to measure, for obvious reasons."

"Okay, let's stick with point-three-six. Did you weigh the body?"

"I did, as always. That's standard procedure."

"And how much did he weigh?"

"One hundred and ninety-seven pounds."

"He was thirty-three years old and weighed one ninety-seven, right?"

"Correct, but his age should not be factored in."

"Okay, let's forget his age. For a man his size, and with that much alcohol, how would you describe his ability to operate a vehicle?"

Dyer stood and said, "Objection, Your Honor. This goes beyond the scope of his testimony. I'm not sure this expert is qualified to give such an opinion."

His Honor looked down at the witness and asked, "Dr. Majeski, are you qualified for this?"

He smiled with arrogance and said, "Yes, I am."

"Objection overruled. You may answer the question."

"Well, Mr. Brigance, I certainly wouldn't want to be in the car with him."

This drew a few brief smiles from some of the jurors.

"Nor would I, Doctor. Would you describe him as being completely impaired?"

"That would be a non-medical term, but, yes."

"And what are the other effects of so much alcohol, sir, in non-medical terms?"

"Devastating. Loss of physical coordination. Greatly reduced reflexes. Walking or even standing would require assistance. Slurred or indistinguishable speech. Nausea, vomiting. Disorientation. Severe increases in heart rate. Irregular breathing. Loss of bladder control. Memory loss. Perhaps even unconsciousness."

Jake flipped a page on his legal pad to allow these frightening effects to rattle around the courtroom. Then he stepped to the defense table and picked up some papers. Slowly, he returned to the podium and said, "Now, Dr. Majeski, you said you've performed over two thousand autopsies in your distinguished career."

"That's correct."

"How many of those deaths were caused by alcohol poisoning?"

Dyer stood again and said, "Objection, Your Honor, on the grounds of relevance. We're not concerned here with the death of anyone else."

"Mr. Brigance?"

"Your Honor, this is a cross-examination and I'm given wide latitude. The drunkenness of the deceased is certainly relevant."

"I'll allow for now but let's see where it's going. You may answer the question, Dr. Majeski."

The witness shifted his weight but was obviously enjoying the chance to discuss his experience and knowledge. "I'm not sure, exactly, but there have been several."

"Last year, you did the autopsy for a fraternity boy down in Gulfport. Last name of Cooney. Do you remember that one?"

"I do, yes, very sad."

Jake glanced at his paperwork. "You concluded that the cause of death was AAP, acute alcohol poisoning, correct?"

"Correct."

"Do you remember the kid's BAC?"

"No, I'm sorry."

"I have your report right here. Would you like to see it?"

"No, just refresh my memory, Mr. Brigance."

Jake lowered the papers, looked at the jury, and said, "Point-three-three."

"That sounds accurate," Dr. Majeski said.

Jake returned to his table, shuffled some papers, withdrew a few, and returned to the podium. "Do you recall an autopsy you performed in August of 1987 on a Meridian fireman named Pellagrini?"

Dyer stood with stretched arms and said, "Your Honor, please. I object to this line of questioning on the grounds of relevance."

"Overruled. You may answer the question."

Dyer fell hard into his chair, and his theatrics drew a harsh look from the bench.

Dr. Majeski said, "Yes, I remember that one."

Jake scanned the top sheet, though all the details were memorized. "Says here he was forty-four years old and weighed one hundred and ninety-two pounds. His body was found in the basement of his home. You concluded that the cause of death was AAP. Does this sound right, Doctor?"

"Yes it does."

"Do you happen to recall his BAC?"

"Not exactly, no."

Again, Jake lowered the papers, looked at the jury, and announced, "Point-three-two." He glanced at Joey Kepner and saw the faint beginnings of a smile.

"Dr. Majeski, is it safe to say that Stuart Kofer was near death from his alcohol consumption?"

Dyer bounced up again and angrily said, "Objection, Your Honor. This calls for an opinion that is far too speculative."

"It does indeed. Objection sustained."

After a perfect buildup, Jake was ready for the punch line. He stepped toward his table, stopped, looked at the witness, and asked, "Isn't it possible, Dr. Majeski, that Stuart Kofer was already dead when he got shot?"

Dyer yelled, "Objection, Your Honor."

"Sustained. Don't answer that."

"Nothing further," Jake said as he glanced at the spectators. Harry Rex was grinning. On the back row, Lucien beamed at his protégé and could not have been prouder. Most of the jurors appeared to be stunned.

It was almost three and His Honor needed another round of meds. He said, "Let's take the afternoon recess and get some coffee. I'd like to see the lawyers in chambers."

———

LOWELL DYER WAS still fuming when they gathered around the table. Noose had disrobed and was lining up little bottles of pills as he stretched at his desk. He gulped them down with a cup of water and took a seat at the table. He smiled and said, "Well, gentlemen, with no insanity to fight over, this trial is moving right along. My compliments to both of you." He looked at the prosecutor and asked, "Who's your next witness?"

Dyer tried to shrug it off and appear as cool as his opponent. He took a deep breath and said, "I don't know, Judge. I planned to call Kiera Gamble to the stand, but right now I'm somewhat reluctant. Why? Because we'll get into the abuse. As I've said before, it's simply not fair to allow these people to testify to matters that I cannot effectively rebut on cross-examination. It's not fair to allow them to slander Stuart Kofer."

"Slander?" Jake asked. "Slander implies false testimony, Lowell."

"But we don't know what's false and what's true."

"They'll be under oath," Noose said.

"True, but they'll also have every reason to exaggerate the abuse. There is no one to rebut it."

Jake said, "The facts are the facts, Lowell. We can't change them. The truth is that these three were living in a nightmare because they were abused and threatened, and the abuse was a major factor in the killing."

"So it was for retribution?"

"I didn't say that."

"Gentlemen. We've been discussing this for some time and I have been briefed by both sides. I am persuaded that the case law in this state leans toward the exploration of the reputation of the deceased, especially in a factual setting like this. Therefore, I will allow it, to a point. If I believe that the witnesses are exaggerating, as you say, Mr. Dyer, then you can always object and we'll revisit the issue. We'll take it slow. We have plenty of time and there is no hurry."

"Then the State rests, Your Honor. We've proven our case beyond a reasonable doubt. The intoxication of the deceased does not alter the fact that he was murdered by Drew Gamble, whether on duty or not."

Jake mumbled, "What a ridiculous law."

"It's on the books, Jake. We can't change it."

"Gentlemen." Noose grimaced in pain and tried to stretch. "It's going on four o'clock. I have an appointment with a physical therapist at five-thirty. I'm not whining but my lower lumbar needs some work. It is difficult to sit for more than two or three hours at a time. Let's dismiss the jury, take an early recess, and re-convene in the morning at nine sharp."

Jake was pleased. The jurors would go home with Kofer's blackout drinking fresh on their minds.

45

Dinner at Jake's office was another round of sandwiches, though far tastier. Carla rushed home from the trial, gathered Hanna, and together they grilled chicken and put together gourmet-style paninis. They delivered them to the office and ate with Libby, Josie, and Kiera. Portia was at home checking on her mother and would rejoin the team for another late session. Harry Rex was at his office, putting out fires, while Lucien begged off and needed a drink.

As they ate, they replayed the day's events, from the prosecutor's opening statement through all the testimony. As upcoming witnesses, Josie and Kiera were still banned from the courtroom and were eager to hear what had transpired. Jake assured them that Drew was holding up just fine and being taken care of. They worried about his safety but Jake said he was well guarded. The courtroom was full of Kofers and their friends and it was undoubtedly a painful spectacle for them to endure, but, so far, no one had misbehaved.

They talked about the jurors as if they were old friends. Libby thought number seven, Mrs. Fife, was particularly disgusted by Kofer's drinking. Number two, Mr. Poole, a deacon in the First Baptist Church and strict teetotaler, seemed bothered by it too.

Jake said, "Wait till they hear the rest of the story. The drinking will seem like child's play."

They covered all twelve. Carla didn't like number eleven, Miss Twitchell, age twenty-four, the youngest and the only one not married. She had a sneer that never went away, and she continually glared at Drew.

At eight, Hanna was bored with whatever the adults were doing in the big room and wanted to go home. Carla left to put her to bed. Despite the boredom, she was thoroughly enjoying the trial itself because the long days were being spent with Jake's parents.

Portia returned and went to the library for some research. Jake said, "Okay, Josie, you're the first one up tomorrow. We're going to talk through your testimony again, word for word. Libby will play the role of the prosecutor and fire away whenever she wants."

"Again?" Josie asked, already tired.

"Yes, again and again. And Kiera, you're next. Keep in mind, Josie, that after you testify, you will be released and you can stay in the courtroom. Kiera will be called next, so I want you to listen and observe everything she says and does as we go through it again."

"Got it. Let's have it."

ANOTHER STORM AT daybreak knocked out the electricity. An automatic generator in the courthouse failed to kick on, and by 7:30 the elderly janitorial crew was scrambling to fix the problems. When Judge Noose arrived at 8:15 the lights were at least flickering, a hopeful sign. He called the power company and raised hell, and half an hour later the lights came on for good. The window units sputtered to life and began straining to combat the thick humidity in the courtroom. When he assumed the bench at 9:00, his robe was already wet around the collar.

"Good morning," he said loudly into his mike, which was working at full volume. "Seems as though we lost power in a storm a few hours ago. It has been restored but I'm afraid the heat will be with us for a few hours."

Jake cursed him for selecting that badly designed and dilapidated old building for a trial in August, but only in passing. He had more important matters on his mind.

"Bring in the jury," Noose said.

They filed in, dressed for the day in short-sleeve shirts and cotton dresses. As they took their seats, a bailiff handed each a funeral fan—a decorative piece of cardboard glued to a stick—as if flapping it back and forth in front of their noses would bring relief from the stifling heat. Many of the spectators were already waving them.

Noose said, "Ladies and gentlemen of the jury, I apologize for the loss of power, and the heat, but the show must go on. I will allow the attorneys to remove their jackets, but keep the ties please. Mr. Brigance."

Jake stood and smiled as he turned the podium to face the jury. With his jacket still on, he began with "Good morning, ladies and gentlemen. I'm allowed at this time to make a few remarks about what I hope to prove in the defense of Drew Gamble. Now, I am not going to risk losing credibility with you by suggesting that there might be questions about who shot Stuart Kofer. It's pretty clear. Mr. Lowell Dyer, our fine district attorney, did a masterful job yesterday proving the State's case. Now, it's up to the defense to tell you the rest of the story. And there is so much more to the story.

"What we will attempt to do is describe the *nightmare* that Josie Gamble and her two children were living." With a clenched fist he tapped the podium in rhythm as he said, "It was a living hell." He paused for a second, then tapped out "They are lucky to be alive."

A little too dramatic, Harry Rex thought.

Not nearly loud enough, Lucien said to himself.

"About a year ago, Josie and Stuart met in a bar, which was fitting for both of them. Josie had spent plenty of time in bars and honky-tonks, as had Stuart, and it should be no surprise that that's where they met. Josie told him she lived in Memphis and was visiting a friend, one who did not happen to be in the bar. She was alone. It was a lie. Josie and her two children were living in a borrowed camper on the property of a distant relative who had told them to leave. They had no place to go. A romance of sorts quickly ensued, with Josie in hot pursuit once she learned that Stuart owned his own home. And he was a deputy in Ford County, a man with a good paycheck. She's a cute girl, likes tight jeans and other clothing that might be considered suggestive, and Stuart was smitten. You'll meet her in a minute. She's our first witness, the mother of the defendant.

"With Josie pushing hard, Stuart invited her to move in. He didn't want her kids because, by his own admission, he wasn't cut out for fatherhood. But it was a package deal. For the first time in two years, the Gambles had a real roof over their heads. For about a month things were okay, tense, but survivable, then Stuart began complaining about how much the arrangement was costing him. The kids ate too much, he said. Josie was working two jobs, at minimum wage, that's all she's ever earned, and trying her best to support the family.

"Then the beatings started, and violence became a way of life. Now, you've heard a lot about Stuart and what kind of person he was when sober. Mercifully, that was most of the time. He never missed a day of work, never showed up drunk. Sheriff Walls said he was a good deputy and really enjoyed law enforcement. When he wasn't drinking. But once on the bottle, he became a vile, vicious, violent man. He loved the honky-tonks, the nightlife, hard drinking with his buddies, and he was a brawler, loved a good fistfight, liked to shoot dice. Almost every Friday and Saturday night after work he hit the bars and would come home drunk. Sometimes he was aggressive and looking for trouble, other times he just went to bed and passed out. Josie and her kids learned to leave him alone and hide in their rooms, praying there would be no trouble.

"But there was trouble, and plenty of it. The kids begged their mother to leave, but there was no place to go, nowhere to run. As the violence grew worse, she begged him to get help, to cut back on the drinking, and to stop hitting them. But Stuart was out of control. She threatened to leave him on several occasions, and this always sent him into a rage. He called her names, cursed her in front of the kids, made fun of her because she had nowhere to go, called her trailer park trash."

Dyer stood and said, "Your Honor, I object on the grounds of hearsay."

"Sustained."

Jurors number three and nine lived in trailers.

Jake ignored Dyer and Noose and concentrated on the faces of three and nine. He continued, "On Saturday night, March twenty-four, Stuart was out. In fact he'd been gone all afternoon, and Josie was expecting the worst. They waited as the hours passed. Midnight came and went. The kids were upstairs in Kiera's room with the lights off, hiding, hoping their mother wouldn't get hurt again. They were in Kiera's room because her door was sturdier and the lock worked better. They knew this from experience. The previous door had been kicked in by Stuart during one of his rages. Josie was downstairs, waiting for the headlights to appear in the driveway." He paused for a long time, then said, "You know, I'll let them tell the story."

He stepped behind the podium, glanced at his notes, and wiped sweat from his forehead. But for the funeral fans and the constant hum of the window units, the courtroom was silent and still. "Ladies and gentlemen, this is not a clear-cut case of premeditated murder, far from it. We will prove that during that horrifying moment, with his mother unconscious on the kitchen floor, with Stuart blind drunk and stomping through the house, with his sister crying and begging their mother to wake up, with both children alone and vulnerable, with the history of indescribable violence scarred into their frightened souls, with the belief that they were not safe and would never be safe from that man, what little Drew Gamble did was entirely *justified*."

Jake nodded at the jurors and turned to face the judge. "Your Honor, we are ready with our first witness, Josie Gamble."

"Very well. Please call her to the stand."

No one moved as Josie made her entrance. Jake met her at the railing, opened the low gate of the bar, and pointed to the witness stand. Because she had been superbly coached, she stopped by the court reporter, offered her a smile, and swore to tell the truth. For the occasion, she wore a simple sleeveless white blouse tucked into a pair of black linen slacks, and brown flat sandals. Nothing was tight or revealing. Her short blond hair was pulled back. No lipstick, little makeup. Carla was in charge of her appearance, and after studying the five female jurors she had loaned her the blouse and sandals and bought the slacks. The goal was to appear attractive enough to please the seven men but simple enough not to threaten the women. Her thirty-two years had been hard and she looked at least ten years older. Still, she was younger than most of the jurors and in better shape than virtually all of them.

Jake began with some basic questions, and in doing so elicited her current address, which until then was unknown. The bill collectors had not found her in Oxford and he had debated which address to use. Without too much detail, they went through her past: two pregnancies before she was seventeen; no high school diploma; two bad marriages; the first conviction for possessing drugs at the age of twenty-three, a year in the county jail; the second drug conviction in Texas that landed her in prison for two years. She owned her past, said she was not proud of it and would give anything if she could go back and change things. She was at once stoic and vulnerable. She managed to smile at the jurors a time or two without making light of the situation. Her biggest regret was what she had done to her children, the lousy example she had set. Her voice cracked slightly when she talked about them, and she wiped her eyes with a tissue.

Though every question and answer was thoroughly scripted, the conversation seemed genuine. Her story unfolded with ease at times, and with pain at other times. Jake held a legal pad as if he needed a prompt, but every word had been committed to memory and rehearsed. Libby and Portia could recite the exchange verbatim.

Switching gears, Jake said, "Now, Josie, on December the third of last year, you made a 911 call to the county dispatcher. What happened?"

Dyer stood and said, "Objection, Your Honor. Why is this relevant to the murder on March the twenty-fifth?"

"Mr. Brigance?"

"Your Honor, this 911 call is already before the jury. Sheriff Walls testified about it yesterday. It's relevant because it goes to the abuse, violence, and fear these people were living with leading up to the events of March twenty-fifth."

"Overruled. Mr. Brigance."

Jake said, "Josie, tell us what happened on December the third?"

She hesitated and took a deep breath, as if dreading the recall of another bad night. "It was a Saturday, around midnight, and Stuart came home in a foul mood, very drunk, as usual. I was wearin' jeans and a T-shirt, no bra, and he began accusin' me of sleeping around. This happened all the time. He liked to call me a slut and a whore, even in front of my children."

Dyer jumped up again and said, "Objection. This is hearsay, Your Honor."

Judge Noose said, "Sustained," and looked down at the witness. "Ms. Gamble, I'll ask you not to repeat specific statements made by the deceased."

"Yes sir." It happened just the way Jake said it would. But her words would not be forgotten by the jurors.

"You may continue."

She said, "Anyway, he flew into a rage and slapped me across the mouth, busted my lip, and there was blood. He grabbed me and I tried to fight him, but he was so strong, and angry. I told him that if he hit me again I was leavin', which made matters worse. I managed to get away and ran to the bedroom, locked the door. I thought he was gonna kill me. I called 911 and asked for help. I cleaned up my face and sat on the bed for a while. The kids were upstairs hidin' in their bedrooms. I listened to see if he was botherin' them. After a few minutes I came out, went to the den. He was in his recliner, a chair we couldn't touch, drinkin' a beer and watchin' television. I told him the cops were on the way and he laughed at me. He knew they wouldn't do anything because he knew them all, they were his buddies. He told me that if I pressed charges he would kill me and the kids."

"Did the police arrive?"

"Yes, Deputy Swayze came out. By then, Stuart had settled down, and he did a good job of fakin' it, said everything was okay. Just a little domestic spat. The deputy looked at my face. My cheek and lips were swollen and he noticed some blood at the corner of my mouth. He knew the truth. He asked me if I wanted to press charges and I said no. They left the house together, went outside, smoked a cigarette, just a couple of old friends. I went upstairs and spent the night with the kids in Kiera's room. He didn't come after us."

She dabbed her eyes with the tissue and looked at Jake, ready to proceed.

He said, "On February the twenty-fourth of this year, you called 911 again. What happened?"

Dyer stood and objected. Noose glared at him and said, "Overruled. Continue."

"It was a Saturday, and that afternoon a preacher, Brother Charles McGarry, had stopped by the house, just payin' a call, you know. We had been visitin' his church down the road and Stuart didn't like it. When the preacher knocked on the door, Stuart got a beer and went into the backyard somewhere. He didn't go out that night, for some reason, just hung around the house watchin' basketball games. And drinkin'. I sat with him and tried to have a chat, you know. I asked him if he wanted to go to church with us the next day. He did not. He didn't like church and didn't like preachers and told me that McGarry was not welcome ever again in his house. It was always 'his house,' never 'our house.'"

Charles and Meg McGarry sat two rows behind the defense table, waiting for Josie to join them.

"Why did you call 911?" Jake asked.

She patted her forehead with the tissue. "Well, we started arguin' about the church and he told me I couldn't go back there. I said I'd go anytime I wanted. He was yellin' and I wasn't backin' down and suddenly he threw a can of beer at me. It hit me in the eye and cut my eyebrow. I was covered in beer and I ran to the bathroom and saw the blood. He was bangin' on the door, cussin' like crazy, callin' me all the usual names. I was afraid to come out and I just knew he was about to kick in the door. He finally quit and left and I heard him in the kitchen, so I ran to the bedroom, locked the door, and called 911. It was a mistake because I knew the police wouldn't bother him, but I was scared to death and wanted to protect the kids. He heard me on the phone and started bangin' on the bedroom door, said he would kill me if the cops showed up. After a few minutes, he settled down and said he wanted to talk. I didn't want to talk but I knew if he blew up again he might hurt me or the kids. So I came out, went to the den where he was sittin', and, for the first and only time, he said he was sorry. He begged me to forgive him and promised to get some help with his drinkin'. He seemed sincere, but he was only worried about the 911 call."

"Had you been drinking, Josie?"

"No. I have a beer every now and then, but never in front of my kids. I really can't afford to drink."

"When did the police arrive?"

"Around ten. When I saw their headlights, I went outside to meet them. I said I was okay, things had settled down, it was just a misunderstandin'. I was holdin' a bloody rag over my eye and they asked what happened. I said I fell in the kitchen, and they seemed eager to believe this."

"Did they talk to Stuart?"

"Yes. He came outside and I went in. I could hear them laughin' as they smoked a cigarette."

"And you didn't press charges?"

"No."

Jake walked to the defense table and took off his jacket. His armpits were soaked with sweat and the back of his light blue Oxford cloth was stuck to his skin. He returned to the podium and said, "What efforts did Stuart take to control his drinking?"

"None whatsoever. It just got worse."

"On the night of March twenty-fifth, were you at home with your children?"

"Yes."

"Where was Stuart?"

"Out. I don't know where he was. He'd been gone all afternoon."

"What time did he come home?"

"It was after two in the morning. I was waitin'. The kids were upstairs, supposedly asleep, but I could hear them movin' around quietly. I guess all of us were waitin'."

"What happened when he got home?"

"Well, I put on a little negligee, one that he liked, thinkin', you know, that maybe I could get him in the mood for a little romance, anything to prevent more violence."

"How'd that work out?"

"It didn't. He was blind drunk, had trouble walkin' and standin' up. His eyes were glazed over, his breathin' was very heavy. I'd seen him plenty drunk, but nothin' like that."

"What happened?"

"He saw what I was wearin' and didn't like it. He started his accusations. I didn't want another fight because of the kids. God, they heard so much." Her voice cracked and she broke down. Her sobbing was unscripted, but real and perfectly timed. She closed her eyes and covered her mouth with the tissue as she fought the tears.

Libby noticed number seven, Mrs. Fife, drop her head and clench her jaws, seemingly ready to shed a sympathetic tear.

After a painful, silent moment, Judge Noose leaned over and said softly, "Would you like to take a break, Ms. Gamble?"

She shook her head firmly, gritted her teeth, and looked at Jake.

He said, "Josie, I know this is not easy, but you have to tell the jury what happened."

She nodded rapidly and said, "He slapped me, hard, across the face, and I almost fell down. Then he grabbed me from behind, had his thick forearm around my neck and was chokin' me. I knew it was the end, and all I could think about was my kids. Who would raise them? Where would they go? Would he hurt them too? It all happened so fast. He was growlin' and cussin' and I could smell his awful breath. I managed to elbow him in the ribs and tear myself away. Before I could run, he hit me hard with his fist. That's the last thing I remember. He knocked me unconscious."

"You don't remember anything else?"

"Nothing. When I woke up I was in the hospital."

Jake stepped to the defense table where Libby

handed him an enlarged color photo. "Your Honor, I'd like to approach the witness."

"Proceed."

Jake handed the photo to Josie and asked her, "Can you identify this photograph?"

"Yes. It was taken of me the followin' day in the hospital."

"Your Honor, I'd like to enter into the record this photo as defense exhibit number one."

Lowell Dyer, who had copies of eight photos taken of Josie, rose and said, "The State objects on the grounds of relevancy."

"Overruled. It is admitted into evidence."

Jake said, "Your Honor, I'd like the jury to see this evidence."

"Proceed."

Jake took the remote, pressed a button, and the startling image of a battered woman splashed onto the wide screen on the wall opposite the jurors. Everyone in the courtroom could see it. Josie in the hospital bed, the left side of her face swollen grotesquely, her left eye shut, thick gauze covering her chin and wrapped around her head. A tube ran into her mouth. Others hung from above. Her face was unrecognizable.

Every juror reacted. Some shifted uncomfortably. Some leaned forward as if a few inches would provide a better look at what was perfectly clear. Number five, Mr. Carpenter, shook his head. Number eight, Mrs. Satterfield, stared openmouthed, as if in disbelief.

Harry Rex would later say that Janet Kofer dropped her head.

Jake asked, "Do you know what time you woke up?"

"Around eight that mornin', they said. I was on painkillers and other stuff and pretty groggy."

"How long were you in the hospital?"

"That was Sunday. On Wednesday they moved me to the hospital in Tupelo for surgery to reset my jaw. It was shattered. I was released on Friday."

"And did you make a full recovery from your injuries?"

She nodded and said, "I'm fine."

Jake had other photos of Josie in the hospital, but at that moment they were not needed. He had other questions, but Lucien had taught him years ago to quit when you're ahead. When you've driven home your points, leave something to the imagination of the jurors.

He said, "I tender the witness."

Noose said, "Let's take a break. Fifteen-minute recess."

LOWELL DYER AND his assistant Musgrove huddled in a first-floor restroom and tried to decide what to do next. Normally, a convicted felon was easy to cross-examine because his or her credibility was questionable. But Josie had already talked about her convictions, and some of her other problems as well. She was forthcoming, credible, sympathetic, and the jury would never forget the image of her in the hospital.

They agreed that they had no choice but to attack. From some angle.

When Josie retook the stand, Dyer began with, "Ms. Gamble, how many times have you lost custody of your children?"

"Twice."

"What was the first time?"

"Approximately ten years ago. Drew was around five or so, Kiera was three."

"And why did you lose custody?"

"They were taken away by the State of Louisiana."

"And why did this happen?"

"Well, Mr. Dyer, I was not a very good mother back then. I was married to a small-time drug dealer who peddled his goods out of our apartment. Someone complained and social services came in, got them, and took me to court."

"Were you selling drugs too?"

"Yes, I was. I'm not proud of it. I wish I could do many things over, Mr. Dyer."

"What happened to your kids?"

"They were placed in foster care, in good homes. I got to see them occasionally. I split up with the guy, got a divorce, and managed to get my kids back."

"What happened the second time?"

"I was livin' with a house painter who also sold drugs. He got caught and plea-bargained his way out by tellin' the authorities that the drugs belonged to me. A bad lawyer convinced me to plead to a lesser sentence and I got sent away to a women's prison in Texas. Served two years. Drew and Kiera were placed in a Baptist orphanage in Arkansas and were treated very well."

Don't volunteer too much, Jake had warned her repeatedly. At the moment, she felt as though she knew every question Dyer might throw at her.

"Do you still use drugs?"

"No sir, I don't. I quit years ago, for the sake of my kids."

"Did you ever sell drugs?"

"Yes."

"So you admit that you've used drugs, sold drugs, lived with drug dealers, been arrested, how many times?"

"Four."

"Arrested four times, convicted twice, and served time in prison."

"I'm not proud of any of that, Mr. Dyer."

"Who would be? And you expect this jury to believe in your credibility as a witness and believe all of your testimony?"

"Are you calling me a liar, Mr. Dyer?"

"I'll ask the questions, Ms. Gamble. Your job is to answer them."

"Yes, I expect the jury to believe every word I've said because it's all true. I may have lied before, but I assure you that lyin' was the least of my sins."

The smart move would be to stop the bleeding. She was scoring far more points than the prosecutor. Brigance had her prepped to the max and she was ready for anything.

Dyer was a smart man. He fumbled with some papers and finally said, "Nothing further, Your Honor."

46

Kiera entered the courtroom with a bailiff trailing behind. She walked slowly, looking down to avoid the stares. She wore a simple, drip-dry cotton dress that was tight around the middle. By the time she stopped and faced the court reporter, everyone in the courtroom was staring at her belly. There were whispers in the gallery and several of the jurors glanced around, as if embarrassed for this poor child. She backed into the witness chair and sat gingerly, obviously uncomfortable. She glanced at the jurors as if ashamed, a terrified kid facing an adult's screwed-up world.

Jake said, "You are Kiera Gamble, sister of the accused, correct?"

"Yes sir."

"How old are you, Kiera?"

"Fourteen."

"You are obviously pregnant."

"Yes sir."

Jake had played this scene a thousand times, had lost hours of sleep over it, and had argued and debated and dissected it with his wife and his team. He couldn't blow it. Calmly, he asked, "When is your baby due, Kiera?"

"Late next month."

"And, Kiera, who is the father of your child?"

As coached, she leaned a bit closer to the mike and said, "Stuart Kofer."

There were gasps and loud reactions, and almost im-

mediately Earl Kofer yelled, "That's a damned lie!" He
stood and pointed at her and said, "That's a damned lie,
Judge!" Janet Kofer shrieked and buried her face in her
hands. Barry Kofer said, loudly, "What a crock of shit!"

"Order! Order!" Noose yelled back angrily. He
rapped his gavel as Earl yelled again, "How much more
of this shit do we have to take, Judge? It's a damned lie."

"Order in the court! We will maintain decorum!"
Two uniformed bailiffs were scurrying to Earl on the
third row behind the prosecution. He was waving his
finger and yelling, "This is not fair, Judge! My boy is
dead and they're lyin' about him! Lies, lies, lies!"

"Remove that man from the courtroom," Noose
barked into his mike. Cecil Kofer stood next to his father as if ready for a brawl. The first two bailiffs to reach
them were seventy years old and already winded, but
the third was a rookie who stood six-five, was ripped at
two-forty, and held a black belt. He lifted Cecil under a
wet armpit while grabbing Earl by the elbow. He
dragged them, cussing and twisting, to the aisle where
they were met by other bailiffs and deputies and quickly
realized the futility of any further resistance. They were
shoved to the door, where Earl stopped and turned
around and yelled, "I'll get you for this, Brigance!"

Jake, along with everyone else in the courtroom,
watched and listened in stunned silence. Other than
Janet Kofer's sobbing, and the window units, there were
no other sounds as the moment passed. Kiera sat in the
witness chair and wiped her eyes. Lowell Dyer glared at
Jake as if he might throw a punch. The jurors appeared
to be overwhelmed.

His Honor quickly regrouped and barked at a bailiff,
"Please remove the jury."

They hurried out of the box as if they had been released for good. As soon as the door closed behind

them, Dyer said, "Your Honor, I have a motion, and it should be heard in chambers."

Noose glared at Jake as if he might disbar him on the spot, then grabbed his gavel and said, "Let's take a break. Fifteen minutes. Miss Gamble, you may go sit with your mother for a moment."

THE WINDOW UNIT in Noose's chambers was working nicely and the office was much cooler than the courtroom. The judge flung his robe in a chair, lit his pipe, and stood behind his desk with his arms crossed, obviously upset. He glared at Jake and demanded, "Did you know she was pregnant?"

"Yes I did. So did the district attorney."

"Lowell?"

Dyer was red-faced and furious, with sweat dripping off his chin. "The State moves for a mistrial, Your Honor."

"On what grounds?" Jake asked coolly.

"On the grounds that we've been ambushed."

"That won't fly, Lowell," Jake said. "You saw her in court yesterday and commented to me that she was pregnant. You knew there were allegations of sexual abuse. Now there's proof."

Noose asked, "Jake, did you know Kofer is the father?"

"Yes."

"And when did you know this?"

"We found out in April that she's pregnant, and she's always maintained that it was Kofer. She is prepared to testify that he repeatedly raped her."

"And you kept this quiet?"

"Who was I supposed to tell? Show me a statute or a rule or procedure that requires me to tell anyone that the sister of my client was being raped by the deceased. You can't find one. I had no duty to tell anyone."

"But you kept her in hiding," Dyer said. "Away from everyone."

"You asked me twice to make her available to you and I did so, in my office. Once on April the second, then on June the eighth."

Noose shot a flamethrower into the bowl of his pipe and exhaled a fog of blue smoke. No windows were cracked. The tobacco relaxed him and he said, "I don't like ambushes, Jake, you know that."

"Then change the rules. We have unlimited discovery in civil cases and almost none in criminal cases. Ambushes are a way of life, especially by the prosecution."

"I want a mistrial," Dyer said again.

"And why?" Jake asked. "You want to come back in three months and do it again? Fine with me. We'll bring the baby and show it to the jury, defense exhibit number one. The blood test will be exhibit two."

Dyer's mouth dropped open; stunned again. He managed to say, "You're pretty good at hiding witnesses, aren't you, Jake?"

"You've already used that cheap shot. Find some new material."

"Gentlemen. Let's talk about how to proceed. We're all in a bit of a shock, I'm afraid. First the pregnant witness, then the outburst by the family. I'm worried about our jury."

Dyer said, "Send 'em home, Judge. We'll try it again later."

"No mistrial, Mr. Dyer. Motion denied. Mr. Brigance, I assume that you and this witness are about to discuss the matter of sexual abuse."

"She's fourteen years old, Your Honor, far too young

to consent. He was twenty years older. Sexual relations between them were illegal, nonconsensual, criminal. She is prepared to testify that he repeatedly raped her and then threatened to kill her and her brother, the defendant, if she told anyone. She was too frightened to talk."

"Can we limit some of this, Judge?" Dyer pleaded.

"How graphic do you plan to get, Mr. Brigance?"

"I have no plans to discuss body parts, Your Honor. Her body speaks for itself. The jurors are smart enough to understand what happened."

Noose discharged another cloud of blue smoke and watched it swirl toward the ceiling. "This might get ugly."

"It's already ugly, Judge. A fourteen-year-old girl was raped repeatedly and impregnated by a brute who took advantage of her situation. We can't change the facts. It happened, and any effort on your part to limit her testimony will give us plenty of ammo for the appeal. The law is clear, Your Honor."

"I didn't ask for a lecture, Mr. Brigance."

Yeah, well maybe you need one.

A moment passed as Noose chomped on the stem of his pipe while adding to the fog above the table. Finally, he said, "I'm not sure how to gauge that outburst. Never seen anything like it, really. Wonder how it plays with the jury."

Dyer said, "I see no way it helps us."

"It doesn't help either side," Jake said.

Noose said, "I've never had one of my lawyers threatened like that, Jake. I'll deal with Mr. Kofer after the trial. Let's proceed."

No one in chambers wanted to return to the courtroom to hear Kiera's testimony.

OMAR NOOSE WAS determined to conduct an efficient and safe trial on his home turf, and he had harangued the sheriff into posting every possible deputy—full-time, part-time, reserve, volunteer—in and around the courthouse. After Earl's outburst, and threat, even more muscle was present when the lawyers took their places and the jurors filed in.

Kiera returned to the stand, with a tissue, and braced herself.

From the podium, Jake said, "Now, Kiera, you said that Stuart Kofer is the father of your child. So, I have to ask you a series of questions about your sexual relations with him, okay?"

She bit her lip and nodded.

"How many times were you raped by Stuart Kofer?"

Dyer was quick to rise and object. He should have remained quiet. "Objection, Your Honor. I object to the word 'rape,' which implies a—"

Jake went berserk. He turned to Dyer, took a step, and yelled, "Good God, Lowell! What do you want to call it?! She's fourteen years old, he was thirty-three."

"Mr. Brigance," Noose said.

Jake ignored him and took another step toward Dyer. "You want to use something a bit lighter than 'rape,' say 'sexual attack,' 'molestation,' 'sexual abuse'?"

"Mr. Brigance."

"You pick the words, Lowell. The jury's not stupid. It's obvious what happened."

"Mr. Brigance."

Jake took a deep breath and glared at the judge, as if he might attack him when he was finished with the district attorney.

"You're out of order, Mr. Brigance."

Jake said nothing, just kept glaring. His shirt was even wetter, the sleeves rolled up, as if he was ready to start swinging.

"Mr. Dyer?"

Dyer had actually stepped back and was reeling. He cleared his throat and said, "Your Honor, it's just that I object to the word 'rape.'"

"Objection overruled," Noose said clearly, loudly, and with no doubt that Mr. Dyer should remain in his seat whenever possible. "Proceed."

As Jake stepped back to the podium, he glanced at Joey Kepner, number twelve, and saw a contented face.

"Kiera, how many times were you raped by Stuart Kofer?"

"Five."

"Okay, let's go back to the first time. Do you remember the date?"

She pulled a small, folded sheet of paper from a pocket and looked at it. It wasn't necessary because she and Jake, along with Josie, Portia, and Libby, had covered the dates so often that all the details were memorized.

"It was a Saturday, December the twenty-third."

Jake slowly waved his hand at the jury box and said, "Please tell the jury what happened that day."

"My mother was workin' and my brother was at a friend's house. I was alone upstairs when Stuart came home. I locked my door. I had noticed him starin' at my legs and I just didn't trust him. I didn't like him and he didn't like us, and, well, things were pretty lousy around the house. I heard him walk up the stairs and then he knocked on the door and rattled the knob. I asked him what he wanted and he said we needed to talk. I said I didn't want to talk and maybe later. He rattled the doorknob again and told me to unlock the door, said it was his door, his house, and that I had to do what he said. But he was kind of nice for a change, he wasn't yellin' or cussin', and said he wanted to talk about my mother, said he was worried about her. So I unlocked the door and he came in. He was already undressed and was wearin' nothin' but his boxer shorts."

Her voice broke and her eyes watered.

Jake waited patiently. No one was about to rush this testimony. A good cry was always helpful. Carla, Libby, and Portia were locked onto the female jurors, watching every reaction.

Jake said, "I know this is difficult but it's very important. What happened next?"

"He asked if I'd ever had sex and I said no."

Dyer reluctantly got to his feet and said, "Objection. Hearsay."

"Overruled," Noose snapped.

"He said he wanted to have sex and wanted me to enjoy it with him. I said no. I was terrified and tried to back away from him, but he was very strong. He grabbed me, threw me onto the bed, ripped off my T-shirt and shorts, and he raped me." She burst into tears as her entire body shook. She shoved the mike away and sobbed with both hands over her mouth.

Half the jurors watched her break down, the other half looked away. Number seven, Mrs. Fife, and number eight, Mrs. Satterfield, were wiping their eyes. Oddly enough, number three, Mr. Kingman, believed by the defense to be one of the staunchest defenders of law and order, glanced at Libby with a curious look, and she caught the unmistakable glow of moisture in his eyes.

After a moment, Jake asked her, "Would you like to take a break?"

The question was rehearsed, as was the answer. A

quick "No." She was a tough girl who had survived a lot and could get through this.

"Now, Kiera, what happened after he was finished?"

"He got up, put on his boxer shorts, and told me to stop cryin'. He said that I'd better get used to it because we were gonna do it all the time, as long as I lived in his house."

On the way up, Dyer said, "Objection. Hearsay?"

"Overruled," Noose said without looking at the prosecutor.

On the way down, he tossed a legal pad that fell off the table and landed on the floor. Noose ignored that too.

Jake nodded at Kiera and she continued, "He asked me if I liked it and I said no. I was cryin' and shakin' and I thought, you stupid man, how can you think I'd like it? As he was leavin', I was still in the bed, under a sheet, and he walked over to me and slapped me in the face, but not too hard. And he said that if I told anyone, then he would kill me and Drew."

"What happened next?"

"As soon as he left, I went to the bathroom and took a bath. I felt dirty and didn't want his smell on me. I sat in the tub forever and tried to stop cryin'. I wanted to die, Mr. Brigance. That was the first time in my life that I thought about suicide."

"Did you tell your mother?"

"No."

"Why not?"

"I was afraid of him, we all were, and I knew he would hurt me if I told anyone. As it went on and on, I realized that I might be pregnant. I felt bad in the mornings, got sick at school, and I knew that I would have to tell Mom. I was planning on it when Stu got killed."

"Did you ever tell Drew?"

"No."

"Why not?"

She shrugged and said, "I was too afraid. And what was he supposed to do? I was scared, Mr. Brigance, and I didn't know what to do."

"And so you told no one?"

"No one."

"When was the next rape?"

She looked at her sheet of paper and said, "A week later, December the thirtieth. It was like the first one, at home, on Saturday, with no one else there. I tried to push him away but he was so strong. He didn't slap me, but he threatened me again when it was over."

With a loud gasp, almost a shriek, Janet Kofer launched into another round of crying. Noose pointed to her and spoke to a bailiff, "Please remove that lady from the courtroom."

Two deputies escorted her to the door. Jake watched the disturbance, and when it was finally over, he looked at his witness. "Kiera, please tell the jury about the third rape."

Kiera was rattled by the outburst and wiped her cheeks. Take your time, Jake had told her over and over. There is absolutely no rush. It will be a short trial anyway, and no one is in a hurry. She leaned closer to the mike and said, "Well, I had to change things for Saturday, so I asked Drew to stay home with me, and he did. Stuart left. A couple of weeks went by and I managed to stay away from him. Then one afternoon Stuart picked me up from school." She looked at her notes. "It was Tuesday, January sixteen, and I had to stay late to work on a play, a theater project. He volunteered to get me, in his patrol car, and we stopped for ice cream. It was gettin' late and, lookin' back, I think he was just killin' time until it was dark. We drove home, but he took a side road not far from the church, Good Shepherd, and stopped behind an old country store, one that has been closed for a long time. It was very dark out there, not another light anywhere. He told me to get in the backseat. I had no choice. I begged him not to and I thought about screamin', but no one would hear me. He left a rear door open, and I remember how cold it was."

"And he was in uniform?"

"Yes. He took off his gun and just pulled down his pants. I was wearin' a skirt. He wrapped it around my neck. When we were drivin' home I couldn't stop cryin', so he took his gun and punched it into my ribs, said to stop it, said he would kill me if I breathed a word. Then he laughed and said he wanted me to walk into the house like nothing had ever happened, said he wanted to see how good an actor I was. I went to my room and locked the door. Drew came to check on me."

As gripping and lurid as her testimony was, Jake knew it would be a mistake to punish the witness and the jury with the details of all five attacks. They had endured enough, and he had plenty of ammo for the rest of the trial. He stepped to the defense table to get some notes, a legal pad for a prop, and glanced at Carla on the third row. With perfect timing, she did a quick slit of the throat with an index finger. Red polish. Cut. Move on.

He returned to the podium and continued. "Kiera, on the night Stuart died, you were home with Drew and your mom, correct?"

"Yes sir."

Dyer stood and said, "Objection, Your Honor. This is leading."

With irritation, Noose said, "Sure, it's leading, Mr. Dyer, but it's going into the record anyway. Overruled. Please continue, Ms. Gamble."

"Well, we were home, waitin' as usual. He was out, late, and the situation had become much worse. Drew and I were beggin' Mom to leave before somebody got hurt, and I had made the decision to tell her I thought something was wrong with my body, that I might be pregnant, but I was still afraid because of him and because there was no place for us to go. We were trapped. If she had known about the rapes and all she would, well, I'm not sure what she would have done. But I was still afraid of him. So, anyway, long after midnight we saw the headlights. Drew and I were huddled together on my bed with the door jammed for protection. We heard him come in, Mom was waiting in the kitchen, and they got into a fight. We heard her get slapped and she yelled and he cussed her, and it was just awful." More tears, another brief delay as the witness fought to control herself.

She wiped her eyes and moved closer to the mike.

"Did Stuart go upstairs?" Jake asked.

"He did. Suddenly everything was quiet down there and we heard him on the stairs, staggerin', fallin'. Obviously drunk. He was stompin' up the stairs, callin' my name, sort of singing it like an idiot. He rattled the doors, yelled for us to open them. We were so afraid." Her voice cracked and she cried some more.

The terror she and Drew felt at that moment was now palpable in the courtroom. Watching that poor girl cry and wipe her face and try to be strong after all she had endured was heartbreaking.

Jake asked, "Kiera, would you like to take a break?"

She shook her head, no. Let's get it over with.

Once Stuart backed away and went down the stairs,

she and Drew knew something terrible had happened to their mother. Otherwise, she would have fought him on the stairway. They waited in the dark, curled up together, both crying, as the minutes passed. Drew went down first, then Kiera, who sat on the kitchen floor with their mother and tried to revive her. Drew called 911. He was moving around the house but Kiera did not know what he was doing. Then he closed the bedroom door, and she heard the shot. When he came out she asked him what he did, though she knew. Drew said, "I shot him."

Jake listened carefully and occasionally glanced at his notes, but he managed to steal looks at the jurors. They were not watching him. Every eye was on the witness. "Now, Kiera, when you came down the stairs and found your mother, were you still worried about Stuart?"

She bit her lip, nodded, "Yes sir. We didn't know what he was doing. Once we saw Mom on the floor, we figured he'd kill us too."

Jake took a deep breath, smiled at her, and said, "Thank you, Kiera. Your Honor, the defense tenders the witness." He sat down and loosened his collar. It, along with the rest of his shirt, was soaked with sweat.

Lowell Dyer approached the podium with trepidation. He couldn't attack such a vulnerable and wounded girl. She had the jury's complete sympathy and any unkind word from the prosecutor would only play in her favor. He began a disastrous cross with "Ms. Gamble, you keep looking at some notes you have there. May I ask about them?"

"Sure." She pulled the folded sheet of paper from under her leg. "Just my notes about the five rapes."

Jake could not suppress a grin. He had laid the trap and Dyer was blindly walking into it.

"And when did you make these notes?"

"I've worked on them for some time. I went back through some calendars and made sure I had the dates right."

"And who asked you to do this?"

"Jake."

"Has Jake told you what to say here on the witness stand?"

She was ready. "We've gone through my testimony, yes sir."

"Has he coached you on how to testify?"

Jake stood and said, "Objection, Your Honor. Every good lawyer prepares his witnesses. What's the point, Mr. Dyer?"

"Mr. Dyer?"

"I'm just probing, Your Honor. It is a cross-examination and I'm allowed some latitude here."

"If relevant, Your Honor," Jake said.

"Overruled. Continue."

Dyer asked, "Could I see your notes there, Ms. Gamble?"

Written materials used for reference by witnesses were fair game, and the instant Dyer saw her glance at her notes he knew he would get them. In a moment, though, he would wish he had ignored them.

She held them up, as if to offer them to the prosecutor, who asked, "Your Honor, may I approach the witness?"

"Sure."

He took a single sheet of paper and unfolded it. Jake let the mystery of its contents hang in the air for a few seconds, then jumped to his feet. "If it pleases the Court, we'll be happy to stipulate and admit Kiera's notes into evidence. We even have copies here for the jurors to look at." He waved some papers.

The notes, written in her own hand and in her own words, were Libby's idea. She had seen the ruse before in a rape case in Missouri. At the direction of the defense lawyer, the victim had prepared little reminders to help her through the ordeal of testifying. A hard-charging D.A. had demanded to see her notes, and it had been a fatal mistake.

Kiera's written accounts of the five rapes were far more graphic than her testimony. She wrote of the pain, fear, her body, his, the horror, blood, and the ever-increasing thoughts of suicide. They were numbered, Rapes 1 through 5.

Once Dyer held the sheet of paper, and glanced at its contents, he realized his blunder. He handed it back, quickly, and said, "Thank you, Ms. Gamble."

Jake, still standing, said, "Hang on, Judge. At this point the jury has the right to know about the notes. The State has put them into question."

Dyer said, "The State has the right to be curious, Judge. This is a cross-examination."

Jake said, "Of course it is. Your Honor, Mr. Dyer went after the notes because he was fishing and trying to prove that this witness has been coached by me and told how to testify. He thought he had caught us when he saw the notes. Now, though, he's backing down. The notes are in play, Your Honor, and the jury has the right to see them."

"I'm inclined to agree, Mr. Dyer. You asked to see them. It doesn't seem fair to keep them away from the jury."

"I disagree, Your Honor," Dyer said in desperation, but could offer no reason.

Jake, still waving copies, said, "I submit the notes into evidence, Your Honor. Let's not keep this from the jury."

"Enough, Mr. Brigance. Just wait your turn."

After the fourth rape, Kiera had written: "I'm getting used to the pain, it goes away after a couple of days. But I haven't had a period in two months and I'm often dizzy in the morning. If I'm pregnant he'll kill me. And probably Mom and Drew too. It's better if I die. I read a story about a teenager who cut her wrists with razor blades. That's what I'll do. Where to find them?"

Reeling, Lowell Dyer asked for a moment to confer with Musgrove. They whispered, both shaking their heads as if they had no earthly idea what to do next. Dyer had to do something, though, in order to discredit a sympathetic witness, and salvage a disastrous cross, and somehow save his case. He managed to nod at Musgrove, as if one of the two had hit the nail on the head. He stepped to the podium and gave her another drippy smile.

"Now, Ms. Gamble, you say you were sexually assaulted by Mr. Kofer on a number of occasions."

"No sir. I said I was raped by Stuart Kofer," she said with ice. Another response scripted by Libby and Portia.

"But you never told anyone?"

"No sir. There was no one to tell."

"You were enduring these terrible attacks, yet you never sought help?"

"From who?"

"What about law enforcement? The police?"

Jake's heart froze at the question. He was stunned by it, but prepared, as was his witness. With perfect timing and diction, Kiera looked at Dyer and said, "Sir, I was being raped by the police."

Dyer's shoulders sagged as his mouth dropped open and he searched for a snappy retort. None arrived, nothing but warm air rushing over a parched tongue. He was suddenly mortified at the prospect of serving up another fat pitch that might land in the upper deck with the others. So he simply smiled and thanked her, as if she had really helped him, and retreated as fast as any prosecutor could possibly scurry away to the safety of his chair.

Noose said, "It's almost noon. Let's take a long lunch break and give the AC time to catch up. It's already a bit cooler in here, I think. Jurors, I ask that you all go home for lunch and we'll reconvene at two sharp. The usual precautions are still in order—do not discuss this case with anyone. We are in recess."

47

Josie was parked behind the courthouse in a small, shaded gravel lot she had found on Monday. She and Kiera were almost to her car when a man with a gun approached. He was thick-chested, with a short-sleeved shirt, knotted tie, cowboy boots, and a black pistol on his hip. "Are you Josie Gamble?" he demanded. She had seen the type many times before, and he was either a small-town detective or a private investigator.

"I am. Who are you?"

"Name's Koosman. These papers are for you." He handed her a legal-sized envelope stuffed with folded papers.

"What is it?" she asked, reluctantly taking the envelope.

"Buncha lawsuits. Sorry." He turned and walked away. Nothing but a process server.

They had finally found her—the hospitals and doctors and their bill collectors and lawyers. Four lawsuits for unpaid bills: $6,340 to the hospital in Clanton; $9,120 to the hospital in Tupelo; $1,315 to the doctors in Clanton; and $2,100 to the surgeon in Tupelo who reset her jaw. A total of $18,875, plus interest and attorney's fees of an undetermined amount. All four filed by the same collection lawyer in Holly Springs.

The car was like a sauna and its AC did not work. They rolled down the windows and sped away. Josie was tempted to grab the lawsuits and toss them in a ditch. She had more important things to worry about and she couldn't remember all the times some shifty collection lawyer had tracked her down.

"How'd I do, Mom?" Kiera asked.

"You were brilliant, baby, just brilliant."

BRILLIANT WAS INDEED the verdict as the defense settled around the table in Morris Finley's rather chilly conference room. For relief, his secretary had turned the thermostat down as low as possible. They ate quickly and savored Kiera's brilliance and the collapse of the prosecution. Victory was still a long shot, but she had evoked enormous sympathy from the jury. However, the problem was obvious—Kiera wasn't on trial.

Portia passed around a memo with the names of eleven witnesses and brief descriptions of their expected testimony. The first was Samantha Pace, ex-wife of Stuart Kofer. She now lived in Tupelo and had grudgingly agreed to testify against her ex-husband.

"Why would you call her?" Harry Rex asked with a mouth full of chips.

"To prove he beat her," Jake said. "I'm not advocating this, Harry Rex, this is just an exercise to make sure we cover everything. This is our witness list, the same one we filed before the trial. Frankly, I'm not sure who to put on next."

"I'd forget her."

"I agree," said Libby. "She might be unpredictable, plus you've already proven abuse."

Lucien was shaking his head.

"Next is Ozzie and three deputies. Pirtle, McCarver, and Swayze could testify about the 911 calls to the house. They saw a battered woman who refused to press charges. They filed paperwork that Ozzie can't find.

Someone, presumably Kofer, filched the incident reports to cover his trail."

"Portia?"

"I don't know, Jake. This is already in evidence and I wouldn't trust the cops right now. They might say something that we're not expecting."

"Perfect instincts," Lucien said. "Leave 'em alone, because you can't trust 'em on the stand."

"Carla?"

"Me? I'm just a schoolteacher."

"Then pretend you're a juror. You've heard every word of testimony."

"You've already proven the domestic abuse, Jake. Why go through it again? I mean, all the jury needs to see is the photo of Josie's face. A picture is worth a thousand words. Let it go."

Jake smiled at her, then looked at Harry Rex. "You?"

"Right now these guys are meetin' with Dyer, who's tryin' to figure out some way to save his case. I wouldn't trust 'em. If you don't need 'em, don't call 'em."

"Lucien?"

"Look, Jake. Your case is as strong right now as it will ever be. There is not a witness on this list who can make it stronger, yet every one of them can be potentially damaging."

"So the defense rests?"

Lucien nodded slowly and everyone absorbed it. The strategy of resting after calling only two witnesses had not been discussed, had not even been contemplated. And it was frightening. The defense just put plenty of points on the board, and it had more points to add. Walking away with uncalled witnesses seemed like retreating.

Jake looked at the memo and said, "The next four, starting with Dog Hickman, are the drinking buddies who'll give the down-and-dirty details of Kofer's last binge. They're all here, all under subpoena, missing work and pissed off. Libby?"

"I'm sure they'll be good for some comic relief, but do we really need them? Dr. Majeski's testimony is much more powerful. The point-three-six BAC has been seared into the brains of the jurors and they'll never forget it."

"Harry Rex?"

"Agreed. You can't be sure what these clowns might say. I've read your summaries and all. They're pretty stupid and they still think they might be implicated. Plus they'll always be sympathetic to their buddy. I'd leave 'em alone."

Jake took a deep breath and looked at his list. "We're running out of ammo," he said under his breath.

"You don't need anymore," Lucien said.

"Dr. Christina Rooker. She examined Drew four days after the shooting. You've read her report. She's ready to testify about his trauma and what an emotional and mental wreck he was. I've spent hours with her and she will make an impressive witness. Libby?"

"Don't know. Still undecided about this one."

"Lucien?"

"There's a huge problem—"

Jake interrupted with, "And the problem is that, by putting Drew's mental state into issue, Dyer can then call a carload of shrinks from Whitfield to rebut anything and declare him perfectly sound, both now and on March twenty-fifth. Dyer has three of them on his witness list and we've researched them, tracked down their testimonies. They're always in lockstep with the State. Hell, they work for the State."

Lucien smiled and said, "Exactly. You can't win that fight, so don't start it."

"Anybody else?" Jake looked around the room and met the gaze of every member of his team. "Carla, you're the juror."

"Oh, I'm hardly unbiased."

"But how many of the twelve will vote to convict Drew right now?"

"Several. But not all."

"Portia?"

"Agreed."

"Libby?"

"My record at predicting verdicts is less than spectacular, but I don't see a conviction, nor an acquittal."

"Lucien?"

He took a sip of water and stood to stretch his back. He walked to the end of the room as everyone watched and waited. He turned and said, "That girl's testimony is the most dramatic moment I've ever witnessed in a courtroom. It surpasses even your closing argument in the Hailey trial. Now, if you call more witnesses, then Dyer calls more in rebuttal. Time passes, memories begin to fade, the drama lessens somewhat. You want those jurors to go home tonight and think about Kiera—young, pregnant Kiera—not some bozos drinking moonshine, not some fancy shrink with a big vocabulary, not some county deputy trying to cover for a fallen comrade. You have Dyer on the ropes, Jake; don't make a mistake and let him wiggle free."

The room was silent as they weighed his words. After a moment, Jake asked, "Anybody disagree?"

Eyes met eyes as they studied each other, but no one spoke.

Jake finally said, "And if we rest, then the State is done because there is nothing to rebut. Dyer will be surprised. We'll immediately go to the jury instructions, which we'll have ready but he won't. Then we'll do our closing arguments, and I'm guessing his is not quite ready. Resting this early is another ambush."

"I love it!" Harry Rex said.

"But is it fair?" Carla asked.

"At this point, everything is fair," Harry Rex said with a laugh.

"Yes, dear, it's quite fair. Either side can rest with no warning to the other."

Lucien sat down, and Jake looked at him for a long time. The others waited as they finished their chips and tea and wondered what was next. Finally, Jake asked, "And Drew? Would you put him on?"

"Never," Harry Rex said.

"I've spent hours with him, Harry Rex. He can do it."

"Dyer will eat him alive because he's guilty, Jake. He pulled the damn trigger."

"And he won't deny it. But he has some zingers ready for Dyer, just like his sister. I mean, 'I was being raped by the police' might go down in history. Lucien?"

"I rarely put the defendant on the stand, but this kid looks so young, so harmless. It's your call, Jake. I haven't spent time with him."

Carla said, "Well, I have, many hours, and I believe Drew is ready. He can tell a powerful story. He's just a boy who's had a hard life. I think most of the jurors will show a little mercy."

"I agree," Libby said softly.

With that, Jake glanced at his watch and said, "There's plenty of time. Let's all stand down. Carla and I need to take a long drive. Meeting adjourned."

JUDGE NOOSE SENT word through his bailiff to Ozzie who was waiting for the Kofers when they returned to the courthouse. A meeting was offered, and at 1:45 Earl, Janet, Barry, and Cecil walked into the empty and somewhat cooler courtroom, and found His Honor, robeless and sitting not on the bench but in the jury box, rocking in a comfortable chair with his bailiff nearby. Ozzie led them through the bar and they stopped in front of the judge.

Earl seemed angry, even belligerent. Janet looked thoroughly defeated, as if she had given up the fight.

"You disrupted my courtroom," Noose said sternly. "That is unacceptable."

"Well, Judge, we're just sick of the damned lies, that's all," Earl said, as if ready for a fight.

Noose pointed a crooked finger and said, "Watch your language, sir. Right now I'm not concerned with the lawyers and witnesses. It's your behavior that bothers me. You caused a disturbance, had to be escorted out, and threatened one of my lawyers. I could hold you in contempt right now and have you jailed. Do you realize that?"

Earl did not. His shoulders sagged and his attitude vanished. He'd accepted the invitation to this little meeting because he had a thing or two to tell the judge, without a passing thought about going to jail.

His Honor continued, "Now, here's the question. Do you want to watch the rest of this trial?"

All four nodded, yes. Janet wiped her cheeks again.

"Okay. That third row over there behind the prosecutor will be reserved for you. Mr. Kofer, I want you to take the aisle seat. If I hear another sound or if you disturb my proceedings in any way, I'll have you taken out again, and with consequences. Understand?"

"Sure," Earl said.

"Yes sir," Barry grunted.

Janet dabbed her eyes.

"All right. We have an understanding." Noose leaned forward and relaxed. The heavy work was over. "Please allow me to say this. I am very sorry for your loss and I've prayed for you since I heard the news. We are not supposed to bury our children. I met your son briefly one day in court in Clanton, so I can't claim any friendship, but he seemed like a fine young officer. As this trial has progressed, I have felt sympathy for you as you sit out there and hear some terrible things said about your son. I'm sure it's just awful. However, we cannot change the facts, or the allegations. Trials are often messy and ugly. For that, I am sorry."

They were not prepared to respond, nor were they the kind of people who could simply say "Thanks."

AS JAKE AND Carla ducked through a rear door of the main courthouse building, Dumas Lee popped up from nowhere and said, "Hello, Jake, got time for a question?"

"Hello, Dumas," Jake said politely. They had known each other for ten years and the guy was just doing his job. "Sorry, Dumas, but I can't talk. Judge Noose has told the lawyers to shut up."

"A gag order?"

"No, a shut-up order, issued in chambers."

"Will your client testify?"

"No comment. Come on, Dumas."

That morning's weekly edition of the *Times* had neglected all county news except for the trial. The entire front page was covered with photos—Jake entering the courthouse, Dyer doing the same, the defendant exiting a patrol car in a coat and tie and duly shackled. Dumas wrote two long articles, one about the alleged crime and all the players, one about jury selection. To embarrass a neighboring county, the editor even included a bad photo of the old courthouse. The caption under it described it as "built in the last century and in need of renovation."

"Later, Dumas," Jake said as he led Carla down a hallway.

The news vans were gone. The Tupelo paper ran a short front-page story on Tuesday. Jackson ran the same story on page three. Memphis wasn't interested.

48

When court was called to order at 2:05, the courtroom was at least ten degrees cooler and much less humid. Judge Noose again invited the attorneys to work without jackets, but they left them on. He looked at Jake and said, "Call your next witness."

Jake stood and said, "Your Honor, the defense calls Mr. Drew Gamble to the stand." There was a rustling through the crowd at this unexpected move. Lowell Dyer shot Jake a wary look.

Drew rose and marched to the court reporter, took his oath, and settled into the witness chair. He was startled by the entirely different view of things. Jake had told him this would happen, said it would be shocking at first to see all those adults staring at him. His written instructions read: "Look at me, Drew. Look me in the eyes at all times. Do not look at the jurors. Do not look at your mother or sister. Do not look at the other lawyers, nor the people out there in the audience. Everyone will be looking at you, so ignore them. Look me in the eyes. Don't smile, don't frown. Don't speak too loud, nor too soft. We'll start with some easy questions and you'll get comfortable. You're not in the habit of saying 'Yes sir' and 'No sir,' but DO IT EVERY TIME when you're on the stand. Start practicing now with me and the jailers."

In his cell, late at night, Jake had shown him how to sit and keep his hands still, how to stay six inches from the mike, how to frown at a confusing question, what to do if the judge spoke to him, how to sit passively if the lawyers got into an argument, and how to say, "Sir, I'm sorry, but I don't understand." They had practiced for hours.

The easy questions and answers did indeed settle his nerves, but then Drew felt oddly at ease to begin with. For a day and a half he'd sat between his lawyers as witnesses came and went. As Jake had instructed, he watched them carefully. Some were good, others were not. Kiera had been visibly frightened, but her fear had connected with the jurors.

He had learned a lot about testifying just from being there.

No sir, he had never known his father, nor his grandfathers. He did not know any of his uncles or cousins.

Jake asked, "Now, Drew, how many times have you been arrested?"

It was an odd question. Youth court convictions were off-limits. The State certainly couldn't mention them. But, as with Josie, Jake wanted transparency, especially when it benefitted the defense.

"Twice."

"How old were you the first time?"

"Twelve."

"What happened?"

"Well, me and a buddy named Danny Ross stole two bicycles and got caught."

"Why did you steal bicycles?"

"Because we didn't have one."

"Okay, and what happened when you got caught?"

"We went to court and the judge said we were guilty, and we were. So they put me in a juvenile detention center for about four months."

"And where was this?"

"Over in Arkansas."

"Where were you living at the time?"

"Well, sir, we were, uh, livin' in a car."

"With your mother and sister?"

"Yes sir." With a quick nod, Jake invited him to continue. Drew said, "My mother didn't object to me goin' to the juvenile jail because at least I would get somethin' to eat."

Dyer stood and said, "Objection, Your Honor. Relevance. This trial is about capital murder, not a stolen bike."

"Sustained. Move along, Mr. Brigance."

"Yes, Your Honor." But Dyer did not ask for the response to be stricken from the record. The jury heard that the kids were hungry and homeless.

Jake asked, "And what was the second arrest?"

"When I was thirteen I got caught with some pot."

"Were you trying to sell it?"

"No sir. It wasn't much."

"What happened?"

"They sent me back to the same place for three months."

"Do you use drugs now?"

"No sir."

"Do you drink alcohol?"

"No sir."

"Have you been in trouble with the law in the past three years?"

"No sir, other than this."

"Okay, let's talk about this." Jake stepped away from the podium and looked at the jury. If Jake did so, then it was okay for Drew to have a quick look too. At that moment, the jurors were watching Jake.

"When did you first meet Stuart Kofer?"

"The day we moved in. I don't remember when it was."

"How did Stuart treat you in the beginning?"

"Well, we sure didn't feel welcome. It was his house and he had a lot of rules, some he made up on the spot. He had us do a lot of chores. He was never nice to us and we knew right away that he didn't want us in his house. So we, me and Kiera, tried to stay away from him. He didn't want us at the table when he was eatin' so we took our food upstairs, or outside."

"Where did your mother eat?"

"With him. They argued a lot, though, right from the beginnin'. Mom wanted us to be a real family, you know, do things together. Have supper, go to church, things like that, but Stu couldn't stand us. He didn't want us. Nobody has ever wanted us."

Pitch-perfect, thought Jake, and with no objection from Dyer. He wanted to pounce and object to the leading questions, but at the moment the jurors were captivated and would resent the interruption.

"Were you physically abused by Stuart Kofer?"

Drew paused and looked confused. "What do you mean by 'physically abused'?"

"Did he hit you?"

"Oh, yeah, I got slapped around a few times."

"Do you remember the first time?"

"Yes sir."

"What happened?"

"Well, Stu asked me if I wanted to go fishin', and I really didn't want to because I didn't like him and he didn't like me. But my mom had been buggin' him to do something with me, you know, like a real father, throw a baseball, go fishin' or something fun. So he got his boat and we went to the lake. He started drinkin' beer and that was always a bad sign. We were in the middle of the lake when a big fish hit my hook hard and took off. I was surprised and didn't grip the rod fast enough, and so the rod and reel disappeared underwater. Stu went crazy. He cussed like a dog and slapped me twice in the face, hard. He was out of his mind, yellin' and cussin' and sayin' that rig cost him over a hundred dollars and I had to pay him back. I thought he might knock me out of the boat. He got so mad he cranked the engine, flew to the ramp, got the boat out, and headed home. He was still cussin'. He had a terrible temper, especially when he was drinkin'."

Dyer finally stood and said, "Your Honor. Objection. Leading and relevance. I'm not sure what's happening here, Your Honor, but this is a direct examination and this witness is being allowed to ramble on forever."

Noose removed his reading glasses and chewed on a stem for a moment. "Agreed, Mr. Dyer, but this testimony is coming in regardless, so let's allow the witness to testify."

Jake said, "Thank you, Your Honor. Now, Drew, what happened as you were driving home from the lake?"

"Well, when we got close to the house, he kept lookin' at me and saw that my left eye was swollen where he'd hit me. So he told me not to tell my mom. He told me to say that I slipped and fell as we were loadin' the boat."

Dyer stood and said, "Objection. Hearsay."

"Overruled. Continue."

Jake had instructed him to immediately continue when the Judge said "Continue." Don't wait on the lawyers. Finish the story.

Drew said, "And then he threatened to kill me."

"Was that the first time he threatened you?"

"Yes sir. Said he would kill me and Kiera if we ever told Mom."

"Was he physically abusing Kiera?"

"Well, we know it now, I guess."

"Okay, Drew, before he died, did you know that Stuart Kofer was sexually assaulting your sister?"

"No sir. She didn't tell me."

Jake paused and checked some notes on a legal pad. The courtroom was quiet, but for the window units. The temperature was improving as a layer of clouds moved in to block the sun.

Jake stood beside the podium and asked, "Drew, were you and Kiera afraid of Stuart Kofer?"

"Yes sir."

"Why?"

"He was a tough guy with a bad temper, a mean drunk, and he had plenty of guns, plus he was a deputy and liked to brag that he could get away with anything, includin' murder. Then he started beatin' Mom and things just got so bad ..." His voice trailed off and he dropped his head. He was suddenly sobbing and shaking as he fought to keep his composure. A painful moment passed as everyone watched him.

Jake said, "Let's talk about the night Stuart died."

Drew took a deep breath, looked at his lawyer, and wiped his cheeks with the back of a sleeve. Because he and Kiera had been so thoroughly prepped, their stories matched perfectly until they reached the critical point when they found their mother unconscious and apparently dead. From then on, they were not thinking clearly and certainly couldn't remember their exact words and movements. Both were crying and at times hysterical. He remembered moving around the house, looking at Stuart on the bed, looking at Kiera holding Josie on the kitchen floor, listening to her as she begged her to wake up, and waiting at the front window for help to arrive.

And then he heard something. A coughing, snorting

sound, and the squeaking of the box spring and the mattress. Stuart was moving back there, and if he got up, as he had done a month earlier, he would fly into another rage and probably kill them all."

"And I went to the bedroom and he was still on the bed."

"Had he moved?" Jake asked.

"Yes. His right arm was now across his chest. He wasn't snorin'. I just knew he was about to get up. So I got his gun off the table where he always kept it, and I left the room with it."

"Why did you take the gun?"

"I don't know. I guess I was afraid he might use it."

"What did you do with the gun?"

"I don't know. I walked back to the window and waited some more, just kept waitin' for blue lights or red lights or someone to come help us."

"Were you familiar with the gun?"

"Yes sir. Stuart took me out in the woods one day for some target practice. We used his service gun, his Glock."

"How many times did you fire it?"

"Three or four. He had a target on some hay bales. I couldn't hit it and he laughed at me, called me a sissy, among other things."

Jake pointed to exhibit number one lying on the table. "Is that the gun, Drew?"

"I think so. Sure looks like it."

"So, Drew, you were standing at the window, waiting, holding that gun there, and what happened next?"

Staring at Jake, he said, "I remember hearin' Kiera, and I remember bein' so scared. I knew he was gettin' up, comin' after us, so I went to the bedroom. My hands were shakin' so bad I could barely hold the gun. And I put it next to his head."

His voice cracked again and he wiped his eyes.

Jake asked, "Do you remember pulling the trigger, Drew?"

He shook his head. "No, I don't. I'm not sayin' I didn't do it, I'm just sayin' I don't remember it. I remember closin' my eyes, and the gun shakin' so hard, and I remember the sound."

"Do you remember putting the gun down?"

"No."

"Do you remember telling Kiera that you shot Stuart?"

"No."

"Well, Drew, what do you remember?"

"The next thing was sittin' in the police car, with handcuffs, flyin' down the road and wonderin' what I was doin' there and where was I goin'."

"Was Kiera with you in the police car?"

"I don't remember."

"No further questions, Your Honor."

LOWELL DYER HAD never believed for an instant that he would have the chance to cross-examine the defendant. At every turn in the pretrial, Jake had indicated that Drew would not testify. And, most crafty defense lawyers kept their clients away from the witness stand.

Dyer had spent little time preparing for the moment, and his trepidation was compounded by the fact that both Josie and Kiera had been so thoroughly coached they had actually scored more points than the D.A. during their cross-examinations.

Attacking the witness because of his criminal record wouldn't work. Drew had already confessed, and, besides, who really cared about a stolen bike and a few ounces of pot?

Attacking anything in the kid's past would backfire because it was unlikely that a single person on the jury had endured such a harsh childhood.

Dyer glared at the defendant. "Now, Mr. Gamble, when you moved in with Stuart Kofer, you were given your own bedroom, right?"

"Yes sir."

Nothing about the shaggy-haired kid suggested the title of "Mister" was appropriate. Dyer, though, had to play it tough. Being too familiar would be a sign of weakness. Perhaps using the title might make him seem older.

"And your sister was just across the hall, right?"

"Yes sir."

"Did you have plenty of food to eat?"

"Yes sir."

"Did you have hot water for showers and clean towels and such?"

"Yes sir. We did our own laundry."

"And you were in school every day?"

"Yes sir, almost every day."

"And in church occasionally?"

"Yes sir."

"And before you moved in with Stuart Kofer, I believe the family was living in a borrowed camper, is that correct?"

"Yes sir."

"And from the testimony given by your mother and sister, we know that before the camper you lived in a car, in an orphanage, in foster care, and in a juvenile detention center. Anywhere else?"

What a stupid mistake! Bust him, Drew, Jake wanted to yell.

"Yes sir. We lived under a bridge one time for a couple of months, and there were some homeless shelters."

"Okay. My point is that the home Stuart Kofer provided was the nicest place you ever lived, right?"

Another mistake. Do it, Drew! "No sir. A couple of the foster homes were nicer, plus you didn't have to worry about gettin' slapped around."

Dyer looked at the bench and pleaded, "Your Honor, would you instruct the witness to respond to the questions without expounding on his answers?"

Jake expected a quick response, but Noose mulled it over. Jake stood and said, "Your Honor, if I may. Counsel described the Kofer home as 'nice' without defining what that means. I submit that any home where a kid lives with abuse and the threat of more is anything but 'nice.'"

Noose agreed and said, "Please continue."

Dyer was too stung to continue. He huddled with D. R. Musgrove and they again tried to find a strategy. He nodded smugly, as if he'd found the perfect line of questioning, and returned to the podium.

"Now, Mr. Gamble, I believe you said that you didn't like Stuart Kofer and he didn't like you. Is that correct?"

"Yes sir."

"Would you say you hated Stuart Kofer?"

"That's fair, yes sir."

"Did you want to see him dead?"

"No sir. What I wanted was just to get away from him. I was tired of him beatin' my mother and slappin' us around. I was tired of the threats."

"So when you shot him, you were killing him to protect your mother and sister and yourself, right?"

"No sir. At the time, I knew my mother was dead. It was too late to protect her."

"Then you shot him out of revenge. For killing your mother. Right?"

"No sir, I don't remember thinkin' about revenge. I

was too upset at the sight of Mom lying on the floor. I was just afraid that Stuart would get up and come after us, like he did before."

Come on Dyer, take the bait. Jake was chewing on the tip of a plastic pen.

"Before?" Dyer asked, then caught himself. Never ask a question if you don't know the answer. "Strike that."

"Isn't it true, Mr. Gamble, that you deliberately and intentionally shot Stuart Kofer, with his own gun, one that you were familiar with, because he beat your mother?"

"No sir."

"Isn't it true, Mr. Gamble, that you deliberately and intentionally shot and killed Stuart Kofer because he was sexually molesting your sister?"

"No sir."

"Isn't it true, Mr. Gamble, that you willfully shot and killed Stuart Kofer because you hated the man and you were hoping that if he were dead, your mother would get to keep his house?"

"No sir."

"Isn't it true, Mr. Gamble, that when you leaned down and put the barrel an inch from his head, that at that crucial moment, Stuart Kofer was sound asleep?"

"I don't know if he was sound asleep. I know he'd been movin' around because I heard him. I was afraid he would get up and go crazy again. That's why I did what I did. To protect us."

"You saw him asleep in his own bed, and you took his own gun and put it an inch from his left temple, and you pulled the trigger, didn't you, Mr. Gamble?"

"I guess I did. I'm not sayin' I didn't. I'm not sure what I was thinkin' at that moment. I was so scared and I just knew he had killed my mother."

"But you were wrong, weren't you? He didn't kill your mother. She's sitting right there." Dyer turned and pointed an angry finger at Josie in the front row.

Drew summoned his own anger and said, "Well, he tried his best to kill her. She was on the floor, unconscious, and as far as we could tell she wasn't breathin'. She sure looked dead to us, Mr. Dyer."

"But you were wrong."

"And he had threatened to kill her many times, and us too. I thought it was the end."

"Had you ever thought about killing Stuart before?"

"No sir. I've never thought about killin' anybody. I don't have guns. I don't get in fights and stuff like that. I just wanted to leave and get away from that house before he hurt us. Livin' in a car again was better than livin' with Stuart."

Another one of Jake's lines, perfectly delivered.

"So, when you were in prison, you didn't get into fights?"

"I wasn't in prison, sir. I was in a juvenile detention facility. Prison is for adults. You should know that."

Noose leaned down and said, "Please, Mr. Gamble, hold your comments."

"Yes sir. Sorry, Mr. Dyer."

"And you never got into fights?"

"Everybody got into fights. Happened all the time."

Dyer was treading water and slowly drowning. Arguing with a sixteen-year-old was rarely productive, and at the moment Drew was gaining the upper hand. Dyer had been burned by both Josie and Kiera, and he preferred to avoid additional damage with the defendant. He looked at the bench and said, "Nothing further, Your Honor."

"Mr. Brigance."

"Nothing, Your Honor."

"Mr. Gamble, you may step down and return to the defense table. Mr. Brigance, please call your next witness."

At full volume, Jake announced, "Your Honor, the defense rests."

Noose flinched and appeared surprised. Harry Rex would later say that Lowell Dyer shot Musgrove a look of bewilderment.

The lawyers met at the bench where His Honor slid the mike away and addressed them in a whisper. "What's going on, Jake?" he demanded.

Jake shrugged and said, "We're done. No more witnesses."

"There are at least a dozen on your witness list."

"I don't need them, Judge."

"It just seems a little abrupt, that's all. Mr. Dyer? Any rebuttal witnesses?"

"I don't think so, Judge. If the defense is finished, so are we."

Noose glanced at his watch and said, "This being a capital case, the jury instructions will take some time and we can't get in a hurry. I'll recess now until nine in the morning. Y'all meet me in chambers in fifteen minutes and we'll hammer out the jury instructions."

49

Lucien invited the team to his house for dinner and would not accept no for an answer. With Sallie gone, and with absolutely no culinary skills of his own, he had leaned on Claude to prepare catfish po'boys, baked beans, sweet slaw, and a tomato salad. Claude owned the only black diner in downtown Clanton, and Jake ate lunch there almost every Friday, along with a few other white liberals in town. When the café had opened thirty years earlier, Lucien Wilbanks was there almost every day and insisted on sitting in the window to be seen by white folks passing by. He and Claude shared a long and colorful friendship.

Though he couldn't cook he could certainly pour, and Lucien served drinks on the front porch and encouraged his guests to sit in wicker rockers as the day came to a close. Carla had managed to find a last-minute babysitter because she rarely had dinner in Lucien's home and wasn't about to miss the chance. Portia was equally curious, though she really wanted to go home and get some sleep. Only Harry Rex begged off, claiming his battle-hardened secretaries were threatening a mutiny.

Dr. Thane Sedgwick from Baylor had just arrived in town in the event he would be needed to testify during sentencing. Libby had called him the day before with the news that the trial was moving much faster than anticipated. After a few sips of whiskey he was off and running. He said, in his thick Texas drawl, "And so I asked her if I would be needed. And she said no. She is not anticipating a conviction. Is she alone?"

"I don't see a conviction," Lucien said. "Nor an acquittal."

Libby said, "At least four of the five women are with us. Ms. Satterfield cried all day long, especially when Kiera was on the stand."

"And Kiera was effective?" Sedgwick asked.

"You have no idea," replied Libby. This led to a long replay of the epic day the Gamble family had in court as Josie and her children tag-teamed through their sad, chaotic history. Portia set the stage for Kiera's dramatic testimony about the father of her child. Lucien laughed when he repeated Drew's testimony about the nice foster homes where he didn't worry about getting slapped around. Libby was astonished at the way Jake had slowly brought out the details of all the miserable places the family had lived. Instead of dumping them all on the jury in his opening statement, he had carefully dropped one bomb after another, to great dramatic effect.

Jake sat next to Carla on an old sofa, with his arm over her shoulders, sipping wine and listening to the different perspectives on what he had seen and heard in court. He said little, his mind often wandering to the challenge of his closing argument. He worried about resting his case so abruptly, but the lawyers, Libby, Lucien, and Harry Rex, were convinced it was the right move. He had lost sleep worrying about putting his client on the stand, but young Drew made no mistakes. All in all, he was pleased with the case so far, but he kept reminding himself that his client was guilty of killing Stuart Kofer.

At dark they moved inside and settled around Lucien's handsome teak dining table. The house was old, but the interior decorating was modern, with plenty of glass and metal and odd accessories. The walls were adorned with a baffling collection of contemporary art, as if the king of the castle rejected everything old and traditional.

The king was enjoying his whiskey, as did Thane, and the war stories began, long tall tales of courtroom dramas over the years, all with the raconteur himself as the hero. Once Thane realized he probably wouldn't be needed on Thursday, he poured another drink and seemed ready for a late night.

Portia, being a young black woman who'd grown up on the other side of town, was not to be shut out. She told a startling story of a military murder she had worked on in the army in Germany. And that reminded Thane of a double murder somewhere in Texas in which the alleged killer was only thirteen.

By 10:30 Jake was ready for bed. He and Carla excused themselves and went home. At 2:00 A.M. he was still awake.

THE COURTROOM ROSE almost in unison to honor the appearance of Judge Omar Noose, who quickly waved them off and asked them to sit down. He welcomed the crowd, commented on the cooler temperature, said good morning to his jury and asked, gravely, if anyone had tried to contact any of them during the recess. All twelve jurors shook their heads. No.

Omar had presided over a thousand trials, and not once had a juror raised a hand to admit that he or she had been contacted out of court. If there was contact, it would probably involve the payment of cash, something no one would ever talk about in the first place. But Omar loved his traditions.

He explained that the next hour would probably be

the dullest portion of the entire trial because, as required by law, he would instruct the jury. He would read into the record, and for the benefit of the jurors, the black letter law, the state's statutes, that would dictate their deliberations. Their duty was to weigh the evidence and apply it to the law, and to take the law as it was written and apply it to the facts. Listen carefully. It was very important. And for their benefit, copies of the jury instructions would be available in the jury room.

When he had them thoroughly confused, Judge Noose began reading into his mike. Page after page of dry, verbose, complicated, badly written statutes that tried to define intent, murder, capital murder, murder of a law enforcement officer, premeditation, guilt, and justifiable homicide. They listened intently for about ten minutes, then began peeling off with glances around the courtroom. Some fought mightily to hang on every word. Others realized that they could read that stuff later if they wanted to.

After forty minutes Noose abruptly stopped, to the relief of everyone. He slapped his papers together, squared them up nicely, smiled at the jury as if he'd done a fine job, and said, "Now, ladies and gentlemen, both sides will be given the opportunity to make closing arguments. As always, the State goes first. Mr. Dyer."

Lowell stood with great purpose, buttoned the top button of his light blue seersucker jacket, and walked to the jury box—the podium was optional at that point—and began. "Ladies and gentlemen of the jury, this trial is almost over and it has moved along more efficiently than expected. Judge Noose has given each side thirty minutes to summarize things for you, but thirty minutes is far too long in this case. Half an hour is not needed to convince you of what you already know. You don't need that much time to decide that the defendant, Drew Allen Gamble, did indeed murder Stuart Kofer, an officer of the law."

A great opening, Jake thought. Any audience, whether twelve jurors in a box or two thousand lawyers at a convention, appreciates a speaker who promises to be brief.

"Let's talk about that murder. Tuesday morning, when we started, I asked you to ask yourselves, as you listened to the witnesses, if, at that horrible moment, did Drew Gamble have to pull the trigger? Why did he pull the trigger? Was it in self-defense? Was he protecting himself, his sister, his mother? No, ladies and gentlemen, it was not in self-defense. It was not justifiable. It was nothing but cold, calculated murder.

"Now, the defense has had a field day slandering the reputation of Stuart Kofer."

Jake jumped to his feet, raised both hands, and interrupted with, "Objection, Your Honor. Objection. I hate to disrupt a closing argument, Your Honor, but the use of the word 'slander' means the spreading of falsehoods. False testimony. And there is absolutely nothing in the record to even remotely indicate that any of the witnesses, for the State or for the defense, has lied."

Noose seemed ready for the interruption. "Mr. Dyer, I ask you to refrain from using the word 'slander.' And the jury will disregard the use of that word."

Dyer frowned and nodded, as if he was being forced to accept the ruling but didn't agree with it. "Very well, Your Honor," he replied.

"Now, you've heard a lot from the three Gambles about what a terrible person Stuart Kofer was, and I won't rehash any of it. Just keep in mind that they, the Gambles, have every reason, every motive to tell only one side of the story, and to perhaps embellish and exaggerate here and there. Tragically, Stuart is not here to defend himself.

"So let's not talk about the way he lived. You're not here to judge him or his lifestyle, his habits, his problems, his demons. Your job is to weigh the facts regarding the way he died."

Dyer stepped to the exhibit table and picked up the gun. He held it and faced the jury. "At some point during that terrible night, Drew Gamble took this gun, a Glock 22, forty caliber, fifteen in the magazine, issued by Sheriff Ozzie Walls to all of his deputies, and he held it and carried it around the house. At that moment, Stuart was sound asleep on his bed. He was drunk, as we know, but the alcohol had rendered him helpless. A blacked-out drunk, snoring away, not a threat to anyone. Drew Gamble held the gun and he knew how to use it because Stuart had taught him how to load it, hold it, aim it, and fire it. It's rather ironic, and tragic, that the killer was taught to use the murder weapon by the victim himself.

"I'm sure it was a terrible scene. Two frightened kids, their mother unconscious on the floor. Minutes passed and Drew Gamble had the gun. Stuart was asleep, in another world. An emergency call had been made, the police and rescue personnel were on the way.

"And at some point, Drew Gamble made the decision to kill Stuart Kofer. He walked to the bedroom, closed the door for some reason, and he took the gun and placed the barrel an inch or two from Stuart's left temple. Why did he pull the trigger? He claims he felt threatened, that Stuart might get up and harm them, and he had to protect himself and his sister. He wants you to believe that he had to pull the trigger."

Dyer slowly returned to the exhibit table and laid down the gun.

"But why then? Why not wait a moment, or two? Why not wait to see if Stuart was getting up? Drew had the gun. He was armed and ready to defend himself and his sister in the event Stuart somehow managed to revive himself and come after them. Why not wait until the police arrived? Why not wait?"

Dyer stood squarely before the jurors and looked at each one of them. "At that moment, he did not have to pull the trigger, ladies and gentlemen. But he did. And he did so because he wanted to kill Stuart Kofer. He wanted revenge for what happened to his mother. He wanted revenge for all the terrible things Stuart did to them. And revenge means premeditation, and that means the deliberate act to kill.

"Ladies and gentlemen, premeditation equals capital murder. Enough said. I urge you to retire for your deliberations and return a just and true verdict. The only verdict that fits this crime. A verdict of guilty for the capital murder of Stuart Kofer. Thank you."

It was a fine closing. Well planned, to the point, persuasive, and concise, something rare for a prosecutor in a big case. Not a single juror was bored. Indeed, each one seemed to follow every word.

"Mr. Brigance."

Jake stood and tossed his legal pad on the podium. He smiled at the jurors and looked at each one of them. About half watched him, the rest stared straight ahead. He began with "I don't blame the State for asking you to downplay much of what you've heard. It certainly isn't pleasant to talk about abuse, and rape, and domestic violence. They are ugly topics, awful things to discuss anywhere, especially in a courtroom with so many people listening. But I didn't create the facts, nor did you, nor did anyone but Stuart Kofer.

"The State tries to suggest, tries to imply, that perhaps the three Gambles are prone to embellish, to exaggerate. Seriously?" Suddenly, he raised his voice and was angry. He pointed at Kiera on the front row behind the defense table. "You see that little girl right there? Kiera Gamble, age fourteen and over seven months pregnant by Stuart Kofer? And do you think she's exaggerating?"

He took a deep breath and let the anger pass. "When you deliberate, look at the photo of Josie Gamble in the hospital, with her jaw shattered, her face bruised, her eyes swollen, and ask yourselves if she's embellishing. They're not lying to you. Quite the contrary, they could tell many more stories about the horror of living with Stuart Kofer.

"What happened to Stuart Kofer? What happened to the local boy who joined the army and wanted to make it a career before being asked to leave? What happened to the fine young deputy known for his bravery and his involvement with the community? Where did the dark side come from? Perhaps something happened in the army. Perhaps the pressure of his work got to him? We'll never know, I guess, but we can all agree that his loss is a tragedy.

"His dark side. We can't understand what makes a man, a big strong tough cop and ex-soldier, kick, hit, and slap around a woman who weighs a hundred and twenty pounds, breaking her bones, her teeth, busting her lips, knocking her unconscious, then threatening to kill her if she tells anyone. We can't understand why Kofer physically abused and threatened a skinny little kid like Drew. We can't understand how a man becomes a sexual predator and goes after a fourteen-year-old girl just because she's available, because she lives in his house. Nor can we understand how a man chooses to drink himself, time and time again, into a state of raging violence and unconsciousness. We can't understand how an officer of the law, one known to be tough on drunk drivers, could spend the whole day drinking and saturate himself with alcohol to the point of passing out, then waking up and deciding it's okay to get behind the wheel of a car. Point-three-six."

Jake paused and shook his head as if disgusted by the ugliness of his own words. All twelve were staring at him, all uncomfortable at the ugliness.

"His house. A house that became a living hell for Josie and her kids. A house they wanted so badly to leave but had nowhere to go. A house that grew more terrifying each weekend. A house that was like a powder keg, where the stress and pressure mounted day by day until it became inevitable that someone was going to get hurt. A house that was so awful that Josie's kids were begging her to leave.

"Now, the prosecution wants you to ignore all this, and concentrate instead on the last ten seconds of Stuart's life. Mr. Dyer suggests that Drew should have waited. And waited. But waited for what? There was no one to help them. They had waited before for the police to come. They came all right, but they didn't help. They had waited for weeks and months, desperately hoping that Kofer would find help and get a handle on his drinking and his temper. They had waited for hours during those long, terrifying nights, waiting for the headlights of Stuart's car in the driveway, waiting to see if he could actually walk himself into his house, waiting for the inevitable fight. They had waited all right, and the waiting only brought them closer to disaster.

"Okay, I'll take the bait. Let's talk about the last ten seconds. As his mother lay unconscious and apparently dead, and with his sister tending to her and pleading with her to wake up, and with Kofer making noises in the bedroom, my client felt a fear and a danger that was unbearable. He feared great bodily harm, even death, not only for himself but for his sister, and he had to do something. It is wrong to take those last ten seconds and dissect them here in this courtroom, some five months after the crime, and far, far removed from the horror of the scene, and say, well he should have done this or he should have done that. Not a single one of us can know or predict what we would do in a situation like that. It's impossible.

"However, what we do know is that we will take extraordinary measures to protect ourselves and those we love. And that's exactly what my client did."

He paused and took in the stillness of the courtroom and the rapt attention from everyone watching and listening. He lowered his voice and took a step closer to the jurors. "Josie and her kids have had a chaotic life. She was very honest about her mistakes and she would do anything to go back and do it all over. They haven't had much luck, if any. And look at them now. Drew is on trial for his life. Kiera is pregnant after being raped repeatedly. What kind of future do they have? I ask you, ladies and gentlemen, to show a little mercy, a little compassion. When you and I leave here we'll go home and get on with our lives, and with time this trial will become a fading memory. They're not so lucky. I plead with you for compassion, for understanding, for mercy to allow this sad little family—Drew, Kiera, Josie—the chance to rebuild their own lives. I plead with you to find Drew Allen Gamble not guilty. Thank you."

WHEN THE JURY was gone, Judge Noose said, "We'll be in recess until two o'clock, at which time we'll reconvene and check the status of the deliberations." He tapped his gavel and disappeared.

Jake walked over and shook hands with Lowell Dyer and D. R. Musgrove and congratulated them on a fine job. Most of the spectators drifted out of the courtroom, but some stayed, as if waiting for a quick verdict. The Kofer gang didn't budge and whispered among themselves. Drew was led away by three deputies and taken to his holding place, the meeting room of the Van Buren County Board of Supervisors.

Morris Finley's mother lived on the family farm, deep in the countryside, ten miles from the courthouse. He met the defense team there for a pleasant lunch on a shaded patio with a lovely view of pastures and the pond where he had learned to swim. Mrs. Finley had been recently widowed and lived alone, and she relished the chance to throw a big lunch for Morris and his friends.

Over grilled chicken salads and ice tea, they rehashed the closing arguments and compared notes on the facial reactions and body language of the jurors. Harry Rex ate quickly and left to get to his office in Clanton, but Lucien hung around. He had little else to do and wanted to hear the verdict. "They're all hung up," he said, more than once.

Jake couldn't eat and was exhausted. A trial was nothing but stress, but the worst part was waiting for the jury.

50

The first fight was verbal, though another angry word or two and it could have easily escalated into a punching match. It erupted over lunch when John Carpenter, juror number five, and without a doubt the one most feared by the defense, resumed his aggressive push to be elected foreman. By then the deliberations were hardly an hour old and Carpenter had done most of the talking. The other eleven were already tired of him. The twelve of them sat around a long table, eating quickly, choking down sandwiches, not sure what to do next because the tension was already palpable.

Carpenter said, "Well, does anybody else want to be foreman? I mean, look, if nobody else wants it then I'll do the job."

Joey Kepner said, "I don't think you should be the foreman, because you're not impartial."

"The hell I'm not!" he shot across the table.

"You are not impartial."

"Who the hell are you?" Carpenter said loudly.

"It's pretty obvious you've already made up your mind."

"I have not."

"Your mind was made up Monday," said Lois Satterfield.

"It was not!"

"We heard what you said about the girl," Joey said.

"So what? You want the job, hell, you be the foreman, but I'm not voting for you."

"And I'm not voting for you!" Joey yelled. "You shouldn't even be on the jury."

The two bailiffs tending to the jury stood just outside the door and looked at each other. The loud voices were easily heard and seemed to be getting louder. They opened the door, stepped quickly inside, and things were instantly silent.

"Can we get you anything?" one bailiff asked.

"No, we're fine," Carpenter said.

"So you can speak for all of us?" Joey asked. "Just like that. You're our self-appointed spokesman. Sir, I'd like some coffee."

"Sure," said a bailiff. "Anything else?"

Carpenter glared at Joey with hatred. They ate in silence as coffee was served. When the bailiffs left, Regina Elmore, juror number six, a thirty-eight-year-old housewife from Chester, said, "Okay, this appears to be just another boy fight. I'll be happy to serve as foreman if that will settle things down."

Joey said, "Good. You have my vote. Let's make it unanimous."

Carpenter shrugged and said, "Whatever."

One bailiff stood by the door while the other reported to Judge Noose.

AN HOUR LATER they were yelling again. An angry male voice said, "I'll kick your ass when this is over!" Another responded, "Why wait? Just do it now!"

The bailiffs knocked loudly as they entered and found John Carpenter standing on one side of the table being restrained by two men. On the other side Joey Kepner was standing, red-faced and braced for hand-to-hand combat. They relaxed somewhat and stood down.

The tension was so thick in the room that the bailiffs were eager to leave. They reported again to Judge Noose.

AT 2:00 P.M. the lawyers and spectators gathered again. The defendant was brought in. A bailiff whispered to Jake and Lowell that the judge wanted to see them in chambers, just the two of them.

Noose was at his conference table, without his robe, and smoking a pipe. He looked troubled as he waved the lawyers in and gestured at their seats. His first words were music to Jake's ears.

"Gentlemen, it appears as though the jury is at war. The bailiffs have had to break up two fights in the first three hours. I'm afraid this does not bode well for the trial."

Dyer's shoulders sagged as Jake tried to suppress a smile. Neither spoke because neither had been asked to speak.

Noose continued, "I'm going to do something that I've done only once in my many years on the bench. It has been frowned on by our Supreme Court but not disallowed."

The court reporter knocked and entered, followed by a bailiff and Regina Elmore. Noose said, "Ms. Elmore, I understand you've been chosen as the foreman."

"Yes sir."

"Good. This is an informal hearing but I want the court reporter to record it all, just to have it. The lawyers, Mr. Dyer and Mr. Brigance, will not be allowed to say anything, which will be painful for them."

Everyone snickered. Ha, ha. How clever. Regina appeared rattled and uncertain.

"Now, I don't want you to name names, or to tell us

how you see this case, or how the jury is leaning. But I know there is some conflict back there and I feel the need to intervene. Is the jury making progress?"

"No sir."

"Why not?"

She took a deep breath and looked at Noose, then Jake, then Lowell. She swallowed hard and began, "Okay, now, I can't use names, right?"

"That's correct."

"Okay. There is one guy back there who shouldn't be on the jury. Let me go back to something that he said yesterday. Is that okay?"

"Yes. Go on."

"After Kiera testified yesterday morning, we were having lunch, and this guy made a crude comment to another man on the jury. They kinda stick together. And I assure you, Judge, we have heard your warnings and there has been no discussion of the case until, well, until yesterday."

"What was the crude comment?"

"Referring to Kiera, he said Kofer probably wasn't the father since the girl probably started screwing, pardon my language, when she was twelve, just like her mother. The other guy laughed. Most of us did not. I heard it and I was appalled. Almost immediately, Joey, oh, I'm sorry, I used his name. Sorry, Judge."

"That's okay. Keep going."

"Joey didn't like his comment and called him out. He said we're not supposed to be talking about the case, and they went back and forth for a few minutes. It was pretty tense. Neither guy will back down. And so today, as soon as we retired, this guy tried to take over, wanted to be the foreman, wanted to vote immediately. It's obvious he wants a guilty verdict and the death penalty. He wants the kid strung up tomorrow."

Jake and Lowell were fascinated by her narrative. They had never heard a juror discuss deliberations before reaching a verdict. Jurors could be contacted after the trial and quizzed about what happened, though most declined. But to hear a firsthand account of what was happening in the jury room was mesmerizing.

Obviously, Jake was far more pleased with her story than Lowell.

She continued, "Personally, I don't think he should be on the jury. He is a bully and tries to intimidate us, especially the women, which is why he and Joey are clashing. He's abusive and vulgar and dismissive of any argument he disagrees with. I don't think he approached his jury service with an open and impartial mind."

Noose could not remove a juror until he or she did something wrong, and swearing to be impartial while holding a secret bias was not unusual.

He said, "Thank you, Ms. Elmore. In your opinion, will it be possible for this jury to reach a unanimous verdict?"

She actually laughed at the judge, not out of disrespect, but out of surprise at such an absurd question. "Sorry, Judge. But no. First we went through all the exhibits, like you said, then we read the instructions again, just like you told us to. And this one guy, same guy, started pushing for a vote. Finally, after lunch, and after he and Joey were separated the first time, we voted."

"And?"

"Six–six, Judge, with no wiggle room anywhere. We're even sitting on opposite sides of the table now. You can keep us here until the cows come home, but it's a hard six–six. Me, I won't vote to convict that boy of anything, not after what Kofer did to them."

The judge showed her his palms and said, "That's

enough. Thank you again, Ms. Elmore. You are free to go."

"Back to the jury room?"

"Yes ma'am."

"Judge, please, I really don't want to go back in there. I can't stand that nasty man and I'm tired of him. All of us are, even the ones who agree with him. It's pretty toxic in there, Judge."

"Well, we have to keep trying, don't we?"

"There's gonna be a fight, I'm warning you."

"Thank you."

After she left, Noose nodded at the court reporter who hustled out of the room too. Alone with the lawyers, Noose relit his pipe, blew some smoke, and looked thoroughly defeated.

He said, "I'm looking for some brilliant advice, gentlemen."

Dyer, eager to salvage his case, said, "Why not excuse Kepner and the bad guy and replace them with the two alternates?"

Noose nodded. It was a decent idea. "Jake?"

"Kepner is obviously in our camp and he's done nothing wrong. That might be a tough one to defend on appeal."

"Agreed," said Noose. "They were properly chosen. I can't dismiss them because they're arguing too strenuously. We can't quit after only three hours of deliberation, gentlemen. Let's meet in the courtroom in five minutes."

With great effort, Jake managed to continue to suppress a smile as he entered the courtroom and sat next to his client. He leaned back and whispered to Portia, "Six–six." Her jaw dropped before she caught herself.

There were no smiles either from the jurors as they filed in and took their seats. Noose watched them carefully and when they were settled, he said, "Ladies and gentlemen, the court has been advised that you appear to be deadlocked."

There were noises from the spectators—gasps, murmurs, shifting.

His Honor then unloaded what was commonly referred to as the Dynamite Charge: "Each of you took an oath to weigh the evidence with an open and impartial mind, to bring no personal biases or preferences into the courtroom, and to follow the law as I have given it to you. I now instruct you to return to your deliberations and do your duty. I want each of you, regardless of how you now feel about this case, to begin anew from the position of accepting the opposing view. For a moment, look at the other side and tell yourselves that it might just be the correct one. If you now believe Drew Gamble to be guilty, then, for a moment, tell yourself that he is not, and defend that position. Same if you believe he is not guilty. Look at the other side. Accept the other arguments. Go back to square one, all of you, and begin a new round of deliberations with the goal of agreeing on a final, unanimous verdict in this case. We are in no hurry, and if this takes several days then so be it. I have no patience with a hung jury. If you fail, then this case will be tried again, and I assure you that the next jury will not be any smarter, or better informed, or more impartial, than you are. Right now you're the best we have and you are certainly up to the task. I expect nothing less than your full cooperation and unanimous verdict. You may retire to the jury room."

Chastened, but unmoved, the jurors retreated like first graders headed for the time-out chair.

"In recess until four P.M."

———

THE DEFENSE TEAM huddled at the end of a cramped hallway on the first floor. They were elated but tempered their desire to celebrate.

Jake said, "Noose brought in the foreman, Regina Elmore. She said they've had two fights and expects more. Nobody's giving an inch. She described the split as 'a hard six–six' and said everybody wants to go home."

Carla asked, "What will happen at four?"

"Who knows? If they make it until then without killing each other, I expect Noose to lecture them again, maybe send them home for the night."

"And you'll move for a mistrial?" Lucien asked.

"Yes."

Carla said, "Well, I'm going to get our daughter. See you at home." She kissed Jake on the cheek and left. Jake looked at Portia, Libby, and Thane Sedgwick, and said, "You guys kill some time. I'm going to see Drew."

He walked to another hallway and found Moss Junior Tatum and a local deputy sitting in chairs outside the meeting room of the Board of Supervisors. He said to them, "I'd like to see my client." Moss Junior shrugged and opened the door.

Drew was sitting alone at the end of a long table with his jacket off, reading a Hardy Boys mystery. Jake sat across from him and said, "How you doing, pal?"

"Okay. Kinda tired of this crap."

"Yeah, me too."

"What's happening out there?"

"Looks like a hung jury."

"What does that mean?"

"It means you won't be found guilty, which is a major win for us. It also means they'll take you back to the jail in Clanton and you'll wait there for another trial."

"So we have to do this again?"

"In all likelihood, yes. Probably a few months from now. I'll try my best to get you out, but that's not likely."

"Great. And I'm supposed to be happy with this?"

"Yes. It could be a lot worse."

Jake pulled out a deck of cards and said, "How about some blackjack?"

Drew smiled and said, "Sure."

"What's the score?"

"You've won seven hundred and eighteen games. I've won nine hundred and eighty. You currently owe me two dollars and sixty-two cents."

"I'll pay you when you get out," Jake said, and he shuffled the deck.

AT FOUR, THEY filed in, angry and defeated, and took their seats, careful not to brush against each other. Three of the men immediately folded their arms across their chests and glared at Jake and his client. Two of the women were red-eyed and just wanted to go home. Joey Kepner glanced at Libby with a confident smirk.

His Honor said, "Ms. Elmore, as foreman, I ask you if the jury has made any progress since two o'clock. Keep your seat."

"No sir, not at all. Things have just gotten worse."

"And what is the vote?"

"Six guilty of capital murder, six not guilty on all charges."

Noose stared at them as if they had disobeyed him, and said, "Okay. I'm going to poll the jury by asking each of you one question. A simple yes or no will suffice. Nothing more is needed. Juror number one, Mr.

Bill Scribner, in your opinion, can this jury reach a unanimous verdict?"

"No sir," came the quick response.

"Number two, Mr. Lenny Poole?"

"No sir."

"Number three, Mr. Slade Kingman?"

"No."

"Number four, Ms. Harriet Rydell?"

"No sir."

All twelve responded firmly in the negative, their body language more emphatic than their verbal responses.

Noose took a long pause as he scribbled some meaningless notes. He looked at the prosecutor and said, "Mr. Dyer."

Lowell stood and said, "Judge, it's been a long day. I suggest we recess now, let the jurors go home and rest on this for a few hours, come back in the morning and try again."

Most if not all of the jurors shook their heads in disagreement.

"Mr. Brigance."

Jake said, "Your Honor, the defense moves for a mistrial and the dismissal of all charges against the defendant."

Noose said, "It appears as if further deliberations will be a waste of time. Motion granted. I declare a mistrial. The defendant will remain in the custody of the Ford County sheriff." He rapped his gavel loudly and left the bench.

AN HOUR LATER, Libby Provine and Thane Sedgwick left the courthouse and headed for the airport in Memphis. Lucien was already gone. Jake and Portia loaded their files and boxes into the trunk of the new Impala and headed to Oxford, forty-five minutes away. They parked on the square and went to a burger joint, one of Jake's favorites from his college days. It was the ninth of August and the students were trickling back to town. In two weeks, Portia would be back as a first-year law student and she was counting the days. After two years as Jake's secretary and paralegal, she was leaving the firm and Jake had no idea what he would do without her.

Over beers they talked about law school, not the trial. Anything but the trial.

At seven sharp, Josie and Kiera walked in smiling; hugs all around. They gathered at a table and ordered sandwiches and fries. Josie had a thousand questions and Jake patiently answered as many as possible. The truth was that he didn't know what would happen to Drew. He would certainly be re-indicted on the same charges, and there would be another trial. When? Where? Jake didn't know.

They would worry about that tomorrow.

51

Late Friday morning, Jake grew weary of the unanswered phone ringing incessantly and decided to leave his gloomy office. Portia had the day off, at his insistence, and no one else was there. The calls were coming from reporters, and a few lawyer pals who wanted to chat, and several strangers who did nothing but rant without identifying themselves. There were no calls from potential new clients. He listened to the messages as they came in and realized that work was impossible. He reminded himself that in the business of criminal law a mistrial was a victory. The State, with all its resources, had failed to meet its burden. His client was still not guilty, and Jake was pleased with the defense he had mounted. But the State would be back, and Drew would be tried again, and again if necessary. There was no limit on the number of hung juries a defendant could face for a crime, and the murder of a police officer would keep the same indictments coming for years. But, that was not an altogether depressing thought. Jake had found his home in the old courtroom. He had thrived on the pressure. His witnesses had been thoroughly prepared and performed beautifully. His strategies and ambushes had worked to perfection. His appeals to the jury had been carefully rehearsed and nicely delivered. Most importantly, Jake had reached the point of not giving a damn about what others thought. The police, the opposing lawyers, the crowd watching, the entire community. He didn't care.

His job was to fight for his client, regardless of how unpopular the cause.

He walked down the street, ducked into the Coffee Shop, and found Dell at the counter drying glasses. He gave her a quick hug and they huddled in a booth in the rear.

"You hungry?" she asked.

"No. Just coffee."

She went to the counter, returned with a pot, filled two cups, sat down and asked, "How you doing?"

"I'm good. It's a win but it's only temporary."

"I hear they'll do it again."

"I'm sure you've heard a lot this week."

She laughed and said, "Yes, I have. Prather and Looney were in this morning and there was plenty of talk."

"Let me guess. Brigance pulled another slick one and got the boy off."

"Several versions of that, yes. The guys were pretty ticked off because you kept them in court all week over there under subpoena, then didn't call them to the stand."

Jake shrugged it off. "That's part of their job. They'll get over it."

"Sure they will. Prather said you ambushed them with the pregnant girl, said you kept her in hiding."

"It was a fair fight, Dell. Lowell Dyer got out-lawyered and the facts fell our way. And the boy's still in jail."

"Can he get out?"

"I doubt it. He should get out, you know? He's still innocent until proven guilty. Was that ever mentioned?"

"No, of course not. They said the testimony was pretty ugly, said you made Kofer look like a monster."

"I didn't change a single fact, Dell. And yes, Stuart Kofer got what he deserved."

"Old man Hitchcock stood up for you. Said that if he ever got in trouble you'd be the first lawyer he called."

"That's just what I need—another client who can't pay a dime."

"It's not all bad, Jake. You still have some friends here, and on some level there's a certain amount of admiration for your skills in the courtroom."

"That's nice to hear, Dell, but I really don't care anymore. I've starved for twelve years because I've worried about the gossip. Those days are over. I'm tired of starving."

She squeezed his hand and said, "I'm proud of you, Jake."

The bell on the door rattled and a couple walked in. Dell smiled at him and left to see what they wanted. Jake stepped to the counter and picked up a copy of the Tupelo paper. He returned to the booth and sat with his back to the door. There was a photo of Drew on the front page, under the headline: "Judge Declares Mistrial After Jury Splits." He had read the story hours earlier and didn't need to read it again. So he flipped to the sports page and read a preview of the SEC football season.

PORTIA WAS AT her desk clipping newspaper articles. Jake walked in and asked, "What are you doing here?"

"Got bored just sitting around the house. Plus, Momma's in a mood this morning. I really can't wait to get out and go to law school."

Jake laughed and sat across from her. "What are you doing?"

"Putting together your scrapbook. You gonna talk to

any of these reporters? All the articles say: 'Mr. Brigance had no comment.'"

"Mr. Brigance has nothing to say, and the case is not over."

"Well, you sure had plenty to say back in the Hailey trial. I've read your file full of clippings for that one, and Mr. Brigance thoroughly enjoyed talking to reporters back then."

"I've learned. Lawyers should stick with 'No comment,' but they find it impossible. Never stand between a hotshot lawyer and a television camera. It's dangerous."

She shoved the clippings away and said, "Look, I know I've said this before, but I want to say it again before I leave. What you and Judge Atlee did with the Hubbard money was just wonderful. Because of the education fund, me and my cousins get to go to college. My law school is paid for, Jake, and I'll always be thankful."

"You're welcome. It's not my money, I just get to control the checkbook."

"Well, you're a great trustee, and we appreciate it."

"Thank you. It's an honor to dole out the money for worthy students."

"I'm gonna do well in law school, Jake, I promise. And when I finish I'm coming back here to work."

"Looks like you're already hired. You've had this office for two years and most of the time you act like you own the place."

"I've even learned to like Lucien, which, as we know, is not that easy."

"He likes you, Portia, and he wants you here. But you'll get offers from big firms. Things are changing and they're looking for diversity. You perform too well in law school and they'll throw money at you."

"I have no interest in that. I want to be in the court-room, Jake, like you, helping people, my people. You gave me the chance to sit through that trial, just like I was a real lawyer. You've inspired me."

"Thanks, but let's not get too carried away. I may have won the case, but I'm broker now than before I met Drew Gamble. And he's not going away."

"Yeah, but you'll survive, Jake. Won't you?"

"I will, somehow."

"Well, you gotta hang on until I finish law school."

"I'll be here. And I'll need you over the next three years. There's always plenty of research to do." Jake glanced at his watch and smiled. "Hey, it's Friday, white folks' day at Claude's. Let's do a firm lunch."

"Can the firm afford one?"

"No," he said with a laugh. "But Claude will extend credit."

"Let's go."

They walked around the square to the restaurant and arrived just before the noon crowd. Claude hugged them both and pointed to a table near the window. He had never seen the need to invest in printed menus, and his customers were offered whatever he happened to be cooking, usually ribs, catfish, barbecue chicken, baked beans with plenty of vegetables.

Jake spoke to an elderly couple he had known since high school. No one seemed even remotely interested in the Gamble trial. Portia ordered ribs and Jake was in the mood for catfish. They sipped sweet tea and watched the place fill up.

"A question," she said. "Something has been bother-ing me."

"Let's hear it."

"I've read all of the reports from the Hailey trial, five years ago. You did an interview with a Mr. McKittrick from *The New York Times,* and you gave a fairly spirited defense of the death penalty. You said, among other things, that the problem with the gas chamber was that it wasn't used often enough. I know you don't feel that way now. What happened?"

Jake smiled and watched the foot traffic on the sidewalk. "Carl Lee happened. Once I got to know him, and his family, it hit me pretty hard that he could well be convicted and sent to Parchman for ten or fifteen years while I fought his appeals, and that one day the State would strap him down and turn on the gas. I couldn't live with that. As his lawyer, I would spend his last moments with him in the holding room, next door to the gas chamber, probably with a minister or a chaplain, and then they would take him away. I would walk around a corner to a witness room and sit with Gwen, his wife, and Lester, his brother, and probably other family members, and we would watch him die. I lost sleep with those nightmares. I studied the history of the death penalty, really for the first time in my life, and saw the obvious problems. The unfairness, the inequalities, the waste of time, money, and lives. I'm also struck by the moral quandary. We treasure life and can all agree that it is wrong to kill, so why do we allow ourselves, through the state, to legally kill people? So, I changed my mind. I guess it's part of growing up, of living, of maturing. It's only natural to question our beliefs."

Claude practically tossed the two baskets on the table and said, "You got thirty minutes."

"Forty-five," Jake said, but he was already gone.

"Why do so many white people love the death penalty?" Portia asked.

"It's in the water. We grow up with it. We hear it at home, at church, at school, among friends. This is the Bible Belt, Portia, eye for an eye and all that."

"What about the New Testament and Jesus's sermons on forgiveness?"

"It's not convenient. He also preached love first, tolerance, acceptance, equality. But most Christians I know are quite good at cherry-picking their way through the Holy Scriptures."

"And not just white Christians," she said with a laugh. They ate for a few minutes and enjoyed Claude's verbal assaults on three black gentlemen in nice suits. One made the mistake of asking to see a menu. They were laughing by the time the abuse was over.

All tables were taken by 12:15 and Jake counted seven other white folks, not that it mattered. For a brief interlude, good food was more important than skin color. Portia ate in small bites with perfect manners. She was twenty-six now, and thanks to the army had seen more of the world than Jake or anyone he knew. She was also having trouble finding a suitable boyfriend.

"You gotta boy?" he asked, looking for trouble.

"No, and don't ask." She took a bite and looked around. "What are the prospects in law school?"

"Black or white?"

"Come on, Jake. If I brought a white boy home my family would go nuts. Surely there'll be some talent in law school."

"I doubt it. I finished twelve years ago and we had three blacks in our class."

"Let's talk about something else," she said. "You sound like Momma. Always pecking away about me not getting married. I remind her that she got married and look how that turned out." Her father, Simeon Lang, had a rough history and was currently serving time for vehicular homicide. Her mother, Lettie, had divorced him two years earlier.

Claude walked by and frowned at their baskets. He glanced at his wristwatch as if they were out of time.

"How are we supposed to enjoy lunch under this much pressure?" Jake asked him.

"You're doin' a pretty good job. Hurry up, though, I got folks waitin' outside."

They finished and Jake left a $20 bill on the table. Claude did not accept credit cards or checks and the town loved to speculate about how much money he made. He had a nice house in the country, drove a beautiful Cadillac, and had sent three kids to college. It was generally assumed that his disdain for printed menus, receipts, and credit cards also extended to the notion of income taxation.

On the sidewalk, Jake said, "I think I'll walk over to the jail and sit with Drew for an hour or so. Kid's cleaning my clock in blackjack and I need to get my money back."

"Such a sweet boy. Can't we get him out, Jake?"

"It's not likely. Can you visit him tomorrow? He really likes you, Portia."

"Sure. I'll make some brownies and take 'em over. The jailers love my double fudge. Not that they need any."

"I'll be back in a couple of hours."

"Whatever, Jake. You're the boss, for now anyway."

52

Monday morning, Jake finished tallying up his hours and expenses for the defense of Drew Gamble, and faxed his bill to the Honorable Omar Noose.

Since the judge's first phone call on Sunday, March 25, the actual date of Stuart Kofer's death, Jake detailed 320 hours, or about a third of his total time. He added 100 hours for Portia's work, and he billed every possible minute related to the case—driving time, phone time, everything. He padded his time sheets generously and did so with no guilt. The approved rate for court-appointed work was only $50 an hour, a paltry sum for any lawyer's time. The most expensive attorney in town was rumored to be Walter Sullivan, who boasted of charging $200 an hour. The corporate firms in Jackson and Memphis were billing as much. Two years earlier, in the Seth Hubbard will contest, Judge Atlee had approved $150 an hour for Jake, and he considered himself worth every penny.

Fifty bucks an hour barely covered his overhead.

His total was $21,000, or $20,000 more than the statute allowed for capital murder, and as he submitted it he doubted he would ever see the money. For that reason alone, the thought of a retrial was depressing.

What was a reasonable fee? It was difficult to say because people of means were rarely indicted for murder. Three years earlier, a wealthy farmer over in the Delta was charged with killing his wife with a twelve-gauge. He hired a well-known trial lawyer and was acquitted. The fee was rumored to have been $250,000.

Those were the cases Jake wanted.

Thirty minutes later, Judge Noose was on the phone. Jake swallowed hard and took the call. "Seems reasonable to me," His Honor said. "You did a fine job, Jake."

Relieved, Jake thanked him and asked, "What's next, Judge?"

"I'm faxing your bill to Todd Tannehill right now with instructions to tell the board to write a check."

Give 'em hell, Judge. He thanked him again and hung up. The Board would decline, and the plan was for Jake to then sue the county in circuit court, Omar Noose presiding.

An hour later, Todd Tannehill called. Todd was a good lawyer and had been the attorney for the Board of Supervisors for many years. Jake had always liked him and they had even gone duck hunting together. Todd said, "Congratulations on the win, Jake."

"Thanks, but it's only temporary."

"Yeah, I know. Look, the fee is quite reasonable and I'd love to write you a check, but there's this statute staring us in the face."

"I'm looking at it too."

"Well, I'll submit the bill. The Board meets this afternoon and I'll put this at the top of the agenda, but we both know the Board will decline. Noose said you'll probably sue the county."

"That's always an option."

"Good luck. I'll get the ball rolling."

TUESDAY MORNING, Jake received a faxed letter from Tannehill.

Dear Mr. Brigance:

On Monday, August 13, the Ford County Board of Supervisors was presented with a bill for your court-appointed services in the defense of Drew Gamble. Your request exceeds the amount authorized by state law. Therefore, the Board has no choice but to decline to pay your bill. At your request, the Board will pay the statutory maximum of $1000.

Regretfully,
TODD TANNEHILL

Jake prepared a simple one-page lawsuit against the county and showed it to Lucien, who was in his room downstairs. He loved it and said, "Well, if these God-fearing creatures around here love the death penalty so much they can certainly pay for it."

Because Dumas Lee combed the court records each Tuesday afternoon in search of news, Jake decided to wait a day or so before filing. The newspaper went to press at ten each Tuesday night, and the next day's edition would undoubtedly scream about the mistrial in the Kofer murder. A story about Jake suing the county for his fees would just add fuel to the fire.

LOWELL DYER SHOWED no such restraint. On Tuesday afternoon, he convened the grand jury in a special session and walked them through the murder once again. Ozzie testified and produced the same crime scene photos. In a unanimous vote, Drew Gamble was re-indicted for capital murder and served with papers in his cell. Dyer called Jake afterward and the conversation was tense.

Not that the timing really mattered. The fresh indictment was expected. And with a possible reelection looming, Dyer needed to do something dramatic to mitigate his defeat.

EARLY WEDNESDAY MORNING, Jake read the *Times* over coffee with Carla. There was hardly enough room on the front page for all the bold headlines about the hung jury, and the photos, and the breathless reporting by Dumas. The new indictment was on page two. Still no comment from Mr. Brigance.

ON THURSDAY MORNING, Jake filed his lawsuit against the county. He also sued the estate of Stuart Kofer for $50,000 for Josie's medical bills, along with some extra for her pain and suffering. Two other lawsuits were being discussed around the office. One was his own against Cecil Kofer for medical expenses from the beating. The other was another suit against Stuart's estate for Kiera's care and treatment, as well as support for her child, yet unborn.

The suing was therapeutic.

Portia was cooking up a lawsuit of her own. Jake, like most small-town practitioners, never dealt with habeas corpus cases. Habeas work was almost exclusively done by lawyers representing prisoners claiming to be wrongfully detained, and virtually all of it was in federal court. But, as she learned, there was no prohibition against seeking habeas relief in state court. Late Thursday, she presented Jake with a lawsuit and a thick brief to support it. He looked at the heading—*Drew Allen Gamble v. Ozzie Walls, Sheriff of Ford County*—and said with a smile, "We're suing Ozzie now?"

"That's right. Habeas lawsuits are filed against the person holding the plaintiff. It's usually the warden of some prison."

"That should make his day."

"He's not on the hook for any damages. It's more of a formality."

"And in state court?"

"That's right. We have to exhaust all state remedies before we can go to federal court."

Jake read on, smiling. The lawsuit alleged that Drew was being unlawfully detained because the court (Judge Noose) considered the charge of capital murder to be a non-bailable offense. He had served over four months in the county jail while presumably innocent. The State had tried to convict him and failed. Because of his age, he was being held in solitary confinement and being denied educational opportunities.

"I love it," Jake mumbled as he read. Portia beamed proudly at her handiwork. At the rate Jake was suing, there was little doubt he would file it promptly.

Ford County and the Twenty-second Circuit Court were violating the Eighth Amendment's prohibition against cruel and unusual punishment by incarcerating a minor in an adult jail with no chance of making bail.

Jake put down the lawsuit and picked up her supporting brief. As he began to read it, she said, "It's just a rough draft. Still got some work to do."

"It's brilliant. You don't need law school."

"Great. Just get me a license."

He read slowly, flipping the pages, kept smiling. When he finished, she handed him more papers.

"What's this?" he asked.

"The federal lawsuit. Once Noose says no, then we run to federal court where the judges know a lot more about habeas corpus."

"Yeah, they hate it."

"True, but they hate it because they are inundated with filings from jailhouse lawyers who have little else to do. Every inmate has a beef, whether it's a legitimate claim of innocence or a rant about leaky toilets and bad food, so they flood the courts with habeas petitions. This is different and might just be taken seriously."

"Same allegations?"

"Yes, pretty much the same lawsuit."

Jake put it down and stood and stretched. She watched him and said, "And I think you should ask Noose to recuse himself. After all, he's part of the problem because he won't consider an appropriate bond. We should ask for another judge, one from outside the district."

"Oh, that'll make him happy. Here's an idea. I have a meeting with Noose in the morning, with Dyer, post-trial stuff. He's in town for first appearances and bail hearings. What if I show him and Dyer the habeas petition, with the brief, and threaten to file it here, then take it to federal court if necessary?"

"Has he ever seen a habeas petition?"

"I doubt it. I'll suggest a recusal and demand an expedited hearing. He knows it'll get to the press and he might want to avoid the hassle. Dyer can bitch and moan and posture for the public. The end game is to pressure Noose to set a reasonable bond so our client can bail out."

"How can Drew afford any bond?"

"Great question. Let's worry about that when the time comes."

53

The courtroom was busy at nine on Friday morning as lawyers milled about and gossiped and told stale jokes. Families of freshly indicted young men watched from the pews and worried. Clerks scurried about with paperwork and flirted with the lawyers. Jake was the man of the hour and several of his rivals were forced to offer congratulations on the win over in Chester. This stopped, however, when Lowell Dyer arrived on behalf of the State.

A bailiff fetched Jake and Todd Tannehill and said His Honor wanted them in chambers. Noose was waiting, standing and stretching and in obvious discomfort, when they walked in. He greeted them warmly with handshakes all around and pointed to the chairs at the table. When seated, he said, "We have a busy docket this morning, gentlemen, so let's get right to the point. Jake, you've filed your lawsuit for your fees. Todd, how soon can you file your answer?"

"Real soon, Judge."

"I'm afraid that's not good enough. The complaint is a simple one-pager, a real rarity in this business, with Jake's bill attached. I'm sure your answer will be even briefer. Denials all around. Right?"

"Afraid so, Judge."

"You've consulted with your clients and I assume all five supervisors are in agreement."

"Yes sir."

"Good. I want you to hustle back to your office,

prepare a one-page answer, bring it back over here, and file it while I work through my docket."

"File it today?"

"No sir. File it before lunch. The trial will be set for next Thursday in this courtroom, a bench trial with me presiding. Jake, do you anticipate calling any witnesses?"

"No sir. I really don't need any."

"Nor do you, Todd. It will be a very short trial. I want all five of the supervisors in the courtroom. Jake, subpoena them if you have to."

"That won't be necessary, Your Honor," Todd said. "I'll get 'em here."

"Okay, but if one fails to show, then I'll issue a warrant."

Todd was taken aback, as was Jake. The idea of arresting an elected county supervisor and hauling him into the courtroom was startling.

Noose wasn't finished. "And, Todd, I suggest that you quietly remind the five that there are two lawsuits pending in this court in which Ford County is the primary defendant. One involves a contaminated landfill owned by the county and alleged to have polluted some drinking water. The plaintiffs are asking for a lot of money. The second concerns an accident involving a county dump truck. Both claims appear to have merit. I want Jake to get paid. The county has the money because I've seen the books. They are, as you know, public record."

Even more startling was the less than subtle threat by a presiding judge to show favor in unrelated cases. Tannehill was stunned and said, "Judge, pardon me, but that sounds like a threat."

"It's not a threat. It's a promise. I dragged Jake into the Gamble case with the assurance that he would get paid. His fees are reasonable, don't you agree?"

"I have no problem with his fees. It's just that—"

"I know, I know. But county supervisors have wide latitude in budgetary matters and they can pay this money out of unrestricted funds. Let's get it done."

"Okay, okay."

"You're dismissed, Todd. Please file your answer before noon."

Tannehill shot Jake a bewildered look, then scurried out of the room. When he was gone, Noose stood and stretched again. "How many cases do you have this morning?"

"Two first appearances, plus Gamble. I don't suppose you want him in court today."

"No. We'll do it later. Let's get through the morning's business and meet back here for lunch, with Lowell."

"Sure, Judge."

"And Jake, order us some catfish po'boys from Claude's, okay?"

"You got it, Judge."

THE LAWYERS TOOK off their jackets and loosened their ties, at His Honor's suggestion. His robe hung by the door. The po'boys were still warm, and delicious. After a few bites and a round of small talk, Noose asked, "Do you have your calendars?"

Both nodded and reached into their briefcases.

Noose looked at some notes and asked, "How does December the tenth sound for the retrial?"

Jake had nothing scheduled past October. Dyer's trial calendar revolved around Noose's. Both said they were clear for December 10.

"Any idea where it might be?" Jake asked, hoping

fervently that it would not happen again in Van Buren County.

"Well, I've been thinking about that," Noose said as he took a bite and wiped his mouth with a paper napkin. "We should keep this show on the road. Things didn't work out too well in Chester. We're not doing it here. Tyler County is Lowell's backyard, so it's out. That leaves Polk and Milburn counties. I'll pick one in due course and we'll tee it up there. Any objections?"

Lowell said, "Well, of course, Judge, we'll oppose any motion for a change of venue."

Neither side was eager for a rematch. Dyer feared another loss and Jake was worried about a possible bankruptcy.

"Of course you will," Noose said. "But don't spend a lot of time opposing it."

And with that, the court had ruled.

His Honor kept eating and talking. "Not that it matters. We could pick twelve people off the streets in any of the five counties and get the same result. Gentlemen, I've thought of little else since the mistrial, and I do not believe any jury will convict this boy, nor will any jury acquit him. I'd like to hear your thoughts."

Jake nodded and demurred and Dyer said, "Well, we certainly have to try again, don't we? I can see the same challenges, but I'm confident of getting a conviction."

The standard response from every prosecutor.

"Jake?"

"I agree with you, Judge. The votes may vary a little, probably not an even split, but a unanimous verdict is not imaginable. The only fact that will change is that Kiera will give birth next month so there'll be a child. We, of course, will have the blood test to prove it's Kofer's."

"And there's no chance otherwise?" Dyer asked politely.

"I believe the girl," Jake said.

"So you'll lose the ambush angle?"

"Maybe, or maybe I'll have another one."

"Gentlemen. We'll try him again, on December the tenth, and there will be no more ambushes. If the jury cannot agree, then we'll go from there. No chance of a plea agreement?"

Dyer shook his head and said, "Not now, Judge. I can't agree to a plea to anything less than capital murder, not for a dead officer."

"Jake?"

"Same. I can't ask a sixteen-year-old boy to agree to a deal that gives him the next thirty or so years in prison."

"I assumed as much. Gentlemen, I see no way out of this mess. The facts are what they are and we can't change them. We have no choice but to keep trying."

Jake pushed his sandwich away and reached for some papers. "I guess that brings us to the issue of bail. So far, my client has served five months for nothing. He is, as we all know, presumed to be innocent. The State has tried once to prove him guilty and the State failed. It is not fair to keep him locked up. He is as innocent as we are, not to mention he's a minor, and he deserves the chance to get out."

Dyer shook his head as he took a bite.

Noose, surprisingly, said, "This has been on my mind too. It's troubling."

"It's worse than that, Judge. The kid was two years behind in school back in March. As we've learned, his education has been rather spotty. He's now incarcerated far away from any classroom."

"I thought your wife was working with him."

"Several hours a week, Judge, and it's a temporary arrangement at best. It's not enough. The kid has shown some interest in learning, but he needs to be in a real school with teachers and other kids, and with lots of tutoring after hours." Jake handed both some paperwork. "This is a petition for a writ of habeas corpus I plan to file on Monday in circuit court. And I'll ask you, Judge, with all due respect, to recuse yourself. If we fail in circuit court, then I'll go federal and get some relief. The kid is being unlawfully detained and I can convince a federal judge of that. The petition claims a violation of the Eighth Amendment prohibition against cruel and unusual punishment on the grounds that he is a minor being held in an adult facility, and in solitary confinement, and with no access to educational resources. We've found two cases on point, from other jurisdictions, and they're covered in our brief. If we get relief, and get him out, then both of you can blame someone else, and not worry about any political fallout."

This irritated Noose and he flashed an angry look at Jake. "I don't think about the politics, Jake."

"Well, you're the first politician who doesn't think about the politics."

"I'm offended. Do you consider me a politician, Jake?"

"Not really, but your name will be on the ballot next year. Yours too, Lowell."

"I don't allow politics to enter my considerations, Jake," Lowell said, a bit too piously.

"Then why not let him out?" Jake shot back.

They took a deep breath as Noose and Dyer skimmed the petition. They were obviously caught off guard and not sure what they were reading. After a moment, Jake said to Noose, "I'm sorry if I offended you, Judge. I did not intend to."

"Apology accepted. We need to be honest here and agree that allowing a capital murder defendant out of jail would upset a lot of people. Do you have a plan?"

"Yes. An appearance bond is used to ensure that a person accused of a crime will show up and face the charges. I promise you both that if and when you want Drew, his mother, or his sister to appear in any court, they will be there. You have my word. My plan is to get him out and take him to Oxford where Josie and Kiera are living, and get him in school in a couple of weeks. Kiera will start school after she has the baby. No one knows them over there, though I guess their address is now in the record. Both Drew and Kiera need tutoring and some counseling, and I'll try to arrange things."

"Is the mother working?" Noose asked.

"She has two part-time jobs and is looking for a third. I found them a small apartment and I'm helping with the rent. This will continue as long as I don't go broke."

"There has to be a secured bond, Jake. How can they afford it?"

Jake handed him a document and said, "This is the deed to my home. I'll put it up as security. And I'm not afraid to do so because I know that Drew will appear in court."

"Come on, Jake," Dyer said, shaking his head.

"You can't do that, Jake," Noose said.

"There's the deed, Judge. Mind you, the house is heavily mortgaged, like everything else I own, but I'm not worried."

"What if they skip out again?" Dyer asked. "They have a history of living on the run."

"Then I'll track down the little asshole and haul him

back to jail." The humor hit where it was supposed to and they enjoyed a good laugh.

"What's the value of the house?" Noose asked.

"I have one of those friendly, drive-by appraisals at three hundred thousand. And a mortgage to match it dollar-for-dollar."

"We're not using your house, Jake. What if I set the bond at fifty thousand dollars?"

"No sir. That means we, or I, will have to scrounge up five thousand cash for the bondsman. It's a racket and we all know it. Right now I don't have five thousand bucks to spare. Take the deed, Judge. The kid'll be in court when he's called."

Noose tossed his copy of the deed on the table. "Lowell?"

"The State will oppose any bail for this defendant. It is capital murder."

"Thanks for nothing," Jake said.

Noose slapped a hand to his chin and began scratching. "All right. The deed will suffice."

Jake reached for more papers and handed them over. "I've already prepared an order for you to sign. I'll talk to the clerk in just a moment. Then I'll talk to Ozzie, if he'll take my call, and arrange the transfer. I'll pick up the kid first thing in the morning and take him to Oxford. Look, we were friends when this started and we'll be friends when it's over. I need your help in keeping this as quiet as possible. Josie owes money and has already been served with lawsuits. Kiera is having a child out of wedlock but no one in Oxford knows anything about it. I'd like her to start school as just another fourteen-year-old girl, not a young mother. And there might be some people who would like nothing more than to find Drew walking down the street. Secrecy is important here."

"Understood," Dyer said.

Noose waved him off as if he didn't need the warnings.

LUCIEN WANTED A Friday afternoon drink on his porch and was pushy about the invitation. Jake didn't want to hang around his office, and after he finally got Ozzie on the phone and worked out the details of the release, he drove over and parked behind the old Porsche. Lucien, of course, was sitting in his rocker, drink in hand, and Jake wondered how many he'd already knocked back.

Jake took a seat in another rocker and they chatted about the heat and humidity. Normally, Sallie would eventually materialize and ask about a beverage, then bring one as if she was doing him a favor.

Lucien said, "I invited you for a drink. The bar hasn't moved and there's beer in the fridge."

Jake left and returned with a bottle of beer. They drank for a while and listened to the crickets. Finally, Jake said, "You wanted to talk about something."

"Yes. Reuben stopped by yesterday."

"Judge Atlee?"

"How many Reubens do you know around here?"

"Why are you always the smart-ass?"

"Practice."

"I actually know another Reuben. Winslow. He goes to our church so you wouldn't know him."

"Now who's the smart-ass?"

"It's a defensive measure."

"Reuben and I go way back. We've had our differences, but we still talk."

It would be impossible to find any lawyer, judge, or

elected official in Clanton who had not had their differences with Lucien Wilbanks.

"And what's on his mind?"

"He's worried about you. You know Reuben. He fancies himself as the shepherd of all legal matters in town and quietly keeps up with things. Little happens in the courthouse that he doesn't know about. He knew almost as much about the Gamble trial as I did and I was in the courtroom."

"Sounds like Reuben."

"He was not surprised at the hung jury, nor was I. They can try that boy ten times and won't get a conviction, or an acquittal. Your defense was masterful, Jake. I watched you with great pride."

"Thank you." Jake was touched because compliments from Lucien were rare. Criticism was the norm.

"A strange case indeed. Impossible to convict, impossible to acquit. I'm sure they'll try again."

"December tenth, either in Smithfield or Temple."

Lucien absorbed this and took a drink. "Meanwhile, he sits in jail, an innocent boy."

"No. He gets out in the morning."

"How'd you do that?"

"I didn't. Portia did. She prepared a habeas corpus petition, wrote a compelling brief, and I showed it to Noose this morning. I threatened him with it, said I would file it here then take it federal."

Lucien laughed for a long time, rattling his ice. When the humor passed, he said, "Anyway, back to Reuben. He's bothered by some things. *Smallwood*. He doesn't like the railroad and thinks it has operated dangerously around here for decades. He told me that thirty years ago a friend of his came within an inch of hitting a train at that same crossing. Guy got lucky and avoided an accident. Reuben has had Central in court a few times over the years, condemnation suits and such. He finds its people arrogant and stupid and just doesn't care for the company."

"I have the documents," Jake said casually, though he had perked up considerably.

"And he's bothered by the mystery witness, what's his name?"

"Neal Nickel."

"Reuben being Reuben, he's read the court file from front to back, and he's bothered by the fact that this guy was at the scene for three hours, cops everywhere, and he said nothing. Then he went home and hoped it would go away. Then he showed up the Friday before the trial wanting to testify. That strikes Reuben as being unfair."

"Well, it was definitely a shock. But why is Reuben reading the court file? Surely he has enough work on his desk."

"Says he reads files for pleasure. And he's bothered by the child, the family's only survivor, and is worried about her future. You set up the guardianship in Reuben's court and he approved it, so he has a right to be concerned. He wants the child taken care of."

"The child is being raised by Sarah Smallwood's sister. It's a decent home. Not great, but okay."

Lucien drained his glass and stood slowly. Jake watched him walk away as if cold sober, and knew that the story was far from over. If it was headed in the right direction, Jake's entire future might improve dramatically. Suddenly anxious, he gulped his beer and thought about fetching another.

Lucien returned with a fresh whiskey and began rocking again. "Anyway, Reuben doesn't like the way the case is going."

"Nor do I. I'm in debt because of it."

"A good strategy might be to non-suit the case in circuit court, then refile in chancery."

"The old non-suit trick," Jake said. "We studied it in law school."

A non-suit allowed a plaintiff to file a lawsuit, then dismiss it for any reason under the sun before a verdict, then refile it when convenient. Sue, and if discovery goes badly, non-suit and walk away. Sue, get to trial, get a rough-looking jury, then non-suit and fight another day. There was a famous case from the Gulf Coast in which a plaintiff's lawyer panicked when jury deliberations dragged on and he thought he was about to lose. He announced a non-suit and everybody went home. The next day it was revealed that the jury had just decided to give his client a generous verdict. He refiled, tried the case a year later, and lost. His client sued him for malpractice, and won. Defense lawyers hated the rule. Plaintiffs' lawyers knew it was unfair but fought to keep it. Most states had moved on to more modern procedures.

"What an archaic rule," Jake said.

"True, but it's still on the books. Use it to your advantage."

Jake finished his beer. It was obvious that Lucien was in no hurry and was enjoying the moment. Jake asked, "And what might happen in chancery?"

"Good things. Reuben assumes jurisdiction of the case because of the guardianship and his responsibility to protect the child. He sets a trial date and off you go."

"A bench trial, no jury."

"Correct. The defense might request a jury, but Reuben will say no."

Jake took a deep breath and said, "I need a shot of that brown stuff."

"The bar hasn't moved. Careful, though, or your wife might hit you."

"My wife might be drinking too when she hears this."

He left and returned with a Jack on ice. "If you will recall, Lucien, Harry Rex and I debated this very issue before we filed suit. I think you might have been in the room during one or two of our conversations. We decided to avoid chancery court because the Honorable Reuben Atlee is so damn tightfisted with money. To him, a hundred-thousand-dollar verdict is obscene, a violation of the rules of an orderly society. He's a miser, a skinflint, a cheapskate. Lawyers have to beg to get a few bucks for their guardians."

"He was generous to you during the Hubbard will contest."

"He was, and we talked about that too. But there was so much money on the table it was easier to be generous. We filed *Smallwood* in circuit court because we liked our chances better with a jury."

"True, Jake, and you wanted a big courtroom victory, a record-setting verdict that would put you on the map as a trial lawyer."

"I did. Still do."

"Well, you're not getting that verdict with *Smallwood,* not in circuit court."

"So, Judge Atlee wants to preside over the trial?"

"There won't be a trial, Jake. He'll force the railroad to settle, something he's very good at. He did it with Hubbard."

"He did, but after I won the trial."

"And the settlement was fair, everybody got something, and the appeals were avoided. Right?"

"Right."

"Same here. Refile in chancery and Reuben will take over. He'll protect the child, and the lawyers too."

Jake took a long sip, then closed his eyes and rocked gently. He could feel the pressure lift from his shoulders, the stress ooze from his pores. The alcohol was settling in and his breathing relaxed. For the first time in months there was a light in the distance.

The fact that Judge Atlee was sitting in the same rocker twenty-four hours earlier and telling Lucien what he should tell young Jake was difficult to absorb.

But then, it sounded just like Reuben.

54

Ozzie was waiting at the jail when Jake arrived early Saturday morning. He was cordial enough but did not offer a handshake. Mr. Zack fetched the prisoner, and Drew appeared at the desk with an army surplus duffel stuffed with everything he owned. Jake signed several forms and Drew signed an inventory sheet. They followed Ozzie through a back door to where Jake was parked. Outside, Drew stopped for a second and looked around, his first taste of freedom in almost five months. When Jake opened his driver's door, Ozzie said, "How 'bout lunch next week?"

"I'd like that, Ozzie. Anytime."

They drove away without being seen and five minutes later parked in Jake's driveway. Carla met them on the patio and grabbed Drew for a long, fierce hug. They went inside to the kitchen where a feast was being prepared. Jake led him downstairs to his bathroom and gave him a towel. "Take a hot shower, as long as you want, then we'll have breakfast."

Drew emerged half an hour later with wet hair, wearing a cool Springsteen T-shirt, denim shorts, and a pair of brand-new Nikes, which he said fit perfectly. Jake handed him three $1 bills and said, "For blackjack. Keep the change."

He looked at the money and said, "Come on, Jake. You don't owe me anything."

"Take the money. You won it fair and square, and I always pay my gambling debts."

Drew reluctantly took the money and sat at the table where Hanna was waiting. Her first question was "What was it like in jail?"

Jake said, "No, no, we're not talking about jail. Pick another topic."

"It was awful," he said.

Over the course of the summer, Drew and Carla had spent many hours together studying history and science and reading mysteries, and they had become close. She placed a plate of pancakes and bacon in front of him and ruffled his hair. "Your mom's gonna get you a haircut as soon as you get home."

He smiled and said, "I can't wait. And it's a real apartment, right?"

"It is," Jake said. "It's not very big but it'll do. You'll like it over there, Drew."

"I can't wait." He crammed a piece of bacon into his mouth.

"What was the food like in jail?" Hanna asked, staring at him.

"Hanna, eat your breakfast and no talk about jail."

Drew demolished a stack of pancakes and asked for more. At first he said little, but was soon chatting away as he ate. The pitch of his voice rose and fell and squeaked at times. He had grown at least two inches since April, and, though still rail thin, he was looking more and more like a normal teenager. Puberty was finally arriving.

When he was stuffed, he thanked Carla, gave her another fierce hug, and said he wanted to go see his mother. On the road to Oxford, he grew quiet as he took in the sights with a pleasant smile. Halfway there, he began to nod and soon fell asleep.

Jake watched him and couldn't help but wonder about his future. He knew how precarious Drew's freedom would be. He did not share Noose and Lucien's confidence that a conviction was unlikely. The next trial would be different—they always were. A different courtroom, a different jury, different tactics by the State.

Regardless of a win, a loss, or another draw, Jake knew that Drew Gamble would be a part of his life for years to come.

ON MONDAY, Jake non-suited the *Smallwood* case in circuit court and sent a copy to opposing counsel. Walter Sullivan called his office three times that afternoon, but Jake was not in the mood to chat. He owed no explanation.

On Tuesday, he filed a wrongful death lawsuit in chancery court and faxed a copy to Judge Atlee.

On Wednesday, the *Times,* as expected, ran a front-page story under the headline "Kofer Suspect Released From Jail." Dumas Lee did him no favors. His reporting was slanted and gave the impression that the defendant was being treated with leniency. Most galling was his reliance on comments made by former district attorney Rufus Buckley, who said, among other cheap shots, that he was shocked that Judge Noose would allow the release of a man indicted for capital murder. "It's unheard of in this state," Buckley said, as if he knew the history in all eighty-two counties. Not once did Dumas mention the fact that the defendant was presumed to be innocent, nor had he bothered to call Jake for a comment. Jake figured he had offered so many "No comments" that Dumas was tired of asking.

True to form, Buckley seemed to have plenty of time to talk. He had never met a reporter he didn't like.

ON THURSDAY, Judge Noose convened the trial in the matter of *Jake Brigance v. Ford County*. The main courtroom was practically empty. The five supervisors sat together in a front row, arms crossed over their chests, their frustration evident as they all glowered at Jake, the enemy. They were veteran politicians who had ruled the county for years, with little turnover in their ranks. Each came from a specified district, a little fiefdom where the boss doled out paving contracts, equipment purchases, and jobs. As a group they were not accustomed to being shoved around, not even by a judge.

Dumas Lee was there to snoop and watch the show. Jake refused to look at him but really wanted to curse him.

His Honor began with "Mr. Brigance, you're the plaintiff. Do you have any witnesses?"

Jake stood and said, "No, Your Honor, but, for the record, I would like to say that I was appointed by the court to represent Mr. Drew Gamble in his capital murder trial. He was and still is quite indigent. I would like to introduce into evidence my statement of fees and expenses for his defense." Jake walked to the court reporter and handed over the paperwork.

"So admitted," Noose said.

Jake sat down and Todd Tannehill stood and said, "Your Honor, I represent the county, the defendant, and acknowledge receipt of Mr. Brigance's bill, which I submitted to the board. Pursuant to the Mississippi Code, the maximum to be paid by any county in such a matter is one thousand dollars. The county is prepared to tender a check for this amount."

Noose said, "Very well. I'd like for Mr. Patrick East to come to the witness stand."

East was the current president of the board and was

obviously surprised to be called. He made his way forward, was sworn in, and settled into the witness chair. He smiled at Omar, a man he had known twenty years.

Judge Noose asked a few preliminary questions to establish his name, address, and position, then picked up some papers. "Now, Mr. East, looking at the county's budget for this fiscal year, I see that there is a surplus of some two hundred thousand dollars. Can you explain that?"

"Sure, Judge. It's just good management, I guess." East smiled at his colleagues. By nature he was folksy and funny and the voters loved him.

"Okay. And there is a line item labeled 'Discretionary Account.' The balance is eighty thousand dollars. Could you explain that?"

"Sure, Judge. It's sort of a rainy day fund. We use it occasionally when there is an unexpected expense."

"For example?"

"Well, last month we needed new lights at the softball complex over in Karaway. It wasn't in the budget request, and we voted to spend eleven thousand dollars. Just stuff like that."

"Are there any restrictions on how this money can be spent?"

"Not really. As long as the request is proper and approved by our attorney."

"Thank you. Now, when the board was presented with Mr. Brigance's bill, how did the five of you vote?"

"Five to zero against it. We're just following the law, Your Honor."

"Thank you." Noose looked at the two lawyers and asked, "Any questions?"

Without standing, both shook their heads in the negative.

"Very well. Mr. East, you are excused."

He returned to his colleagues on the front row.

Noose said, "Anything else?"

Jake and Todd had nothing.

"Very well. The court finds in favor of the plaintiff, Jake Brigance, and orders the defendant, Ford County, to proffer a check in the amount of twenty-one thousand dollars. We are adjourned."

ON FRIDAY, Todd Tannehill called Jake with the news that he had been ordered by the board to appeal the decision. He apologized and said he had no choice but to do what his client wanted.

An appeal to the state supreme court would take eighteen months.

FRIDAY WAS PORTIA'S last day at work. She would start classes on Monday and she was ready to go. Lucien, Harry Rex, Bev, Jake, and Carla gathered with her in the main conference room and opened a bottle of champagne. They toasted her, with a few light roasts in between, and each took a turn with a little speech. Jake went last and suddenly had a knot in his throat.

The gift was a handsome chestnut and bronze plaque that read: OFFICE OF PORTIA CAROL LANG, ATTORNEY AT LAW. It was to be mounted on the door of the office she had occupied for the past two years. She held it proudly, wiped her eyes, looked at the group, and said, "I'm overwhelmed, but then I've been overwhelmed many times around here. I thank you for your friendship, you have been dear. But I also thank you for something far more important. It is your acceptance. You have accepted me, a young black woman, as an equal. You have given me an incredible opportunity, and you have ex-

pected me to perform as an equal. Because of your en-
couragement, and acceptance, I have a future that, at
times, I cannot believe. You have no idea what this
means to me. Thank you. I love you all—even you,
Lucien."

There were no dry eyes when she finished.

55

On the third Sunday in September, with the summer heat finally breaking and a hint of autumn in the air, the Brigance family, running late as usual, was trying to leave for services at the Good Shepherd Bible Church. Carla and Hanna were in the car and Jake was about to set the house alarm when the phone rang. It was Josie, anxious with the news that Kiera was in labor. She was in a hurry and promised to call when she could. Jake calmly set the alarm, locked the door, and got in the car.

"We're even later," Carla growled.

"The phone rang," he said, backing out of the driveway.

"Who was it?"

"Josie. The hour has come."

Carla took a deep breath and mumbled, "She's early." They had not yet told Hanna.

The child missed nothing, and from the backseat she asked, "Is Miss Josie okay?"

"She's fine," Jake said. "It was nothing."

"Then why'd she call?"

"It was nothing."

After a sermon that seemed far too long, they visited with Pastor McGarry and Meg for a moment, then got away. They hustled home and ate a quick lunch while staring at the phone. Hours passed. Hanna's birth had been a nightmare, and they remembered all the things that could go wrong. Jake tried to watch a football game while Carla puttered in the kitchen, as close to the phone as possible.

Finally, at four-thirty, Josie called with the news that the baby had arrived. Kiera had been a rock star. Mother and child were doing fine with no complications. Seven pounds, four ounces, and of course he was beautiful and looked just like his mother. Hanna knew something strange was going on and watched every move.

On Monday, she and her mother left for school as usual. Jake was at his office, reviewing paperwork. He called his attorney in Oxford, a friend from law school, and they walked through their plan. He called his parents with the news. Carla had called hers Sunday night.

After school, they dropped off Hanna at a friend's house and drove to the hospital in Oxford. Kiera's room was a wreck because both Josie and Drew had spent the night there on foldaway beds. The family was ready to go home. Drew seemed particularly bored with it all.

At Jake's insistence, Kiera had not seen her baby. He walked them through the procedures and explained the legalities. Kiera was emotional and cried through most of the meeting. Carla stood by her bed and patted her arm. She looked even younger than fourteen.

"That poor child," Carla said, wiping her cheeks as they left the room and walked away. "That poor child."

Jake almost said something banal, like the worst was behind them and now they could move on, but with Drew's legal problems hanging like a sword it was difficult to be optimistic. By the time they got to the maternity ward, though, the sadness was gone. After a quick peek at the baby, they declared him to be just perfect.

That night they finally sat down with Hanna and broke the news that she was about to get a little brother. Her days as the only child were coming to an end. She was thrilled and had a thousand questions, and for hours they talked about his arrival, and his name, and his room, and on and on. Jake and Carla had decided to postpone any discussion of the mother's identity. They described her only as a beautiful young girl who couldn't keep her baby. This mattered little to Hanna. She was ecstatic over the idea of her new brother.

Jake worked late into the night assembling a new crib they had hidden in a storage closet, while Carla and Hanna unwrapped new gowns and blankets and baby clothes. Hanna insisted on sleeping with them that night, not an unusual occurrence, and they almost had to muzzle her to get some sleep.

They awoke early for the big day and dressed like they were going to church. Hanna helped pack a diaper bag with more stuff than any newborn could possibly need. She chattered all the way to Oxford while her parents tried in vain to answer all her questions. At the hospital, they parked her in a waiting room with strict instructions and stopped by to see the administrator, who reviewed the paperwork and signed off. They went to Kiera's room and found her and Josie packed and ready to leave. Drew was already at school. The doctor had signed the discharge forms and the Gambles had had enough of the hospital. With hugs and tears they said goodbye and promised to get together soon. Then they raced to the maternity ward to collect the boy. The nurse handed him over to Carla, who was speechless, and they hurried away to the waiting room where they presented him to his big sister. Hanna, finally, was speechless too, for a moment. She cuddled him like a doll and insisted that he wear a soft blue outfit, one she had selected and that was more appropriate for the occasion.

They would call him Luke, a name that Hanna approved. On his amended birth certificate his legal name would be Lucien, a name that Carla had at first resisted. Naming their child after the biggest rogue in Clanton might present all sorts of problems, but Jake was adamant. By the time the kid was ten, Lucien Wilbanks would be gone and forgotten by most of the town. Jake, though, would treasure his memories for the rest of his life.

They drove to the square and parked in front of the office of Arnie Pierce, a close friend of Jake's from their law school days. Before she met Jake, Carla had once dated Arnie, so the relationships were old and trusted. They walked across the street to the Lafayette County Courthouse where Pierce had arranged a special appointment with Chancellor Purvis Wesson, a youthful judge Jake knew well. They gathered in his chambers for a private hearing with a court reporter present. Like a priest at a christening, Judge Wesson held the baby, examined him, and declared him ready to be adopted.

Portia arrived just in time for the occasion. Three weeks into the grind of law school, she was more than willing to skip a class or two and witness the adoption.

With Arnie feeding him paperwork, Judge Wesson waived the three-day waiting period and the six months probation. He examined the petition and the consent forms signed by Josie and Kiera. For the record, he read the specifics from the father's death certificate. He signed his name twice, and little Luke Brigance became the legal son of Jake and Carla. The final matter was an order locking up the file and keeping it away from the public records.

Thirty minutes later, they posed for photos and said goodbye.

For the ride home, Hanna insisted that Carla ride in the rear seat with her and her brother. She had already assumed possession of the child and wanted to give him a bottle. Then she wanted to change his diaper, something Jake heartily endorsed. She could change all of them she wanted.

The drive to Clanton was a joyous moment, something Jake and Carla would relive for years. At home, lunch was waiting, along with Jake's parents and Carla's, who had flown into Memphis early that morning. Harry Rex and Lucien arrived for the homecoming. When Jake announced the child's name, Harry Rex feigned irritation and asked indignantly why Lucien was chosen. Jake explained that one Harry Rex in the world was more than sufficient.

The grandmothers took turns squeezing the boy, all under the watchful eyes of his big sister.

The friends and family would go to great lengths to bury as many of the details as possible. People would talk, though, and the town would eventually know.

Jake didn't care.

AUTHOR'S NOTE

I began writing *A Time to Kill* in 1984 and published it in 1989. A long time passed before Jake returned in 2013, in *Sycamore Row*. In between, other books set in the same fictional place were published—*The Chamber, The Last Juror, The Summons,* and my only collection of short stories, *Ford County.* Now, with the addition of this novel, a lot has been written about Clanton and many of its characters: Jake and Carla, Harry Rex, Lucien, Judge Noose, Judge Atlee, Sheriff Ozzie Walls, Carl Lee, and so on. Indeed, I've written so much about Ford County that I can't remember all of it.

The point of all this is to apologize for any mistakes. I'm just too lazy to go back and read the earlier books.

Thanks to some old lawyer pals in Hernando who helped me remember details from an earlier career: James Franks, William Ballard, Chancellor Percy Lynchard. They explained the laws correctly. If I modified them to fit the story, then so be it. It's my error, not theirs.

The same is true for any number of statutes and procedural rules in my home state. As a young attorney so many years ago I was bound to follow them to the letter of the law. Now, as a writer of fiction, I feel no such bondage. Here, as before, I have changed laws, twisted them, even fabricated them, all in an effort to drive the narrative.

And a big special thanks to Judy Jacoby for the tit

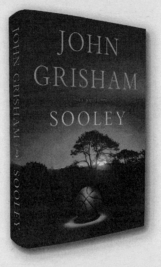